ERICA HAYES

I'm an Aussie living in northern England, where at least the hospitality and the beer are warm. I write in coffee shops, feed my enormous cat, and watch TV or read until far too late at night. If it's got serial killers, superheroes, monsters or spaceships – preferably all four – I'm there.

On the big issues: Captain Picard is cooler than Captain Kirk, Batman would beat up Superman, and vampires are hotter than werewolves any day. See, I knew we'd get along.

You can follow me on Twitter @ericahayes.

Scorched

ERICA HAYES

A division of HarperCollins*Publishers*
www.harpercollins.co.uk

HarperImpulse an imprint of
HarperCollins*Publishers* Ltd
77–85 Fulham Palace Road
Hammersmith, London W6 8JB

www.harpercollins.co.uk

A Paperback Original 2014

First published in Great Britain in ebook format by HarperImpulse 2014

Cover images © Shutterstock.com

Erica Hayes asserts the moral right
to be identified as the author of this work

A catalogue record for this book is
available from the British Library

ISBN: 978-0-00-810501-3

This novel is entirely a work of fiction.
The names, characters and incidents portrayed in it are
the work of the author's imagination. Any resemblance to
actual persons, living or dead, events or localities is
entirely coincidental.

Automatically produced by Atomik ePublisher from Easypress

1

I'm not a bad person.

I repeat it, over and again until the words scorch into my brain. *I'm not a bad person. I don't deserve this.*

It's the white room again. I'm strapped to the hard metal chair, my eyelids taped open. A dangling light bulb flickers. My feet are bare, my half-shaved hair a knotted mess under the heavy alloy helmet they've bolted around my skull to neutralize my power. I'm sweating in my gray hospital smock. It itches and stinks of piss. I don't remember pissing myself.

I don't remember much about anything.

But I'm not a bad person. They can't trick me into believing I am. Hour after hour, I repeat the words, so they can't make me forget: *My name is Verity Fortune. I'm thirty-one years old. I'm not a bad person.*

In the dim control room behind safety glass, the pretty doctor pushes her glasses up on her nose. She's the one I call Dr. Mengele, blue eyes like ice and a thick blond braid over her shoulder. She wears a clean white coat. She twiddles knobs on her machine and hurts me.

I brace for the next assault, struggling to keep my thoughts untangled. They can't make me forget. I know who she works for. My archenemy, the psychopath who locked me up in this place. He's the evil one, not me. If I ever get out of here...

Mengele presses one of her buttons. Current crackles along my skin, and the tiny hairs on my arms jerk taut. My muscles crunch and twist in agony. An angry bonfire ignites behind my eyeballs, and even after so many days—even though I know it's what she wants—I can't help it.

My power flexes, a warm muscle in my head. I remember that, all right. I can break glass, crush concrete, move objects at will. But nothing happens. The augmentium helmet just heats up, absorbing my telekinetic energy. Electrodes sizzle. My skin burns, the stink of singed hair. I gnash my teeth. Spit bubbles on my lips, coppery with blood.

"Zero point three micra on the left frontal." Dr. Mengele's voice, distorted over the tannoy.

The orderly waddles closer, his grin full of bad teeth. It's the fat one today. The fat one likes to hurt people, and his greasy hospital greens are already pinpricked with blood—mine or from one of the other poor fools they've got locked up in this dungeon. A black expanding baton dangles from his thick waist. The nametag sewn onto his shirt says *Frank*.

I've been watching the orderlies, while each day they tie and untie me, shove me from room to room, bring my plastic trays of pureed food. Fat Frank is slower and stupider than the others. And today, I'm more awake than he thinks.

Last night I choked up my meds, mashed peas and acid and two little red capsules of mindfuck. Again this morning. I'm feeling more alert, more alive than I have in weeks. And for the past few days, I've been giving Frank attitude. Making wise-ass remarks. Spitting stewed apple in his face. He's already blacked one of my eyes, and he wants to hurt me more. He's easy game.

Frank looms over me, his globular shadow blotting out the light. I whimper, like I usually do. Let myself drool. Fight to keep my senses sharp, though the raw-scraped nerves in my brain scream for silence and surrender.

Keys jingle on Frank's belt. My ears twitch. I can smell the peculiar sweetness of his breath, like spoiled flowers. His sour body heat is an unpleasant caress. His thigh squashes mine. He reaches for my helmet to make the adjustment.

Clickety-snap. The vise-tight band around my skull loosens, just a fraction.

I sink my teeth into his fat wrist.

Blood spurts. Frank howls, and slaps me upside the head. My ears ring, and the helmet knocks crooked, just an inch or two.

Told you he was stupid. An inch or two's all I need.

I let loose with a clumsy surge of power, and rip the buckle from my left wrist. I'm out of practice—creaky, like a rusty cell door in some ancient prison—but the leather tears clean off its studs. A crushing ache squeezes my skull, but I don't care.

Mengele shouts. Frank's already lurching for me like a bleeding ox. But he's too slow. With my free hand, I tear the helmet from my head. Horrid thing, now I see it, wires and clamps and a rusty bolt at the back. I throw it across the room, and I'm free. My power thrashes and screams, a tortured beast released at last, and I pick Frank up with a huge invisible fist and slam him into the wall.

He hits with a splat like the blubbery sack of shit he is, and slumps. Blood trickles from his nose to stain his shirt. Never mind. A few drops more won't make a difference.

I crack my neck, satisfied. See? A bad person would have killed Frank. But Frank—so far as I can tell from the way he's groaning—isn't dead.

I rip off my restraints. Tear the tape from my eyelids. Blink, one-two-three-four-five-six. Ah, sweet relief. In the control room, Mengele's reaching for the alarm, calling for her heavies to come pin me down.

The glass pane judders in my unseen grip, and the window explodes. I dive through headfirst, hit the console and tumble onto the floor in a glittering hail.

Mengele backs off, stumbling for the door. I slam the bolts shut and jump up.

She cowers, alone. In close-up, with no glass separating us, she looks slender and breakable. Her fear smells rotten, like she's crapped herself. Maybe she has. But that sly headshrink's guile still glints in her gaze. "Okay, I can see you're upset. Would you like to talk? We can talk about whatever you want—"

"Shut up!" My voice is rusty, too, like I've forgotten it or screamed too long. "Give me my files."

"I can't divulge personal information."

I fling out my hand, palm outwards, and an invisible force rams her against the wall. My hands quiver in memory of everything she's done to me, the machines, the voltage jerking my muscles tight, the agony chewing in my skull as she tortured me. I'm sweating, shaking. My breath's on fire. My power is starved and vengeful, hungry for prey. A bad person would squeeze the life from her.

I ease up, just a fraction. "Give me the goddamn file before I crush your throat."

"Okay." Mengele's voice strangles. Her face gleams bloodless. She believes me. "On the shelf, white document box. Just let me go."

I let her go and tear the box from the shelf. It's empty but for a single pink slip of paper, duplicate to a form headed INPATIENT ADMISSION. The carbon-copy handwriting is dusty and black. I blink stinging eyes, confused. I don't recognize the name or birthdates. My thoughts swirl and tangle, sinking into chaos…

No. I grit my teeth. I know who I am. I'm Verity Fortune. I'm thirty-one years old. These details are fake. They just don't want anyone to find me.

Date of admission: October 2nd. Must be what, three weeks ago now? Addresses, phone numbers, none of which I recognize. Ten square boxes for my fingerprints, but the ink doesn't show on this copy. A scrawled signature at the bottom that I can't read.

The space for Discharge Date is blank.

My knuckles crack white, and the paper crushes in my fist. It's not enough. I need details. Proof. Once I'm gone, they'll deny everything. "Where's the rest of it?" I demand.

Mengele swallows. She's stalling. "It's digital. That's the only paper copy."

"Then download it—"

The door implodes, and her heavies pile in. Six of them, armed with batons and capsicum spray and hissing tasers. One of them's holding an iron-ribbed strait jacket.

Fine. Screw details, if that's the way they want it.

I stuff the paper into my itchy gray scrubs—no pockets—and fight.

Ten minutes later, I'm done. Outside, on the mountainside, it's nighttime, the wispy fog drifting though fragrant eucalyptus trees. It's warm for October, and in the valley, Sapphire City's towers glitter like frosted flames. Smoke roughens my throat. Shadows flicker, and behind me, someone screams.

I leap the fence and run into the forest. The dirt feels good under my bare feet.

Before I left, I opened all the doors and set the asylum on fire.

2

By the time I reached the city, it was long past midnight. Behind me, fog wreathed the tree-lined hills, grasping wispy fingers down into the valley. Stars wheeled overhead, their constellations strange and lopsided. Street lights burned oddly bright. Even the air smelled weird. Freedom. I never wanted to forget it again.

I stole some clothes from a hobo's shopping cart in some alley off Castro Street. Distant sirens howled. A painted mural rainbowed the wall where the hobo slept, and he muttered and rolled over, wrapping himself in his greasy jacket and a mist of stale rotgut whiskey. Rats scuttled under a trashpile as I rifled the cart. It was very warm for October, and shorts and a T-shirt would have done. But I needed to stay hidden, so I chose a dirty black hoodie, grimy jeans and a pair of flip-flops, and threw my piss-stinking hospital gear in the dumpster.

A discarded pizza box lay half crushed in the gutter, a rat poking his long nose inside. My stomach grumbled, but I left it alone. Not quite that desperate, yet.

Clothes sorted. Nothing I could do about my beaten-up face, or the ragged state of my hair. I looked exactly like an escaped mental patient. I stank like one, too, and my head ached like... well, like

I'd had a metal helmet bolted to my skull for three weeks. But I couldn't go home. *His* goons would be hunting me. I had no cell phone, no cash, not even a dollar for a phone call.

And truth was, I felt naked and helpless without my mask. Sure, that foul helmet was gone, and I was strong again, but these days you couldn't just flash your powers around in Sapphire City and expect to avoid attention. There's a reason we augmented folks have secret identities.

In the real world, we're called *augmented*, see. Life isn't a comic book. I'm not from another planet, and I didn't get bitten by a mutant spider or drown in toxic waste only to be resurrected with super powers. I was just born this way. It didn't make me good or evil. That's a choice we all make, one way or another.

But wielding powers attracted unwanted attention, whether from the villains, the lynch mob or the press, all equally dangerous in different ways. That's why we wear masks and costumes to work: what we do isn't safe. And without my mask—or any idea of what had been going on since I'd somehow pissed the villains off enough to get locked in some prehistoric loony bin—I was trapped like a bug in a jar inside my own cover story. *Hi, I'm Verity Fortune, freelance journalist. Who's that, you say? The Seeker? Black vinyl catsuit and mask? Fights crime? She's just a rumor, friend. She's not real. Trust me, I'm a reporter. If she was real, I'd know, wouldn't I?*

No, I had to stay incognito until I got a grip on the situation. For the moment, I was just plain Verity, but I still had villains on my trail who'd happily carve my brain into cat food, or worse. Which meant I needed to see my father, and pronto.

My father was Thomas Fortune, owner and chairman of Fortune Corporation, a multi-million-dollar company specializing in security and weapons technology. By night, he was Blackstrike, Sapphire City's best-loved crime-fighter, wielding his dark mastery of shadow to defeat the Gallery, our local gang of villains. Only our family knew that Tom Fortune was Blackstrike (for a guy his age, I've gotta say, Dad still looks rockin' in that black trench coat) and that FortuneCorp was just a front for the real family business: fighting evil.

Augmentation came with the Fortune blood: me, my two brothers, my sister, my uncles, our cousins. Though we didn't always get along—big sister, in particular, had the mother of bad attitudes—Dad kept us in line, and he didn't risk unmasking himself without good reason. Still, the bad guys had just benched me for three weeks in the middle of a cease-fire, and FortuneCorp couldn't take a hit like that without fighting back. Dad would know what to do.

But my wits spun in drunken circles, and my vision blurred with fatigue. I couldn't remember Dad's phone number. And I couldn't just turn up at FortuneCorp HQ without being sure I wasn't followed. I'd just have to stick with what I did remember.

I tugged my hood forward as far as it would go, and walked on.

Broken glass littered the sidewalk on Market Street, where galleries and colorful boutiques squeezed in beside restaurants and crowded bars. Garbage piled in the gutter, spilling onto the street, and a few pale people in shapeless clothes picked through it for food. Yellow hybrid taxi cabs cruised for customers, amongst zipping traffic, bicycle couriers, rattling painted trolley cars.

I passed some drunken guys in suits, a gang of teenagers riding skateboards, and prostitutes, the expensive ones in thigh boots and fishnets, as well as their poorer, more desperate sisters, wearing whatever skimpy clothes they could scrounge. Homeless dudes harangued passers-by for change or booze. Graffiti on the brick alley walls read U.S. OUT OF IRAN and SAVE OUR CHILDREN: VOTE NO TO PROP 101 and GOD HATES AUGMENTS, but one phrase in particular stood out...

It was everywhere. Scrawled in chalk on the broken sidewalk. Spray-painted in fat scarlet letters like blood-soaked balloons. Etched on a window with bold, sharp strokes beneath a blotch of melted glass:

My thoughts melted like ghosts, a haze of glassy memory come alive. *Flames lick the hot metal walls. Radiant heat scorches my face, inexorable, hungry. No. I fling out my hand, grasping for my power. Chilling laughter taunts me, and flame stings my palm in warning, a threat or a caress...*

My shoulder bounced hard off a lamp post, and I stumbled. I blinked to clear my head and walked on.

I stole some change from the tip jar in a fire-bright trance bar and caught the trolley car, downtown where neon-lit doorways beckoned and people spilled out onto the streets in their clubbing gear, tight rubber dresses and high-cut leather jackets and the silky slide of Lycra. Searchlights split the sky between skyscrapers and old town houses, amid sirens and thudding helicopter blades. One of the clubs was gutted by fire, just a charred shell, sprouting twisted metal and glittering with broken glass. Yellow crime scene tape strung tight across the gaping hole, and black-uniformed cops with truncheons moved people along.

I stared, pressing my nose to the trolley car window. The Gallery's work, no question. One entire corner of the building had been chopped off and burned debris littered the sidewalk. The exposed steel beams had bubbled at the ends, the ragged brickwork melted. Cauterized. Like a white-hot razor had sliced it clean through.

BURN IT ALL

I shuddered, and looked away.

The sidewalk was crowded with street performers and food carts selling pizza slices or hot dogs. Mmm, real food. My mouth watered at the delicious salty scent. We passed a police blockade, then another, the cops with their holster-locked sidearms and polycarbonate riot shields checking IDs. Gangs of youths in baggy jeans and hoodies slunk around and glared at each other. No one walked alone.

I frowned. Tense. Had the war erupted again? More work for FortuneCorp?

The tram turned right and rattled along the waterfront where, through the palm trees, the double-decked Bay Bridge suspended creaking across the water, its sweeping neon arcs glistening in misty moonlight. Overhead, seagulls wheeled and squawked. On the opposite shore, suburban lights sparkled like scattered jewels.

I hopped off and walked two blocks south, to an ornate redbrick apartment building, its gilt-etched windows hidden behind security mesh. I strolled casually to the next corner. Didn't see or hear anyone. No one did a sudden double take, or grew a lizard's skin and attacked me, or carved the street open down to the subway with burning razorwhips. When the Gallery are involved, you have to guard against everything.

I slipped alongside the building and jumped up to the second floor fire escape. My flip-flops slapped on the metal landing. Inside, a shadowy living room beckoned. No lights. No movement. No one was home. Fine. I'd just go inside and wait.

I twisted the security screen aside with a swift tug of mindsense, unlocked the window and quietly slid the sash upwards.

Cold hands grabbed my throat, and dragged me inside.

3

Lights flared, blinding me. I hit the floor, my bones jarring, and scrambled to my feet, ready to fight by ear and scent. A steely arm caught me across the chest, and slammed me into the wall. My breath sucked away. Struggling, I grabbed an invisible handful of power and prepared to throw it, hard.

"Verity?" The grip on my throat loosened. My vision cleared, revealing curly blond hair, broad shoulders. I smelled leather and cologne, and memory twinkled bright. "Is that you?"

I choked, eyes watering, and let my power ebb away. Damn, his voice felt good in my ears. "Christ on a cheeseburger. That's no way to greet your sister."

My big brother wrapped me in a hug, crushing my breath away all over again. I clung to him, overcome. He was so warm. So human. His voice muffled against my hair. "Verity. Holy Jesus. I can't believe it's you. Where the hell have you been?"

"Steady on," I grumbled, and pushed him away, but I couldn't help a tired grin. Adonis Fortune is sixteen months older than I am and, unlike me, he inherited Dad's patrician good looks: six foot two, blond and blue, with a smile that kills at twenty paces. No joke.

Adonis works for FortuneCorp in public relations, but he's also Narcissus, vigilante crusader for peace, wielding the power of charisma. Which sounds like a pretty lame augment, until you consider all the crazy things people will do if they think they're in love with you.

I've seen Adonis charm hardened criminals into giving up their weapons, talk suicidal teenagers down from the edge with a wink and a smile. Once, last year, when Razorfire and the Gallery were terrorizing the dockyards, we were holed up in this greasy warehouse and—

The world blotted black, and I stumbled to my knees in a dizzy whirlpool of misery.

Razorfire.

Goddamn it. I said his name.

It pierced my ears, mocking me, echoing like his eerie laughter, and jagged memories hacked deep into my brain.

I cling to the side of the skyscraper, my fingers wrapped tight around a glassy ledge. Raindrops sting my face, the October breeze chilled with the promise of winter. My hair blows wild. I grit my teeth and climb. My feet slip on the glass. Only seconds now, until the weapon goes off...

Dad calling my name, his shadows curling...

...silvery metal glints in the spotlights, a glass canister of poison gas on a cell phone timer. It's an aerosol weapon, ionized particles for maximum adhesion. The building is fifty-six stories high. From this altitude, the poison will spread rapidly, blanketing the city center within minutes. Maximum loss of life. Not a moment to lose. My hands shake. I reach for it, grasping...

...don't hurt her... last chance...

Something slams into my face, and I fall into iron-strong hands. Coiled lightning whips an inch from my cheek, searing me. I struggle, blood streaming into my eyes, but it's no use. They grab my legs, my arms, wrap a fist in my hair. I'm taken...

"Verity, stay with me." Adonis gripped my shoulders, dragging me from the shattered mess of my mind. His cool fingers stroked my face. "My God. What happened to you?"

I throttled down a scream, and forced my eyes open, willing the nightmare to leave me be.

BURN IT ALL. Razorfire, archvillain, wielder of flame and poison. My nemesis. Hell, that raging psycho was everyone's nemesis. Ruthless, rage-riddled, driven by indomitable conviction that he was smarter and stronger and better entitled to be alive than everyone else. But us augmented folks at least rated a fight and a wise-ass remark or two while he preached his hatred. Regular people weren't even fit to breathe the same air.

I'd crippled his weapon at the last second, stopped his insane poison plan. But I hadn't gotten away clean. Oh, no. I'd swallowed the full, sick force of his vengeance. Three endless weeks in that mediaeval torture chamber...

Adonis shook me gently. "Listen to me. Stay with me. What did they do to you?"

"What happened?" I gasped, blood trickling hot from my nose. "That night. Tell me. Did he... did Razorfire...?"

"He got away, Verity!" Adonis's words cracked like whip leather. "Don't you remember? We looked everywhere for you."

"They locked me up!" My scream broke, glass shattering on iron. I twisted from my brother's grip. "They bolted my head in augmentium so I couldn't do anything, and they tortured me. There was no point to it. They didn't ask me any questions. They just..."

Adonis stared, pale. He'd cut his hair, I noticed, and grown a short beard. Since when?

"Don't stare at me like that! Why didn't you come for me?" Hot liquid rage welled in my eyes. I knew it wasn't Adonis's fault. Razorfire was clever. He'd hidden me well.

But that didn't quench my anger. And I couldn't bear my brother's silence. I needed him to talk to me, to prove I existed in the real world, and not just in a rusty white cell, or the broken wasteland of a tortured mind. "You left me there," I accused, shaking. "You left me in that forsaken place—"

"Everyone thought you were dead." The dimple in his handsome chin tightened. He was just as furious. "You were gone so long, and we looked everywhere..."

"So long? You gave up pretty damn fast. It's only been three weeks!"

Adonis eyed me, incredulous. "Three weeks? Verity, it's July."

My vision doubled. "Huh?"

"It's July. You've been gone for over nine months."

Flame flashes, the dark depths of a pit, the agony in my head flaring like a supernova...

I swallowed, sour. "Th–that can't be right. I counted. It was only..."

Oh, shit.

I stalked to his computer, and swiped the screen to wake it up. The date glared at me like an evil eye from the top corner. July 12th. I scrabbled through the glossy marketing magazines on his desk. June issue, a year I thought hadn't yet begun. The *Financial Times*, July 12th, the Dow Jones down again, the new deutschmark tumbling, riots in Zurich, some crisis in Chinese fusion energy production.

The sweat slicking my forehead suddenly taunted me, cackling in my head like a witch. Stupid me, I'd thought the warmth unseasonable. Evil laughter, clanging in my ears, metal clamps grinding tighter and tighter...

Panicked, I sucked in air, hyperventilating, the taste of rust invading my lungs, stewed apples, my bitter medication, the saccharine moisture of Frank's breath...

"I am so sorry, Verity." Adonis's face was wan with shock. "If I'd known, I never would have... Hey, easy. It's all right." He stilled my twitching hands, tried to make me sit. "I'm just happy you're alive. Let's get you a shower and some food and we can talk."

My tired body whimpered in response. Food sounded great. A

shower, even better. But I didn't have time for comforts. "Look, I just need to talk to Dad. He can sort this out. I've lost my cell phone, my memory's a bit hazy, can you...?"

My brother's gaze blackened like a thundercloud.

"What?" The word parched my throat.

"Don't you remember?"

My pulse squirted cold. "What? Tell me!"

"Dad's gone, Vee." His eyes glittered, sky-blue to the brim with anguish and rage. "The night you were caught. He tried to help you, and Razorfire killed him."

4

I must have fainted, because next thing I knew, I woke in Adonis's bedroom, with sunlight pouring in the window. His red feather quilt was tucked around me. I groaned, and rolled over. A pair of black lacy panties scrunched under the pillow. They weren't mine. Apparently some things hadn't changed.

From the next room, I could hear Adonis, arguing on the phone. His closet lay open, the mirrored door pushed aside to reveal tailored suits, expensive knitted sweaters, soft leather jackets, perfect shoes. Sharp fashion sense was another trait of Dad's that I'd somehow missed out on. I was a T-shirt-and-favorite-jeans kinda girl, and with a pang of dread, I wondered what had happened to all my stuff after nine months. Had they kept my apartment? My clothes? My costumes?

I levered myself out of bed, a mess of headache and bruises and broken heart. Enough feeling sorry for myself. Time to get back to work. I hadn't forgotten that Dad was dead because of me. Murdered. Razorfire's sweet-sick revenge.

But mine, I vowed, would be sweeter still. Adonis and I would see to that. Thomas Fortune wasn't an affectionate father. More the aloof, practical type. But he'd loved us. Trusted us. Treated us as equals. I didn't know how Adonis had been running things at FortuneCorp while I was gone, but I knew I wouldn't let Dad's murder go unpunished. No way.

I still wore my greasy hoodie and jeans, and they stank real bad. I peeled them off and stumbled under the shower. At the first flush of hot water, I shivered in bliss. I'd forgotten what it felt like, clean water flooding my skin, sloshing through my filthy hair. Dirt swirled over the rough creamy tiles and down the drain.

The welts on my skin stung, but I polished off half a bar of Adonis's musk-scented soap and three handfuls of shampoo before I was satisfied. Still, I'd have to squeeze in a rare visit to the salon. I'm not a beauty-product girl—not much point—but I could really use a manicure, not to mention a wax. I twisted the water off and stepped out onto the mat, and the misted mirror reflected my face.

I froze, towel halfway to my dripping hair. Leaned closer. Slowly wiped the mirror clean.

A horrid sickle-shaped scar curled over my left cheek, from my temple to the side of my nose. The skin there was seared away, replaced with shiny red scar tissue. Half my eyebrow had burned away for good. My cheekbone was dented, and when I touched it, it ached faintly, the echo of something lost.

Christ on a cracker. I'd never been pretty. But this…

Memories of pain scorched my mind. The helmet, current arcing blue, skin sizzling to the backdrop of my screams…

I wanted to scream again, claw at my face. They'd carved me up pretty good. I should be thankful my eye had been saved. That the damage was only cosmetic.

But it wasn't.

The bruises, the welt where the augmentium helmet had cut into my scalp: they'd heal. But the burned scar was too old, too brutally deep. I'd never fix this. I'd have to live with it forever. And every time I touched it—every time I glimpsed my reflection, in a mirror or a window or someone else's eyes—I'd remember what Razorfire had done to me.

Guess it was lucky for me I wore a mask most of the time, then.

I let out a deep breath, and stared my scarred reflection down. I had stuff to do. No point crying over what was lost.

Not that I ever rated much in the beauty department to start with, right? The Seeker, in her mask and tight leather, attracted far more interest from the opposite sex than plain Verity ever did, and that suited me just fine. Lots of guys thought it was kinky to sleep with a masked vigilante. They never wanted her phone number afterwards. But relationships are a tedious mess of half-truths when you've got a secret identity to protect, and the Seeker just took what she wanted and vanished into the night. Fun all round, no one gets hurt.

But still, as I studied my new scar-bright face, the hungry hate-seed inside me burrowed fresh poison shoots into my heart. This went above and beyond normal hostilities. The damage was spiteful, unnecessary. When I finally caught up with Razorfire— and I would, so help me, if it sucked out every last drop of my strength—maybe I'd return the favor before I killed him.

I dried off and hunted for something to wear. My body was skinny and malnourished, and Adonis's clothes were too big for me at the best of times, but I found a Versace T-shirt and some sweats that didn't fall off once I tied knots in strategic places. Shoes were more of a problem. I opted for the hobo flip-flops, once I'd given them a good scrubbing.

I slouched into the living room. Sunlight slanted in, glinting on polished oak floorboards. Adonis's apartment was meticulously tidy, telling a familiar tale of paid housekeeping and too many hours spent at work. White Italian sofa, plush rugs, four televisions on mahogany shelving, tuned to four different news channels with the sound muted. An array of computers sat on the glass-topped desk, alongside three cell phones. Through the open glass doors lay a sparkling view of the bay, and a saxophonist's melancholy wail mingled with the sounds of traffic and café customers. The smells of bacon and French toast made my mouth hurt, and my empty stomach protested with a growl.

Adonis's voice drifted in from the sun deck, with that sarcastic edge that meant he was talking to our sister. "Yeah, whatever. I'll bring her in, you can talk to her yourself… Well, cancel the fucking meeting, then… Jesus, E., don't go out of your way or anything."

My mouth twisted. That was my sister, all right. Not *Thank God Verity's still alive!* or *Is she okay?* or even *Where the hell's she been all this time, I'll wring her telekinetic neck for making me worry.*

Just grief about cancelling some damn meeting.

I raided the fridge while I waited, hunting for waffles or eggs. I pushed aside a bottle of Moet, a gift box of Belgian chocolates, a wheel of triple cream brie. "Jeez, don't you do anything but seduce debutantes? Haven't you got any real food?"

"Blow me," came the reply.

"The places you've been? Not likely." I grabbed the OJ and swigged, a fresh burst of sweetness. Finally, I unearthed a box of Pop-Tarts and dropped four into the stainless steel toaster. My mouth watered harder at the fruity scent. How long since I'd eaten properly?

The tarts popped, and I burned my mouth wolfing the first one down. Oh, God. My knees weakened, and my taste buds had their own little private moment on that hot strawberry goodness. Mmm.

I unfolded the *Sapphire City Chronicle* on the breakfast bar as I munched, wiping drool from my chin. All those computers and Adonis still had this thing for newsprint. **VILLAINS ON THE RISE!** yelled the headline, above a half-page, blurry security camera photo of masked bandits heisting an armored van. They had balls, to rip off a van in full view of the cameras. Hubris, not to shoot the cameras out first. Arrogance, even. The guy in front was giving the camera the finger, his sawed-off shotgun brandished above his head in victory.

I peered closer. A glint showed on that cheerily-displayed middle finger, so tiny you could barely see it. But I knew what it was. A Gallery ring, marking him as one of Razorfire's petty minions. His

Archvillain-ness despised normals, sure. Didn't stop him recruiting all kinds of petty criminals and bad-asses to wreak havoc and perpetuate the kind of climate he reveled in: fear.

As I read, I frowned. The article listed a grotesquery of heists, sieges, kidnappings, shootings, and assorted mayhem, all in the last couple of weeks. A crime wave, in fact.

Adonis walked in, dropping phone number four into his jacket pocket. He looked great in black, and his suits always fit him perfectly, from square shoulders to neat white cuffs to the green or violet or sapphire-blue ties he liked. He flipped a tart from the toaster and bit into it. "Typical. Back for five minutes and already you're into my secret stash."

"Hey, I'm the one who's been eating stewed puke for nine months. Give over." I swiped the tart from his hand with my talent, and it flew across to splat onto my plate. But an ache flared in my skull. I couldn't control it. The plate spun onto the floor and smashed to shards.

"Sorry." My cheeks burned, and I felt queasy. Had they broken me in that place? If I couldn't control my talent, I was useless. I knelt and scrabbled for the mess, but my fingers were just as clumsy. I smeared strawberry jam, splinters stabbing my knees.

Adonis knelt beside me. "It's okay."

The broken plate cut into my fingers. I didn't care. I had to fix it, make it right. *Chipped glass slices my palms as I climb... the poison vial, smooth and cool under my fingertips. I reach for my mask, force my thumbs underneath, drag it off...*

"Verity, stop." Adonis's voice pulled me back to the present. He grabbed my hand, forcing me still. "It's okay, damn it!"

I shook my dizzy head to clear it. "Uh... sure. It's all good. I just made a mistake, that's all. Tired, I guess."

He helped me up. "I heard you last night. Didn't sound like nice dreams."

I didn't remember. Probably a good thing. I'd had enough night-mares to last a lifetime. I shrugged, and reached for another tart.

Adonis watched me. He hadn't said anything about my face, and I was grateful. What was there to say? "Finish up, already. Big sister wants to see you."

"Whatever. Like she cares." I pushed the newspaper over the counter towards him, my mouth full of strawberry goo. "What's wrong with this picture?"

He shrugged, avoiding my gaze. "What do you mean?"

"You know what I mean." I stabbed my finger at the photo. "Where are FortuneCorp in all this? Are we letting the Gallery get away with this stuff now? Jeez, I take a few months off and the place goes to hell."

"Did you read further down?"

"Huh?"

He flipped the folded newspaper over. Bottom half of page one, beneath the crime picture.

MAYORAL RACE HEATS UP ON CRIME
Villains Won't Drag Us Down, Says Fortune

Sapphire City's mayoral race is still too close to call, after candidates campaigned yesterday in the inland suburbs, the scene of many of the violent incursions that have terrorized citizens in recent weeks. Experts are predicting that policies on law and order will play a decisive role in the poll, to be held in just under two weeks, and it seems the candidates agree. The newest man in the race, local businessman Vincent Caine, visited a Bayview housing project where he promised long-time residents that, under his governance, their community would not be forgotten. "Too long, our disadvantaged communities have been easy prey for the unchecked violence of these power-augmented criminals," Mr. Caine said. "Only by regulating these people's activities and neutralizing their psychotic outbursts will our citizens once again feel safe." To that end, Mr. Caine promised the *Chronicle* that he will make an announcement on his innovative law and order policy in the next few days.

By contrast, the opposing candidate, Assistant District Attorney and socialite Equity Fortune, gave an impassioned speech at a charity luncheon, saying that she will not rest until the violence is stopped—but that conciliation, not regulation, is the key. "All Sapphire City's citizens must have a voice," Ms. Fortune said, "and that includes those with whose methods we do not necessarily agree. Freedom of speech is sacrosanct, and if sectors of our community must resort to unsavory acts in order to be heard, it is because we are not listening. If you elect me your mayor, I promise you, citizens: I will listen."

I tossed the paper away, disgusted. Typical. Equity was the eldest, and she'd always liked getting on TV, either with her mask on as Nemesis, the bringer of justice, or in the clear as assistant DA, trying high-profile cases and putting the villains away. "Our sister's running for mayor? God help us. What's all this crap about conciliation?"

Adonis shrugged, and flipped the paper back to the security photo. "As you see. FortuneCorp's taking a step back."

"So Equity can win votes from the bleeding-heart civil liberties sector? Give me a break. Has she unmasked? Told the world she's augmented?"

"Of course not."

"Of course not," I echoed ironically. "Even the bleeding hearts wouldn't vote for that, would they? And who's this other moron...?" I checked the name. It seemed familiar. "Local businessman Vincent Caine," I read. There was a picture of him, typical guy-in-a-suit. I squinted at it, trying to remember. "Oh, right. The smartphone guy?"

"That's him."

"'Neutralizing their psychotic outbursts', huh? Nice. Sounds like a hater to me." A few of Sapphire City's prominent citizens insisted all augments were bad news, whether good or evil, and that we should all be locked up for public safety. Apparently, this Caine was one of them.

"Maybe. A clever one, if he is. His company invents new-generation IT hardware, and they say he's still the brains behind it. But he's got the common touch. Self-made man, and all that. A lot of people like what he's got to say."

"People with crappy lives always like what scaremongers have to say. It justifies being afraid of their own shadows."

"Maybe," Adonis said again. "Or maybe they're just hardworking normals who've had their businesses torched by Razorfire, or their kids held hostage by some Gallery scumbag. Powers all look the same to people who don't have any."

"Yeah, well, there'd be a lot more scumbags holding kids hostage if you and I weren't around," I pointed out. "People always hate what they don't understand. Doesn't make it right."

"If you say so. But Caine's popular. Loaded, too, if the color of the campaign he's running is any guide."

"More loaded than the family Fortune?" I scoffed. "Say it ain't so."

"I know. Unthinkable, isn't it?"

I swallowed the last mouthful and smacked my lips. "Whatever. Let Equity play at politics. You and me against the world, eh? Let's get to work and kick some villainous butt."

"It's not that simple, Vee."

I cocked one singed eyebrow. "Villain's ass, my boot. Seems pretty simple to me."

"I told you. Equity wants FortuneCorp to take a step back."

I snorted. "Good thing Equity's not in charge, then."

Adonis just looked at me.

My bones chilled. "But... you're Dad's favorite. You know the company inside out. We always thought... You're the only one who can do what Dad did. It has to be you!"

"Equity's the eldest. It's how he wanted it." His eyes glinted, a flash of ocean-blue resentment. Gone so swiftly I could have imagined it.

But I knew I didn't, and my heart broke for him, like it had already broken for Blackstrike, our father, murdered at the ugly hands of Razorfire. Dad could have left anyone else in charge—his superconducting brother Illuminatus, for instance, or even Phantasm, our tetchily invisible cousin—and Adonis would have understood. But Equity?

She'd always treated me with disdain, because I spoke my mind instead of weighing every word for political correctness. I'm named for truth, after all, and in strategy meetings Dad always relied on me to tell it how it was. Still, it saddened me that she and I weren't closer, because on those rare occasions when she forgot to be a bitch, we actually got along okay.

But Equity resented Adonis. Not just for being Dad's favorite—like every guy of his generation, Dad wanted a son—but because Adonis was everyone's favorite. It wasn't enough for Equity to be strong, intelligent, a kick-ass attorney, and master of the power of light. She wanted to be glamorous, too. Adonis had the augment that Equity longed for, and she hated him for it.

It didn't make sense. Everyone knew Equity lived on celery sticks and jealousy. So why the hell had Dad left her in charge?

My stomach squirmed. I knew how it felt to believe your family had abandoned you. "Jeez. I don't know what to say."

"Say nothing. It's done. Equity's the new boss."

"And you're on board with that?"

"I have to be. What am I gonna do, go work for another secret crime-fighting family? Oh, wait, there aren't any." Adonis sounded resigned, like he'd already thought this over too many times. Didn't stop him sounding angry, too.

"But we're still equal shareholders, right? What about Chance?" Our littlest brother, with his cheeky surfer-boy smile and careless charm, was the only one Equity had any time for, probably because he made it easy for her to feel superior.

"You know Chance. Doing his own thing, as ever." Adonis's tone twinged sharp.

I understood his frustration. Chance didn't take the family business seriously. Sure, Adonis parties hard, but he'll drop it all in a heartbeat if there's work to be done. As a geeky teenager, I used to be jealous of Adonis's girlfriends, until I learned it's never the sister who gets her heart broken.

Chance, on the other hand, has talent up to his baby-doll eyelashes, but by Dad's standards, he's the family screw-up: instead of fighting crime, Chance prefers to use his lucky augment to risk his life at extreme sports, win the long odds at roulette and pick up girls.

Chance follows his heart; Adonis locks his heart away. I know who I trust more. "But what if—"

"It doesn't matter what Chance says, even if we could get the cocky little shit to turn up. The chairperson has the veto. Always did. You know that. Forget it, okay?" Adonis pushed me towards the bedroom. "Big sister awaits. Go get ready."

I chugged more OJ from the bottle and jammed it back in the fridge. "I am ready," I announced.

He eyed me critically. "Wearing that? You look like a hobo."

I snorted, glad of the change of subject. "Hey, they're your clothes. And oh, look." I patted my nonexistent pockets and frowned. "I seem to have misplaced my crime-fighter's spring collection while I was in the nuthouse. So sad. C'mon, we can worry about my fashion sense later."

"Just a sec." He vanished into the bedroom, and soon reappeared with a black suitcase, which he dumped on the table before me. "You might want these."

I unzipped it. Folded neatly inside lay my clothes. Some of them, anyway. My favorite blue jeans, soft from months of wearing. My T-shirts, even the wise-ass ones I knew he hated, and my leather belt. My old black lace-up boots, scuffed and charred from fighting. Even—bless him—a set of my knife-proof leathers.

And my mask.

I fingered the soft black leather. So familiar. My suit still smelled of flame and city dirt, a faint whiff of some perfume I didn't remember wearing.

All still here, even though I'd vanished. With this stuff, my brother had kept me alive.

My eyes burned. I was real after all. Or rather, the Seeker was real, and she was the important part of me. The Seeker was strong. Verity was weak. Nine months bolted into an augmentium helmet had proved that.

Without my power, I was nothing.

Adonis shrugged, sheepish. "They gave away your apartment after the memorial service. I couldn't keep everything. But I wanted... I couldn't just let you disappear."

I struggled to swallow on a lumpy throat. "You always were a sentimental idiot, Ad."

"You're welcome." He hugged me, one arm around my shoulders. "I'm glad you're home, Vee."

Home. It sounded good. I hugged him back, and his warm spritzy scent unleashed a fresh flood of memory. Only this time, they were good memories. I wasn't alone.

Adonis kissed my bruised forehead. "Go get changed. You don't want to be late. Equity's skipping a meeting, don't you know?"

5

We stepped from the elevator on the top and fifty-sixth floor of the FortuneCorp building. The long fluoro-lit lobby with its pewter-colored carpet still looked the same. On the way in, we passed Illuminatus, Dad's younger brother. He looked like an older, silver-frosted version of Adonis, and he threw me a handsome grin as he passed. His superconducting alloy bracelets crackled with static charge. "Verity. Heard you were back. Good to see you, girl."

"Thanks, Uncle Mike. You too." I grinned back, but it soon faded. Illuminatus and Blackstrike. Sapphire City's original crime-fighting duo. They'd never fight together again.

A skinny receptionist wearing too much makeup sat behind a curved glass desk. Adonis flicked her a smile, and she picked up the phone, frowning. "Ms. Fortune? Mr. Fortune and Ms. Fortune are asking to see you. Adonis and... and Verity."

I laughed. "Yeah, right. Pretty please. Whatever." When this was Dad's office, any of his kids could just walk right in. And I felt fine and belligerent once more in my jeans and kicker boots. My black T-shirt read I'M ONLY NICE TO ONE PERSON PER DAY, and then underneath, it said TODAY IS NOT YOUR DAY. It pretty much summed up how I felt.

I strode up to the frosted glass door and turned the handle. It wouldn't open.

Frustrated, I tried again, harder.

Adonis put a cool hand on my shoulder. "It's just security—"

"Security, my ass." I broke the lock with an angry flash of talent. The handle snapped downwards with a crunch, and I shoved the door open and stalked in, ignoring the receptionist's protests.

Afternoon sun streamed in the floor-to-ceiling windows. Below, the city glittered, the sunlight flashing on metal and glass skyscrapers, gloating over the flat summer waters of the bay. I squinted in the harsh glare, wishing I'd remembered to bring sunglasses. Equity has a natural affinity with light, and she likes it bright. The vast corner office was lined with ugly green plants that turned their faces sunwards, and at the far end, behind Dad's big blondwood desk, sat our sister.

She came around the desk to greet us. Tall and gangly as ever, she wore a neat navy-blue suit and heels. A rope of black pearls coiled around her neck over her white silken blouse. Her makeup was flawless, and she'd dyed her straight-bobbed hair, from plain old brown like mine to lustrous news-anchor auburn. She and I had inherited Mom's coloring. Like me, Equity would never be beautiful, but she looked elegant. Professional. Like a politician.

"Verity," Equity said, with all the warmth she could muster, which wasn't much. "Welcome back."

"Hey, E.," I replied grudgingly. If my ruined face shocked her, she'd hidden it admirably, and it cost me nothing to be pleasant. "Nice haircut. You look like President Palin. I'd vote for you."

Equity smiled, gracious. Obviously, she'd been practicing. "Adonis told me your tale." The smile vanished as quickly as it had appeared. "I'm sorry for what happened to you. That was a vicious attack. Quite uncalled for. I'm glad you're safe."

She sounded like she meant it. "Thanks," I muttered. "Listen, I want to get back to work—"

"Of course. Please." She ushered us to her little plush sofa arrangement by the sunlit window. A vase of silk orchids sat on the glass coffee table. Dad never liked fake flowers. I missed his big Chesterfield armchair, his smell of leather and cigarettes. When I was little, he'd play hide-and-seek with us, me and Chance and Dad's shadows. Equity had spoiled the game then, too.

I sat opposite her, and Adonis stood by the window, sunlight gilding his hair. Equity crossed her long legs, stockings gleaming. "How are you feeling, Verity?"

Dr. Mengele's blue gaze stabs mine like an iced needle. Her finger-tips cool my fevered cheek. Static prickles in my hair, the stink of ozone and sweat. "How do you feel now?" she asks. My stomach knots in terror, and I vomit in her lap...

I blinked, dizzy. How the hell did Equity think I felt, after nine months in the loony bin? "I feel fine."

She and Adonis exchanged glances. "You've had a horrible experience," she said. "It's only natural you'd be suffering some ill effects—"

"So my head hurts," I interrupted, scratching my itchy palms. On the way here, I'd filled Adonis in on everything they'd done to me. What had he told her? "Yours would, too, if you'd had the Augmentium Helmet of Death bolted to your skull. I'm fine."

"Even so," Equity said coolly, "you should see a doctor."

"No!" I'd jerked from my seat before I realized I'd moved. My guts cramped, and for a horrible moment I thought I'd wet myself. "A shrink, you mean. No fucking way. Never again!"

Sweat stung my burned cheek. My palms hurt, and I realized I'd jammed my nails into them. I was shaking. Jesus.

Adonis touched my arm. "Steady, Vee," he whispered. "No one's making you. She's just worried about you."

I sucked in deep breaths, trying to quiet my screaming nerves. I stuck my hand in my pocket, where I'd shoved my mask. It felt smooth and warm, soothing. I gripped it tightly for a moment. Only one thing could put the howling horror in my soul to sleep: Razorfire, drained and dying at my feet. "I don't need a doctor,"

I insisted. "What I need is to get back to work. Dad's dead, and R—and *he's* still out there, spouting his burn-it-all bullshit. I'm gonna remedy that."

"I'm afraid that will have to wait." Equity poured me a frosted glass of water from the carafe, her favorite set of gold bracelets clinking on her wrist.

I gulped the drink. "What? Why?"

"The situation is very delicately balanced out there. I've put a lot of work into negotiating a peace."

I snorted. "Yeah. I saw the police barricades, the shitfight on the front pages. Gallery goons running amok all over town. How's that peace working out for you?"

She strode to the window, and rounded to face me, hands clasped behind her. "Be sensible, Verity. If we've learned one thing in all these years, it's that you don't provoke this psychopath. If you go after Razorfire, the city will erupt. It's what he wants. Now's not a good time."

"Not a good time?" Water splashed my hand, and I set the glass down hard before I broke it. Muscles twitched in my thighs. I wanted to kick something. "He murdered Dad, E. He had me tortured. He tried to poison the whole damn city, and you don't think it's a *good time*?"

Equity eyed me coldly, augmented light glinting fiercely in her eyes. "This campaign is important. If we win, we'll have a blank slate to start making changes. I won't have you stirring up trouble."

"Stopping villains is not stirring up trouble," I retorted. "It's what we're here for. Razorfire is a murdering bastard. He doesn't deserve to live. If Dad was still alive—"

"I'm in charge now!" Angry white light flashed from Equity's fist. Swiftly, she quenched it, her jaw popping with the effort. "Dad's policies were outdated. Times have changed. War is no longer our objective. You'll do as you're told or I'll have you suppressed."

"Suppressed?" I repeated in astonishment. "What the hell does 'suppressed' mean? You gonna arrest me, is that it? Lock me up?"

"If I must."

Adonis raised his hand. "Calm down, kids—"

"No," I interrupted, furious. "I want to hear this. Let me get this straight, Equity. Razorfire has been our archenemy ever since we were kids. We've fought him and his filthy Gallery on the street since forever. Dad devoted his entire life to this war. Now Razorfire's winning, and you want to back off?" My fist clenched, warm. It felt good, after all, to say his name. It gave me power.

"No one's backing off." Her glib politician's tone only infuriated me more. "We're rejecting violence as a solution."

I guffawed, it was so ridiculous. "Are you insane? I bet the Gallery are just hanging out to renounce violence."

"I don't care what the Gallery want. Sinking to their level is no longer acceptable."

"Sinking, my ass," I snapped. "What are you so afraid of?"

She flushed, ugly. "I'm not afraid."

I strode up and stared her down. She was taller than me. I didn't care. "The hell you aren't," I said, my voice shaking. "You're a coward, Equity."

Adonis tugged his hair behind his neck and sighed. "Verity, chill out, will you?"

"Shut up, Ad. You know it's true." I laughed, and it tasted bitter. "Sure, let's sit down with Razorfire. It'll be fun. Hell, I'll even buy the sick freak a beer, just to let him know it's okay that he murdered our father!"

Equity's face stormed over, like it did when we were kids and I stole her toys, and I knew I was going too far. But I couldn't stop. The truth just frothed up, tainted with rage, and I spat the words into her face like poisoned darts. "He might as well kill the rest of us, too. Torture us, do whatever he wants. No need to worry, because FortuneCorp is rejecting violence as a solution!"

"Oh, grow up, Verity," Equity snapped at last. "There's more at stake here than the mess on your ugly face."

My throat swelled shut and, inside, my mind exploded in blood.

I shrieked, and slapped her. The crack of her cheek on my palm was loud, satisfying. But it wasn't my slap that sent her flying across the room.

My power erupted, thundering like monstrous drums in my head. Equity flew backwards into her desk. Paper and hardware scattered. A glass globe on the desk shattered, falling shards prisming in the sun.

Equity stumbled to her feet. Her mouth twisted, and she flung up one angry fist and hurled light at me.

So bright, my skin scorched like sunburn. My retinas seared blind. I screamed, and something in my brain stretched itself to the limit and tore. Somewhere, a window exploded, and dimly, I felt Adonis crash-tackle me to the floor.

My head clanged. Water poured from my eyes. My throat was swollen, I couldn't breathe. I wheezed, gulping for air.

Gradually, the glare faded. Adonis hovered into focus above me. I blinked, reeling, my eyes burning like acid. He gripped my wrists, shaking me. "Verity. Let it go. Chill. C'mon."

"Okay... Fine... Get off me." I scrambled to my feet, panting. The window behind me was smashed, and breeze swirled in, ruffling the plants and scattering paper on the floor like tumbleweed. What the hell had I done? Equity pissed me off, but attacking her was uncalled for. "Jesus. I'm sorry, E. I didn't mean it. Guess I'm still a little tense."

"I think you should leave now." Equity advanced on me, her eyes alight with chilly fury. Silver light glittered between her fingers, and sparks crackled from her hair. "I don't want to see you. I don't want to talk to you. See a doctor, don't see a doctor, I really don't give a shit. But I swear to you, Verity, if you interfere with my campaign I will come down on you like an act of God. Now get out of my office, and don't come back."

My vision swirled. "What? I said I didn't mean—"

"Didn't you hear me? You're fired. Get out."

"What?" Adonis was incredulous. "Jesus, E. Give her a break."

I laughed. "I'm a Fortune. You can't fire me."

Equity smiled back, thin and cold. "I can. I just did. Get out."

My jaw dropped. Speechless, I looked to Adonis for something—anything—but he just gave a tight shrug, his gaze guarded. *Later,* it promised. *Don't make this worse.*

I swallowed. Flexed my fingers. Coiled my power tightly. "Fine," I said calmly, and walked out. Behind me, Adonis swore and started arguing with her. I didn't stop. Didn't look back.

On the way down in the elevator, I let my forehead fall against the cold metal wall, and closed my eyes. She'd fired me. My own damn sister. Fine, I shouldn't have hit her. But she was letting my enemy get away with murder...

Wind whips my hair back. Tears scorch my chilled cheeks. I scrabble for the poison vial. It's just out of my reach. I stretch out with my power, but something yanks me backwards. I fall. My face slams into metal, and a lick of razor-sharp flame slices the floor apart an inch from my nose...

My head swam, images and memories mingling like water. FortuneCorp were the good guys. We were meant to fight villains, not encourage them. Not—the word stung sour in my mouth—*negotiate* with them.

I stood straighter, and scraped my hair back, automatically checking my look in the mirror, a second before I remembered what I'd see.

My stomach tilted, sick. My eyes looked dark and hollow, my mouth a tight line. Still burned. Still scarred. Still hideous.

There's more at stake than your ugly face.

Oily rage boiled inside me, and I shoved it away, pounding my fists against my thighs until my burning blood subsided. She was wrong. Yes, I wanted revenge. For my face, my shattered memory, all those months of agony. I wanted to make Razorfire suffer like I'd suffered, scrape that knowing smile from his lips, watch the fire flicker out in his hate-bright eyes and whisper, *this is for what you did to me.*

But it wasn't just about my face. It wasn't even that Razorfire killed Dad and had me tortured until my mind nearly shattered. Razorfire was a public menace. A terrorist and mass-murderer. A psychopath who despised everyone and everything, who'd stop at nothing until he owned the world, or burned it all.

He didn't deserve to live. And I wasn't going to let him.

Hot determination forged to steel in my heart. I pulled my mask from my pocket and wrapped it tightly around my fist. The leather's soft stretch across my skin felt safe. It gave me strength. If Equity wasn't on my side, fine. I'd talk to Adonis, our cousins, Dad's old friends, even Chance. And if they wouldn't help me? I'd just have to do it on my own.

The elevator pinged as it reached street level. The doors slid aside, and I walked out.

Into two big guys, who grabbed my shoulders and yanked me forwards.

I stumbled, but they dragged me to my feet. A woman in a pale suit smiled at me. A blond woman with glacial blue eyes, who held a gleaming silvery helmet.

Dr. Mengele.

No. My blood screamed cold. My muscles spasmed in terror, the remembered stink of piss and fear. *I'm not a bad person. I can't go back there. I can't.*

Someone had betrayed me. They were sending me back to the asylum.

A wail of denial ripped my lungs raw. *Escape, or die.*

6

I yelled, and let my power explode.

The glass walls shattered, and crashed in silvery waterfalls. Breeze swept in from the street, dragging my hair wild. People in the double-story lobby screamed and ran. The two heavies stumbled, and something sharp scraped the skin between my neck and shoulder, the hot sting of a needle. A plastic syringe tumbled onto the tiles. They'd been about to stick me, fill me full of sleepy-time shit so I wouldn't struggle.

Good luck with that.

Mengele kept coming. *Should have killed the evil bitch when I had the chance.* More of her people came out of nowhere on all sides, running for me. Behind the reception desk, the lobby security guy reached for his radio. I crouched, panting, and sized up my enemy. Surrounded. No way through. No way out.

I gathered my power beneath me, and leapt.

Force flung me skywards. I somersaulted, and fell, dragging the air downwards with all the strength I could muster. The heavies looked up. I landed in a crouch in their midst, slamming my fist into the tiles with a crack like thunder.

Boom! The shock wave rippled outwards, shattering ceramic

as it went. The floor quaked. Mengele and her heavies staggered, and I sprang to my feet and sprinted for freedom.

I hurdled spiky broken glass and screeched out onto the sunlit street. People gawked. I shoved them aside. Behind me, heavy footsteps pounded, Mengele's goons coming after me. I had a few seconds' head start, if that. Better make the most of it.

I ran across the street, dodging honking traffic. Despite the danger, it felt good to run, wind in my face, blood pumping in my legs. But my scratched shoulder felt hot and numb at the same time, and I knew with a sinking stomach that some of their helljuice had made it into my system. It was only a matter of time before I fell and couldn't get up. If I wasn't safe before that happened...

I ran faster, my thighs protesting with a fresh burst of lactic acid. Tires squealed and drivers yelled abuse as the goons followed, not as agile as I was. I ducked through a corner coffee shop, leaping the tables with a flex of power. The goons would have to go around. Score another few seconds for me. I skidded around another corner, out of sight for a few precious moments. A brick two-story was jammed in between two ten-floor glass office buildings. An old guest house or something, converted into a bank, its sloping tiled roof shimmering in the sun.

No time to think. I leapt onto the roof, and crouched beside the chimney pot, dying to gasp for breath but barely daring to inhale.

The goons tumbled around the corner. My chest ached for air. I didn't dare move. Sweat trickled down my neck. My shadow loomed frighteningly large on the roof tiles. Surely, they'd see me. The buildings either side were too tall, even for me. I can jump, sure, but I can't fly. And I couldn't climb those smooth glassy walls...

My sweaty fingers slip as I clutch the glass. The stairway's cut off, enemies everywhere. I have to climb. Fifty stories below, the ground looms. Swirling wind threatens to sweep me away. My stomach plummets, but I scrabble and drag myself skyward...

I swallowed, dry. The numbness in my shoulder was spreading.

I had nowhere else to run. Surely, they had to see me.

But the goons didn't look up. They just kept running.

I let out my breath in a rush, and gulped for air. They weren't dumb. I didn't have much time before they realized their mistake and came back. Gotta get out of here.

I stood, and dizziness rinsed my balance thin. I staggered, clutching the chimney. Jesus. My fingers were numb. I couldn't stand straight. Fighting creeping nausea, I crawled to the rear of the building and peered over the edge.

The ground telescoped, shimmering. I closed my eyes, lowered myself over the gutter. Dropped to the ground, cushioning my landing with a clumsy flex of power.

The narrow alley was shadowed and caked with grime. A few plump black trash bags heaped next to a dumpster. I leaned against the wall for a second or two, sweating, struggling to straighten my thoughts.

I had no other clothes. Couldn't disguise myself. And I had nowhere to run to. I couldn't go back to Adonis's place. Someone in my own family had betrayed me, and they'd know where to look. I was on my own...

Someone shoved me, and I bounced off the brick wall and fell.

Terror squeezed my guts. I scrabbled to get up, run. But a boot slammed my shoulder, pinning me down. A smoke-roughened voice taunted me. "What have we here, lads? An uppity little augmented bitch, that's what."

Huh? I fought to clear my vision. Big blond kid, sleeveless black hoodie, steel hoop earrings. Not a Mengele goon. Three of his friends slouched behind him. A skinhead one spat nonchalantly on the sidewalk, the chains on his jeans clanking. A dreadlocked girl popped pink bubblegum, stretching it around one tattooed finger. Another fat one sweated, his pasty skin gleaming, and clutched something shiny and round in his fist.

Haters. Great.

I struggled to rise, but my thigh muscles softened like pudding, and the ground kept sliding out from under me. Frustration jabbed me sharp in the belly. I didn't have time for this. "Look, just lemme 'lone, 'kay."

"I seen you jump onto that roof, bitch." The leader prodded my collarbone with his boot, cracking my head back into the bricks. "Who the fuck you think you are, Supergirl? You're not welcome here. Geddit?"

"Uh-huh. Whadebba..." My mouth was stuffed with sticky string. Goddamn it. I tried to focus, to stretch the air like elastic and fling these assholes away from me, but I couldn't concentrate. I couldn't flex. I was just plain Verity, and I couldn't get away.

Shit.

He kicked me. I barely felt the pain, just my ribs bending under the force, my skin swelling. Again, more, all four of them getting into the act.

Hysterically, I laughed. These morons would kick me to death before Mengele's goons could get to me. And thanks to the drug, I couldn't even feel it. That was some funny shit.

I tried to crawl away, to cradle my head in my arms. The sidewalk scraped my elbows raw. Crimson splotched from my nose. A punch slammed me into the wall, dizzy. I spat red, and crawled some more. What else could I do?

The leader loomed over me, his spiked blond hair dripping with sweat, and dragged my chin up with a fist in my hair. "Like that, bitch? Where's your power now?"

Dimly, I fumbled for my list of oh-so-witty replies. *Up your butt, you stinky hater. Your momma wears jackboots.* Or just plain *screw you.* That's always a good one.

The fat one gave a slobbery grin. "You ever make an augmented bitch squeal, Bro?"

"I don't believe so, Slugger." Bro's smile split wider. "I'm thinking we should see to that."

"I'm thinkin' you're right."

The girl popped her bubble gum, shuffling. "Jesus Christ. You

43

can't do that."

"Shut up, Cookie." Bro dragged my head back harder, and reached for his belt buckle.

I coughed out a bloody mouthful. *Take that out and I'll bite it off, you whiskey tango son of a bitch,* I tried to say. "Urrphh..."

He screamed, and clawed at his own face.

I scrambled back, bewildered.

He kept screaming. Kept digging his fingers deeper into his own eyes. The others did the same, howling and flailing about in unseen agony, and finally they hurled curses and staggered off.

Huh? I hadn't done that. I *couldn't* do that. What the hell just happened...?

The air shimmered like heat haze, and a shadow coalesced on the bloodstained concrete.

A tall, broad shadow, in the shape of a man.

I scuttled away like a dizzy crab, fumbling on the rough side-walk. Who the hell was that?

But my eyelids drooped. My numb lips drooled. I dragged my swimming head up, forcing my blurry eyes to focus. There he was, leaning against the dumpster. Long legs in jeans and boots, a scuffed leather coat. A glimpse of tousled black hair and white teeth, mingled with shimmering shadows. I couldn't see his face. *Need to see...*

I fought my clogged tongue, my sinking wits. *Who are you?* I wanted to say, but the drug overcame me. I caught the warm scent of vanilla as the stranger lifted my limp body in his arms, and the world dissolved into murky nothing.

7

I awoke sluggishly, in dim electric light that hurt my eyes. Soft cushions squished beneath me, a whiff of dark vanilla. An ancient incandescent bulb swung above on its cord, an inch one way, an inch the other. The tiny breeze stirred my hair. The air smelled crisp, recycled. Overhead, I heard rushing water, and something large and mechanical rumbled distantly.

The subway, I registered dimly. I was underground. But where? And how?

I sat up on the bed, wincing. Thirst tore my throat, and my body ached like poison. I stretched, popping my vertebrae one by one. Bruises everywhere, purple and yellow. Those assholes had really kicked the shit out of me. And… uh.

I wore a man's white shirt. Soft and clean, buttoned over my chest. Underneath, I was naked.

My ribs itched, and when I scratched them I found gauze and white paper tape. Someone had washed me, tended my bruises. I touched my face gingerly, and my fingers came away clean and smelling of antiseptic ointment.

Whoever had tended me, they didn't necessarily mean well.

But hey, at least I wasn't wearing hospital scrubs and an

augmentium helmet. That had to be an improvement. Right?

I swung my legs over the bed's edge and tried to stand. Instead, I fell, a six-foot drop. I landed, shaken, on a cool concrete floor. Roughly, I tugged the shirt down over my butt. Very funny.

The bunk bed was jammed into an alcove behind me. I squinted into the gloom. Large square room, low ceiling, walls fading into darkness. Next to the bed, in another alcove, sat a claw-foot bathtub with a rusted shower. Somewhere, a generator hummed, and a keyboard clattered as someone typed.

I swallowed, my throat crispy. Would I discover my shadowy rescuer's identity at last? I might not like what I found. Sapphire City vomited up new villains as fast as we could wash the old ones down the drain.

But I had to know. Mr. Mysterious had probably saved my life—not to mention my dignity—from the haters at least, and probably from Mengele's goons too. Presuming it wasn't all a trap, of course. If we didn't get along, I'd just flip him a quick *thanks for nothing* and run again. I was getting good at running.

I followed the clickety-clack of keys, tiptoeing past gray metal shelves loaded with books, files, boxes of photographs, newspapers, cables and electrical components I didn't recognize. Light flickered between the shelves. I clenched my fist, readying my power for a swift onslaught, and crept out.

A double row of screens gleamed—websites, television channels, CCTV—above a long desk covered in a mess of paper and photographs six inches deep. In a high-backed chair hunched a long lean figure, his shadow looming huge and monstrous on the wall.

He didn't stop typing. Didn't look up. Just jerked his head towards the corner of the room. "Door's that way."

So much for stealth. I cleared my throat, and stepped out where he could see me. But I still clasped my hands tightly behind my back, ready. "Excuse me?"

"You can leave whenever you want. I won't stop you. No need to break things." His voice was rough and rich, like old bourbon.

His battered leather coat hung over the back of his wheeled chair. He finished whatever he was doing, and swung his chair around, skidding into the light.

Strong, lean, the same tight black T-shirt and jeans he'd worn before. A few days of beard shadowed his chin, dark against his olive skin, and his wild black hair had a single albino splash at the front. He wore a leather band buckled around one wrist, and a silver ring on his right ring finger.

Intriguing. Younger than I'd expected, for a guy who'd sent a gang of haters screaming. Warmer, somehow. I wanted to see the rest of his face.

But I couldn't. He wore a mask. A black one, like mine, tied at the back of his head and cut around sharp cheekbones that made him look feral or crazy. All I could see were his eyes, deep and starlit black.

Uh-huh. I wanted to fidget. Handsome devil, to be sure. The crazies often are, in that offbeat, intriguing sort of way. It's a rule of the universe, or something. Sick equals sexy.

But suddenly I was conscious of my scarred cheek, my bruises, the fact that I was wearing his shirt and nothing else.

I dragged in a fistful of power and swept a pile of books off his desk. "That's close enough."

Paper drifted in dust, and settled. He didn't move. Just glanced at the mess I'd made, and then back at me. His black-and-white hair stuck up in odd directions, like a skunk who'd partied too hard. He reminded me of my little brother Chance, only Chance was cheerful and careless. This guy looked neither. "Threat taken," he said calmly. "You done?"

I studied him, wary. No reaction. No move to retaliate. Whatever his augment was, he was keeping it holstered for now. Was that stripe in his hair real? He didn't seem the type to make like a skunk. "For the moment," I said at last. "But you'll talk, or maybe I will start breaking stuff. Starting with you. Who are you?"

"You can call me Glimmer."

I recalled my assailants, clawing for their eyeballs though nothing was there. *Glimmer.* A hypnosis trick, maybe? "Is that what your friends call you?"

"I don't have any friends." He folded his arms, and muscles bulged in the sleeves of his T-shirt.

"Figures. You always wear your mask in the house, Glimmer?"

"I have a guest. It's only polite… oh, wait." He stuffed a hand into his back pocket and offered me a little black bundle. "This was in your jeans. I kept it for you."

My mask. I snatched it, careful not to touch him, and unrolled it, enjoying the warm softness in my fingers. It smelled of him: vanilla and danger.

Okay. So he knew I was augmented. I knew the same about him. Not a recipe for friendship.

Glimmer smiled, bittersweet. "Don't mention it."

"I didn't. How did you chase those idiots away?"

Strange watery shadows flickered over his face, from no light source that I could see. "I poured acid in their eyes," he said at last, and his black eyes gleamed with eerie starlight.

"No, you didn't," I accused. "I was there."

He scrunched his hair in one fist, and showed me a crooked smile. Bashful. Harmless. For an instant, I almost believed it. "Very astute. Of course I didn't. But they didn't know that. It's just a little illusion."

"A *glimmer?*"

"If you like."

"Okay." I fidgeted, relaxing only slightly. We had mindbenders at FortuneCorp. Adonis, for one, and our shifty cousin Ebenezer with the feartalent. If this Glimmer used his hypno-mojo on me, he'd be sorry. "Why did you help me?"

He shrugged. "I don't like haters."

"Not good enough." It came out harsher than I'd intended. I was grateful, after all, that he'd saved me from another round of Dr. Mengele's sadistic games. But it didn't mean I had to like this, or him. "You could've chased them off and left me."

"I was passing by. You needed help. And you were drugged, probably against your will. Somehow, I didn't think hospital was a good idea. I'm no medic, but..." He indicated my bandages. "You feeling okay? You've been out for two days."

Great. More lost time. I shrugged, brusque. "What've you done with my clothes?"

"There was blood. I washed 'em." He pointed to a pile on a chair, my jeans and T-shirt with boots on top. "You hungry?"

Inwardly I cursed, but too late. My stomach croaked audibly.

He laughed, warm whiskey. "C'mon, lady, chill out. If I was your enemy, you'd already be dead. Whoever you're running from, they haven't found you so far. Will a few more minutes kill you?"

I sighed, defeated. "Okay. Fine. Can I wash up? And can I, uh, use your phone?"

"You gonna call the cops?"

"No." Like I'd tell him if I was.

"Then knock yourself out." Glimmer tossed me a cell phone, swiveled back to his glowing screens, and ignored me.

I grabbed my clothes and headed out back to the bathroom. My wound dressings got in the way of having a shower, but I washed up as best I could with a towel. The water from the bath taps tasted coppery, but it was hot, and his soap smelled of vanilla and spice. My freshly washed jeans felt crisp against my skin. I didn't see a washing machine. Had he done them by hand?

I pulled my T-shirt over my head, uneasy. Maybe he truly didn't mean me any harm. Then again, I'd heard of serial killers who treated their victims like pets.

I tied my boots and smoothed my damp hair. The mask, I stuffed into my pocket. He'd already seen my face, and clearly knew I was augmented. Probably knew everything else about me, too. What did I have left to hide?

I studied the cell phone he'd given me. Full reception, even though we were underground. Maybe he had a repeater or something. I squirmed, suspicious. It was a risk. But I didn't know what else to do. No one at FortuneCorp had this number. If I didn't stay on the line for very long, they'd never find me. Right?

I held my breath, and dialed my brother's number, the only one of his four that I could remember. Despite everything that had happened, I couldn't believe Adonis would lie to me.

He picked up after three rings. "PR."

I swallowed, dry. "Hey. It's me."

"Jesus." A muffled sound, like he'd put his hand over the phone. "Where are you?" he whispered. "Are you okay? What happened?"

"The doctor from the asylum. Someone told her where I was. I…" Stupid tears blinded me. Fuck. I'd forgotten how much I'd missed his voice. How much he gave me strength. "Someone's after me, Ad. I don't know what to do."

"Okay. Verity, listen to me." Calm, collected, in charge, like always. "You can't come home. It's not safe for you here. Find somewhere to hole up, and I'll sort this out. Equity will listen to us once she's calmed down. I know she will. But I can't protect you unless I know who your enemies are."

Relief sweetened my blood, but at the same time, tiny poisoned claws pricked my heart, sour with suspicion. *He would say that, wouldn't he?* a harsh voice hissed in my ear. *If he was in on it, that's exactly what he'd say. "She'll listen to you, Verity, just tell me everything…"*

No. It wasn't true. If he was in on it, he'd say, *"Come home, Verity, I'll take care of you, it's not safe for you out there. Come home."*

Adonis loved me. He was on my side. I knew it in my heart.

But that didn't mean his phone wasn't tapped. I struggled to keep my voice low. "No. I have to do this on my own. I'll get to the bottom of this, I promise. I'll be in touch. I… I just wanted you to know I'm okay."

"But—"

"Talk soon, Ad." I ended the call, and broke the phone open with shaking fingers. Pulled out the SIM card, and crushed it beneath my boot. Now, no one at FortuneCorp could trace me. At least, I hoped not.

I wiped my leaking eyes. Enough with the self-pity. I had things to do.

Taking a steadying breath, I walked back into the room. The delicious smell of cooked tomato and oregano watered my mouth. Glimmer was messing about in his little kitchenette, his crazy hair sticking up like a mad scientist's. He looked like a cross between Dr. Jekyll and Pepé le Pew.

It was unsettlingly charming.

I held out the gutted phone. "I, uh, had to break your SIM. Sorry."

He shrugged. "It's okay. I go through dozens." He yanked a bowl from his microwave and shoved it across the cracked bench towards me. "Hungry?"

My stomach grumbled. Lasagna, my favorite, homemade, steaming hot and dripping with herbed tomato sauce and cheese. Beat the hell out of Pop-Tarts. "Um—"

"Eat," he insisted. "I've had a dozen chances to poison you already. You've got serious trust issues, you know that?"

I snorted. "Hey, pal, you're the one with the secret underground lair."

That crooked smile. "Yeah. Well. A little paranoia is an occupational hazard."

"Uh-huh. And what is your occupation, exactly?"

"I watch things. Record them. Do a little cleaning up. As you see." He extended his hand in an *after-you* gesture. His wrist was scarred on the inside, I noticed, old pale lines criss-crossed over the veins. I looked away, uncomfortable. He wouldn't be the first augment to loathe his own skin. *Steel slicing soft flesh, warm blood spurting, the bitter taste of copper...*

I took the bowl and spoon and headed back to his desk. He sat, bathed in his screens' pale light. I took a cautious bite of lasagna. Mmm. Delicious herbs and roasted tomato made my mouth weep, and I gave up and dug in.

"What's all this?" I mumbled, my mouth full. Touchscreens, data flows, a virtual display projecting fine white light in three dimensions. It reminded me of the set-up in Adonis's living room, only bigger, flashier, more sinister and a whole lot cooler.

"My eyes and ears." Glimmer's fingers darted over the keyboard, and real-time CCTV flashed up, fuzzy black-and-white video of bright-lit shelves of cigarettes and snack food, a security grille, logo-painted windows. "Will you look at this? That's the fourth time the Gallery have robbed that same convenience store in six months. Someone forgot to pay their protection."

Curiosity got the better of me, and I leaned over his chair. Twenty-four-hour news channels, local and national, video upload websites. Stock market watch lists. *Sapphire City Chronicle* website. Bank and tax records. Police department database, dispatch comms, vehicle movement maps. Custom search engines, automatically sorting and filing hits. An optical satellite tracking system, GPS, cell phone grid triangulations, all overlaid on a digital map of Sapphire City. His own files, reams of information, dates and names and events meticulously catalogued. And all of it about crime and criminals.

Here were images, filed and numbered, mug shots, security cameras, paparazzi snaps and surveillance shots. I swiped through them on the big touchscreen. Gallery hooligans, the unaugmented kind with shotguns and pistols, robbing banks and gas stations, holding hostages, fighting with riot police, whipping up violence at mass demonstrations against poverty or war. Torched housing projects, the charred shells of stores and warehouses. Corpses, shot, burned and mutilated, the victims of gang violence and other angry Gallery shenanigans.

But also the augmented, masked and costumed. I leaned closer, spooning in another tomato-drenched mouthful. Damn, he could cook. This image showed a skinny African-American woman, in a fish-tailed black Goth skirt criss-crossed with scarlet ribbons. Her arm was cocked back, long-nailed fingers bent like talons, midway through hurling a cloud of screeching insects at a fire engine. Her hair flew in a bright crimson tangle, and her eyes were painted with cruel black makeup like a mad Egyptian queen.

"That's Witch," Glimmer said absently, typing as he talked. "She's Gallery. Real name Patience Crook. Owns an occult shop, crystals, tarot cards, all that quasi-Wiccan stuff. Only she's the real deal."

I raised my eyebrows. Nice. We'd never been able to track her true identity down. I swallowed the last of my dinner—mmm, delicious, he'd make some woman a good wife one day—and left the bowl on the desk. "You got some good info here. How come I never heard of you?"

"Maybe I don't want to be famous."

"Give it a rest, Glimmer. You know what I am. We're in the same game. How come we never met?"

He shrugged, but his black gaze darted away. "I keep to myself."

"Right." I flicked to the next image. Another Gallery villain, a stocky guy with long greasy hair, slamming his fist through a shopping mall's glass ceiling and freezing it to glittering icicles. "Awesome," I remarked. "My good buddy Iceclaw. Charming son of a devil. Nearly lost three fingers to frostbite one time because of him…"

I bit my tongue, appalled. Jeez, did I just share? What was this, a crime-fighters' coffee club? For all I knew, this Glimmer character was Gallery too, and playing sly tricks with me.

But I didn't think so.

Call me naïve, but some fragile instinct warmed my blood about him, and it wasn't just that he was sorta cute and smelled great and cooked like a punk-ass Jamie Oliver. He was good-guy material, no question.

And I had to admit, it felt good to be back in the game.

"Likewise," Glimmer said, either oblivious or pretending not to notice my discomfort. "Iceclaw's real name is Declan Finney. He doesn't have a regular job. Just hangs around the docks, crushing knuckles and collecting tribute money from the Dockside Boys."

I wrinkled my nose, disgusted. "Charming. One of those guys who just likes wrecking stuff. He giggles when he freezes things, d'you know that? Like an evil little boy killing ants with a magnifying glass."

The next image popped up, and I had to bite my tongue again. My uncle Mike, masked in silver, his bracelets alight with charge. He crouched on the roof of a trolley car, blue lightning crackling from his fingers.

I stiffened, unwilling to speak. How much did Glimmer know about our family?

"Illuminatus," supplied Glimmer. "With an augment like that, he could be a terror. I'm still figuring out who's who in the zoo around here. Luckily, this guy seems to be on our side."

I snorted. Fishing for information? Good luck with that. I wasn't about to tell him, for instance, that Uncle Mike was basically a human lightning rod, and that if he ever took those bracelets off, there'd be charred ground and broken glass from here to Oakland. "*Our* side?"

"Yeah." Glimmer slanted warm dark eyes at me. "Y'know. Truth, justice, freedom from violence. That sort of thing?"

"Uh-huh." I folded my arms, defiant. "Let me give you some advice, young Jedi. Be careful who you trust. You don't know me from a kipper. For all you know, I'm the Gallery's latest trick. What makes you think I give a damn for truth and justice?"

That quirky smile again. "I've had plenty of chances to hurt you, right?"

"Yeah, yeah, we've covered that. Thanks so much, and all. What about it?"

"Well, so have you, lady, and you haven't come at me yet. That's good enough for me." He tilted his chair back. "Now can we move past the Mexican standoff and get down to business? You have enemies, so do I. Maybe we can help each other. But if you want to leave, go right ahead. I won't stop you." He spun back to his screens, dismissing me.

In the screens' eerie glow, his shadow loomed on the wall, distorted, a stick insect with crazy hair. I dragged a hand across my chin, frustrated. He was right. At least he hadn't tried to kill me, or throw me in an asylum, at least not yet. And—be realistic—what other choice did I have?

I had no friends left. I couldn't trust my own family. Adonis's phone was probably tapped. And my power was erratic, at best. I was damaged. Until I recovered from Mengele's screw-your-mind tricks, I wasn't operating at full capacity.

Razorfire, on the other hand, was unharmed, and wreaking havoc unmolested. Apparently, I couldn't defeat him even at the height of my powers, let alone half crippled like this. Add to that his fanatical Gallery chums, augmented and normal, who'd cheerfully hunt me down in a heartbeat on his say-so…

Maybe—just maybe—I couldn't do this alone.

8

"Okay." My mouth dried up like I'd just said *I love you*. Jeez, if Skunkboy went all *welcome-to-the-team* on me, I'd die of embarrassment.

But Glimmer just flashed that crooked smile at me over his shoulder. The pale stripe in his hair glistened silver in the screen-light. "Relax, tough girl. Doesn't mean we're dating, or anything."

Bless his cute little butt. I snorted, grateful. "Not in this universe, pal."

"Famous last words." He pointed at the image of Uncle Mike on the trolley car, and it sprang onto the virtual display, zooming into high resolution on a streetlamp's orange halo. "See? That faint oval shimmer under the streetlamp? That's Phantasm. A light-bender. He's hard to pin down. I only got that shot because of the three-angle shadows."

I peered closer, thankful to get down to work without any more friendly-ass fuss. Heh. So it was: Cousin Jeremiah. Wait till I tell the OCD little brat he's been made. He'll count toothpicks for a week.

Still, I fidgeted, memories dancing an elusive waltz. Uncle Mike saw me outside Equity's office. He could have set Mengele on me, though I had no idea why he'd want to. Hell, for all I knew,

Phantasm-slash-Jeremiah was skulking about in Equity's office the whole time.

Thing was, I hadn't been paying attention. I'd been too damned angry at Equity to care.

I swiped the picture away too roughly, and the display skipped a few. Another pic flashed up, shadow piled upon shadow, a tall dark figure facing a towering wall of liquid fire.

"Blackstrike," Glimmer said, unnecessarily. I'd know my father anywhere, his spare frame, his black coat swirling, his long fingers fashioning those writhing plumes of darkness.

My throat hurt. I wanted to reach out, slide my fingers over the glass. Touch him, give him one of our rare, awkward hugs. Tell him I was sorry he'd died trying to save me.

Too late for that, old girl.

Maybe that was it. Uncle Mike and Dad had been inseparable. Maybe Mike was inconsolable, and blamed me...

"That's my last image of him," Glimmer continued. "Five days after that, he vanished. They say he's dead. I'm not so sure, but he covers his tracks too well. I don't have a real name to trace him with."

Clank! My jaw dropped, along with the penny. "You really don't have a clue who I am, do you?"

His eyes narrowed, midnight slits. "I know you're not Blackstrike, if that's what you mean."

I laughed, dazed. Glimmer didn't know me. Had no idea, in fact. About me, or Dad, or FortuneCorp.

About any of it.

My mind splintered, glitter-sharp. All just coincidence. Maybe Glimmer really did just stumble over me in that alley. Maybe he really had built up all this intel by himself, from nothing. Fact was, I wasn't sensing a single ounce of guile in my glimmery new friend.

Either that, or Mr. Tall-skunk-and-handsome was a most excellent liar.

"Dude, you have so much to learn." I shook my head,

incredulous, and flicked to the next image.

Glimmer spoke, but I didn't hear. I stared, frozen, my vision soaked in crimson death.

Razorfire always wore red.

My pulse pounded. Sick heat washed over me, and I covered my mouth.

Just a sneaky snapshot of him, rounding an office building's corner with his sleek head cocked to one side. Tall, angular, graceful like a shark. He had a fetish for this long close-fitting coat in the Mandarin style, high-collared and shiny red. His hawk-like mask was dark and glassy, some heat-reflective alloy, a rusty color like dried blood. He stared directly at the camera, like he didn't give a shit he was being watched, and though I couldn't see anything burning, his eyes gleamed orange, the triumphant reflection of fire.

Glimmer looked up. "What? You okay?"

I nodded frantically, fingers plastered over my lips. Blood thundered in my skull. I wanted to scream. I wanted to be sick. I wanted to smash the screen, clamber through the shards into that little glass world and squeeze the sick bastard's throat in my bleeding hands until he choked his last. "It's..." I spluttered, and forced my hands down. "Razorfire," I managed, strangled. "What have you got on him?"

"More than I want to." Glimmer reached for the screen, ready to access more, but glanced at my face and apparently thought better of it. Instead, he skidded his chair back. "But less than I need," he admitted. "He always slips my surveillance. It's like he knows he's being watched, and can disappear at will—"

"You got a name?" I interrupted. "A picture in the clear? Anything?"

A soft laugh. "You're kidding, right? Believe me, lady, that one's personal. If I knew who Razorfire was, I wouldn't be sitting here with my thumb up my—"

"What about the night Blackstrike died? Have you got CCTV?"

"Nope. I've got nothing. It's the damnedest thing. Everything from that night has been erased…" He narrowed black eyes at me again. "What do you know about that?"

"Blackstrike's dead," I repeated flatly. "Razorfire killed him. I was there. You can add that to your file."

Glimmer leaned forward, elbows on knees, clasping his strong hands together. "Lady," he said slowly, "I think it's time you told me who you are."

My stomach twisted tight, laundry in a wringer. Damn it if I didn't want to trust him. But could I?

Did I have a choice? I was safe here, at least so far. I'd no one else to confide in. Nowhere else to go.

No one else who gave a shit.

"Long story," I offered at last, trying to keep it light.

"I've got all night—" An electric alarm screeched, and he spun his chair around to face the screens. "Uh-oh. It's on."

I leaned over him. "What was that?"

"I've got alerts set on CCTV and satellite surveillance. My algorithm matches known villains with suspicious activity, police comms traffic, emergency calls, that sort of thing. Not always accurate, but it lets me sleep." He pointed, and virtual video burst forth in black and white. "Look. Hostage situation. Looks like… the Bay Bridge."

I peered closer, and my pulse quickened. A thin figure in a shiny black catsuit leapt about like a big insect on the five westbound lanes of the upper deck. Her long black hair flew in the breeze. She was tossing cars left and right with what looked like a lasso made of thick glassy rope.

"Fuck." My fists clenched. "I know that skinny Gallery bitch."

"Arachne." Glimmer typed swiftly, his dark gaze darting from screen to screen. "Last week she cleared an attempted murder rap for crashing a trolley car. Looks like she's getting her own back." He jumped up, scooped his long leather coat from the desk and tossed it to me. "You up for some action?"

Nonplussed, I caught it. The worn leather warmed my fingers.

"Uh. Sure."

He unearthed a pistol—matte black, semiautomatic—from the junk on his desk, and swiftly checked the magazine. Smart lad. I approved. Like I said, life isn't a comic book, and all the augments in the world won't save you from a bullet in the neck. Only an idiot takes anything less than a gun to a gunfight. "Good," he said, clearing the chamber with a *snap!* "Put that on and let's go."

"But it's not cold," I protested, more out of contrariness than any distaste for wearing his coat. *Au contraire.* Clever, cute, reclusive, a disarming touch of paranoia. He could even cook. Hell, I could learn to like this Glimmer character, if his bleeding heart didn't get us both killed first.

I blushed, though he couldn't hear my thoughts. Or at least I hoped he couldn't. Jeez. Did I have a fever, or was that a soft spot coming on?

"It will be, on the bike." He caught my amused glance, and paused, the magazine halfway back in and a bruised expression on his face. "What?"

I laughed, and it felt good in my belly. "Because you couldn't just drive a car, or anything uncool like that. The dark and dangerous mystery man. Hell, I bet the girls really go for that."

Shadows flickered over his face, so brief I almost missed it. And then he finished with the pistol and clipped it to his belt, and wrinkled his cute upturned nose at me in a smile. "I'll let you be the judge. You ready?"

I shrugged his coat on, and cracked my neck, flexing the warm invisible muscle of my power. "Let's go."

9

Traffic clogged the on-ramp to the bridge's lower deck, horns honking in the warm night air. We passed a couple of black police LAVs, en route to the carnage but as caught in traffic as everyone else. Luckily for us, we wanted the upper level. The one where we were heading in the opposite direction to everyone else.

When you're doing this? There's no point in driving like you give a shit.

Glimmer gunned the motor, and scooted over the median strip and up the wrong side of the interstate. Drivers swerved, cursed, flipped us the bird. Moonlight rippled through wispy fog as he weaved the bike in and out, headlights flashing at us. Heh. It was fun. The swaying was exhilarating and calming at the same time.

I held on, Glimmer's back warm against my cheek. He felt strange but familiar, like a friend long lost, a blurred memory of someone I once knew. Maybe he just reminded me of Chance, with his crazy hair and wild-thing smile, but there was a fair slice of Adonis in him, too, the determination that hardened his stubbled jaw, the tension in his lean muscles. A serious young thing. Weight of the world, and all that. What had happened to him, I wondered, to make him so intense?

We crossed above the waterfront and out over the wide dark expanse of the Bay. Salty seaside breeze dragged my hair back from my masked face, fingered beneath my clothes. I huddled tighter in his coat. I didn't know much about bikes, but this one was gleaming chrome and ruby-red, well cared for, but not polished within an inch of its life like he had nothing better to do. We'd emerged from his underground ramp onto some dark backstreet, a couple of blocks from the docks, warehouses and freight company offices and yards crammed with shipping containers stacked four high. The engine's sweet note rattled in my ears, and red taillights flashed in the mirrors as we canted to the side to get around a truck.

Ahead, I could hear screams, amid the crunch and crash of abused metal and glass. Now the lines of traffic were crooked, cars bunched together like they'd stopped in a hurry. A few had collided, their fenders dented and headlights smashed, and glass fragments littered the road amid swearing drivers.

Wreckage littered the bridge across all five lanes. One car lay upturned with wheels spinning, another had slammed into the suspension cables and nearly sliced in two. A minivan lay on its side, and its dazed occupants clambered out through jagged glass to crawl away.

And in the middle of it all, Arachne leapt and wailed like a triumphant banshee. She wore shiny black leggings and heavy boots, beneath a tight black scoop-necked top that covered her skinny arms to the wrist. Her waist-length black hair flapped. She flung out her arm, snapping her rigid palm outwards, and her augment uncoiled itself: a glassy rope, like the silken line a spider makes, only thicker and much, much stronger.

It speared from the center of her palm, ten, twenty, thirty feet, and split, into three grippy glass claws that slapped across a shiny black car's roof and lodged there, sharp points stabbing through the steel.

People screamed, and scattered. Arachne just laughed, a horrid shrieking sound like a thousand cicadas in agony, and *pulled*.

The rope retracted, back to where it had come from, almost too fast for me to watch. Her claws unhooked, and the car sailed through the air and hit the suspension cables. *Crash!* The thick steel bars thrummed, a deep-throated harp. The car's windows shattered, the screeching buckle of steel. Arachne's glassy hookvine broke, and fell to the road, where it splintered into a thousand tiny fragments. She hopped like a dervish in delight, and flung out another, heaving a second car high into the air and dashing it to mangled scraps on the road.

My heart clogged my throat. That one was empty. The next might not be.

Glimmer skidded the bike to a halt, and we jumped off. Already, the bridge began to shake. My pulse raced. Too much more of this, and there'd be serious damage as the wires stretched and bent. Not to mention injuries, broken cars, the traffic snarl from hell...

Glimmer cocked his pistol and wiped sweat back into his hair with his forearm. His midnight eyes glittered inside his mask, no longer warm but sharp black icicles, deadly. "Can you lift a car?"

"Sure." I cracked my neck, left and right. Hell, I hoped so. My power hadn't exactly been cooperative over the last forty-eight hours. Still, a car shouldn't be a problem. Putting it down quietly might be another matter, but Glimmer didn't need to know that.

"Then stop her breaking anything else." And he ducked for cover and ran. Leaving me no time to argue or say no.

Gallant little skunk, wasn't he? I swore, and got on with it.

Arachne saw us, and hooted laughter. "Pretty things in masks," she gloated. Augmented fire ignited in her eyes. Her scarlet-painted lips curled, a sharp bloody smile soaked in hatred. "Come get it."

Glimmer leveled his pistol at her, two-handed. "First, last and only chance, lady. Give yourself up."

"Go fuck yourself." She rolled her skinny wrists, and flashed out twin glassy vines. They crawled across the ground like psycho snakes, searching for prey.

Glimmer didn't say anything. He just fired. I like a man who keeps his promises.

Quick as a jumping spider, Arachne leapt, impossibly high. The bullet sang harmlessly between the steel cables. Her vines split, their evil claws glistening like wet glass, and crunched onto the roof of an orange-striped white bus. People still clambered about inside, the ones who hadn't worked up the guts to run. Now, escape was impossible. They screamed, slapping their palms on the windows, wild and ripe with terror.

Arachne landed in a whippy-legged crouch, hair streaming aloft. She let loose a triumphant wail that shivered my bones, and *pulled*.

I sprinted, heart thumping, and flung out a wall of power on one outstretched fist. Hot wind seared my face. The bus slammed into my invisible wall and stuck there, shuddering on its side in mid-air, her hooked vines still attached to the roof.

Inside, the people tumbled and squeaked like trapped rats. A window broke, and a girl fell out, dropping twenty feet to the road. She lay there moaning, and Glimmer ran for her and dragged her from the bus's looming shadow.

Arachne cursed, spitting little drops of poison that caught the air like a cloud of angry gnats, and dived for me. The backs of my hands blistered. I braced myself, legs apart, and held on. Arachne yanked her vines harder, gritting her teeth. Still I held on. The bus shuddered and groaned, metal twisting under the opposing forces. Sweat poured down my temples, soaking my mask. My head ached, bright and stinging like sunburn. I couldn't see. The stink of hot metal choked my nose, and I could feel my back stretching under the stress, muscles popping fibers and bones twisting.

But damn, it felt good to let my power loose.

I flexed my fist, and the bus's steel shell twisted, just a few inches. The metal creaked in protest. My blood burned, urging me to more, harder, darker. A bad person would crush Arachne with this bus. Hurl it on top of her and grind her to bloody pulp, and damn the consequences...

Glimmer ran forward. Now he was between Arachne and the

bus. Damn it. I gritted my teeth, and held on.

Arachne spat poison at him, and whipped her wrists down-wards. Her vines snapped off, only a few inches from her palm. The long ends dangled from the bus, slapping lifelessly onto the ground. Quick as a striking snake, she speared them out anew, five wicked barbs on each, like twisting hands clawing for Glimmer's face.

I wasn't sure whether what happened next was real.

Glimmer ducked, so swift he blurred. The snaking spikes shot past him, writhing, searching blindly for prey. She howled and tried to whirl, to re-attack from a different angle. But Glimmer kept running at her. He grabbed her hair and yanked, forcing her to look at him, and snapped his fingers an inch from her eyes. "Watch me," he commanded.

Her flame-bright eyes shuttered black.

She froze, her body motionless except for her flapping hair. The fierce glassy vines halted, rigid, snapped frozen in mid-air.

I stared, warm and chilled at the same time. That was some hypno-mojo.

"Lose the spikes." Glimmer's voice was calm, cold, resonating, even above my bus passengers' screams. He didn't drop his dark gaze. Didn't blink. Didn't let her go.

Arachne obeyed, staring blankly into his eyes. The glassy spikes sucked back into her palms, a slicing sound like sword blades. No blood. No ripped flesh. Just something she was born with. Did it hurt, I wondered, when she let them out?

"Cross your arms," Glimmer ordered softly. "Palms on your chest. Then don't move."

She did as he told her. Like a black leather mummy, those dangerous palms pressed flat to her own shoulders. If she spiked now, she'd run herself through. Clever.

I licked dry lips, sympathy itching. I was a freak, sure. But my freakdom was invisible compared to hers. If I had glassy spikes growing inside my hands, what would my life have been like? Would it be so easy for me to choose good over evil?

I flexed my aching fist, and slowly lowered the bus to the ground.

Crunch! The dust settled, and people started climbing out. One guy was already filming us on his smartphone. A few windows were broken, but all in all, I'd done well. Probably a good thing I hadn't squashed Arachne. But like always, it niggled me like a phantom itch that being a good guy meant leaving the sick mofos alive.

I popped my stiff spine, twisting left and right. Ahh. Inside my head, my power coiled and relaxed, and a pleasant afterglow ache flooded my muscles from head to toe. I stretched, lazy and content despite my raging headache. My thighs tingled. Someone pass me a cigarette. Was it wrong that my augment felt better than sex?

Was it like this for other augmented? I'd never asked. It wasn't the kind of thing I liked discussing, especially not with Dad or Adonis, and I sure as hell wasn't about to ask Glimmer. Maybe I was just doing the sex thing wrong.

Whatever. I didn't have time to ponder my choice of pleasures now. At last, the distant howl of frustrated police sirens from the east inched closer. We didn't have much time. Even with FortuneCorp's full powers at my back—we helped the police, they helped us, it had been that way ever since the PD realized all those years ago that Blackstrike and Illuminatus were in Sapphire City to stay—I'd only ever had an uneasy relationship with cops. Now I was a loner. A vigilante. An outlaw. Cops were bad news.

Seemed Glimmer knew it too. He jerked his chin at me, never taking his eyes from Arachne's. "Duct tape, please. On the back of the bike."

I scrambled over broken iron and glass to the bike. Sure enough, in the little saddlebag was a fat black roll of tape. I tossed it to him. He caught it, and ripped the end free with his teeth. I stepped up to help, and in half a minute, Arachne looked even more like a mummy, wrapped from collarbone to solar plexus in tape, her hands bound immovably to her chest. Another couple of twists bound her ankles tight.

Still she stared straight ahead, into Glimmer's masked eyes.

Her red lips had dried. She didn't lick them. Didn't move. Didn't even blink.

"Nice," I commented, tossing the empty roll away. "Remind me never to let you tie me up." Or hypnotize me, I added silently. Like I'd be able to do anything about it if he did, judging from the way Arachne stared like a dead thing into his eyes.

Glimmer plastered the last scrap of tape over her lips. Gently, sufficient to silence her but not hard enough to tear the skin. "Should stop her spitting. Any poison get you?"

"A little. Nothing I can't scratch off."

"You did good with the bus."

"Thanks." Behind us, motorbike engines rattled to a halt, and tires screeched. "Time to go," I said.

"Yeah." He passed his hand in front of her face. "Arachne?"

"Mmph." Her voice clogged through the tape.

He clicked his fingers. "Wake up."

Her eyes snapped golden. Scarlet shame bled in, stained black with poisoned fury. Glimmer grinned, and we ran.

Two motorcycle cops ran for us, guns drawn. They still wore their helmets, visors down. "Freeze!" one yelled, muffled.

Yeah, okay. Let me wait here while you arrest me. Idiot.

Arachne struggled and cursed, vile and skin-crawling even through the tape on her lips. Glimmer jumped on his bike and kicked the engine. I vaulted on behind him, and he gunned it, the back end sliding out.

The cops shot and missed. Bullets zinged. I held on tight, ducking my head against his back. Glimmer rode for the piled-up cars, and instinctively I squeezed my eyes shut. The engine revved, brutal. Suddenly we were airborne, weightless for a few glorious, ear-splitting seconds. And then we hit the road, and bounced, my bones jarring.

The engine grunted in protest. I whooped, exhilarated. He skidded the bike into a turn, scattering broken metal fragments, and we howled away.

10

By the time we reached Glimmer's hideout, dawn's gleaming fingers crept along the horizon. No streetlamps lit the back alley where he eased the bike down the ramp. Somewhere in the dark, the iron grille clattered aside, and we rolled in. Once the grille slammed shut, orange security lights popped on, revealing a deserted underground parking lot, and he stopped the bike in its alcove and shut off the engine.

I climbed off, stiff and weary, my nerves still jangling. I hadn't forgotten how easily he swept Arachne under his power. Sure, I was dangerous, too, but at least everyone could see what I was doing. Glimmer's augment was insidious, invisible, unknowable.

My stomach turned over, watery. Mindbenders gave me the creeps. What had I let myself in for?

An electric combo-locked steel door like a safe led to his lair. Inside, his screens still flickered, information and images flowing, collating, like the thing had a brain of its own. Cool, but spooky, too. Glimmer tossed his gun onto the desk-shaped mess and headed for the fridge. "Want a beer?"

"Huh?"

He paused, the door half open. "Beer. You know. A drink?"

"Uh. Sure." I dragged off my sweaty mask, uneasy. I was thirsty. That wasn't the problem. I'd already taken too much from him. Taking meant debt, and I wasn't sure owing a dark and mysterious mindfucker who wouldn't take off his mask was a particularly stellar idea.

He tossed me a bottle, and I caught it. At the sight of the amber fluid, my mouth stung. I sure could use one. Screw it. I wrenched off the top and chugged. Mmm. Cold, bitter, bubbly. All that a beer should be.

Except free.

He cleared a space on his dusty sofa, pushing aside a pile of green circuit boards and memory chips. "Have a seat. Make yourself at home. *Mi casa*, and all that."

I sat, fidgeting. Did he think I was going to stay here, in his place? Fact was, I hadn't thought about what I'd do next. Could I sleep here, with him around?

Did I have anywhere else to go?

I took another bitter swig. Damn him. Damn them all. Razorfire, Equity, Mengele, Arachne, those cops on the bridge, whoever it was at FortuneCorp who'd dumped me in this mess. Once, I had a life. Now, I had nothing.

Except my revenge, and this flashing time bomb of an ally.

Watch me, he'd said. And Arachne stared into his eyes, and her will dissolved.

Glimmer slouched in his desk chair, stretching his long legs, and leaned over to clink bottles with me. "Cheers. Here's to another Gallery shitball in custody." He swallowed half his beer in a long chug, cold drips running down his strong forearm. He had a long, lean throat, olive skin dappled with soft dark stubble...

Uh-huh. Staring. Not cool.

I coughed, and dropped my gaze. He still hadn't taken off his mask. Didn't seem inclined to, at least not in front of me. Heh. Maybe I should creep up on him while he slept and take a peek, like lovesick Psyche, who couldn't resist shining a lamp on her mystery boy toy.

Yeah. Because that ended well. Boy toy turned out to be Cupid, and Psyche lost him forever. Secret identities, see. They never work out for the best.

"Ah. That goes down fine." Glimmer wiped his mouth with the hand holding the beer. "You up for breakfast? I do a mean omelet—"

"Could I stop you?"

He paused, beer halfway to his mouth. "What?"

"If you pulled your *look-into-my-eyes* trick on me." I took a hot breath. "Would I even know about it?"

He studied me, silent, his midnight eyes warm and inscrutable. "Probably not," he admitted at last.

"Could I stop you?"

"Maybe. I don't know. I never know until I try."

"That's not an answer." My mouth crisped. I swallowed more beer. It didn't help.

"It's the only answer I can give you. You're a force-bender. That power comes from your mind. You might have some resistance—"

"Don't bullshit me!" I slammed my bottle down and jumped up, pacing.

"You want me to do it to you? So you know how it feels?"

"Why the fuck would I want that?"

"Hell, I don't know." For the first time, tension stretched his whiskey voice to a harsh edge. "I'm trying here. I've been by myself a long time. I don't know what else to give you."

"But—"

"Think!" He spun his chair and pointed at the desk, where his pistol lay. "You could shoot me right now. Hell, I imagine you could cave the roof in and crush me to pulp any time you wanted. So why don't you?"

Because I'm not a bad person. I cleared my throat. "I hardly think that's—"

"There's nothing in it for you, that's why." He ruffled his hair, weary or frustrated. "I told you. We can help each other. I couldn't have trapped Arachne without you. If you weren't there, I'd probably be dead right now, so tell me why the hell I'd want to hypnotize you!"

To make me stay. My mouth opened, the words alive on my tongue.

I swallowed them.

I've been by myself a long time. His words echoed, bitter. I'd seen the look on his face when he spoke them. I'd worn it myself, through long hours abandoned in Mengele-inflicted agony, and as I looked at him, my heart swelled hot and uncomfortable.

I knew how it felt, to be so utterly alone it hurt. He needed a friend. And—God help me—so did I.

I stalked up to the console, and poked the touchscreen until it exploded with virtual 3D images. I flicked through the pile, keeping some, discarding the ones I didn't want. Finally, I flipped the whole thing though ninety degrees so he could see, and pointed at the first one, a handsome blond guy in a designer suit. "Who's this?"

Glimmer didn't blink, or argue. "Narcissus. A mindbender, like me."

"My brother, Adonis Fortune. He's a PR consultant at my father's company."

His eyes slitted inside his mask. But he didn't laugh, or claim I was lying. Just went along with me.

I flipped to the next image: the trolley car, same as Glimmer showed me before.

"Illuminatus and Phantasm?"

"My uncle, Michael Fortune, and his son Jeremiah. You don't have one of Ebenezer, but they don't let Eb out much. Augments run in my family, okay? We're called Fortune Corporation."

"As in, *the* Fortune Corporation? Defense and security contracts? That big flashy skyscraper in the financial district?"

"Our cover story is security and weapons technology, yeah, but our mission is to fight the Gallery and keep the city safe."

I flicked up the picture of my father, wreathed in shadow and flame, and another one, showing a dark-haired woman in dusty leathers, a black mask covering her eyes, dragging boulders from a pile of rubble.

"Blackstrike," I confirmed. "Thomas Fortune, my father. Late chairman of FortuneCorp. And me. Verity Fortune, also called the Seeker. Last October, Razorfire murdered Blackstrike, and imprisoned me in a lunatic asylum, where his minions tortured me until I escaped three days ago."

Glimmer rubbed his chin. "Uh-huh," he said blankly, like it was all he could come up with to say.

"I don't remember exactly what happened, but I know those assholes who were chasing me when you found me were Razorfire's people. Someone in my family set them back on me, when I thought I was safe." I swallowed on bitter grit, and flicked to the next image, a woman wearing reflective silver armor, a slender knight brandishing a fistful of light. "This is—"

"Nemesis," Glimmer cut in swiftly, as if suddenly I wasn't talking fast enough for him. "Some kind of photonic power… This is extraordinary!" His dark eyes danced. "These are the links I've been searching for. God, I'm so *slow*. To think this was all there, right before my eyes the whole time…"

"Nemesis is Equity Fortune, assistant district attorney," I interrupted. "My sister. She took over FortuneCorp when Dad died."

"The Equity Fortune who's running for mayor?"

"The very same." My throat stung, and I sucked in a steadying breath. "I think… maybe she's the one who betrayed me. I wanted to avenge Dad's death, but she didn't want me stirring up trouble during her campaign. She's initiated a policy of non-violence against Gallery villains."

Glimmer nodded. "Okay. That explains a lot. Gallery activity has been escalating. But doesn't that mean that…?" He looked askance, haunted. He didn't want to say it.

Hell, I didn't want to say it either. "Somehow, Razorfire's gotten to her." My tongue stung sour. I wanted to spit, wash my mouth out, make those words untrue again.

But I didn't know how. I didn't know what else to think. Damn her. It had to be her. No one else had a motive that I knew about... or did they? I recalled Uncle Mike, smiling at me in the fifty-sixth floor lobby. He'd always liked me, or so I thought...

"I'm sorry," said Glimmer softly, and damn it if he didn't look like he meant it.

"Yeah, well, I'm sorry, too." Stupid tears swelled my eyelids. God, I wanted to let them fall. Wanted to let Glimmer be sorry for me, comfort me, stroke my hair and tell me everything would be okay.

Fuck.

I coughed, and blinked fiercely, dragging my mind back to problems I *could* solve. "It doesn't matter, okay? You said you had a problem with Razorfire? Well, so do I. We can help each other."

Glimmer scrunched his hair, considering. "And that would involve...?"

"Your information, my experience. Let's put them together. Work as a team. If Equity is Razorfire's latest trick, we can't let her take charge. FortuneCorp won't fight the Gallery? Fine. You and I can do it alone. We'll hunt the evil bastard down like the shitworm he is!"

My own vehemence startled me. Jeez. I sounded like I wanted it. Believed it, even.

But could I be a team player again, after it bit me so savagely in the ass last time? Could I work with this Glimmer, whoever he was and whatever crazy havoc his powers might wreak with my already busted-to-shit mind?

But my bones burned deep inside, the bitter fury of retribution denied, and I knew that wasn't the real question.

The real question was: could I afford not to?

Glimmer watched me, inscrutable. "And when—if, that is—we find Razorfire... What will you do?"

Kill the bastard! My blood boiled. *Rip that shiny mask from his face and put the wicked motherfucker down like a sick dog.*

But I recalled Glimmer's behavior tonight, skipping between Arachne and my Dangling Bus of Death. Keeping his hypnotic commands strictly above the waist, when he could have humiliated her if he wanted to. Wrapping her with duct tape and handing her over to the cops, when he had a perfectly serviceable pistol in his pocket.

My skin prickled a warning, and I decided that *claw the bastard's eyeballs out!* wasn't the answer Glimmer needed to hear.

"Well," I said, keeping my voice steadfast, "that'll depend on him."

I almost flushed, the lie came so easily. It stung my heart like poison to deceive Glimmer, after he'd been so forthright with me. But deep inside me that cruel and hungry vengeance-beast laughed, and part of me laughed with it.

Glimmer perched his butt on the desk's edge and leaned on his palms, his shoulders hunched. "So that's what you want, then? A reckoning?"

I nodded, fierce and alive. Oh, yes. I wanted that, all right. Right before I blew Razorfire's sniggering head off.

"Then let me tell you what *I* want."

The force in his voice shocked me, and I almost fell a step back.

His dark eyes glittered, starlit with rage and loss that matched my own. "Yes, I want Razorfire, and believe me, it's for selfish reasons. This power of mine has cost me my life. My family. Everything I loved… but that wasn't Razorfire's fault. I don't want revenge for something he didn't do."

I gulped, nonplussed. "But—"

"What I want," said Glimmer fiercely, "is justice for what he *did* do. For every child who grows up hating augments, because their mother got killed or their big sister was raped or their family's business got burned down. For every shopkeeper whose kids go hungry because he paid half his earnings in protection. For every woman who won't go out alone in the dark in case some Gallery scumbag decides it's his lucky night. For the politicians who'll vote for Proposition 101 because they think all augments are psychotics who need to be identified and tested and controlled. For every good-hearted person who can't bear the sight of—" His whiskey-rough voice cracked, and quickly he angled away, so I couldn't see his eyes.

My heart bled for him. He had rejection issues of his own. I didn't know what to say. Best to say nothing at all.

When he turned back, his eyes shimmered. But a crusader's holy conviction burned there, too. "For everyone who lives in terror of people like you and me," he finished shortly. "That's what Razorfire did. What he's still doing with every poisoned breath he takes. And I swear to you, Verity Fortune, I'll see him brought to justice if it takes every second of every hour of the rest of my life."

Stun me speechless. A genuine white knight.

Dark triumph stirred with trepidation in my blood. I had myself an ally... and a better one than I'd ever have found at FortuneCorp. Because I knew the truth about Glimmer now, and it tingled sweetly over my skin like a treacherous lover's caress.

Glimmer, bless his skunky head, was a true believer.

His heart was pure. He'd never give up. Never lose interest, or call in sick, or betray me to the highest bidder for a lark. All I had to do was keep the faith—live up to his standard—and retribution would be mine.

He didn't need to know that my bruised soul thirsted for a darker, bloodier, less honorable end than justice. And if Razorfire ended up dead when we were finished?

Well, best to worry about one problem at a time.

Daring, I touched Glimmer's shoulder. He turned to face me, stormy shadows flitting across his face. I could feel the heat of his conviction, burning in his blood, radiant like fever on my skin. Maybe, it'd sustain me, too.

I held out my hand. "Amen," I said softly.

His night-black eyes caught mine, afire. For a moment, I thought

I saw knowledge there, accusation, disappointment… and my courage quailed.

And then, slowly, he shook my hand. "Amen."

11

That night, I slept the warm black slumber of satisfaction.

Glimmer's bed was fresh and comfortable. I would've refused it, but I was too tired to argue, and he claimed he was happy with the sofa. I fell unconscious as soon as I dragged the quilt over my head. If my nightmares visited me—if I dreamed in fever-soaked delirium of Razorfire's flaming scarlet eyes—I didn't remember it.

Next morning (or was it afternoon?) I crawled out like a crusty, bad-tempered turtle, raking my fingers through knotted hair.

I'd slept in my clothes, and I wrinkled my nose at the peculiar smell: dirt and sweat, mixed with that sweet vanilla-spice scent that followed Glimmer around. I sure could use some fresh gear. Only I couldn't go home, and I had no cash, no debit card, no credit I could call in without giving myself away.

Great. Dad had brought us up to be frugal, but still, I was used to a limitless stream of funds at my fingertips. Would this be my first day as a petty thief?

Glimmer had arisen before me—if he'd even slept—and he sat at his desk, typing and fiddling with his console like always. He still wore his mask. Maybe he really did sleep in the damn thing. On the desk beside him, an empty plate lay dotted with crumbs, and the smell of buttery waffles and honey tempted me.

"I've been going over what you told me," he said as I emerged, like our conversation hadn't stopped. "This is incredible. How did you ever keep your entire company a secret for… how long did you say?"

"Nearly thirty years," I admitted, yawning and stretching my arms behind my back. My muscles still ached distantly, afterburn from using my power, but it was a good ache. "Dad and Uncle Mike started FortuneCorp. The Gallery weren't around then… well, I mean, they were, but they didn't get properly organized until later. Dad used to tell us kids stories."

I half-smiled in memory. Dad in his leather armchair, eight-year-old Adonis and me cross-legged on the floor at his feet. "Razorfire wasn't even on the scene back then. Their archenemy was this crazy mofo called Obsidian who could turn things to stone. Dad and Uncle Mike chased that lunatic all over Sapphire City. Once they saved an entire subway train full of people, and…" My smile twisted, and I swallowed it, bitter.

"Obsidian," mused Glimmer. "Never heard of him. What happened to him?"

Memory dazzled me sick. Noises in the middle of the night, the front door crashing open. Dad, his shiny black coat torn and dusty, stained with blood, carrying my mother in his arms.

I'd never seen Dad weep before. In that moment, as he slumped to his knees stroking dark tangles from Mom's granite-marbled face, I realized for the first time that he wasn't immortal, and that I probably wasn't either.

I gulped. We all grew up that night, or chose not to. Eleven-year-old Equity took one look at what Obsidian had done to Mom and threw up. But I remembered Adonis, just a little boy but already a miniature version of Dad, calling 9-1-1, giving them our address, telling them to hurry. I grabbed water and towels from the kitchen to mop up the blood. Chance was only four, and he wouldn't let me hold him or quieten him down. He just wailed and banged his little fists on the carpet, not understanding that his luck couldn't fix things this time.

A few weeks later, Obsidian disappeared. Dad never told me what happened, and Uncle Mike still refused to talk about it. But we never heard from Obsidian again.

I blinked, fierce. The awful images shattered, slicing deep like glass. "I don't remember," I said shortly. "So what's the plan? Crime-fighters 'R' us?"

Glimmer folded his hands behind his head. His skunk stripe stuck up, making him look young and harmless. I reminded myself that he was neither. "Well, I figured you'd need a few things if you're going to stay here. Clothes, and stuff like that."

"Jeez, you sound like my brother," I grumbled. "What's wrong with my clothes?" But a pang of loss soured my stomach. My leathers were gone. The costumes Adonis had saved for me; I couldn't go back for them. I had nothing left of the Seeker, except a mask and some broken memories.

Could I rebuild her now, in a new and stronger image? Or was she doomed, stripped naked, lost forever?

"You wanna hunt villains in a wise-ass T-shirt? Be my guest."

"Right. Because you're all over the secret identity thing." I waved my hand at his black clothes, all he ever seemed to wear. "How many of those outfits you own, anyway?"

He grinned. "Lots. But I'm thinking it's time we suped it up a bit. Made a spectacle of ourselves."

"O-kaay. Because calling attention to ourselves would be a good idea, all of a sudden?" I shoved hands in pockets, ready to argue.

"Exactly." He turned to his screens and flicked up a dozen news reports, the *Chronicle*, websites, CNN, the national airwaves. "Sapphire City's crime rate is on the rise, both from the Gallery's augmented villains and regular criminals. It correlates with what you've told me about your sister's new policy at FortuneCorp. Which sounds like a shit idea to me, if you don't mind me saying."

I snorted. "No argument here. So?"

He flipped up another data screen. A folder opened, and buckets of images and data tumbled out. "This is what I've got on Razorfire, and so far it's led me nowhere. Unless you've got something new to add, I'm as clueless as I was before."

"So?" I repeated, impatient.

"So, let's stop looking for him. Let's make him look for us." He stabbed at the crime reports, and the images cut themselves out and pasted in a neat array. Bank jobs, arson, convenience store robberies, home invasions, vandalism, mob murders. The usual rogues' crew. "We start at the bottom. Make ourselves known. Video of us and Arachne is already online. So let's get famous. Glimmer and the Seeker, Sapphire City's newest crime-fighting duo, taking up the slack after Blackstrike's tragic death."

"Uh-huh."

"Get it out there that every villain who pulls a job in this town is calling down the thunder. Make enough of a ruckus, and maybe Razorfire will come to us."

"Steal enough souls, and the devil will come calling," I mused. "I like it. It could work."

"It has to work. It's all I've got."

"And in the meantime, we can investigate what's going on at FortuneCorp," I added.

Glimmer chewed his bottom lip. "Are you sure you want to go there?"

"Equity didn't think this up on her own," I insisted. I wasn't interested in discussing it. I just wanted to act. "Someone's pouring poison in her ear. I want to find out who, and put a stop to it. That's Dad's company, Glimmer. It's not hers to ruin."

"And then what?" Glimmer's candid gaze bored deep. "Say you root the villains out, whoever they are. Say you can even do it without blowing the company's cover, which doesn't seem very likely. What then? Your family will all just forget about it, and crack on with crime-fighting?"

"Yeah. Why not?" Conviction boiled cold in my blood, ice in

fire. But that horrid voice still sniggered and taunted, chewing on my mind's edge like a hungry rat. *You know they won't*, it cackled. *FortuneCorp is dead, Verity. Poisoned. You can't ever bring it back to life.* "Adonis will be in charge, like he should always have been," I insisted, more for myself than for Glimmer. "And the company will be like Dad wanted. You got a problem with that?"

Glimmer warded me off, palms outwards. "Okay. I'm in, Verity. You know that. I'm just playing devil's advocate here."

"I know. It's just..." I gritted my teeth. I hadn't meant to snap at him. But this ravenous rage roiled over me like a fever, blotting out my sense until all I could do was scream inside. I struggled for breath. Jeez. Was it Mengele's abuse that made me into such an angry bird? Or was I always this way?

"It's okay." He soothed me with a warm black glance. "So, what's the plan?"

My nerves ratcheted back, just a notch or two, like I'd swallowed whiskey or taken a pill. A born defuser, this Glimmer... *or he's using his power on you...*

I chose to ignore that little voice this time. Already my mind tumbled over, sorting ideas. I could use my press connections to dig up the dirt. With the election coming up, everyone would be fighting for the scoop on Equity and that other guy. The traitor at FortuneCorp would soon know I was onto them, but hell, they knew that already. If I was careful, I'd be one step ahead.

"Verity Fortune is a journalist," I offered. "She knows a few tricks."

"Yeah?" He sounded impressed. "The Clark Kent of the *Chronicle*. An oldie but a goodie."

"Mmm," I said absently. An idea popped. *The other guy.* The smartphone guy, Caine. I vaguely recalled meeting him once, at some press shindig or other, when he'd made the cover of *Richest Bastards in Town* or whatever. One of those ruthlessly confident business types. I recalled Adonis's words: *a hater, but a clever one.* Every politician dug for dirt on his opponents, and corporate sharks like Caine were the experts at it. He might have information I could use, an angle I could push.

Yes. I could pull some strings, get an interview. Pretend I was writing a feature article, sympathetic to his anti-powers campaign. At least talk to his people, find out what kind of man he was.

Besides that, though, I needed the good oil on what was happening *inside* FortuneCorp. Someone was in cahoots with the villains. I needed to know who, and why, and what their plan was. And no one knew FortuneCorp's workings as well as I did.

I eyed Glimmer's array of CCTV, audio recordings, footage from hidden video cameras. "I'm thinking you know a thing or two about surveillance."

Glimmer winked, star-bright. "Oh, honey. Surveillance is my middle name."

"Brilliant. Here's hoping 'disguise' is your other middle name."

"Why? Where are we going?"

"The FortuneCorp building's CCTV is on a shielded interior circuit, not on the main city network. We'll have to break in there to get it..." Shards of memory spun and sliced, stinging. I squeezed my eyes shut. *Glass walls, slipping under my sweaty palms. My hair flaps in the wind. At last, I haul my body over the roof's edge, and lie there for a second or two, panting. Not a moment to lose. I drag myself to my feet, and light like a blood-soaked angel's glory dazzles me blind...*

Snap! Back into the present, dizzy. Whoa. I sucked in cool air, soothing my scorched lungs. Damn. It always felt so real...

Glimmer eyed me, concerned. "You okay?"

"Sure. Yeah. Um... what were we talking about?"

The tilt of his stubbled chin suggested he didn't believe me. But he didn't accuse. "CCTV," he said simply. "You had this strange idea that I can't hack into a shielded circuit?"

"Are you saying you can?"

He grinned, and his skunk stripe stuck up, a crazy splash of challenge. "Watch me and weep, sister."

Sure enough, before I'd finished my breakfast—waffles and syrup, which I cooked in his little electric frypan—he'd hooked into the security surveillance circuits at FortuneCorp and dragged down their signal. Odd, to see the familiar sights on his screens, that distorted monochrome look of security footage. The entry lobby, tall and glass-lined, tiles still cracked and surrounded with striped caution tape where I'd smashed them. Inside, the elevators, one to six, chrome and shining glass. The underground parking lot. A maze of corridors, our office managers and temp staff and PR people walking beneath the cameras, oblivious.

The technical drawing and inventors' labs, where our cover story was sustained by every now and then producing some actual weapons that worked. The cameras there were digitally blurred, deliberately kept slightly out of focus, so no corporate secrets could be revealed. You couldn't read any of the plans laid out on the big design desks. I squinted, vague memories baffling me. *Flicking through papers, abstracts, technical designs, line diagrams melting together in squiggles to baffle me. A chart's edge slices my finger. Ouch. Paper cut. I pop it in my mouth, blood salty on my tongue...*

And Dad's office, bright and shiny, the window already repaired. Not on video—no continuous recording in the boss's office, again a matter of secrecy—but a series of stills, a few seconds apart, cobbled together like a jerky cartoon.

I stared, my throat tight. Equity wasn't there. Probably on the campaign trail, or at one of her endless meetings.

Maybe she was out colluding with villains right now.

That steaming rage boiled my organs again, and I clenched my fists and fought it back down, forcing myself to concentrate on the issues. "This is amazing. We always thought our system was secure."

Glimmer didn't pause. He just sat there, typing and looking pleased with himself. "It is. Just not from me."

Curiosity sparred with my purposeful lack of interest, and won.

"Where'd you learn all this stuff? CalTech? Prison? X-Box Live?"

His expression darkened. "In another life."

"Oh." I hesitated. "You a systems analyst, or a security guru or something?"

"Or something."

"Uh-huh. So what happened?"

"*This* happened." He tapped his temples with both hands, a rough gesture of disgust or frustration, and went back to typing. "I like microprocessors better than people. They don't have minds, or thoughts, or irrational fears."

And they aren't afraid of you.

His shoulders stiffened to stone, and I realized I'd said it aloud. Acid guilt scraped my bones. "Shit. I didn't mean that."

"Don't apologize for the truth." He flashed me a masked glance, inscrutable.

Gritty confusion rubbed me even rawer. Was that an invitation to ask what had happened? Or a polite Glimmer get-lost? I had no clue.

Shit. Was I this hopeless at all this friendship stuff before? Or had some delicate connective tissue in the play-nice part of my brain been scraped away in Mengele's torture parlor? "Umm…"

"There we are." Glimmer pointed at the screen, dismissing me. "Done. It's recording all of this. I've set alarms to ping us if anything out of the ordinary happens."

I leaned closer, grateful to talk about something else. I liked him, sure. Didn't mean I wanted to share confidences. "How does it define 'out of the ordinary'?"

"Slowly," he admitted. "Until we've got baseline data to work with—tracked the usual movements for a few days, at least—we'll have to do most of the work ourselves. Still, it's on the way." He shoved his chair back and cracked his fingers. "Meantime, I've been thinking."

"Do tell."

"About our good buddies the Dockside Boys."

89

"Uh-huh," I offered. "Bunch of small-time Gallery thugs. Specialize in fencing stolen goods and threat work. Muscle for hire, basically, for any villain who'll pay their price."

"That's them." His dark eyes twinkled. "Word on the wire is, they're planning a little smash-and-grab down at the waterfront tonight. Seems there's a rival bunch of scumbags trying to muscle in on their drug trade."

"The bastards. Can't you run a decent mob these days without some asshole trying to bring you down?"

"Sounds like a job for Glimmer and the Seeker. Wanna get on TV?"

I grinned back. After last night's fun on the bridge, I was looking forward to flexing my mental muscles again. "Gotta start somewhere."

"Yep." He jumped up, dragging a fist through his crazy hair. "Got a couple of trips to make first. Do some shopping, get some supplies in. You need anything?"

"Umm. A toothbrush. Some socks. That kind of shit. Oh, and can you grab some more beer?" I paused, wincing. I'd forgotten my financial famine. "I, uh, don't have any money."

"It's okay. You can pay me back."

With what? I wondered. But he didn't seem short, with this set-up of his, all this gear. Unless he'd stolen it with his mindfuck tricks, of course.

"You wanna make some calls, get your press mojo happening?"

"Sure. But I, uh, already broke your cell…?"

He rummaged on the desk and unearthed a dented black smart-phone. "Here. It's got a few jamming tricks installed. Can't be traced. No one will find you. Use it for email if you want. Same deal."

He tossed me the phone on his way out. I caught it, and soon, the low rippling note of his bike arced up and dopplered away.

12

WHO ARE GLIMMER AND THE SEEKER?

I sat at Glimmer's console, my feet propped up on the desk, munching on a breakfast of honey waffles and cream as I scrolled through the day's news. About damn time we got some good press. Over the past week, we'd collared a dozen Gallery scumbags, broken a lot of stuff, made some flashy explosions.

The first night, we made page five and a sideline story online. Today, we were front page news plus editorial. **Glimmer and the Seeker: brave crime-fighters or masked menaces?** We were the talk of the town, discussed over coffee or after-work beers, trending on all the social networking sites. Journalists had started asking questions about us in election press conferences. It was fun to watch Equity dissemble, but the other guy, Caine, the hater, just smiled and said we proved his point about augments being dangerous.

Whatever, asshole. We hadn't yet gotten a whiff of Razorfire, or any of his high-level Gallery minions. But we'd only just begun. *Wait till you see Razorfire. Then I'll show you dangerous.*

I quaffed my glass of OJ—I'd gotten used to sleeping all day and having breakfast at twilight, and Glimmer's waffles were nothing short of spectacular—and flicked through the emails on the phone he'd given me. Over the past few days, I'd inboxed my sources in the PD and emergency services. Couldn't remember anyone's contact details, but on the whole, people at their day jobs have no reason to be secretive. They want to be found, so they put themselves on phone lists, email directories, business networking sites. And even if they don't, corporations and government departments are pretty unimaginative when it comes to email addresses. I considered dropping Adonis a line—I'd offer short odds for *adonis@fortune-corp.com*—but I decided it was too dangerous.

I'd also called my contacts at the *Chronicle,* just to say hi and let them know I was finally back in the saddle after my surgery. Yeah, didn't they hear? Dreadful car wreck, some DUI asshole on the interstate wrecked my damn car and nearly took me out. It'd been a long recovery—nine months, and half of it in traction? Jeez—and that damn hospital food sure sucked the big one, but I was out now and back to work. Thinking of doing a human interest piece on the mayoral race... No, both sides. Of course. Really? You've got a number for Caine's press secretary? Wow, that'd be great. Sure, I'll put in a word for you at FortuneCorp PR. Equity loves doing interviews. I'll be in touch, we'll do lunch sometime. Great to talk to you.

Caine's press secretary was ever so nice, but firm: *Mr. Caine's schedule is very busy.* Sure, I understand that. I only wanted a few minutes of his time, a couple questions, specifically on the augmented angle? I really admired his stance on public safety, and I'm writing a feature for the *Chronicle,* syndicated to online media and... Well, I understand. Thank you, ma'am, I sure do appreciate your time anyway. You'll email me his appearance schedule? Generous of you, ma'am, most generous.

I sighed. No luck there. But persistence was my breakfast cereal. I'd get this Caine guy to talk to me if I had to follow his campaign all over town and throw tomatoes.

An engine rumbled into the parking lot and soon Glimmer

emerged, shopping bags bulging in both fists. He liked shopping. Did it every day. He still wore his mask. I hadn't seen him without it yet, in fact. Was he hiding just from me, or did he wear it to the shops, too?

"Hey, hero," I said. "Did you get me a pretty face this time?"

He flashed me a grin. "Wanna get your feet off my desk?"

I smirked, hopped up and walked my empty plate to the kitchen. "You know you love me."

"That doesn't mean you can put your feet on my desk."

"But it's a special occasion," I argued cheerfully. We had this conversation every morning. Along with him cooking me breakfast, it never failed to put me in a good mood. "We made the front page."

"So I see. Good to be famous." He hefted his bags onto the bench.

I helped him, unloading vegetables and fresh pasta from the food markets, beer, chocolate, potato chips and cans of caffeine and cola. All the good stuff. "So what's our good deed for tonight?"

"Well, the word is—"

"Yeah, yeah," I grumbled. Him and his computer wizardry hadn't been wrong yet. "You and your 'word'. What does that even mean, geekboy?"

He grinned, satisfied. "Word is," he repeated, "the Dockside Boys are getting themselves a little weapons delivery at their warehouse tonight." He popped a juicy-looking strawberry into his mouth.

I took one, too, a cool sweet burst of flavor. "And they're not buying from FortuneCorp? Shame on them. Let's kick their asses."

"And take the weapons," reminded Glimmer. Was that a dig at me? I'd controlled my power okay. Hadn't made any really big messes. So my head still ached every time I tried to unleash. Didn't mean I was a liability.

"That too." I frowned at a monstrous jar of stuffed olives. "Jeez. Are we preparing for the holocaust? This'll feed us for a month."

"Not the way you eat." He stuffed a pile of tins and packets of waffle mix into the cupboard under the microwave.

"Screw you. I'm a growing girl."

"I hope not." He handed the last bag to me, a shiny paper one with ribbon handles. Not from the food market. "Then this won't fit you."

I took it, uneasy. The weight felt considerable. "What is it?"

"Take a look."

I tipped out the bundle and tore the white tissue open. Gunmetal-gray fabric gleamed. I unfolded it. It felt satiny and strong under my fingers. A long coat, round-collared and silver-buttoned on wide lapels down the front in the military style. The sweeping tails scalloped into a blunt point. He'd brought me trousers to go with it, slim-fitting ones in the same glistening gunmetal fabric, and new black boots that looked elegant and—cough—feminine, but not ridiculously girly or pointy-heeled or any of those other things I hated.

It was sleek. Smooth. Beautiful. Too beautiful for this ugly chick.

My scarred cheek stung, and I flushed, sick. Jeez. Talk about embarrassing. Was he trying to dress me up? Make me into a girl? Good luck with that.

Glimmer shifted on one foot. "I thought it'd suit you. The Seeker, I mean. If you don't like it…"

"No." I didn't know where to look. This strange, sorrowful boy had given me everything I needed. A place to stay, a purpose, a new life. A friend. "I mean, yes, it's fine… Good, I mean. I, uh… I like it."

"Cool." He didn't seem to know where to look, either, and after an excruciating moment, he turned away.

I cleared my throat. "Glimmer?"

He paused, his back to me.

"Umm… thanks."

I felt him smile, a warm caress that prickled my skin. "You're welcome."

13

The air down at the dockside stung warm and salty in my mouth. A soft breeze blew wisps of hair from my masked face. My new suit fit me perfectly. Quite an eye for ladies' fashion, young Glimmer. When I'd first put it on, I studied the strong, shapely figure in the narrow looking-glass bolted to his wall and didn't recognize myself.

The shiny gunmetal coat buttoned firmly, but not too tight, over my chest—what there was of it—and the twin rows of silvery buttons accentuated my broad shoulders and narrow waist, where my knotted silver belt buckle clipped onto long, close-fitting trousers. The coat's tail swept back, out of my way, and fell in graceful satiny folds to my knees. My new boots fit well, supporting my ankles but not too clunky. I could run, skip, jump. Dance, if I felt like it, though me and dancing were kissing cousins at best.

I'd braided my scorched hair, tucked in the bits that were still too short and slipped my mask over my eyes. I stared at this new Seeker, and warm energy built in my muscles. She looked tough. Cool. Alien, not the kind of lady you wanted to mess with or befriend.

Perfect.

Now, with the sea breeze rolling in over lapping water, I climbed off the back of Glimmer's bike in the sultry shadow of a warehouse, and adjusted my mask with one finger. I'd kept my old mask, though Glimmer had offered to find me another. The soft leather had learned my shapes over the years, and despite my dented cheekbone, it still felt good on my face. I took strength and safety from it that I'd never found anywhere else, and I was reluctant to throw it away, even if it didn't quite match my new outfit.

And even if it still smelled strange, even after a week. That whiff of feminine scent I'd first caught at Adonis's place. I wrinkled my nose, wishing I'd aired the leather out. I never wore perfume. Perfume was for girls. Maybe it had rubbed off from one of Adonis's one-night-stands.

Glimmer rolled the bike into deeper shadow, the ruby-red glint vanishing into the gloom, and re-emerged, wiping sweat back into his stripy hair. He'd glammed himself up, too, after I'd insisted— *I'm not wearing this if you're just wearing jeans,* I'd said, like some virgin schoolgirl who didn't want to be the only one on the beach in a bikini—though I suspected he'd intended to all along, and was only teasing me.

We were supposed to be making a spectacle of ourselves, after all, and Glimmer looked like a character from a futuristic MTV clip, in the most amazing glossy black number that buckled with silver across one shoulder, fit snugly at his waist and left his muscular arms bare. I'd noticed his butt in his worn jeans—oh yes, this girl may be ugly, but she's not blind—and it looked just as tasty in tight gleaming vinyl. He still wore his wrist buckle and ring, but soft half-gloves wrapped his palms, too, keeping his fingers free to work their magic.

Kinky. Just add handcuffs. I wanted to survey and appreciate. Instead, I snorted. "Is that product I see in your hair?"

He ruffled it defiantly, poking up the skunk stripe. Definitely wax-assisted. "Bite me," he suggested, clipping his pistol to his belt.

I didn't have a pistol, and he hadn't offered me one. Suited me. I didn't intend on giving these Dockside creeps enough warning to shoot at me. "Dude, the only person biting you tonight will be some skinny white-trash rent boy with a vinyl fetish."

"Now, you're just jealous."

Dignify that with a response? Think not. "Seriously, what's with the shiny? I figured you for a more casual brand. Y'know, Mr. Inconspicuous, or something."

He shrugged. "I tried that. This is better. If I want to hypnotize someone, they gotta look, just for a second. This makes 'em look."

"Uh-huh. Yeah. I can see where that would work." *Watch me...* His command to Arachne echoed like raindrops in my skull. He'd pulled the same trick a couple of times this week, always with the same result. *Would you know about it? Probably not.* I shivered, despite the summer heat.

He studied me, serious. "You sure you want to do this? We don't have to work tonight if you're not—"

"I'm fine." His solicitousness poked irritable thorns into my nerves, the more so because he'd already unsettled me. "There's nothing wrong with me. Stop babying me. Let's just get on with it."

I pushed past him, and stalked across the street. He didn't argue. He just followed, catching up to me with a few quick strides, and it only annoyed me more. Why did he let me insult him without getting his own back? Emotional denial wasn't supposed to be a one-person game. His silent acceptance just made me feel shitty that I'd snapped at him.

Not how it was meant to work.

"The shipment is due about midnight," he murmured, as we crept in the dark beside the gang's warehouse, a rusted iron behemoth that stretched for a whole block. He didn't even sound pissed at me. Like he hadn't even heard me. "My info says they're buying for a sleazy Gallery augment who calls himself Weasel. Familiar?"

I made a disgusted face in the dark. I'd met Weasel before, on a job with Adonis a while back. The little bastard hacked through some sewer pipes downtown and flooded a hospital, made one hell of a mess before we caught him. An old lady got an infection and died, and Weasel did three undoubtedly miserable years in San Quentin for involuntary manslaughter, one of Equity's better moments in court. "Yeah. Rabid little rat with whiskers and teeth. Always hungry."

"Yeah, well, he's got a rodent's sense of smell, too, so be careful. If we can put him away, so much the better."

We lighted up to a shadowy corner, me first, Glimmer only a breath behind. The sultry air licked my mouth with salt. The water's edge was across the street, with rocks piled up along the breakwater. A parking lot for containers lay behind a chain link fence, the shipping crates piled in towers. Seagulls wheeled, squawking and hunting for food.

The warehouse's doors loomed along this side, big sliding iron sheets thirty feet high to the roof, tarnished with rust. I peered around the corner, breeze whispering in my hair. No one. "Are we early?" I murmured. "What's the plan?"

"I'll surprise 'em, you trap 'em." He craned his neck, gazing up to the warehouse rafters that showed through a rusted gap in the iron. "Can you get up there?"

I shrugged. "Sure."

"I'll hide inside. Wait for it. You'll know when."

"Got it."

"Verity?"

"Yeah?"

He caught my gaze, and inwardly I sighed, waiting for the *don't-kill-anyone* speech. But all he said was, "Be careful."

I flushed. He trusted me? Jeez. Now I really felt bad. "Right. Sure. Uh… you too." I flexed my power, and jumped.

High-pressure air swelled, carrying me aloft. I sailed through the gap, up to the rafters, and grabbed one, slinging myself on top. My butt crunched onto the wide iron strut. The breeze slapped at my coat-tails. I caught my balance, and butt-shuffled into the darkened warehouse.

It stank of rust and stale air. I found a flat place and held on, peering down over my swinging legs. The floor receded into gloom, but a few spotlights had been left on, pooling white light on the concrete. A few empty crates lay discarded, and twin tire tracks in the dust led out under the closed doors onto the street. Against the corrugated iron walls, I could make out shapes, furniture, bedrolls scattered on the floor, fire drums and piles of junk. Some of the Dockside lowlifes camped out here, when they weren't brawling or robbing convenience stores or drinking themselves into a stupor.

The doors edged silently apart, just a whisker, and a shadow slipped inside. Glimmer waved at me. I waved back. He passed both hands in front of him, tracing a swanlike shape. A capsule of air around him shimmered, like heat haze, and Glimmer vanished.

I don't mean slipped into shadow, or hid. I mean *vanished*. Disappeared. Wasn't there any more.

I shook myself, and peered again. Hang on. Wasn't that a shadow? A puff of dust, like footsteps? I strained my ears, and caught the almost inaudible scrape of feet. Heh. Right. It was just an illusion. He was still there, if you knew how to look.

I stretched smugly, enjoying my superior position. These scungy gun-running villains wouldn't have time to figure out Glimmer's tricks. They'd be too busy getting slammed against the walls by me.

As I waited, perched thirty feet above the floor, puffing idly at dust bunnies that drifted by, I recalled that I hadn't discussed with Glimmer exactly what we'd do to these scumbags. So far, we'd wrapped them up and left them for the cops, like we did to Arachne. But tonight, with Weasel involved… Hmm. Lock-up or hospital? That was the question. Personally, I wouldn't mind a little bone-crunching, if it'd get Razorfire's attention…

The metal roof slams into my face. My cheekbone flexes, dangerously close to snapping. I can feel it. Sickness floods my stomach. I'm caught. I can't get up. Can't get to the weapon…

"Don't hurt her. I'm warning you." It's not my father's voice. It's someone else. I gulp a coppery mouthful of air, and try to drag my head up, to see who's got me pinned down, but I can't. He's holding

*me too tightly, his hand jammed into the back of my neck too strong,
his weight more than I can move.*

*I try to flex him off me, but my mindmuscle groans in fatigue
and melts to nothing. I can't. I'm helpless. I yell, rage and frustration
flecking my lips bloody...*

A buzzing electric motor dragged me reeling into the real world.
Fuck. I lurched, dizzy, and grabbed wildly for the rafter to keep
from falling.

Panting, I held on tight. My thoughts tumbled, denial swirling
against terror, the horror of my torture in the asylum biting back
with a vengeance. I'd gotten Razorfire's attention once before. It
didn't turn out well.

Pain sliced into my brain, and I bit back a scream. My eyes
streamed, dust and agony. I fought to catch the drips before they
fell, not to give myself away with a careless blot in the dust all
those meters below. Moonlight knifed in, the blade widening. The
door was opening. They were here.

Excitement sprinted through my veins, and my rushing blood
eased the pain, just a little. I searched for Glimmer, but the moonlight had ruined my night vision. I couldn't see into the shadows.
We had no comms, I realized distantly. If we're gonna be a crime-
fighting duo, we really should see about getting ourselves Bluetooth
or something. Here's hoping the villains were blinded, too.

The doors crunched apart, and in drove a white refrigerated
one-ton truck. My palms itched. The shipment of weapons. What
would it be? Guns? Bombs? Something more exotic?

The truck ground to a stop, and two guys in jeans hopped out.
One was short and nuggetty, the other fat. Both packed pistols in
shoulder holsters. They slouched around to the back, and opened
the truck, and a third guy with a long greasy ponytail jumped out
of a foxhole, brandishing a shotgun. All three wore those silver
Gallery rings on their left hands. Inside the truck lay a row of
yellow plastic crates, the tissue transplantation kind. Four or five
of them, about the size of big lunchboxes, with that quasi-radiation

symbol and BIOHAZARD printed on the side.

Huh? What kind of weapons were these?

"All good?" the fat one asked.

Shotgun hefted his weapon. "If it weren't all good, we'd be a bonfire, JimJim."

Nugget cackled, and slapped fat JimJim's shoulder. "He's got a point, JimJim. Indeedy he does."

Impatiently, I swallowed a sigh. Get on with it, Glimmer. The longer I had to sit here and listen to these morons, the crankier I'd get.

My senses prickled. The sweet, astringent flavor of *augment*, a sherbety shock. Someone was close... I gripped the rafter tighter, flexing my power muscle in readiness.

A black limo cruised in like a shark, its shadow long and threatening. Dark tint obscured the windows. My anticipation whetted. At last, the big fish in this pond. I'd give that Weasel something to chew on, all right.

The limo stopped. The doors popped open, and not one but *two* augmented villains got out.

My pulse quickened. The weedy guy in a greasy shirt was definitely Weasel. I recognized that arrogant swagger, his crooked bowlegs, the scruffy brown hair and ratty mustache. But the other guy...

Stocky, barrel-chested, muscles bulging like a dwarf wrestler's. He wore a tight white T-shirt and blue jeans tucked into motorcycle boots. Unshaven chin, lank brown hair hanging to his waist. He flexed thick hands, his glassy nails long and sharp like a hawk's talons. The cold breeze of his augment swirled around him, stirring the dust at his feet, and his breath frosted white.

Declan Finney.

Iceclaw.

My throat squeezed tight. My power muscle trembled inside me, and I sweated, struggling to stop it from thrashing out in self-defense.

Fuck.

Iceclaw, giggling sociopath, murderer and destroyer of fun for all and sundry. Next to Razorfire, he was our most reviled enemy. My thoughts staggered, trying to recover my misstep. What the fuck was Iceclaw doing here? Whatever shenanigans we'd stumbled on, this was way higher up the Gallery chain than we'd anticipated.

I held on tighter, my palms slick and cold. Weasel was one thing, with his rodent teeth and whip-smart muscles and high-pitched snigger. Rabid and serpent-quick, sure, but no match for me. Weasel, I could handle.

I'd never beaten Iceclaw.

Last time we fought, Adonis got knocked out cold (no pun intended) and I nearly lost a hand to frostbite for my trouble. Word was that Iceclaw and Razorfire—frost and flame, each deadly in his own right—were on speaking terms. That Razorfire treated Iceclaw like he deserved to be alive. You only got that honor if you loathed the human race as much as Razorfire.

Or if you were murderous enough that your ideology didn't matter to him. Razorfire wasn't above manipulating sadists and psychotics into doing his dirty work. Once, Adonis and I arrested a cannibal serial killer who swore on his collection of stuffed corpses that Razorfire told him if he ate enough people, it'd make him superhuman. We'd even brought down suicide bombers who, instead of *God is great* or *fuck the IRS,* screamed *burn it all.*

Whichever one Iceclaw was, master race or lunatic or true believer, he didn't mean well.

I peered down, horrified yet fascinated. No sign yet of Glimmer. I forced myself to relax, wait it out. Treat this like a police operation. No point busting them until they'd had themselves a fine meal of felony stew. If we wanted a conviction, we had to wait for Frosty Ass and Hydrophobia Man here to actually lay hands on the loot.

Or, we could dive in screeching like the wrath of God, and kill them all.

I closed my eyes, glorying in the galloping drumbeat of my

heart. My muscles twitched. My breath burned my lungs, and sweet tension twisted my belly tight. Mmm. *Fight. Scream burning rage to the stars. Rend them limb from limb...*

I forced my eyes open. Gripped my rafter tighter, until the iron sliced my palms bloody. And waited.

Iceclaw shoved spike-clawed thumbs into his belt and swaggered up to the back of the truck, Weasel in his wake. "Evening, boys," Iceclaw said. New Jersey Irish, thick as cold cow shit. "What do we got?"

The three stooges each banged a clenched fist over their hearts, a Gallery genuflect. "Just as the boss ordered," fat JimJim said.

Iceclaw hit him. Full in the face, open-handed. His talons slashed JimJim's cheek apart like razor wire.

Blood spurted. Weasel giggled. JimJim howled, and grabbed his face. Three ragged cuts, dirty and cold to the core. JimJim better watch for gangrene.

"You don't talk about the boss, scumsucker." Iceclaw's drawl made it sound like *bawws.* "You don't smear his name in your monkey-shit mouth. You don't presume to compre*hend* what he's *think*ing! Got it?"

Nugget and Shotgun backed off, placating. "Sure, Mr. Finney," said Shotgun swiftly. "No problem. Just doing the business. JimJim never meant nothing..."

Iceclaw shoved past them, like he'd forgotten they existed. Weasel snickered, frothing at the mouth, and did a little jig, kicking his pointy heels up. His skinny feet were bare under his frayed jeans, and they were furry and long-nailed like a rat's. Word was, he had a tail, coiled inside his pants where no one could see.

I winced, my mouth sour. Jeez. Some guys really got the short stick. Imagine growing up like that. What hope did the poor bastard have of being ordinary? Still, didn't mean he had to hang out with evil death-lovers like Finney. Like I said, we've all got a choice in the end.

Iceclaw gestured impatiently, and Weasel scuttled up into the truck and retrieved a single yellow crate from the stack. He placed it carefully on the ground. On the side, it read:

BIOHAZARD
INFECTIOUS WASTE – DO NOT OPEN
KEEP REFRIGERATED

Clever, whatever was actually inside. Customs and quarantine didn't open BIOHAZARDS, not under normal conditions. And Sapphire City's docks had no infectious disease containment facilities. All you have to do is buy off the right corrupt officials—the Gallery spread rivers of dirty money around, so they've got friends in all kinds of places—and your cargo comes straight in through the regular channels, unopened.

The plastic lid was taped down tightly on all four sides. Iceclaw ran one talon around the edge, slicing the tape, and popped the lid. Inside, surrounded by white plastic packing, was a metal-and-glass globe about the size of a baseball, filled with watery red gel.

A flush of fever dizzied me. *Wind buffets my face, a flash of lightning. The glassy globe glitters like starlight, and I wipe a drop of condensation away...*

I shook myself, memory clanging my head sore. Christ on a cracker. Was it the same stuff? The stuff in the weapon I'd disarmed that night, on FortuneCorp's roof? Poison? A toxic chemical? My skin crawled just looking at that horrid glass globe. Whatever that shit was, it couldn't be good.

I shifted, itching to dive. Come on, Glimmer. Get him, before he smashes that thing and we find out the hard way.

Iceclaw grinned, baring short saber teeth. He bent over, his dirty hair dangling, and hefted the globe in one clawed hand. It sparkled faintly, tiny motes inside catching the spotlights like poisoned rubies. "So this is the new Pyrotox," he commented. "Real nice. I like the new color. Much more sinister than the old clear stuff."

Weasel snickered, and preened his straggly whiskers. "Yeah. That was himself's idea. 'Give me scarlet death, Weasel,' he says to me. 'Let 'em know just who's learning them their lesson.' Or, y'know. Words to that effect."

"Always with the fashion statement," Iceclaw commented dryly. "Does it actually do anything different to the old stuff?"

A sly Weasel wink. "Sure. The biocide's more lethal. And more persistent, too. Sticks like shit to a blanket. But the red's just cosmetic. Why the fuck not, I say?"

I sweated, sick. *Biocide.* Killer of living things. Charming.

"Why the fuck not," agreed Iceclaw. "What is it, a nerve agent?"

"Oh, yeah," said Weasel. "One breath and they're doing the epilepsy tango. Eventually their diaphragms seize up and they die of asphyxiation. So long as they don't burn to death first, of course."

"And the incendiary...?"

"Fourteen hundred degrees, count 'em and cringe. It ignites on contact with air to expel the nerve gas. That's the persistent part. It cleans up the bodies and burns off the excess agent afterwards." Weasel sniggered. "All very tidy. Just like himself ordered."

Iceclaw smiled, and I could see the insane gleam in his washed-blue eyes from here. As if he liked the idea of biocides in general, and asphyxiating incendiary nerve agents in particular.

I shivered. Jesus. A nerve gas that burned at fourteen hundred degrees. Now who did I know who'd think that was cool?

Burn it all. He'd tried once, and failed because of me. Now, with this new improved red death, he'd try again. And only Glimmer and I had the will to stop him.

"You've outdone yourself, Weasel," said Iceclaw, clapping him on the shoulder with an ingratiating smirk. "I think I'll let you live. How soon can we get more?"

Weasel sniffled, and scratched behind one ear. "Soon enough. Them eggheads at the lab are creaming themselves over this shit. 'Twas easy, once we figured out how to synthesize it..."

At the edge of the pool of light, shadows shimmered.

My muscles tightened. Silently, Glimmer eased from the gloom, still covered by his *don't-see-me* illusion. He looked like a smear on glass, an eye-crossing, out-of-focus blob that made your gaze want to slide away. *Move along, nothing to see here...*

Weasel's nose twitched. He frowned. "Hey, Deck...?"

Glimmer edged closer, quasi-invisible, into the spotlight's glow.

"What?" Iceclaw scowled, holding his glittering ruby globe to the light to admire it.

"D'you smell that?"

Now, Glimmer. Run!

Glimmer ran.

He popped into sight, sprinting straight for the truck like a black streak. The Three Stooges cursed and fumbled for weapons. Glimmer flung out his gloved hand in a wide arc. *Bang!* My ears popped, and a shock wave rippled outwards around him, almost too rapid to see. And JimJim, Shotgun and Nugget slumped to the dust, unconscious, eyeballs rolling white.

Weasel sniggered, and rubbed his eyes with a sleepy sigh. But he stayed awake.

Iceclaw just stared at Glimmer, and grinned.

Now or never. I flexed my power, sucking in a hot updraft, and jumped.

Wind swirled. My coat-tails flapped, the stunning sensation of falling. *Crunch!* I landed in a crouch and a swirl of dust.

Behind us, the limo driver jumped out and fled. Glimmer kept running. Iceclaw snarled, and leapt back to earn a second's grace. Weasel's furry paws scrambled in shock. Glimmer sprinted up to him, and dived, knocking the ratty bastard onto his back in the dust. He grabbed that skinny throat, jammed Weasel's head into the floor, and thrust his pistol barrel deep under Weasel's pointy whiskered chin. "Move an inch and I'll shoot, you skanky little rat."

Love me a guy who keeps his promises.

I jumped, and flung a handful of power straight at Iceclaw.

14

Weasel thrashed and squealed in Glimmer's grip. "No, you stupid bitch, you'll kill us all!"

My mouth dried. I tried to pull my power back, but too late.

I'd forgotten Iceclaw still held that glittering ruby globe in his fist.

The invisible force wall slammed him in the face. He staggered, and cursed. Sharp icicles spat from his lips. A cloud of dust blew his hair back. Behind me, the truck lurched and shuddered on its wheels, caught in the draft. I could feel the freezing white wall of Iceclaw's rage. My cheeks stung and blistered, but I stumbled forward, desperate to catch the ugly bastard if he fell, stop that menacing glass globe from shattering and throttling us all.

But he stayed upright.

He rounded on me, white insanity alight in his pale blue eyes. Frost crackled in his dirty hair. His laughter grated, icicles scraping on the blackboard of my nerves. "Long time, no thrashing, Seeker. Nice duds. You're still pig ugly."

"Hello, Ice," I called, shaky. Jeez. I'd nearly killed us all, and for what? "You're looking sick as ever. How I've missed your witty repartee."

He brandished the globe, flashing me a fanged grin. "You want some of this, lass? You and your faggotty boyfriend? You'll die quiet, you know. This shit doesn't even let you scream."

Glimmer jammed his pistol harder into Weasel's throat. "Careful," he warned me. "Back it off. You know the drill."

In his grip, Weasel sniggered. "Do it, you dumb cow. See what happens."

My blood boiled. I flexed, clenching raw power in my fists. It felt warm, smooth, inviting. I burned to let it play. But instinctive self-preservation clawed inside me, and my limbs shuddered, unwilling.

I didn't want to die. Not before I brought down Razorfire and his entire ugly crew. And maybe not then, either.

But this crazy son of a yeti might not care. He might really do it. Smash the globe and kill us all.

Could I really call his bluff?

Or should I back down, and let him walk away? Iceclaw, public enemy number two, Razorfire's BFF. The Sultan of Snow. The Imam of Ice. The Fakir of Frosty Fuck-you.

The cold-eyed maniac who'd asphyxiate the whole of Sapphire City and incinerate the corpses, if I let him.

Fuck that.

A whip of flame, sizzling the metal an inch from my cheek. Shadows flicker and threaten. I try to scream, but I can't make a sound, and warm fingers stroke my neck, hushing me. "It's for your own good. Don't fight. It'll only hurt more." I struggle, useless rage afire in my heart. I want to kill him. I want to slash, crush, rend the twisting metal apart, destroy everything and everyone who's ever tried to hurt me...

Reckless rage scorched my reason to quicksilver. Fucking frosty prick didn't deserve to live.

I grinned, and whipped a tentacle of my power around Iceclaw's throat.

He gurgled. I dragged him closer, making him stumble. "Put

it down, asshole," I hissed. "Carefully. Before I slam you into that wall and kill us all."

"Shoulda iced your ugly tomboy ass when I had the chance," he choked. His gaze glittered with fury, and another cold blast of wind stung my lashes with icicles. Icy moisture dripped from his claws and froze. But he didn't unleash on me.

He couldn't. Not without unleashing on the Truck of Chemical Nasty, too, and I saw in his fury-blue eyes that he didn't want that.

Triumphant insight caressed my skin warm.

Gotcha.

Now, I had his measure, yes indeedy. Iceclaw wasn't a lunatic or a suicide bomber. Just like Razorfire, he was the real deal. Mr. Superiority Complex, a power-mad maniac who thought he deserved to rule the world.

But they have a weakness, these monsters: they need to see the world genuflect at their feet. There's only one thing a true archvillain won't do to win. And that's die.

"Last warning, freak." I clenched my fist, and my power choked him tighter. "Give it over, or we all die horribly. Think your precious boss will give a damn that you miss the show? Not likely. He'll just get himself another minion, and good riddance."

Iceclaw uttered a filthy curse. My skull throbbed and split, the ice-cream headache from hell, and against my better judgment, I blinked.

Flash-quick, he hurled the globe straight at me. Hard.

I yelled, panic screaming at last in my brain. Jesus. I'd actually challenged him while he held our destruction in his hands. Called the psycho's bluff. I could've killed us all, and everyone within a mile's radius along with us.

What a reckless, angry, insane, *stupid* fucking thing to do.

All I had left was instinct. Both my hands flashed out. Fumbled for the globe. Caught it.

But when my concentration slipped, so did my power. And I let him go.

I clutched the globe to my chest, gulping the sweet air of relief. Iceclaw dived for the open limo door. He hit the gas, the door flinging shut as the rear end fishtailed, and screeched away in a stinging hail of icy dust.

Panting, I hugged the globe tightly. It felt cool and smooth in my hands. I stumbled for the empty yellow crate and placed the globe carefully back inside, pressing the lid on tight.

The three normals—Shotgun, Nugget and bleeding JimJim—still slumped in the dust, snoring. Glimmer dragged Weasel to his feet and cuffed his wrists tightly behind his back, spearing me on a dark glance full of inscrutable rage. "Oh, look, scumbag. Your boss left you behind for us. How about you tell us where this stuff came from, and who made it, and maybe we'll let you live to see a courtroom."

Weasel sniggered, spitting froth. Glimmer better get his rabies shot. "Like I believe you. Haven't we had this convo before? Oh, yeah. Right before you beat the living snot out of me. Screw you."

I strode up and aimed a shaking finger into Weasel's face. "We heard everything you said. Where's the lab, Weasel? Who's making this shit?"

His beady black eyes danced. He laughed, squeaky and high-pitched. "That's just beautiful, coming from you. Jesus. Deck always said you was schizo. What about glam-rock kid over here? Doesn't he think you're taking the secret identity thing a tad too far?"

Huh?

A frosty headache sliced my vision to blurry shreds. *A cool white corridor, the smell of lemon carpet deodorizer. I ease the glass door open and creep inside, where it's dim and silent. In the corner of the ceiling, a tiny red LED flashes, but I ignore it. Papers lie unfolded on the light boxes. I flick through them, and paper slices my finger, a blot of bright blood…*

I grabbed Weasel's whiskered chin and forced his head up. "What the fuck are you on about?"

But Weasel just laughed, and started singing a filthy song.

I shoved him away in disgust. He wasn't talking, and I wasn't up for torture. Probably, he was used to other Gallery villains abandoning him or double-crossing him or telling him lies. They had a sacred code, a bit like the Cosa Nostra or the Marine Corps: you didn't rat on your friends. Not even when those friends dumped you in the shit.

Nothing honorable about it, mind you. The Gallery hierarchy's wrath was far more terrifying than any limp-dick vengeance our legal system could cough up. If Razorfire found out that Weasel had squeaked, he'd hunt the stinky little rodent down and skin him alive. Slowly. With a blunt hacksaw. Dipped in chili.

Behind me, Glimmer spoke on the phone, cool and efficient, telling the cops it was a chemical hazard, they'd better bring SWAT and army bomb disposal as well as full NBC protection. It was a good idea. For all we knew, the truck was rigged with explosives, a nasty Gallery booby trap. Just Iceclaw's style.

I sweated, overheating. Glimmer was sharp, his wits always collected. He never lost control. Would I have thought to warn anyone, I wondered? Or just stormed away, angry that Iceclaw had escaped me, and left the cops to figure it out for themselves? What was wrong with me? Didn't I know that people could get hurt? Didn't I care?

Hell, I was just tired and sore from the asylum. Wouldn't be the first time my temper had landed me in trouble.

Speaking of which… I cracked my knuckles, my power coiling warm and hungry inside. We could kill Weasel right here. Put an end to one more Gallery villain who didn't deserve to live. If we let the lawyers deal with him—Christ, Dad had wanted Equity to be the DA, not the goddamn mayor, and why couldn't she just do as she was told for once in her life?—if the lawyers had their way, Weasel would be out again soon enough. Conspiracy to murder was probably the best we'd get, and he'd probably plead that down to an illegal substance trafficking charge.

And Iceclaw was still alive, along with the Three Morons. They'd be sufficient to spread the word about Glimmer and the Seeker. We didn't need Weasel...

I jerked back into the real world. "Huh?"

Glimmer touched my shoulder, and handed me one of the sealed yellow crates. He still wasn't really looking at me, his dark gaze guarded. "We'll take one," he said calmly, but underneath, emotion smoldered, ready to be unleashed once we were alone.

"What for?" I argued, more to forestall his accusations than because I disagreed. "This Pyrotox thing is the stuff that was in Razorfire's bomb the night I was captured, okay? It sounds like VX mixed with fucking napalm. Who invents this shit? And they say we augmented are the psychopaths."

"Preaching to the choir here, sister. If what Weasel said is true? It's super-lethal."

"And illegal, right? Tell me there are laws against this stuff."

"Useless for anything but a chemical weapon? It's very illegal."

"And you really want this shit in your house?"

He produced his phone and snapped pics of the truck, Weasel, the three normals asleep on the ground, the tire marks and scattered frost crystals left by Iceclaw. "For analysis. And for proof, in case some crooked cop tries to sweep this under the carpet." He pocketed the phone. "You good with that?"

I shivered, recalling how stupidly I'd baited Iceclaw. Worked out okay in the end, but that wasn't the point. Whatever nasty rebuke Glimmer was cooking up for me, I probably deserved it. That didn't mean I was looking forward to feeling like a naughty child.

That calm, sinister voice whispered excuses in my head. *I got confused. My head hurts. My memories made me do it. The crazy bastard deserved it.*

I wanted to believe them. But none of them made me feel better. None were good enough.

But sirens already sliced the summer night, howling ever closer. We couldn't afford to be found here. I pulled myself together, and clutched the sharp yellow crate tightly. "Okay. Let's go."

15

Twenty minutes later, I paced before Glimmer's console, yanking my ragged braid over my shoulder. My skin itched like ant bites. My new shiny costume felt too tight, and inside it I sweated, feverish. I tugged my mask off and tossed it aside. It didn't help.

My stomach thrashed like a pit of cobras, bad-tempered and ready to strike. I wanted to kick something, scream, shudder the ceiling loose with my rage. Sweep all those fancy screens to the floor and watch them shatter.

I wanted to shatter *him*.

Because Glimmer didn't shout, or hit me, or demand to know what the fuck I thought I was doing. He hadn't unbuckled his shiny black suit, or washed his skunky head under the tap to fight the heat. He didn't even look like he was sweating.

He just sat there, skewering me with that reproachful gaze. "Are you feeling all right?"

"I'm great," I said shortly. "Why do you ask?"

A light shrug. "Just wondering—"

"Why don't you ever say what you really mean?" I wrenched my coat off and tossed it on the desk. Underneath I wore a tank top, and my bare arms stung with sweat. It didn't cool me down.

"Huh? Stop hiding behind that mask and tell the goddamn truth for once. Because guess what? I don't believe your nice-guy act for one second."

"Verity—"

"Go on. Show me that bad-boy anger." I leaned over, getting right in his face. "You know it's in there, Glimmer. You know you want to let it loose. Hit me. Curse at me. Say, 'What the fuck happened, Verity, you dumb bitch, are you trying to get us killed?'"

He shoved me away, spinning his chair so he could get up, and rounded on me, that smoldering spark igniting a magnesium flashburn. "Okay. Fine. What the fuck happened, Verity? Are you trying to get us killed? Jesus. Do the words 'incendiary nerve agent' mean nothing to you?"

Ha. Got a rise out of him. I should've been triumphant. But I just felt nauseated, fevered, like I had the flu. "What else was I supposed to do?" I demanded. "He had it in his hand. What do you want, that I should just let him go?"

"I want you to use some finesse." He fisted his hair, exasperated. "I want you to think before you hit things. But no, you were too determined to hurt him—"

"Like you were a big fucking help," I interrupted. "If you weren't so damn keen on keeping Weasel alive, you could have helped me."

"What, did you want me to shoot him?"

"Yes, I fucking well wanted you to shoot him!" My nerves hacked ragged, but I was too angry to stop. "What were you saving him for? He's a Gallery scumbag. An accessory to murder. A freak who thinks a truckload of Pyrotox bombs is just a lovely idea. Yeah, he's a real nice guy, Glimmer. Totally worth saving a bullet for."

"This is not about saving bullets. This is about the difference between them and us."

"Oh, yeah?" I jumped closer, furious. "And what's that? Competence? Intelligence? They've got a plan and we don't?"

"No," he retorted, and the air around him shimmered with his frustration. "It's that we're supposed to give a damn who we hurt. And I don't think you do, Verity." He let out a deep breath, calming. "I think you would've let Iceclaw crush that canister and kill us all, not to mention half the damn neighborhood. So long as it meant he'd go down, too. Just to get your revenge."

"Right," I said sarcastically. "Even though it was Razorfire who fucked me over, not Iceclaw. You know so much about me, do you? Then tell me. Revenge for what?"

Glimmer hesitated, and for a moment I really thought he'd back down.

"For making you afraid that you're one of them," he said softly.

My body shuddered, weak like water.

I'm not a bad person. It clanged evil bells in my skull. I wanted to cower, cradle my head in my arms. *I'm not! It isn't true! Don't hurt me...*

I must have staggered, or slumped, because in a second Glimmer was at my side, forcing me back to my feet. He smelled of vanilla, safe and sweet. I tried to shake him off. I was bad. I didn't deserve sweetness or safety. Didn't deserve him, Glimmer, with a heart of gold and conviction forged from steel, who'd never hurt anyone unless they hurt him first and probably not even then, not unless other lives were at stake.

I reeled, and vomit splurted into my mouth.

Glimmer held on as I choked. "Verity, listen." His dark voice was low, urgent, rough with emotion. "I know how it feels, sweetheart—"

"No, you don't!" My voice stretched to a scream, and I fought to shrug him off. "You don't. No one does."

"Believe me," he insisted, gripping my shoulders tightly so I couldn't escape. "I do. I've had those thoughts. I kept it... this thing, you know... I kept it hidden for a long time, until Razorfire called me out. He'd been watching me, see. He knew I was augmented, that I was hiding it out of fear. For him that's an unforgivable sin. He attacked my family, and to save them, I had to show myself for what I am. The way my wife looked at me..."

I gulped, sick. His wife. I didn't want to hear.

But he shook me gently, made me listen. "She was so frightened, so angry with me. She called me insane. Said I'd tricked her, that what we had wasn't real. She took our baby daughter. I haven't seen them in... well, it's a long time. I'll never see them again."

I struggled, unwilling to face him through a haze of guilt. I'd grown up in a family of augments. Always accepted, loved, encouraged. Sure, I had to keep it in the can in public, but at home, at least, I could be myself.

Unwilled, I imagined Glimmer's home, his baby, his beautiful wife, of course beautiful for a guy like him, he was gentle, strong, clever. Perfect. He must have married so young, and then... what? Reality sets in. Always on guard. Never allowed to be himself. Forever hiding, pretending, covering up in case she found out... So tempting, see, when it's in the mind, to take a peek, murmur sweet persuasions in her ear, find out what she wants and give it to her, make her smile for you...

"I wanted Razorfire so badly, after that," Glimmer admitted. "I've never known such hatred, and you know what? It felt damn good. It gave me power. Her leaving me was all his fault, see. If he hadn't forced me to come clean..."

"You'd still be with her today," I finished. My leg muscles watered, and I succumbed, falling on my knees. My voice cracked, raw with acid. "Fuck. Glimmer, I'm so s—"

"No!" He joined me on the floor, brushed the hair from my sweaty forehead. Trapped me with a midnight-rich blink, and wouldn't let me escape. "No, you see. I was wrong. It was *my* fault."

"What?"

"My power didn't hurt her. Only my lies."

"But..." I tried to blink, to run. I couldn't move.

Shit. Was he hypnotizing me? Or was I just transfixed, drowning in my own turmoil, clutching desperately at his words for a lifeline?

"I deceived her," he insisted. "She thought she knew me, and I'd lied to her all along about the most important thing in my life. I should've told her long before, but I was too afraid. I got what I deserved." He sucked in another deep breath. "That makes me a liar, and a moron. But it doesn't make me a villain."

I swallowed, dumbstruck.

"People will love you or hate you for your power, Verity, and nothing you can do will change that. But you *can* control what you do with that power. The world—or God, or whoever, I don't know—something made you strong. It's how you treat the weak that makes you what you are."

What was I, then? I wanted Razorfire. He wasn't weak. By stopping him, I was *protecting* the weak. Wasn't I?

Or was I just protecting myself? Chasing *him* to chase away my demons. Erasing *him* to erase my past.

As if causing him pain could somehow make up for the pain he'd caused me.

Glimmer had tried that. Glimmer was past that. He'd given up on blind revenge, and channeled his rage and loss into helping others.

But had he really?

I shifted, itching to act. Surely, something remained of his dumb animal fury. The jealous, selfish child inside us all, the one that hammers its fists on the walls and howls *I don't deserve this! It's not fair! Someone has to pay!*

I stared deep into Glimmer's eyes, searching for the truth. I could feel his ragged breathing. His pupils dilated. His eyes weren't black, after all, but blue, the endless, strange, midnight blue of starlit space. I couldn't read them. Couldn't see inside.

I lifted a shaking hand. His mask, black and silken under my fingertips. Warm.

He jerked back, instinctive. I followed. "Take it off."

"No." Soft, but certain.

"I need to see your face." Compelled, I slid my thumb along his cheekbone, under the mask.

"No. Please, I can't." He averted his face. But he didn't get up, or run.

I dipped my fingers into his hair, pulling him back around. First time I'd touched it, springy and soft, that delicious scent of vanilla spice.

I trembled, warm. I wanted to bury my face and inhale, bathe in his goodness and let him wash me clean. "I have to. I need to see. What are you afraid of?"

Glimmer grabbed my wrist and forced it away. "Don't you get it? That guy underneath isn't me! *This* is me. *This.*" He pressed my palms to his face, one either side where the mask stretched. "I'm Glimmer. That guy? He's a lie. He's where I go when I can't face myself. But—Verity, listen to me—I stopped avoiding mirrors a long time ago."

"No." I shook. My thumbs dug into his cheekbones. My fingers clawed in his hair. I think I hurt him.

He didn't let me pull back. "Lying to yourself? Pretending it's not real? It just ignores the inevitable. I don't wear a mask to hide. I wear my mask because it's the truth."

My thoughts reeled, and I struggled to pierce the swirling rainbows. The truth? I knew the truth, all right. They can't make me forget. The Seeker's strong. Verity's weak. I'm not a bad person…

My cheeks scorch like sunburn in the hot breeze of the destruction he's wrought. I don't care. I have to know…

I thrust my thumbs beneath my mask. My nails sting my cheeks. I push harder. The stitching rips. I yank it off, and bare my face to the fire. "Look at me!" The scream hurts my lungs, but they're already burning, and I choke on gritty smoke. "Look at what you've made of me. For God's sake…!"

His reply drifts back through the smoke, rich with delight that makes me shiver: "Haven't you learned yet? You have no god but me…"

White light dazzled me, the stinging aftermath of a sucker punch, and my mind stumbled like a drunken dancer. Christ on a cheesy rissole. That was a new one. What the fuck?

I held on tight to Glimmer's strong hands, choking back a gritty sob. *It's how you treat the weak that makes you what you are,* he'd said. He'd sounded so sure.

But what if he was wrong?

What if we had no choice?

What if the villains molded us in their image? Dragged us down to their level? Chipped away at that moral high ground, brick by fragile brick, until it crumbled beneath our feet and we fell... or until we got tired.

Tired of bodies and burning buildings and dead friends. Tired of always being one step behind, forever losing to an enemy who always held one more trick in his hand than we did.

Until we said *the hell with it,* and dived in.

Sinking to their level is no longer acceptable. Equity's words filtered back to me, tainted with new and bitter meaning. Had I misjudged her? What if she'd suffered the same doubts? Faced the same ugly temptations? What if her plan to renounce violence was just that: a last-ditch effort to climb out of the abyss?

Horror slashed my veins, bleeding me raw. *You have no god but me...*

"Verity? Stay with me... Jesus." Glimmer's voice echoed, distant. His warm fingers on my cheeks, tilting my head, trying to keep me upright. I wanted to fall into his arms, pass out, keep the ugly dreams at bay. *Please, let them be dreams. Let them be drug-fucked hallucinations, brainwashing bullshit that Mengele cooked up to confuse me. Just don't let them be real...*

I crunched my tongue in my teeth. Hard.

Blood, tart and coppery, stinging my nerves awake. *Stay conscious, Verity. Face this. Don't let them win.*

I sucked in a hungry breath, willing the oxygen to pump around my tired body. I tried to say it, but my throat squeezed shut, and my thoughts swirled in evil snapping rainbows, blotting out my reason.

"You've got to help me." It tasted strange in my mouth. But it was a sweet, compelling flavor of strange. "I can't do this alone. Please."

"Anything." Glimmer tilted his warm cheek against mine. His sweet scent ached in my throat like honey. I wanted to swallow it. Swallow him, let his goodness blot out my guilt, the warmth of his body next to mine to calm my beastly rage... but damn it, he deserved better than that.

He deserved so much better than me.

"The night I was taken," I gasped. "The night Dad died. I don't remember it. I need to see what happened."

"But... I told you, remember? All the video has been erased."

"I don't care!" I swallowed a shriek, desperate to think past the throbbing in my skull, the selfish need that slicked my body warm. "Search again. Please. Whatever you can find. I need to see, don't you get it? I need to *see*."

"Shh." He brushed his lips across my forehead, a warm electric shock. "I get it. I'll help you. Just relax." And he helped me to my feet, and walked me over to the sofa. His arm was steady around my waist. I wanted to lean on him, but I stumbled best I could. He made sure I was comfortable, and ducked into the kitchen, where I soon smelled coffee brewing. And then he skidded his chair over to the desk, and woke up his console.

The screens shed their familiar greenish glow. The warm light soothed me. Comforting.

I caught my breath, forcing myself to calm down. I'd make it through this, right? I'd find out what happened, and then my night-mares would go away, banished to suffer in whatever screaming hell those imaginary monsters under your bed go to when they die. And at last, I'd know what was real, and what was just a wild, torture-soaked dream.

Glimmer fired up his satellite tracking system. "Nothing to watch on cable tonight anyway, right?" He flashed me his crooked smile.

I dredged up my own in answer. "Probably not. It's all shit since they canned *The Justice League*."

"Preaching to the choir here, sister." He slotted in a few algorithms and brought up that mega-brain search engine of his, info-capture programs already blinking in the corners of his screen. "Okay. Let's look for video first. You got GPS co-ords?"

Glass walls, smooth under my fingertips. The wind buffets my face, and fifty floors beneath me, the city glitters in a wispy wreath of fog, the wide arcs of the Bay Bridge a sprayed neon rainbow...

"The FortuneCorp building," I interrupted. Now was not the time for more misleading hallucinations. "Inside and out. I wanna know where I went, what I did, who else was there that night. Everything."

"Right." Glimmer's fingers already danced over the keys. "Time?"

"No clue. Zero-dark-hundred. It was stormy. But not raining." I struggled with the few fleeting images I could remember. "And there was lightning. A lot of lightning."

A swift smile. "That'll do for a start."

16

"What d'ya mean, there's nothing?" I demanded, an hour later. I was on my fourth cup of coffee. It wasn't helping my mood.

Glimmer shrugged, mellow as usual, even with added caffeine. "I mean, there's nothing. No media files, no swipe card records, nothing. It's like the entire building's security system was down. But look at this." He flicked up a page of gibberish, and pointed. "I checked all the way down to the source code. There's no entry. Not a thing, from a quarter past midnight for a two-hour period. Not even a null reading or a system fail."

"In English, geekboy."

"Either the power grid was down and the emergency generator system didn't kick in…" He jumped to another screen, and in a few moments, a diagram of Sapphire City's power grid popped up, mains and voltages and service channels drawn in black and red. Glimmer did a quick search, and shook his head. "Nope. No faults recorded. The grid didn't fail that night."

"Then what?"

"Someone deleted it, that's what." He scrolled the code again, highlighting a couple of lines. "See those time groups there? One hundred and thirteen minutes apart. Someone wanted to make those two hours disappear."

I leaned closer in my chair, and frowned. All looked like Wingdings to me. "Seems a bit clumsy. Wouldn't they insert false data, to cover it up? Make it seem like the system failed, or something?"

"They might, if it wasn't triple-encrypted. Maybe they didn't expect anyone to decode it. Or anyone to come looking." He slanted me a dark glance. "Someone who thought you weren't coming back?"

I shuddered. It made sense. Razorfire didn't want anyone to know where he'd hidden me. He'd made them all believe I was dead. Maybe the missing footage was a clue he didn't want found.

But how did he gain access to the system? My brow furrowed until I realized that system access probably wasn't much of a hurdle for the Gallery's archvillain. I had Glimmer, after all. Razorfire probably had his own tame computer genius chained up in a vault somewhere.

Either that, or Equity had shown him where to look. Maybe even done it herself…

I blinked that thought away. I still harbored hope that Equity wasn't dirty. That Dr. Mengele's goons had tracked me independently, that somehow I'd given myself away. Heaven knew my brain was at half-mast that night. I'd probably made all sorts of dumb-ass, amateur mistakes.

"Okay," I said. "What else we got? What about cameras across the street, at ground level? Would they show who came and went from the building?"

"They might. It's an old archive, but the files might still be there." Glimmer scanned his CCTV circuit diagram. There was the financial district, the terrace-gardened square where the FortuneCorp building stood. The map showed four cameras in that area, and the real-time view from each soon popped up.

I peered closer, fascinated, feeling a trifle voyeuristic. Two faced the other way across the square, and didn't show our building.

One showed the side street, bathed in morning sunlight, a garbage truck inching along its collection route, and the fourth showed the street out front, morning traffic jerking in five-second jumps, right by the lobby's front entrance. They'd replaced the windows I broke, I noticed. Probably fixed the floor, too. Wouldn't do for Equity's campaign for there to be a mess.

"Right. Now for the archive…" Glimmer searched for the date-time. The four feeds paused for a couple of seconds, and then history flashed up before our eyes. Nighttime, the softly-lit park, car headlamps glaring on the glass windows.

Dizziness flushed me warm. I wobbled in my chair, closing my eyes for a second. It felt strange, peering through this electric window into my past. It felt…wrong.

Glimmer reached for his coffee and teetered back in his chair, stretching his long legs. "Whatever happened was done and dusted in those two hours, right? At five times speed, that's twenty minutes. Think you can stay awake that long?"

"Blow me," I said, my nerves cut sharp. Was he kidding? I was sweating, shaking, perched on my seat's edge. My fingernails ached with anticipation. For this, I'd stay awake all night.

I stared fiercely at the jumping images, determined not to miss an instant. People jerked by, now on one side of the image, now on the other, now gone. It was late, and they were mostly restaurant-goers, in couples or groups, the occasional wino or bunch of slouching teenagers or trio of rifle-armed cops in Kevlar. But no one stopped in front of FortuneCorp. No one went inside. Until…

I pointed, shaking. "There. Wind that back. What was that?"

Glimmer slid his finger across the touchscreen, and the four films reversed as one. He played it again. Now the automatic glass doors were open. Now they were closing again, just a foot of gap remaining between the panes. No one there. A page of newsprint tumbled by, caught in the breeze.

"Again," I ordered.

Newspaper, carried by the breeze. Doors open. Doors in

mid-close, just a foot apart.

"Pause it there." I peered closer, remembering Glimmer's secret snapshot of Phantasm, my invisible cousin. But there was no shimmer. No heat haze. Just that breeze, and then a curl of shadow, coiling like a smoky snake's tail through the gap in the closing door. "Holy crapola. There he is."

Glimmer looked a question.

I stabbed my finger at the picture, my pulse alive. "That shadow. It's Blackstrike. My father just walked through that door."

At forty-seven past midnight. Alone. No Adonis. No Uncle Mike. No me.

Like someone had called him in from home, and he'd showed up as fast as he could. An emergency.

Frustration gnawed at my eyeballs. Fuck it. Razorfire was in that building—maybe right as that picture was taken, I was climbing that smooth glassy wall, racing against time to stop him—and I couldn't see. Couldn't act. Couldn't stop my father striding in, heading inexorably for his death.

"Phone calls." Sweat trickled in my hair. I swiped it back, my heart racing. "Can we check incoming calls for twenty minutes prior? Someone must've called Dad in."

"What's his number?" Glimmer was already typing.

Fuck. I strained my memory, but I couldn't remember his cell. "He lived in Ocean Heights," I said desperately. "You could smell the park."

"First name Thomas, right? Jackson Street?"

"Yes!" Inspiration flashed bright, like fog rubbed from a mirror. "That's it. Can you reverse?"

"Already on it." Glimmer's screen filled with call records. "Twelve fifteen a.m. There you go. Zero zero thirty-four, a fourteen-second call from a cell phone." He read out the number, and did another search. "Which belongs to..."

Another light flashed, dizzying me, and I knew.

"...Adonis Fortune," Glimmer finished with me.

Fierce relief ached in my muscles. So Adonis had been there, just like he said. It had all gone down just as my brother had told me. "Can you get the call? Is it recorded?"

"Uh. Nope. The recording's gone, it's too old. Sorry."

Bugger. But fourteen seconds wasn't long enough to say much more than *Dad, it's me, get your shadowy ass down here*. And if Razorfire was truly inside, up to his Fiery Antics of Doom…

I frowned. Something didn't compute. "Who else did Adonis call? Just Dad?"

Another search. "Yep. No other calls until 3:00 a.m." Glimmer frowned. "Adonis has five… no, six phones. Paranoid much?"

"Doesn't that seem weird to you?"

"Like, weird how?"

"Imagine you're Adonis, from a family of augments. Imagine it really is Razorfire up there. Your archenemy, right there in your inner sanctum, threatening fuck knows what. Wouldn't you call everyone in the entire world to help you? Uncle Mike, Equity, Jem, the rest?" I paused. "Wouldn't you at least call me?"

Glimmer shrugged, cautious. "Maybe he doesn't have time. Maybe Razorfire's right there, or the phone got broken or taken from him. He only has fourteen seconds, so he calls the boss. Makes sense."

"Yeah." Evil warmth crept into my bones, and I shivered. "Or maybe I'm already in there."

"Or already captured?"

"That too… wait a sec. What about me? Did I call anyone?"

"Good question. What was your number?"

I gave him a *duh!* glare.

"Oh, right. Sorry." He blinked sheepishly, and searched. "Uh. Nope. Oh, hang on… I see three calls, all to the same cell, earlier in the night. It rang out each time and you hung up. Your phone hasn't been used since then. It's disconnected." He read out the number I'd called. "Any ideas?"

"Nope. Whose is it?"

"Uh… must be unlisted. Wait one…" He typed, and frowned. "That's strange."

"What's strange?"

"It's not coming up anywhere. Even an unlisted or disconnected number leaves a trail. It's as if someone's deleted this entire phone account."

"From the phone records?"

"From the face of the earth. It's like it never existed."

"Maybe I called the wrong number. One that wasn't in use."

"Three times? In any case, that'd get you the invalid number message, not an empty ring." He lifted his hands. "Sorry. I've got nothing."

"Give me your phone." He gave it to me, and I called. A burst of hash, and then a recorded message chimed in my ear.

I ended the call and cracked my neck, sighing. "Well, it's an invalid number now. So… I pranked someone three times— someone who didn't want to talk to me, apparently—and then I up and disappeared? And Mr. Mysterious has since erased his number?"

"Or Ms."

"Huh?"

"It could be Ms. Mysterious."

"Oh. Yeah, I guess so." An ache rotted my skull from the effort of thinking it through, and I tried to relax, to smooth the wrinkles from my forehead. There must be a simple explanation. A crisis, and Adonis doesn't call me. Why not?

Because he thinks he doesn't need help? Not likely, with Razorfire on the rampage.

Maybe I'm already there, but I'm in no shape to help. Perhaps I'm injured. Or perhaps I'm already captured by the time Dad gets there.

Is that why Adonis calls Dad? Because Razorfire's already got me?

Vaguely, I recalled my brother's words, the night I escaped. *Dad tried to help you, and Razorfire killed him.*

I frowned. Tried to help me what?

Fight Razorfire? Escape? Or defuse that glossy glass weapon I kept seeing in my dreams, the one with the ominous gel-like stuff inside it that looked disturbingly like a clear version of Pyrotox, the Gallery's newest screaming death trick?

Obviously, it didn't go off. So what happened to it? And why wasn't I dead, too?

My memory glittered, bright and then dim and then bright again, like a cloud passed in front of the sun.

Maximum loss of life. Not a moment to lose... *I like the new color,* Iceclaw said, his saber-toothed grin dripping cold with menace, *much more sinister than the old clear stuff...* and my father's voice, piercing my heart like a hot needle, releasing floods of molten guilt: *Don't hurt her. I'm warning you...*

Was it Dad's voice? Smoke twinged my nose, an acrid echo. My vision blurred. I shook my head to clear it. I felt drunk, light-headed. It sounded like Dad. Maybe Uncle Mike. Maybe Adonis. I didn't remember.

Too goddamn much that I still didn't remember...

"Huh?"

Glimmer waved a hand before my eyes. "You still with me?"

"Uh. Sure. Sorry. Just thinking." I crossed damp wrists on my knees. That yellow crate hunkered on the kitchen bench, glaring at me with its yellow BIOHAZARD symbol and its INFECTIOUS WASTE – DO NOT OPEN. I glared back. Something about it bothered me. "What do you know about this Pyrotox gear?"

"Same as you, after tonight." Glimmer shrugged. "A corrosive pyrophoric neurotoxin. Meaning, a substance that ignites on contact with air to produce a nerve agent. You heard Finney. It only has one purpose."

"And this red stuff is the new version they've made, right? Horrible Death Mark II, fresh and improved."

"That's what Ratboy said."

I frowned. "So where'd they get the old version? The weaker stuff, that only killed eight zillion people per cupful, or whatever?"

Glimmer ruffled his stripe. "That's what I hoped Weasel would tell us. I assumed they had some mad neo-Nazi chemist with Zyklon B fantasies locked away somewhere..." He halted in mid-ruffle. "Oh, shit."

He'd figured it, too, and we shared a glance of *oh, yeah*.

Them lab eggheads are creaming themselves, Weasel said. *'Twas easy, once we figured out how to synthesize it.*

Like they didn't already know how.

Like they'd reverse engineered it. Which meant they'd taken the original from someone else.

"So where'd they flog it from?" I demanded.

"Military, maybe? There'd be no patents, nothing on the record. They keep new weapons a state secret."

"Or some other kind of secret," I mused. "Like..."

My throat knotted, slicing off my breath.

FortuneCorp didn't manufacture illegal weapons. It was in Dad's charter. No chemicals, no biologicals, nothing that breached the Geneva laws or the Chemical Weapons Convention. Only chemical defense research allowed.

But sometimes, accidents happen in science. You forget to clean your Petri dishes one weekend and boom, there's penicillin. Or you're trying to invent a better bug spray, and by mistake you get VX. Oops.

And once you've invented something awful? Historically, your chances of stuffing that bad genie back into his bottle aren't good.

"What about a *trade* secret?" I said grimly. "Commercial-in-confidence. Like, I dunno. A private weapons technology company?"

Glimmer stared, and chewed his bottom lip. For once, he didn't know what to say.

I choked on a mouthful of bile. I couldn't go on. I didn't want to go on.

But it made horrible, evil, unthinkable sense.

Razorfire loathed FortuneCorp and everyone in it, from Blackstrike himself down to the janitors. We were weaklings, collaborators, as bad as the human scum we defended. If Equity wanted an entree to the Gallery, she'd need something ultra-cool to bribe him with.

Something ultra-cool, that is, to a genocidal pyromaniac with a god complex.

Something like a weaponized incendiary asphyxiating nerve agent.

"Oh, Jesus," I whispered. "What if... what if some boffin at FortuneCorp invented Pyrotox by mistake? And what if Equity..."

My thoughts scrambled over each other like crabs racing up a beach. That was Pyrotox Mark I inside that rooftop weapon that night. I knew it. Which meant Equity had poached the horrid stuff earlier than that.

Dissatisfied with her work as Nemesis, lady of light. Disgruntled, maybe, that Adonis got all Dad's attention. Starved for the spotlight, hungry for more power, more adoration than her job as assistant DA could provide.

Maybe, even, Razorfire plants that seed. Nourishes it, tempts her with promises of position and influence. He's sneaky like that. She takes her chance to get in good with the Gallery. Then Dad dies, and unknowingly places her in charge—or is that Equity's doing, too? Some clever fudgery of legal documents? She's an attorney, after all. And now, suddenly, she's running for mayor...

With Razorfire's hand stuffed right up her puppety little butt. Fuck.

I spun my chair around too hard, crashing into Glimmer. He caught me. I grabbed his chair, wild. "We have to stop her. If Razorfire's brainwashed her, we can't let her win this election." I realized I was squeezing his hand fit to crush it. He didn't seem to mind. I tried to relax. "We have to unmask her, tell the world what she's done. Now."

Glimmer's eyes shone, a midnight glint of blue. "We could do that."

I glared. "Or what? What's the problem?"

He considered, flexing his hand gently. "She could be innocent."

"Right. Have you even been listening? Jesus Christ on a spit-roast—"

"But even assuming she's guilty," he interrupted firmly, "if you were Razorfire, and someone unmasked your political stooge a week before the election, what would you do?"

I opened my mouth to say *who the fuck cares?* But then I thought about it, and sighed. "Get angry, and burn things," I admitted at last. "But we just stole his Pyrotox samples..."

"That we did. And if you were Iceclaw, and you'd just lost a truckload of crimson death that belonged to Razorfire, what would you do?"

I sighed again. Too damn thoughtful, this Glimmer. "Get him another one before he melts my face off? And pronto. Like, this week."

"And?"

"And... tear a pair of new assholes for the smug crime-fighting bastards who ripped me off?"

"Bingo." Glimmer cracked his knuckles. "Iceclaw will be hunting us down, with the help of every smarmy Gallery snitch he can lay his claws on. And from what I see on the news? Equity's looking solid for a big cut of the vote on Tuesday. Razorfire won't burn the city down when he's about to get the new mayor in his pocket. No, now isn't the time to be unmasking your sister."

"Then when?" I demanded. It itched me raw that he was right. More that I hadn't worked the ideas through myself. Jeez, I was too damn thoughtless for this line of work. Maybe I really did need a sidekick to rein me in.

Glimmer and the Seeker, I mused, considering it seriously for the first time. We did work kinda well together.

"Well?" I added, frustrated. "You want to wait until she wins? It'll be a damn sight harder to un-mayor her than it will be to unmask her."

"True. But we need proof first. That she stole Pyrotox and gave it to Razorfire, and that he's backing her campaign."

"Hmm." Once my hot blood chilled out, Glimmer's plan began to shape itself in my mind, and I liked it. "We find out just what his plan is for the weapon. Watch Iceclaw, see when the next shipment comes in."

"Exactly. Wait until they're ready and cocky and expecting to win." Glimmer's smile twisted, not altogether nice. "*Then's* the time to unmask your sister. We go to the police chief and the DA and the opposing candidate—"

"Don't forget the *Chronicle*," I chimed in.

"And the *Sapphire City Chronicle*. Give them everything we know. Researched, fully documented and undeniable."

I nodded in warm satisfaction. "Heh. Let them try brushing *that* under the rug. But..." I wrinkled my nose. "This other candidate, Caine. He's a hater. Wants to muzzle us and tattoo Danger! on our foreheads, or whatever? Doesn't seem like a grand choice for mayor."

Glimmer shrugged. "Better than a mayor whose patron wants to poison everyone and burn the city to the ground."

"Good point."

"Anyway, weren't you planning to interview him, ambush him with your secret journalist powers? You'll just have to change his mind."

I snorted. "You've seen his speeches. Lock up the psychotics, keep the city safe, blah blah spew. Change his mind with what? A demonstration of how easily I can throw a bus at him?"

"You could try that. But I was imagining you'd use your natural guile, charm and sex appeal."

"Yeah, right. Good plan. You got yourself a wild imagination, Skunkboy."

"Don't sell yourself short." He tilted his crooked smile at me. "You're charming as hell when there's something in it for you."

That smile dazzled me, and I wanted to hide under the table.

I flushed. Did he think I was stupid? Sure, I'd had a moment of weakness back there. I wasn't dead. But I knew how I looked, and I sure as hell knew when a guy was out of my league. If he was fishing for an easy lay, he was wasting his damn time on this ugly chick.

Whatever. I didn't have time to get all hot and bothered about it. Whatever evil shenanigans Razorfire had lined up for the aftermath of election day—and I couldn't help suspecting it had something to do with a truckload of glass globes stuffed with Pyrotox—I had two days to stop it.

Two days to prove my sister was guilty.

Sickness bubbled in my stomach, and I swallowed it down. Or to clear her name, I reminded myself. It was still possible I'd misjudged her. Though if an innocent explanation existed for what had happened that mist-clouded night at FortuneCorp, damned if I was clever enough to see it.

Either way, time was short. Better get on with the fun. Sleep was for weaklings anyway.

Caine would be on the campaign trail today. I had his schedule, thanks to that politely unhelpful press secretary. Time to make a nuisance of myself.

And time to forget about Glimmer's sweet dark eyes and crooked smile. I had too much to do.

"Yeah, well, don't get any ideas," I grumbled, my face hot, and headed for the shower. "It doesn't mean I like you, or anything."

17

At twelve thirty sharp, I sat on twitching hands in my hard-cushioned chair and watched Vincent Caine the Hater walk out onto the stage.

He'd chosen the lobby of his own company HQ for this press conference. Iridium Industries—the big silver sign at the entrance read IRIN—was a sprawling white complex of laboratories, offices, neat green lawn gardens and solar power cells glittering in the sun, set on a couple of dozen acres south of the city.

I'd ridden a cab from the train station, but the driver had to let me off at the big white gates. No fossil fuels allowed, and inside the compound, people scooted around on Segways and white solar-powered golf carts, or glided along on in-line skates. The main building's lobby looked like a technogeek's utopia, with natural light pouring in the clear double-glazed walls, white ergonomic lounge furniture and acres of low-glare flat screen TVs. All it needed was console games on tap and a big environmentally-friendly sign reading DON'T BE EVIL.

Anyway, here I was, yukking it up in the press corps again. I didn't have any business clothes, and I hated suits anyway, so I wore jeans and one of Glimmer's buttoned shirts. Casual, but neat enough that I barely earned a second look.

Around me, reporters chatted, texted, spoke into their cells. Maybe I was risking capture, putting myself out in the open like this. But Equity wouldn't set Mengele's goons on me in front of everyone, not in the middle of an election campaign. No, she'd wait for a private moment to commit her own sister to the loony bin. Couldn't have me making her look bad.

A few people I knew had grinned and shaken my hand, congratulating me on getting out of hospital at last, car accidents sure were a bitch, was I back at work full time, we should catch up for a drink one evening, whaddaya say?

I smiled back and made small talk. But after that first initial shocked glance, their gazes avoided my scarred face. My belly squirmed, strangled by angry snakes. I wanted to grab them by the collar and yank their faces into mine, make them look until they puked. *Oh, I'm sorry, is the big flap of skin that's torn off my cheek making you uncomfortable? Must have forgotten my paper bag. Won't happen again.*

Now, I watched Caine as he stepped onto the carpeted risers. I vaguely remembered him. Younger than I'd expected from the TV, maybe early forties. Not a silvery, old-looking guy like most politicians, but energetic, tall, well built. He wore a charcoal suit—not nasty, not ultra-expensive, though word was he was richer than sin—and a plum-red tie. Short fair-to-chestnut hair, bronzed by the sun. Strong features, not exactly attractive, but compelling. An interesting face. He moved smoothly, no wasted motions, like he meant business but wasn't in a hurry.

I'd been following Caine about on his campaign business all morning, flashing my press credentials to get access. Around me, the other reporters texted and tweeted, messed about on their tablet computers and set their cell phones to record.

I didn't bother with that. I already knew Caine's message. I wanted to know what kind of man he was. What he said mattered less than how he said it, who he chose to say it to, and more importantly, what he *didn't* say.

Luckily for my plan—and unfortunately for Equity, and for all us augmented folks whom he wanted to weld into steel canisters and drop into the ocean, or whatever—he'd yet to falter on any of the three.

Caine's schedule was fierce. First a clothing factory, then a school, a visit to Sapphire City General's pediatric oncology ward, and now he was holding a press conference, and it wasn't yet lunchtime. He hadn't taken a break, only travel time, and he didn't smoke, or chug Red Bull, or even sneak a speed pill and a shot of whiskey so far as I could tell. He'd been followed around all day by his entourage of one, a good-looking kid with neat blond hair, who kept Caine's diary and took notes on a tablet.

Just watching Caine's rate of effort tired me out. He'd been doing this for how many weeks already? I wondered if Equity had it in her to display the same amount of energy, personality, unfailing courtesy and genuine interest in other people.

Because Caine sustained it without stress. He was easy, charming and engaging, whether he was talking industrial relations with factory workers, chatting to school kids about cool gadgets, or coaxing smiles and giggles from the solemn, hairless, big-eyed children in the cancer ward.

The common touch, Adonis had said, and after years spent perfecting his charismatic aura, Adonis was the expert on human relations, even if he did cheat a little.

But it was more than that. If I didn't know better, I'd think this Caine guy genuinely gave a shit.

I yawned, waiting for him to start. It was the middle of the night for me, and I hadn't slept, just come straight from Glimmer's place to follow the campaign. I didn't have my mask on, of course, and I felt naked, exposed. Like everyone was watching me, staring at my scarred cheek. Thinking *that poor girl, how awful* or *eww, what a freak!* or *rather you than me, sister*.

Guess I'd better get used to that.

Hell, I was already used to it. Once people found out about my little move-things-with-my-mind trick, *freak* was at the polite end of what they called me.

Fuck 'em, then. I didn't care.

But a part of me still longed for my mask. Which was stupid, really, because it was my mask that announced me in public as a freak. Sigh. You could do your head in thinking about it.

Caine lifted a hand for silence, and the reporters hushed. Cameras flashed, and behind me a TV network was filming.

"Ladies and gentlemen, thank you all for coming." As he'd done all morning, he spoke without a lectern or notes. As if everything he said came from the heart. Nice politician's trick. No doubt Adonis was advising Equity to do the same.

"I have an exciting announcement to make and I'm pleased you're all here to share in it. You all know that law and order and public safety are the big issues in this campaign. You know that, because you've made it that way. Because our citizens care about public safety. They care about their children's safety. And for the last decade, Iridium Industries have worked in and with the local community, to make Sapphire City a safer place to live and work."

Yeah, yeah.

He touched his fingertips together, a gesture of concern. "You've all seen the news this morning. Another of these vile Gallery criminals apprehended, his vicious schemes thankfully thwarted before any harm could be done, by the good men and women of the Sapphire City PD. And may I commend Chief Paxton and her people for their stellar work."

A polite round of applause. I didn't join in.

He was talking about Weasel. I'd seen the lead article in this morning's *Chronicle*. Nothing about Pyrotox—they'd kept that quiet—or my charming buddy Iceclaw. Apparently, when the police questioned Weasel, he'd told them his name was Fleabag McRatty, and that he taste-tested cheeseburgers for a living. After that, he just sang dirty ditties at them until they gave up in disgust.

We'd gotten good coverage, though. Glimmer had made sure the tip-off wasn't anonymous, and the Three Morons had squawked the story like obedient canaries. Job done.

"But that was this time," Caine continued, and inwardly I snorted. *Now, we get to it.* "Next time, the PD's best efforts could be in vain. Too long we've suffered at the hands of these so-called 'augmented' individuals with their superhuman powers. It's time to level that playing field, ladies and gentlemen. It's time to end the fear. And to that end, I'm proud and excited to announce the latest innovation by our scientists here at IRIN."

He waved at the glass-topped table beside him. In shining sunlight sat a silvery cylindrical object, the size of a sugar canister. It looked a bit like a test tube centrifuge, with little round things sticking out at the top and a brass switch on its squat base. "Ladies and gentlemen, I give you the Sentinel."

A hushed murmur rose. More cameras flashed. The African-American reporter next to me leaned forward, her straight brown bob brushing her jaw. She looked familiar. Maybe I'd worked with her at the *Chronicle* some time.

I eyed the device, uneasy. The Sentinel, huh. Could it bode well? Nope.

"For too long the augmented have lurked as monsters in our midst, undetectable because they look exactly like everyone else. The Sentinel changes all that. Thanks to our state-of-the-art innovations in paracognitive dynamics, this device can detect micro-level fluctuations in the neural force matrix at distances we've never achieved before."

Uh-huh. I twitched, threatened. Did that mean what I think it meant?

"In layman's terms, ladies and gentlemen, the Sentinel detects parahuman powers."

I sucked in a tight breath. Bingo.

And no points for guessing what Caine would do with his nasty little gadget if he got elected.

144

I dragged my attention back to his speech. "If an augmented individual comes within range, the precision alarm activates," he explained. "You'll know within seconds when there's a threat. The range can be set from full physical contact only, like this model, to a distance of up to twenty meters. And of course, we've developed a range of customizable response matrices, to adapt this technology for law enforcement, corporate and private use." He swept the crowd with his gaze. "It's my intention, if I'm elected Sapphire City's mayor, to make this technology available to all our citizens—and to fund the introduction of the Sentinel as part of the standard issue equipment of our police officers. I envisage one on every street corner, one in every home…"

One in the pocket of every augment-hating asshole who thinks it's his lucky night.

Awesome.

This guy might be genuine—hell, he might actually mean well—but he had some twisted fucking ideas about public safety.

My heart contracted. Jesus on a jelly roll. What if he switched it on right now? What if the damn thing actually *worked*? I'd be trapped like a bug in a light bulb.

A hubbub dragged me from my worries. Caine was taking questions. "And who'll manufacture these Sentinels, Mr. Caine?" a journalist asked. Blond French twist, chic designer glasses perched on her nose. I knew her vaguely. Used to work for the *Chronicle*, writing lurid gossip columns and the society pages and complaining that no one took her seriously as a real reporter. "Isn't that profiteering for Iridium Industries?"

Her husky tone and lowered lashes made me smirk. Asking a politician if he's pork-barreling. Helluva way to flirt, sister.

"On the contrary, Ms. Mason," said Caine with a polite smile. "You can tell your good readers at *expose.com* that Iridium Industries won't be licensing manufacture of the Sentinel." A dramatic pause. "We'll be giving it away. Along with all the design, safety and quality control documentation, as well as the full testing regime, to anyone who's interested. We won't be applying for patents. In fact, all the Sentinel's specifications are being posted online in the public domain as we speak."

That got them buzzing over their laptops. "For no cost?" Mason persisted, red nails hovering over her tablet.

"That's what 'public domain' generally means, Ms. Mason."

I snickered. Polite, but lethal. In another life, I could learn to like this guy.

Caine took another question. "Yes, Stuart?"

A shaggy-haired kid in a blue suit coughed. "Stuart Winchester, the *Post*," he said, the customary intro at a press conference, though clearly Caine already had filed away in his rabbit-trap mind who all the reporters were. "Can we have a demonstration, please?"

"Certainly. If there's an augment in the audience, can he or she please step forward?" Laughter. Even Caine smiled.

I scowled, irritated. Like it was only natural that we freaks would want to hide ourselves. I raised my voice. "What about public safety, Mr. Caine?"

Caine's deep gray gaze lighted on me, and my heart fluttered like a girl's. Whoa, baby. He had presence, that's for sure. It reminded me of the few times Adonis had ever unleashed on me. I wanted to stare, wallow in his hypnotic voice, dive in and drown...

I snorted, shaking it off. Just politician's tricks. He'd have to do better than that.

Caine blinked, and the effect shattered. "I'm sorry, Ms....?"

"Fortune," I said steadily. "Verity Fortune. For the *Chronicle*."

A steely glint of size-me-up, and then an easy, flattering smile. "Of course. Ms. Fortune. Glad you could join us. I trust I haven't given away too many campaign secrets to the other side."

More laughter, but good-natured. "What about public safety, Mr. Caine?" I repeated. "Aren't augments *the public*, too? Don't they have the right to free assembly? To mind their own business, and let other people mind theirs?"

"Yes, Ms. Fortune, they do," he said easily. "They also have the right to self-defense. As does every Sapphire City citizen. The Sentinel is an opportunity to improve that defense. For everyone," he added with emphasis. "All our citizens have the right to know what they're up against."

I laughed, disturbed. A reasonable hater. The worst bloody kind. "Augments are concealed weapons, is that what you think? Is intelligence a weapon, Mr. Caine? Is willpower? How about suspicion, or hatred, or fear? If so, you're concealing a few of your own."

His eyes crinkled, amused. "Perhaps I am." A tiny flicker of a smile, just for me. And then he refocused his gaze on the group, and I felt cold, bereft. "Then again, perhaps my weapons aren't so well hidden. Determination, vision and courage, ladies and gentlemen. Those are my weapons. And unlike the augmented who lurk like cowards in our midst, unwilling to reveal themselves honestly, I've no need or wish to conceal those weapons. I'll need every one of them to succeed as Sapphire City's mayor. More questions?"

I looked away, troubled. Confident, eloquent, so certain he was right. How the hell was I supposed to make a dent in that?

And yet… he smiled at me when I challenged him. Just a politician's façade? Or was he truly willing to be convinced?

I scratched my marred cheek, confused. The black woman beside me typed a message into her BlackBerry and sent it, probably texting her editor at whatever website she worked for.

Someone asked a question about Caine's funding plan. I zoned out in the warm sunshine. Hell, he was probably just putting on a show. Afterwards, he'd have words with his efficient, young PA with the blond hair, and they'd never let me into one of his press conferences again.

BlackBerry Chick cursed under her breath, and popped off another text. It was hot in the sun, and she wristed damp brown hair from her cheek… and beneath, a bright red wisp peeked out.

She was wearing a wig.

My mouth dried, like I'd swabbed with cotton, and with a black-silver stab of pain, I remembered where I'd seen her before.

Crimson hair. Pointed nose. Black Cleopatra eye paint, a flash of weird silver in her eyes.

Patience Crook. BlackBerry Chick was Witch.

Fuck.

My palms slicked, warm, and my senses prickled with the telltale flavor of *augment*. It was her, all right. Her makeup was understated compared to her usual war paint, just a bit of eye color like you'd wear to the office, and she wore a conservative blue suit instead of a red-ribboned Goth skirt and boots, but it was her. Her black beaded handbag lay pooled at her feet.

What was in it? What was she doing here? Did she recognize me? Who was she texting? Her Gallery buddies? Razorfire himself?

My muscles itched to act. If she unleashed her power—if she even just had a gun, and fired it... The Gallery, getting rid of the only mayoral candidate willing to stand up to them.

My thoughts spun out of control, a drunken skater on ice. Did I care if Witch killed Caine? He was a fucking hater. Worse: a rich and powerful hater, one people listened to. Good riddance, right?

Maybe. But it'd also be the signal for everyone who'd soaked up his message of fear to rise and take their vengeance on any augments they could find.

It'd make him a martyr for the hater cause, and that I couldn't have.

I had to stop her.

But I couldn't use my powers. Not in front of half the Sapphire City press corps, just dying to plaster my unmasked face all over the front page. And not with Caine standing there, his evil Sentinel ready to finger me for a villain.

Patience's smile curled, satisfied, and she bent to slip her BlackBerry into her bag.

"Gun!" I yelled. "Get down! That woman's got a gun!" And I crash-tackled her, knocking chairs askew.

Chaos erupted. My shoulder crunched into Witch's side, knocking her to the carpet. People screamed and ducked for cover.

A pair of male security guards descended from nowhere, black suits and curly white wires in their ears, and hustled Caine off the stage, and then I lost sight of him.

My head thunked against an iron chair leg. My vision blurred, 3D without the glasses. I held on grimly, my arms about Witch's waist. She screamed and kicked. Her brown wig tore off, and wild crimson hair exploded like a splash of blood.

That seemed to unlock some beast caged inside her, because her eyes rolled back to the whites, and she cackled like a brain-eating monster. "Come get it, bitch," she snarled. Her knuckles cracked into talons, and she unleashed.

A cloud of mutant gnats erupted from her palm and dived for me.

I shoved her, hard, and rolled away. The bugs buzzed greedily, and swirled in a choking cloud over the cowering reporters. I held my breath and covered my face. Bites stung my hands. I resisted the temptation to swat the bugs away, to wave my hands wildly. It just fired them up. I knew that from experience. And sure enough, the little fuckers soon buzzed away to torment someone else.

And that's when I jumped on her.

She was already stretching her arm to unleash another burst. I grabbed her clawing hand, yanking it back fiercely until her shoulder popped. She yelled, and spat, but she couldn't shake me off.

Triumph warmed me. I didn't need my augment to overpower her this time. She didn't have enough space. And she was a skinny thing, whereas I worked out, or at least I had until her boss chucked me in the nuthouse. That'll teach her to aspire to that skeletal look...

More security guards piled in, this time on top of us. One big guy dragged me off her, and another two forced Witch efficiently into a come-along hold, face first into the carpet and hands behind her back.

Blood dripped from her lip, staining the pale floor. Beside her, a pistol gleamed.

Heh. Nice guess. Guns to a gunfight, and all. I'd only suspected she was conventionally armed. But they didn't need to know that.

"You okay, ma'am?" The big rent-a-cop steadied me.

"I'm fine." I shrugged him off. People were climbing out from under chairs. Bugs buzzed far and wide, seeking the sun, banging blindly against the high glass walls. I'd already called too much attention to myself. Time for a quick exit...

But Caine, too, was shrugging off solicitous security guards, and strode over to survey the scene, cracking his knuckles, his face dark with concern.

I sighed inwardly. Here we go. Another speech about augments, the scourge of the earth.

But Caine just clicked his fingers, hand outstretched. "Ashton, fetch me the Sentinel."

His blond PA scrambled to obey, and placed the silvery cylinder in Caine's hand. It looked small there. Harmless. Like it'd never hurt anyone, merely the public safety device he was telling everyone it was.

Fuck.

What if it was directional? What if it pinpointed me, too?

But too late to run for it now.

Caine thumbed the switch. The Sentinel hummed, crackling with electric current, and its metal edges glowed blue. He waved his hand over the plate, like he was testing it was working, and the blue lights flickered, then steadied.

On the floor, Witch screamed. "No! I'm sorry! Doooon't..."

"Give me her hand," Caine said.

The security guards grabbed her thrashing arm, and forced her palm onto the Sentinel's glowing plate. It whined louder, higher, winding up like a runaway train, and the lights flashed from blue to bright red.

It didn't hurt her. Didn't burn or shock or poison.

It just flashed. Accused. And Patience Crook banged her crimson head into the floor and wept.

Everyone stared, waiting for Caine to denounce her for a villain.

But Caine didn't speak.

He didn't have to. Everyone already knew what to think: if he'd had the Sentinel fully operational, Witch might never have gotten near him.

And neither would I.

He flicked the horrid machine off. The lights popped out, and that accusing whine wound down to silence.

Witch lay on the floor, howling like she'd been burned, and the rent-a-cops dragged her away.

A hubbub broke out, everyone chatting into their cells or tweeting or typing furiously on their tablets. The TV crew were still filming.

Caine seemed subdued, frowning at the device in his hand. Ashton whispered to him, and Caine's face cleared. Ashton took the Sentinel and set it carefully back on the table.

I'd seen enough. I turned to go.

"Ms. Fortune."

My stomach wriggled, warm. But I turned back. I had to.

Caine outdid the sunshine with a smile. "Thank you. For your vigilance, and your readiness to put yourself in harm's way. You're a credit to your family, and to our city." He knew the cameras were on him, but still I got the distinct sense that he meant it.

I fidgeted. I'd never been one for taking the credit. I just did the job and got the hell out. "Thanks," I muttered. "It's nothing."

He came closer, and I smelled mint. The fresh kind, leafy and sweet, not gum or breath mints. He was only an inch or two taller than me, and his gray eyes were flecked with black, like storm clouds. "It wasn't nothing. That woman was armed. You risked your life. You're quite formidable."

Okay, great. Now I was blushing. He was good-looking, in a sharp and quirky way, if I forgot that he loathed my very skin and everything inside it. "Not so much. Could've been me she

151

was planning to shoot first."

He laughed. "Ouch. Did I just assume I'm the only one here worth shooting? Yeah. That's one apology I owe. Ashton? Do the honors, please." He touched my arm, polite and professional, yet somehow… not. "Brush up your questions, Ms. Fortune," he murmured. "You might not get this chance again." And he flashed that unreasonably engaging smile, and strode away.

Whoa. Hot in here, or just me?

I blew out a steadying breath. Verity, you are *such* a sucker for the confident ones. When Glimmer said *guile, charm and sex appeal*, he was totally *kidding*.

But I had to admit he intrigued me, this hater. I couldn't figure him out.

I fidgeted, unsettled. Hell, maybe I just needed to get laid. Could be Glimmer's lucky night after all…

Fingers on my elbow made me jerk. "Huh?"

Ashton blinked over-alert blue eyes at me. Maybe he was the one chugging Red Bull, just to keep up with Caine's schedule. He'd already conscripted an army of IRIN nerds and armed them with cans of bug spray, and they ran around the lobby squirting insects and playing aerosol deathmatch. Idiots.

Not that me and my brothers had never done that at FortuneCorp, of course. Put out the lights and hunted each other through the corridors. Chance always found me first, but then I'd whip his lucky ass. Adonis was crap at it—more a lover than a stalker, ha ha—but he played anyway, because it was just us kids and it was fun.

My eyes misted. I blinked, watching the nerds ambushing each other from behind chairs and indoor plants. I envied them their *de facto* family.

Ashton followed my gaze, and smiled, rueful. "Sure is nice to find your tribe."

His *tribe*? Did he read that in a HR manual? I forced a smile, and idly crushed a dead bug with my toe. "Tribes are cool, for sure. And 'the honors' would be…?"

"What? Oh. Sorry." Ashton reached into his immaculate jacket and handed me a white magnetic security card. "His office, fourth floor," he instructed. "He's got seven minutes until he leaves for his next engagement, so make your questions good."

18

Caine's office wasn't on the fourth floor.

It *was* the fourth floor, or near enough.

I stepped from the elevator, which ascended smooth and silent behind a misted glass wall, and boom! There it was, a single room taking up the whole floor, pale carpet and tiles and a high airy ceiling. Sliding windows took up eighty percent of the walls, and they lay open, letting in sunshine and eucalyptus-scented breeze, giving the whole place a fresh, open-air feel. I felt grimy and dim just being here.

His desk sat by one window, facing inwards, and in front of it a virtual display gleamed with prisms and white lights. Caine perched on the edge of his transparent Perspex chair—yeah, you can actually get those, if you're rich enough—and was doing what passed for his lunch, which meant he'd removed his coat and loosened his tie, and was flicking rapidly through correspond-ence on his screen with his right hand, and forking a salad into his mouth with his left.

Just to be sure, I reached out with my invisible senses, hunting for threat, traps, that sweet sherbet tingle of *augment*. Nothing. The place was clear. So far, so good.

I stood there, uneasy. Did I go in? Wait to be asked? Change my mind and run in the opposite direction before he *looked* at me like he had in the press conference and I blurted out anything and everything that was on my mind?

Not that I'd had that problem before, or anything.

No, I decided. He'd invited me, after all. This was my chance to really talk to Caine. To figure out once and for all whether he was an ally worth cultivating, or just a hater who'd never listen. And my seven minutes were slipping away.

I squared my shoulders, and walked in.

He looked up, and flashed that supernova he called a smile. "You eat salad?"

"Huh?"

"Ashton feeds me. Otherwise I forget to eat. You like Moroccan dressing?"

"Uh. Sure, I guess so."

"Have a seat, then. And a fork."

I wandered up, surveying the room. On the minimal wall behind his desk, a glass-framed gadget shone. It was a familiar gadget. Pretty much everyone in Sapphire City owned one. I squinted at it, impressed. "You invented that?"

He followed my gaze, and shrugged. "Conceptualized it. I had help."

I snorted, and settled in the second chair, a white plastic one that looked hard but molded itself gently to my body weight. Cool. "Now who's saying 'it was nothing'?"

Caine laughed. "Fair enough. It did make me my first unmentionably large fortune. All downhill since then, I'm afraid."

"Hell, no one's perfect. Even God rested on the seventh day, right?"

He munched a mouthful of salad. "Probably why he got screwed on the stock options. I'd have held out for exclusive control. Resting is for people with nothing better to do."

"But not for the wicked, I've heard."

"In my experience, Ms. Fortune, the wicked sleep very well. It's conscience that keeps you awake at night."

I picked up a fork and tasted the salad. Lettuce, tomato and couscous, dressed with cumin and spicy yoghurt. "Mmm. Ashton has good taste. If only it were that easy."

"What's that?"

"To tell the difference between heroes and villains, Mr. Caine. Arrest the ones who sleep through the night?"

"Maybe it is that easy. Please, call me Vincent." A glint of brightness in those deep gray eyes. They weren't bottomless, I noticed. On the contrary. They were full. Dark, brimming with something I couldn't quite identify. Smarts, sure. Conviction. Obsession. Warmth?

I twisted the fork in my fingers. Okay, so I was dizzy again. Was that a flirt? Or just a play to get the *Chronicle's* sympathy? Jeez, I was crap at this people stuff, and it seemed I'd blundered into the presence of a master. Great.

"May I call you Verity?" The way he said it, my name sounded gentle, warm, feminine. Vincent and Verity.

Hah. Good luck with that. "Sure. Why not?"

"You asked me some interesting questions, Verity," he said smoothly, putting his fork aside and leaning back in his chair with his fingers linked. Sunshine bronzed his hair. "I get the feeling you have concerns with my policy on the augmented."

I popped my phone onto the desk to record, just like a real reporter. The smartphone, the jamming-enabled one Glimmer had given me. Caine shrugged easily, like he didn't care if this was on the record or not.

I tapped the screen to switch it on, and leaned back. "I have concerns with any suggestion that citizens should prostitute their freedom in return for a vague promise of safety," I said carefully. "Especially when some citizens seem to have the right to be safer than others. We learned this lesson after 9/11, didn't we? Look where the Patriot Act got us. Neck deep in wars we'll never win abroad, and scuttling about afraid of our own shadows at home. Pointing fingers never made anyone safe. It just engenders fear."

"Steady on," he said calmly. "I'd be grateful if you'd reassure your readers at the *Chronicle* that I'm not advocating a police state. The Sentinel doesn't judge. It merely provides information to which I believe we're all entitled."

"Are we? Why is it anyone's business if a person's got talents, so long as they don't use them to hurt anyone?"

He laughed. "You don't really believe that, do you, after your talk of concealed weapons? Fine analogy, by the way. I had to think fast."

I shrugged, blunt. "People have a right to be themselves."

"Even if it profits them at another's expense?"

I waved my hand at his glossy office. "If you don't mind me saying? You don't exactly have a leg to stand on there. I mean, I get the whole IRIN-helps-humanity vibe. Very noble of you. But you're not poverty-stricken out of it, are you?"

"A fair point." He studied me, tapping his fingertips. His fingers were long, masculine, but fine. An artist, not a fighter. At last, he inclined his head at my phone.

Anticipation twinged in my bones. I switched the recorder off.

"Look at me," he said, "and tell me what you see."

A creepy lying bastard who wants to lock me up? "Excuse me?"

"Indulge me. It's not a trick question. Give me your best Sherlock Holmes impression. Tell me about the man you see."

"Okay." I fidgeted, warm. "He's… white, early forties, English-speaking. Sounds educated, college at least, but he still talks like a real person, so practical rather than theoretical. Well-dressed but not extravagant. Wristwatch, nice but not worth an embarrassing fortune. But no glasses or contacts, so at his age he's maybe had laser surgery, and that's not cheap. So I'd say he's well-off enough not to care what people think. Also, he's confident, looks directly at people, doesn't mince words. I'd say he's used to getting his own way, which means he's not a company man. Probably in business for himself."

His mouth twitched, like I'd said something secretly amusing. "Anything else?"

"Umm. No wedding ring. And a career like that eats up all his waking hours. So I'm guessing never married, no kids." I snickered privately, and allowed a smile. "Like I said, used to getting his own way."

He dipped his head in acknowledgment. "Very good, detective. Correct on almost all counts. Now let me tell you what you *can't* see." He studied one fingernail, a soft breeze ruffling his hair. "I have three-fold synesthesia, which means that numbers and colors look like shapes to me. I see spatial relationships in figures that other people don't see. I also have an IQ in the one-sixties. Now, that doesn't make me the world's genius, but it does mean I can think quickly, digest information in high volume. It gives me the creative vision to think up concepts like that"—he flicked his eyebrow at the glass-framed gadget on the wall—"when no one else does. And it's brought me here." He indicated his surroundings, like I had. "So, you see, it's not a magical power, or a genetic mutation, or whatever. But it's something invisible that others don't have. With me?"

"Sure." But my nerves sparkled in warning. I had an idea where he was going with this, and I didn't like it.

"Now, I didn't do anything to deserve this. I didn't earn it. No one checked to make sure I was a good person before they gave it to me. It's just an accident. Yet it made me wealthy and powerful."

"Okay," I said. "We all know life's not fair. But a bit of luck doesn't make you dangerous." I thought of my brother Chance— who went through a phase as a teenager where he liked to play chicken with eighteen-wheelers on the interstate, because, y'know, you'd have to be unlucky—and shrugged inwardly. Well, maybe luck made you dangerous sometimes.

And what about me? I hadn't exactly played it safe last night in that warehouse with Iceclaw... but that wasn't me. That was just Mengele's mindfuck, making me jumpy. Right?

"Doesn't it?" Caine gazed at me, unruffled. "How do you know? You have no idea what I can do."

"Such as?"

"You want a for-instance?" He shrugged coolly. "I have superlative memory. Most number synesthetics do. I could, for example, count cards and cheat you out of your money. Or, I could recall perfectly everything you say, and use it against you later. My condition also means excellent vision—wrong on the laser surgery, I'm afraid, but point taken. I can detect the tiniest tics of body language. That means I can tell when you're lying, give or take. My elevated neurotransmitter levels also mean I sleep only four hours a night. That gives me an advantage my business competitors can never match." He smiled, slight and bashful. Disarming. "I could go on. But do you see my point? My 'accident' gives me power. And there's no defense against it."

"But you can choose not to take advantage of that power," I pointed out. "I don't see you in Vegas at the poker tables—"

"No," he interrupted, "but what about freedom of expression? Didn't you say people have the right to be themselves?"

I frowned. "I don't get it."

"Yes, you do." Deep in his storm-dark eyes, long-shackled emotion sprang alive. It mesmerized me. "You're a smart woman, Verity. A strong and beautiful woman who knows what she wants. You know what it's like to be feared. Don't tell me you've never dumbed down so others won't feel squeamish."

My cheeks flamed, and not just because he said the B word, which was so patently untrue that it made me want to laugh and cringe at the same time. *He knows!* my nerves howled. *Run! Get out of here before he summons his Ashton-robot and has you arrested.*

I forced my screaming senses quiet. He didn't know about my augment. He couldn't possibly know.

But he didn't have to. He still understood.

Involuntarily, I recalled all those times I'd had to hide my power. Pulling my mindmuscle in tight so no one would see. Ignoring those who needed help because there were too many people around, I wasn't wearing my mask, they'd see me, hurt me, lock me up.

All those times I'd been forced to pretend I wasn't me.

Jeez. Not what I expected from Vincent Caine, augment-hater extraordinaire.

I chewed my lip, uncertain. *Get a grip, Verity. He's manipulating you. He's a politician, that's what he does. A dash of creative genius doesn't make him one of us. He'll still skin you alive when he finds out what you are.*

But deep in my heart, something cold and lonely cried out to be known.

He saw my reaction, and nodded, his dark eyes alive. "You know what I mean, Verity. It's no way to live. That's why I created IRIN. To be with others like me, who aren't afraid. Ashton calls it a *tribe*. To me it's more of a garden. Things grow here. I can grow here."

I didn't say anything. I couldn't speak. *You already have a friend,* my inner, sensible voice scolded me. *You have Glimmer. Glimmer understands you. Glimmer will never hate you. Leave this right where it is and back the hell off.*

But I hadn't reacted to Glimmer the way I was reacting now. Glimmer was one of us. He had no choice but to accept me. Caine…

Caine was *normal*. And he accepted me anyway.

"But…" I struggled to grasp the contradiction. "You're not making any sense. Doesn't that mean augments should be allowed to live in peace?"

He laughed, studying his long fingers. "Verity, believe me, nothing would give me greater satisfaction. But it doesn't work like that. History proves it. Look at the zealots in Iran, Nazi Germany, the French Revolution. Offer a small section of the population the chance to gain arbitrary power and influence over the rest, and what happens?"

I cocked an eyebrow. "A fight?"

"They take it," he said calmly. "Create an elite, the chosen get everything and the rest get nothing. I can't have that in my city, do you understand? I won't have that."

"But you're the one who's already *got* everything," I protested. "You're ridiculously wealthy, you own half the city, nine out of ten people own one of your phones. Isn't that 'arbitrary power and influence'?"

"It certainly is. And I intend to use it to protect those who have none."

It's how you treat the weak that makes you what you are.

"But..." Jeez. I was saying *but* a lot. As in, *yes, but...*

As in, he actually made a whole lotta sense. If it didn't involve persecuting me and everyone I cared about.

"But not all the augmented are bad guys," I insisted. "What about Blackstrike? He protected the city from crime for years."

"Sure, that was the effect for a while. But what was really in it for him? How can you know he wasn't just fighting his own private war?"

I opened my mouth, and shut it again. It was a private war. No question. FortuneCorp and the Gallery were mortal enemies. But we fought to protect other people, as well as ourselves. Didn't that make it good?

Or were we just kidding ourselves?

My throat ached. *Because you're afraid you're one of them,* Glimmer had said. Maybe he was right. I'd risked our lives last night, and other people's, all because Iceclaw pissed me off...

No. That was just a mistake. I was still fragile, my power still unreliable. I'd acted without thinking. That made me a damn fool, but it didn't make me a bad guy.

Or maybe that was what all the villains told themselves. *I had to. They made me. It wasn't my choice.*

Caine watched me sort it through, and nodded. "That's the point, see? We can't ever know their motives. And even if we could, nothing comes cost-free."

A dark shimmer in his tone gave me pause. "What do you mean?"

He hesitated, tapping his fingertips again. "You want my example? Hypercognition is double-edged. There's a dramatically increased risk of developing paranoid schizophrenia. I'm probably too old, now, but the odds are still relatively high."

I shrugged, but something warm and painful scraped at my heart. What a waste. "So? Better clever and crazy than sane and stupid."

"Maybe. But it only takes a few delusions before my creative process gets channeled into uglier things. We already have a poisoned garden in Sapphire City. It's called the Gallery."

"Not every augment goes insane!" But I remembered how I'd reacted back on the bridge with Arachne, when Glimmer first showed his colors. I was afraid. *What can he do?* I'd wondered. *How can he hurt me?* I'd assumed he was hostile, because I didn't know what he could do. "You can't persecute people for what they might do. It's inhumane."

A regretful smile. "Next you'll be saying, 'guns don't kill people...'?"

"But we care! That's the difference." The *we* galloped away before I had time to lasso it. "You and me, I mean," I covered desperately. "Blackstrike, the others like him. They care about other people. The Gallery would happily murder thousands."

He chuckled. "Believe me, if I could invent a gadget that could prove I give a shit, I'd be President of the United States by now." His amusement faded. "But that's exactly my point. Intent is unknowable. All I can do is identify capability and threat. People deserve to know who they're dealing with. It's up to them what they do with that information."

Behind me, the door hissed. I turned. Ashton peeked around the elevator's glass screen. "Forgive my intrusion. Mr. Caine, it's one o'clock."

163

"Really?" Caine swallowed one last mouthful of salad, and pushed the rest away. He rose and fixed his tie, efficient but not hurried. "I'm sorry, Verity, time's gotten away from me. But I can see you're still troubled. Why don't you..." He slipped on his jacket and fished in the pocket for a card, on which he scribbled a few lines, and slid it across to me. "Join me tonight, and we can continue our chat?"

I took the card. *Vincent Caine*, it said, *Iridium Industries*, and a cell number and email. I flipped it over. He'd written in black fountain pen, letters slanted to the right. *Corporations Against World Poverty, Crystal City Ballroom, 9:30 for 10:00*. And his initials, VC, bold and confident with a slashed underline.

"It's a charity banquet," he replied to my raised eyebrows. "And a political opportunity, for sure, but it's a worthy cause. I have a special interest in class divides, as you may have noticed. Come by and we'll talk."

I laughed. Likely, they wanted a five-figure donation just to show up. I'd had that kind of money once, though Adonis had done most of the charity gigs back in the day. Dad didn't send me out in public much. I tended to blurt out too much of what I was thinking, and besides, Adonis was handsome and charming, and I was neither. "The air must taste real nice up in that ivory tower," I scoffed. "I'm not on the press list."

"Not as a reporter. As my guest."

Did he mean, like, a date? Please. "But I can't afford this."

"I can." He blinded me with a smile. "Consider a donation made on your behalf. What are friends for?"

"Paying off a journalist? Isn't that thin ice for a politician?"

"All on the public record," he said cheerfully. "It's for charity, after all. Don't see the *Chronicle* donating. Perhaps I'm entitled to a little positive coverage." He finished his glass of water. "Gotta go, Ms. Fortune. I hope I'll see you there." And he offered me his hand.

I stared at it, my knees trembling. Part of me wanted to spit on it, curse him for a dirty manipulative hater. Part of me wanted to crush it, force him to his knees with an effortless flex of mind-muscle, say *this is how it feels, asshole, how's my threat capability now?*

And another, desperately shy part of me just wanted to touch him. Feel his skin on mine, his warmth, the easy, uncomplicated touch of a guy for whom I didn't have to be a masked vigilante to be interesting. Who thought I was normal, but respected me anyway.

I shook, light but firm. "Wouldn't miss it," I said, and Ashton showed me out.

I emerged into the now bug-free lobby, and squinted in the waterfall of sunshine. I should check in, tell Glimmer what I'd found, see if he'd made any progress with our surveillance on FortuneCorp.

I reached for my phone, but it rang before I could dial. Uncanny. "You still out of bed?" I answered.

"Hey." Glimmer's whiskey voice was weary, like he still hadn't slept. "It's me."

"I know that. No one else has this number, idiot." I walked through the big glass doors onto the lawn. Sunshine warmed my skin, pleasant. A beautiful day, fragrant with blossom and euca-lyptus. Fuck, was I smelling the flowers? Jeez. Caine must have really charmed my socks off. Five minutes with him and I was all birds and bees and springtime. "Hey, you're the fashion guru, right? What do I wear to a charity ball?"

"Come again?"

"A charity ball. One of those fancy turns where rich people show off. This Caine guy got me an invite."

"And you're gonna go? Jesus. What did he do, propose?"

"Don't be a wise-ass. So, what do I wear?"

"You're asking me? You're the society girl. A dress, maybe?"

I snorted, plucking a fragrant leaf from a bush and smelling it. "Right. Good luck with that—"

"Listen," he interrupted, "can you come in? I've got something to show you from our surveillance."

My attention sharpened like a blade, and I dropped the leaf. "Like what? Is it Equity?"

"Like, you need to see this. Can you come in?"

"I'll be there in an hour," I said, and hung up on him to call a cab. By the time I walked back up the curving drive to the gate, past golf carts and electric cars that glinted in the sun as they rolled silently by—creepy, if you ask me—my cab had arrived.

I jumped in and gave the driver an address three blocks from Glimmer's.

Caine had me intrigued. Okay, and maybe a little smitten too, curse his oily hide. But I wasn't stupid. And neither was he.

It was a long ride, the traffic thick. I fidgeted, my skin sticking to the warm seat. At last, I jumped out on the curb and paid the driver with Glimmer's cash, looking around to make sure I wasn't followed. Caine had a lot at stake. He'd be checking me out, sure as I was scar-faced.

I'd just have to make sure he found nothing. I was just Verity Fortune, freelance journalist, trying to get a *Chronicle* by-line with a controversial article. If that meant I had to hobnob with the rich and tedious at some glittering society do—wearing a dress, for Christ's sake, and wouldn't that be a sight?—and listen to another hour of Caine's smooth politician's lies, then that's exactly what I'd do.

For that's what they were, right? Lies. He was just another rich asshole who thought he should be in charge. He didn't mean any of that stuff about gardens and tribes and protecting the weak. He was just doing what he thought was popular.

And Witch's attack, right in the middle of his press conference, had played right into his hands. What was she thinking, the stupid Gallery twit...?

I coughed, my throat suddenly gritty with unease.

Witch only unleashed her powers *after* I jumped her.

I recalled her sitting there, her bag at her feet—what was really in that bag?—and her nondescript brown wig curling over her cheeks. Texting on her BlackBerry as Caine spoke.

Caine posed just as big a threat to the Gallery as he did to us. What if Witch was just following Caine around, like I was, pretending to be press? What if Razorfire had sent her merely to check out this Sentinel gadget and report back?

If she hadn't intended on revealing herself until I gave her no choice?

By unmasking her, I'd unwittingly handed Caine the perfect, 'accidental' opportunity to make his point.

I swallowed, suddenly aware I'd blundered into the muddy quicksand of politics. I'd never been any good at this subtext shit. If I wasn't careful, I'd sink too deep and drown.

Witch had played straight into Caine's hands, all right.

And so had I.

19

"Honey, I'm home." I plopped onto the sofa and kicked off my boots.

Glimmer didn't look up from his console. Seriously, was his butt glued to that chair, or what? "Come look at this."

"My day was fine, since you ask," I grumbled. "Witch attacked Caine's press conference. It was awesome. Sorry you missed it."

"So I heard. Your name's all over the news. Verity Fortune, intrepid reporter, hero of the day. Nice work," he added, with a glance that could have meant the opposite.

"Yeah, well, I didn't exactly get the chance to slip into a phone booth and costume up, did I? Did you see that Sentinel thing? Got the slick treatment from this Caine dude, too. He's good, unfortunately. Manages to make his rotten hater crap sound reasonable. I'd say Equity's in trouble." I squinted at the images on Glimmer's screen, and my heart thudded cold. "What's that?"

But I knew what it was.

A FortuneCorp science lab. That fuzzy monochrome footage we'd noted before, the resolution digitally limited to protect company secrets. Benches cluttered with high-tech equipment, drafting tables, filing cabinets, supercomputer terminals with flickering LEDs and fat data conduits stapled to the floor.

I rose and peered closer, leaning over Glimmer's chair. The time stamp in the top corner showed a date last year, only a few weeks before Dad died. Early morning, just before business hours, and the place was ghostly, eerily deserted. No activity. "What am I looking at?"

"Wait for it… There you go."

A fuzzy figure walked in. Dark tapered trousers and jacket, narrow waist, shaped shoulders, a curved figure. A woman.

The outline was fuzzy, her facial features obscured. But I knew who it was. Her hairstyle, before she cut it, caught in a clip and flowing down her back. Her kind of suit, no-nonsense power. Her dark spectacle frames, her favorite set of golden bracelets she wore on one wrist.

Equity, in the lab at 6:45 a.m. I frowned. "What's she doing?"

"Wait and see." Glimmer hesitated. "I couldn't sleep, after what you said about FortuneCorp and Pyrotox. But I couldn't hack into their lab computers, at least not in this lifetime. It's too deeply encrypted. So I ran a search algorithm on the lab cameras."

I watched, fascinated and horrified. Equity walked up to the computer terminal and sat in the padded chair. She clicked something small and rectangular into a slot on the console, and typed something into the machine. Data flashed up, too fuzzy to read, and she did something to her mobile device that made menus and dialog boxes flick up.

I swallowed on hot sickness. She was copying files, or deleting them. But probably copying. No prizes for guessing what they contained.

"Can you be sure?" I demanded. "Can we find out what's in those files?"

"No. Like I said, it's too deeply encrypted."

"She got in, didn't she?"

"She's a board member. She probably has a password. In any case, if she's smart she's copying a whole pile of stuff, to obscure what she really wants."

He was right, I realized. Not standard procedure—typically, at board level, we didn't have hands-on contact with the labs, apart from Dad, who as chairman had approval and veto over every project, and Uncle Mike, who was a techie geek at heart and liked to keep up with the latest. But no one would have refused Equity if she'd applied for access. Wouldn't have been too hard to come up with a plausible need-to-know, some quality audit or legal issue she was responsible for.

Now she disconnected her mobile device and logged off. Her screen flashed blank. And she walked out.

Just like that... "No, wait." I pointed. "Who's that?" A dude in jeans and a Superman T-shirt walked in, and she stopped to talk with him. I didn't recognize him. Probably a lab tech, on an early start or an all-nighter.

They ended their conversation, and Equity walked out. The dude fiddled with some stuff on a desk in the corner for a while, and wandered away.

I frowned. "Why'd he let her just walk out? He didn't even check what she was up to!"

"Why would he?" said Glimmer reasonably. "She's senior management, he's just a boffin. That's why she's there at 6:45. Lawyers work early hours, eggheads get in at midday and work late. It's not middle-of-the-night enough to be suspicious—"

"But early enough that the lab won't be full of people looking over her shoulder," I finished tightly. "Damn her. She's too bloody clever." But acid stung my eyes, and I had to look away.

I didn't want it to be true. Didn't want my sister to be a thief and a villain.

But there she was. In full view of the camera. Hadn't even bothered to delete the footage. Like she expected simply to get away with it, unquestioned.

How superior and villain-esque of her.

My muscles tightened, and my mindsense jabbered to be free.

A sharp ache split my skull. I wanted to reach through the screen and strangle her.

Bright light crunched my vision tight like tinfoil. *Glass, smooth and shiny, cool under my reaching fingertips. Inside, the gel glitters. So pretty. So lethal. Lightning flashes, a burst of thunder. I grit my teeth against the wind, and reach for the globe, my arm stretching.*

"Stop." The voice commands me, an effortless presence, and my insides shrivel. I'm a little girl again, in trouble for some long-forgotten naughtiness. "Get your hands off that. You're not fit to touch it."

My guts convulse, and I laugh, though nothing's funny. It's crazy, unhallowed laughter. The laughter of a fool. I swallow it, clenching my teeth until my gums bleed. My mindmuscle flexes, ready, and I scrape up the last of my strength and turn...

Light splashes bright, I'm blinded. My eyes burn. I scream, and through the throbbing in my ears, another voice slices, strong and urgent and beloved. "No! Verity, for God's sake, you'll kill us all..."

The pain shimmered and dissolved, and my vision cleared.

Fuck! Frustration clenched my fists to rocks. Too soon. It always cleared too soon. Always too vague, too conflicting. I didn't know what was real.

I wanted to scream, claw at my eyes, bang my head against the floor until it cracked open and the poisoned memories poured out...

Glimmer flicked the screen dark, like he knew I didn't want to look anymore. "So. What do you want to do?"

I flopped unsteadily onto the sofa, raking my hair. "What can we do?" I snapped, my nerves still waspish. "It's not enough. You said yourself we can't tell what's in those files she took. It's circumstantial evidence at best. Hell, for all I know, she was just researching for some company lawsuit."

Glimmer eyed me darkly. "Do you think that's likely?"

I set my jaw tight. "No. But that doesn't mean we've got proof."

"So what do you want, a picture of Equity actually putting the

172

stuff in his hand?"

"Gee, d'you think you could? That'd be nice."

"I'll work on it." Glimmer fisted his hair, two-handed this time, a sure sign he was getting tired. "Until then, we should get some sleep. What time did you say this charity ball was?"

I pulled out Caine's card. "It says nine thirty for ten. 'Corporations Against World Poverty'," I read. "Sounds like gangbusters."

"Sounds like a public relations bonanza," corrected Glimmer. "Not to be missed by any grasping politician. You do realize Equity will be there?"

"Yeah. I figure if I stay in public view, I should be okay. She won't arrest her own sister in a ballroom full of potential campaign donors, right?"

"Still," said Glimmer, "I'm coming with you." He folded his arms, muscle bulging, expecting an argument.

Mildly, I arched my brows, just to confound expectations. "Isn't a costume party, so far as I know. You'll have to take your mask off."

He grinned, and with a flick of his fingers, he shimmered himself out of sight for a second or two. "Not if I stay incognito."

I blinked, dizzy. Damn, I hated it when he did that. "Fine," I said grudgingly. "But you have to dress up like an idiot, too. I won't have you embarrassing me in all that polite society, y'hear?"

"Yeah, right. You just want to see me in a tux. So bad it hurts."

"About as bad as you want to see me in a dress, wise-ass."

He winked, midnight-blue and charming. "Can't wait."

There it was again. That flirty-boy glance. My fingers itched, irked. Why did he even bother? Wasn't like I was going anywhere. But before I could tell him just how full of shit he was, my phone rang. Automatically, I pulled it out to answer.

Only then did it occur to me that Glimmer alone knew this number.

My finger halted, an inch from the glass. No incoming ID. I glanced at him, tense. "You give this to anyone?"

"Nope. You?"

Still ringing. "No. Thought you said it was untraceable."

"It is." He shrugged. "Hey, I said I was a genius. I didn't say I was the only SIM card freak in town."

"Right. That's comforting." Still ringing, louder now. Carefully— like swiping slowly could make it safer?—I picked up and put it on speaker. "Joe's Pizza, may I take your order?"

"Seeker." A sharp-frosted laugh. "So it is you, ya skanky whore."

My muscles iced. I'd know that Joisey accent anywhere. Where the hell did Iceclaw get this number?

Glimmer frowned. *Don't provoke him,* he mouthed.

Right. Good luck with that. I grinned, a feral old girl that dripped with menace. "Ice, old buddy, I am *so* glad you called. Glimmer and me were concerned about you, since we kicked your greasy ass so bad the other night. Ooh, and stole your boss's toys, too. Is he pissed? How's that working out for you?"

"That ain't none of your goddamn business. How's that work out for you?" A slurp, like he licked his saber teeth. "Just wanted to say I'll be seeing you. You and your new friend. Tonight."

"Really? 'Cause I figured I'd stay in, catch a little cable…"

Iceclaw chuckled. "No, you won't. Crystal City Ballroom, ten o'clock. Don't be late, Seeker. I might get there ahead of you, prepare you a nice surprise."

"For me? You shouldn't have."

"Only because I like you, bitch. I'll be the one wearing a pink carnation… no, wait. I always get that wrong." His tone froze over, cold as a midnight murder. "*I'll be the one stabbing an ice pick through your face.*"

And the line snapped dead.

Charming.

"O-kaay," I said slowly, checking the phone in case it had recorded any incoming call info. It hadn't. "Forgive me if I'm slow, but… how did he find all that out?"

Glimmer rubbed his stubbled chin, considering. "Maybe Witch recognized you at Caine's press conference, and added two and two. He does mean Caine, right? Your 'new friend'?"

Friend? That was stretching it a bit. I wrinkled my nose, uneasy. "Great. So now we're watching for Iceclaw as well as Equity. And I have to worry about Caine getting whacked, as well as saving our own impeccably-dressed asses."

"And don't forget every other Gallery asshole who thinks it's his lucky night."

"Awesome. Truly. What a grand evening out." A thought struck me, and I grabbed it. "So what's Finney's game, d'you think? Why would he warn us out? Why not keep the advantage of surprise?"

"Maybe he's trying to scare us," Glimmer suggested. "Make us jumpy, put us on edge. Or…"

"Or to make sure we'll be there." Trepidation heated my blood, but anticipation twinged too. "Maybe something's happening that he doesn't want us to miss. Something special."

"Like what?"

"Like… maybe we'll find out what Razorfire's plan is? Villains like an audience, right? Or tonight could be it!"

"Could be," Glimmer agreed, rubbing his eyes wearily. "Could be that Iceclaw just wants to kill us without the trouble of having to find us first. You can't second-guess these maniacs. You just have to be prepared for anything."

"Gee, thanks for that, Obi-Wan." I jumped up and stretched, my spine popping. "Either way, let's take his oh-so-helpful advice and not be late. It's two thirty. You coming?"

He yawned, lean and sleepy-eyed like a big black-and-white cat. "To where? The show's not till ten. I could use some sleep."

"Are you nuts? Like I'll sleep now, after Nanny Iceclaw's charming little lullaby. And shopping, that's where. I've got nothing to wear to this shindig, in case you'd forgotten. You can tell me what…" My voice trailed off. *What looks good*, I'd been about to say. "What doesn't look completely ridiculous," I amended lamely.

He groaned in mock disgust. "Do I have to? Clothes shopping's for girls. Y'know, people like you?"

I slung his leather jacket at his face, and he caught it, grinning. "Yes, wise-ass, you do have to," I retorted, but a smile infected me and wouldn't cure. "You're the one with the cash, remember? And I sure as hell won't fit into your frocks, glamour boy."

"Okay, fine," he grumbled, shrugging his jacket on. "Just this once. But if you start trying on underwear? I am so outta there."

He'd already seen me naked, the night he brought me here. What did I care? But my skin heated at the thought of him watching me, hidden in warm darkness where I couldn't see, his mask covering all but his blue-as-midnight eyes…

"In your dreams, girlfriend," I scoffed, and walked away before he could make me blush yet again.

20

I stepped from the elevator on the top and sixtieth floor, and walked out into a glittering glass heaven. If I wasn't so damn nervous that my jaw had locked up like a clamshell, it would have hit the floor.

The Crystal City Ballroom was the *pièce de résistance* of the Crystal Towers Hotel, and it took up the entire sixtieth floor in a soaring, sepia glass dome, glittering with craftily hidden spotlights and the jeweled echo of summer stars. The slimmest of steel supports criss-crossed the vast glass expanse, like a fine spider's web, adding to the magical illusion.

I gawked up at the ceiling from the little carpeted lobby, dwarfed by the magnificence. Wow. This place was amazing. To one side, on a patch of soft coffee-and-milk carpet, dinner tables were laid with white linen and silver, candles flickering in ornate holders. Behind a glass wall, the kitchen bustled, uniformed chefs and deck hands and waiters in black. Delicious smells of fine food drifted, roasting meat and tomato and herbs. Opposite, past the carpet, shiny black tiles stretched to the glass horizon. Not a speck of dust anywhere.

And the people glittered as brightly, black suits and fine dresses of all colors, the wink of jewels. They chatted, clinked champagne glasses, snacked on expensive canapés. Couples danced, soft piano music rippling. I couldn't see Equity or Caine. But I knew the type—Dad had enough business associates amongst Sapphire City's snooty *nouveaux riches* that even I'd had to deal with them at one time or another—and even the mouthwatering kitchen smells couldn't drown out the stink of money.

Fidgeting, I smoothed my new dress over my hips. Black, silken, subtle highlights sparkling, it reached to my knees, which was as high as I'd been prepared to go. The neckline stretched flat across my collarbones and dipped down towards my butt, leaving my back and arms bare. Glimmer had helped me flick through racks of them (costume party, he'd explained glibly to the teenage shop assistant who eyed his mask uncertainly) and he'd insisted on this one, even though I complained it showed too much skin.

"You've got a lovely back," he'd explained.

Like that made up for all the things that were wrong with my front.

Whatever. He was paying. I was just glad we finished shopping in under an hour.

I'd pinned my hair up best I could with the ragged bits. My face was no fit stage for makeup, not with my scars, so I'd left it mercifully clean.

Still, I felt ridiculous. Not having trousers on made me feel naked, and though I'd bought the lowest heels I could find, a mere two inches, my ankles teetered. I wobbled, and cursed, fighting for balance. High heels were so stupid. How was a girl supposed to run or fight?

"Easy. You look fabulous." Glimmer's unseen fingers on my elbow made me jump.

"Simple for you to say," I whispered. "You're not the one everyone's staring at." The space where he stood shimmered faintly with his mind-bending power, and my eyes boggled and ached.

"They're not staring. They're too busy worrying about themselves. Take it easy."

I snorted, trying to bolster my confidence. Damn invisible folks gave me the creeps. I'd had the same reaction to my cousin Jem whenever he pulled his light-bending tricks. I knew Glimmer was there, beside me, a subtle shift of light and shadow. I could smell him, like his soap, vanilla and spice. That didn't make it any less spooky that he was fucking with my mind.

Or any less irritating that even when he was invisible, I still felt like a spiky weed in a rose garden next to him. He looked every bit as amazing as I'd feared in that tux, and his mask just gave him an even more rakish air. The Dread Pirate Glimmer. All he needed was a golden earring and a cutlass.

I'd stared at us in the mirror at his place before we left. Glimmer and the Seeker, two sleek figures in black. We almost looked good together.

Until you noticed my face, that is. Then you just wondered how much his buddies had bet him to go out on a date with me.

Glimmer's fingers brushed my shoulder, where a wisp of hair curled loose. "Take care," he whispered. "Remember what you're here for. You've got my number?"

"Uh-huh." I squeezed the thin silver strap of my new clutch bag. I had my phone, my mask (just in case) and Caine's card, which I'd stuffed inside the phone case for safekeeping and shown to the impeccably-suited concierge at the bottom so she'd let me up. I didn't have a pistol or a blade. Metal detectors, no weapons allowed. It wasn't increasing my confidence.

"I'll be around. You'll be fine. Just remember to walk like a girl, not an army sergeant." And a dizzy whiff of headache and vanilla-scented breeze told me he was gone.

Walk like a girl. I snickered. Girls wore jackboots, too. I sucked in a breath, taking courage from the warm summer air, and strode into the fray.

The party swallowed me, drowned me in opulence and the perfume of richly-dressed old ladies. A penguin-suited waiter offered me his tray with a polite bow. "Champagne, madam?"

"Why the hell not?" I took a chilled crystal flute and sipped. Delicious, the bubbles tingling my tongue, the piquant flavor warming my belly. Only the best for Corporations Against World Poverty. Probably could've fed some African village for a week on what a bottle of this gear cost. Perhaps they should change their name to Corporations Regurgitating Appropriate Platitudes. A much better acronym.

I swallowed bigger, praying that the alcohol would calm my nerves, and soon I'd downed my second glass and felt pleasantly warm and relaxed. So far, so good.

I grabbed a canapé from another waiter's tray and wandered in further. Might as well get a free feed, and those smoked salmon crusties sure looked fine. The rich people chatted and waved their hands, jewels and fifty-thousand-dollar wristwatches everywhere. Most of them ignored me.

I caught the eye of one old lady with purple hair like Barbara Cartland and a dead fox wrapped around her sequin-clad shoulders. She tilted her nose up at me, a disdainful *who-let-that-trash-in-here* sniff. Obviously, I wasn't wearing enough precious stones. Maybe she thought I was the World Poverty part of the evening.

Then, her face fell, and she looked away, a guilty flush spreading under her rouge.

My cheeks heated, too, and I hated it. I wanted to lean closer, point at my ruined face, scream *take a good look, grandma! Like what you see?* Instead, I raised my glass to her, and munched loudly on my canapé. Mmm, salmon. "Nice fox head," I said with my mouth full. "Did you kill it yourself?"

She simpered—oh, so *now* you're polite, you snotty old cow—and turned away.

I made a rude face at her behind her back. Whatever. I had work to do. Equity, Caine, Iceclaw, Razorfire's deadly games.

I walked on, and paused in the shelter of some tall decorative flowers, a massive spray of orchids and soft greenery. Where was my sister? I scanned the crowd's edges, looking for the telltale security personnel. Sure enough, there they were, unobtrusive, but obvious if you knew how to look. Curly wires and gun-shaped lumps under their jackets, sure, but they were also the only ones not drinking.

I peered deeper into the crowd, past tables and chattering cliques, following the security detail's formation. Somewhere there...

A flash of shining auburn hair, a long silver dress. My mouth dried, and I gulped for champagne, but my glass was already empty.

Equity, angular but elegant in a floor-length silver gown. Her hair hung straight and glossy, parted to the side and brushing one shoulder. She chatted easily with a group of older guys in suits, probably from the chamber of commerce, the merchant banker's guild, some other *we're-filthy-rich-so-screw-you* club. They all laughed, and she tossed her head, charming.

My guts tightened. Had she seen me? Probably not. Too busy chatting up the influential people. And hell, I was wearing a dress. That was a pretty good disguise.

A hand grabbed my wrist, spinning me around.

Shit. I stumbled on my stupid heels, and fell against a hard black-suited shoulder.

"Let go of me!" I yanked back, ready to unleash with a flex of mindmuscle, but strong hands caught my forearms and trapped me there, and I inhaled male cologne and musk, spied a flash of blond hair...

Cold hands pin me to the iron roof. Body weight on my back holds me down, my face pressed into the metal. I struggle, but it's no use. He's too strong, I can't move...

"Jesus. What are you doing here?" Adonis gripped me tightly, fingers digging in.

My heart fluttered, and I almost sobbed in relief. "Fuck," I gasped. "I thought you were someone else..."

He flashed a swift blue glance around, and tugged me deeper into the orchids' shadowy concealment. "Where have you been?"

he whispered. He wore evening dress, his black silken tie gleaming softly in the spotlights. Effortlessly perfect, as ever. "I tried to call you back, but it wouldn't connect. Jesus, I thought something had happened to you…"

That old brotherly concern crept hot tears behind my lids. I swallowed, and rubbed my sore wrists. I'd missed him. "I'm okay," I whispered back. "Really. I just can't… Listen, Ad, I've found out some bad stuff. I think she's doing things she shouldn't." I didn't dare mention her name. Anyone could be listening.

"Like… what?" His blue gaze was steeped in shadows. Behind him, deeper in the scented foliage, the air shimmered softly. Was that Glimmer, watching over me?

"Like, Gallery stuff," I whispered.

Adonis's eyes narrowed. "You can't be serious."

"I don't have proof yet. But it's bad, Ad. We have to stop her."

"Fuck." He yanked his hair at the back of his neck, hard. "This changes everything."

"Damn right it does. What are we going to do? I can't come home, I can't call you…?"

He sighed. "Listen, there's, uh… there's things you should know. I need to show you something—"

"Forgive me. Mind if I cut in?"

The cool voice shattered our bubble. I jumped, nerves jangling.

Vincent Caine, sharp and suave in a tux, sunny-bronze hair gleaming. He was alone, no girl on his arm, no Ashton-robot in sight.

Fuck. I didn't know whether to curse or be thankful that I hadn't heard what Adonis had to say. Show me what? Had he found evidence against Equity too?

Caine favored us with a smile, probably about half wattage for him, but it still dazzled me dumb. "Lovely to see you again, Ms. Fortune," he said. "Glad you could make it." He offered his hand to Adonis. "You know, I don't believe we've actually met?"

Coolly, Adonis shook hands. "Mr. Caine. That's quite a campaign you're running. I congratulate you."

"Don't be coy, Mr. Fortune. I have formidable opponents." Not a power handshake, no fight for dominance. But Caine sized my brother up all right, clear gray eyes on ocean-blue, and Adonis sized him up right back. I wasn't sure who won. You need a penis to understand these things. But I thought I saw Caine's mouth twitch at one corner.

"Well, we'll see about that on Tuesday," said Adonis, that ultra-pleasant tone that meant he was thinking swear words.

"I imagine we will." Caine turned to me. "May I?"

His rainstorm gaze pulled me under, a swift, deep current I couldn't fight, and I flushed, suddenly acutely aware of my ugly-scarred-wearing-a-dress problem.

My thoughtlessness gurgled like warm treacle in my belly, unsettling me. Caine had me at a disadvantage before we'd even begun, and I realized he'd chosen this venue on purpose. He could've scheduled another meeting in his office, a lunch, a few minutes between speeches. But here I was, behind enemy lines, deep in his territory. Clever bastard.

Well, screw him and the ego he rode in on. I'd fought worse odds.

I mustered some attitude and a smile—what did I care how I looked, anyway?—and slipped my hand into his arm. I resisted a chuckle. You watching this, Glimmer old buddy? Practically a proper lady.

Over Caine's shoulder, Adonis flicked me a pleading, *what-the-hell-are-you-doing?* glance.

Talk later, I mouthed, and that was all I had time for before Caine swept me away.

His silky sleeve felt cool in my fingers. He swiped me another champagne from a waiter's tray. I sipped, and managed a dopey-ass smile.

"Your brother's very charming," he observed wryly.

I laughed, almost choking on the bubbly. "He sure as hell didn't charm you, Mr. Caine. You looked like you wanted to eat him alive."

"Mmm. Busted. I confess, I wish he worked for me. Perhaps one day he will." He clinked his glass against mine, and drank, his silver wristwatch glinting.

"Listen, I don't mean to sound stupid, but... My memory's been a bit hazy since my car wreck, and I can't help feeling... Do we know each other?"

"Aside from today? I believe we've attended the same party once or twice. Why?"

"I dunno. I... kind of feel like I know you, Mr. Caine."

"I was hoping you'd say that." A flicker of smile. "And please, it's Vincent. I insist. It's our second date, after all."

Okay, great. Blushing again. Get a grip, Verity. It's not like he's even all that good-looking... but he sure had an interesting face. Strong chin, sharp cheekbones, stirring storm-gray eyes. Made you look, and keep looking.

"Didn't think you had time for dating." I lounged on one foot, fingering my champagne glass.

He smiled, and I caught myself staring at it, at the way his hair glistened under the spotlights. "I don't. It's more profitable to mix my pleasure with business."

Clunk! That's the sound of me put firmly in my place. I sighed. "Well, I guess we'd better get to it, then. You want to tell me more about this Sentinel of yours—?"

"Not particularly. Will you dance with me, Verity?"

"Excuse me?"

"You. Me. Dance. It's not a trick question."

"Huh?" My brain rapidly bogged itself in muddy *what-the-fuck*?

He didn't repeat himself. He just watched, amused, waiting for me to catch up.

Ooh, a challenge. Inwardly I grinned. Fine. If he wanted to play it that way, I was up for it. I'd still get what I wanted out of him, mark my words. He wouldn't trick me.

I smiled back. "That depends on whether it's pleasure or business."

"Business, naturally. What other purpose could I have?" He made to take my glass, put it aside, but his fingers closed over mine and didn't let go. "But still, you should be careful. My true intention might be unknowable."

Unsettling warmth tingled up my arm. I squirmed. That was what he'd said before, about augments. *Their intention is unknowable.* I didn't think that was what he meant this time.

Hmm. Intriguing, cryptic, a hint of danger. I liked it.

Shit. I liked *him*. I liked his attitude, his smarts, the games he played. How he laughed at the serious things and took the funny things seriously. The way his hand touching mine made me feel, all hot and girly inside, yet… special. Powerful.

Okay, don't shoot. I surrender. I am *totally* attracted to this man.

Inwardly, I groaned. Way to go, Verity. What a stellar idea. Never mind that he planned to make my life and the lives of everyone I knew a misery. That he feared everything I stood for.

That if he discovered what I really was, he'd weld me into a steel cell with the rest of my kind and throw away the angle grinder.

"Uh-huh," I said. "So how do I go about figuring you out, then?"

"Perhaps you can't. Perhaps all you have to go on is capability"—he unwrapped my fingers from the glass and brought them to his lips—"and threat."

Just a single kiss, at the very tips of my fingers, and my knees went to water.

Christ on a cracker. Was he actually…? Did he…?

I swallowed, warm. *Say something flip. Show him you know he's not serious, give him the chance to laugh it off with good grace.* "Okay. So which one was that? The threat, or the capability?"

But he didn't take the offered out. His storm-dark gaze didn't let me go. "That's entirely up to you."

Tell me he didn't just go where I think he went… Before I could stop them, possibilities unfolded in my mind. Hot, sultry possibilities that stole my breath.

Fuck. I struggled to keep my mind on the issues. Don't be

186

ridiculous. Put it out of your mind.

But...

Enough with the *buts*. You want reasons? 1) He's a politician, for which you can read *professional asshole*. One way or another, he's playing you. 2) You lift buses with your brain. Enough said. 3) No matter what he told you, he's probably married. They all lie about being married. 4) Even if he isn't, he won't be chasing a steamy affair with a reporter in the middle of his election campaign. 5) Even if he is, it won't be with a tongue-tied man-chick with a face like yours. And 6) Even if you've magically been transported to some dream universe where a man like that could possibly find you attractive, his opponent is your sister. You're poison. If he sleeps with you, he's a moron.

And those were just six of the eight zillion reasons *not* to flirt with this guy.

But I only needed one reason why.

Vincent Caine didn't see my augment, or my mask. He saw *me*. And he liked me anyway.

"Mmm. I haven't decided yet." My lips stung. I wanted to lick them. I wanted to crush that fine crystal glass in my fist, feel his palm pressed to mine, the crunch of broken shards in our skin... Uh-huh. That wasn't weird at all.

"In that case, let's call it a flicker of one, but mostly the other."

"Threat and capability?"

"Business and pleasure."

"Oh. Sure. Suits me." Oh, yes, it suited me all right.

He did put the glass aside, then, so he could take my hand, guide me into his arms. We were already next to the tiles, somehow. Like he'd taken us there deliberately.

Like this had been his plan from the moment he'd interrupted Adonis and me.

Squelch! That's me, headfirst into that quicksand I was talking about. Gritty confusion sucked me under. He had a campaign to run, a public image to uphold. I hadn't heard he had a reputation.

What the hell was on his mind?

But his eyes on mine gave away nothing, and I felt transparent, dreamy, like he could see deep into my soul. He was still a little taller than me, despite my heels, and his arm felt warm and strong on my lower back, just inches below bare skin. I could smell his hair, warm and minty. I wanted to rest my head on his shoulder, ease closer, move my body against his.

Instead, I concentrated on not falling on my ass in these stupid shoes. I still felt like everyone was watching me. Only this time, they probably were. Including Glimmer, I realized, who probably thought I'd gone insane.

Maybe I had. I felt hot, reckless, a little crazy. The champagne, maybe. Or just the man. "Umm… I don't mean to be rude, but isn't this a bit risqué?"

A delighted laugh, like I'd said something fascinating or clever. "I didn't think we'd gotten to that part yet."

Yet? Like, he intended to get to that part? "No," I muttered, sweating. "I mean, this. In front of everyone. I'm Equity's sister, after all. And a reporter, no less. Unconscionable dealings with the press, all that. Aren't you taking a risk?"

"The risk of what?" He inched closer, teasing. "Everyone knows who you are. They know I know who you are. I'd be an idiot to suggest anything inappropriate, wouldn't I?" He sniffed my hair, and exhaled with a tiny murmur of appreciation that suggested he didn't give a damn about *appropriate*. "So what else can this be but a professional discussion, mixed with a little banal socializing of the transparent kind that we politicians tend to go on with?"

"Uh-huh." So close, he was mesmerizing, a drug I wanted to keep on using. "I can see you've thought this through."

A confident grin. "Naturally. Thinking is what I do."

"Right. And you think flirting with me is a good idea." *Bam!* Nice work, Verity. Might as well get it out there.

"Being close to an attractive woman is always a good idea," he murmured, and though our bodies didn't quite touch, warmth tingled in my breasts. "And you are magnificent, Verity, as I'm sure you're aware."

I couldn't help it. I burst out laughing.

He watched me, amusement crinkling his eyes. "That wasn't supposed to be funny."

My eyes watered, and I struggled to talk. "Jeez," I managed at last. "For a creative genius, you're not very bright."

He wrinkled his nose. "Ouch. Did I overstep? As you say, I'm used to getting my own way."

"It's not that. It's just… you had me already, don't you see?"

His fingers tightened on mine. "I don't follow."

I blinked to clear my eyes, a giggle still rich in my throat. Good job I'd decided against that makeup. "All that stuff you told me this afternoon? I *believed* you. I'm already over here thinking, 'jeez, maybe this guy isn't so bad after all!' And you have to go and overdo it by saying something ridiculous like that."

A moment of silence, as if he didn't get me. "I always mean what I say. You're an extraordinarily beautiful woman."

My scars burned, like he'd painted them with fresh acid. Fuck him. I knew I was ugly. Not like I hadn't heard it before. And this guy hated me, or he would if he knew the truth. He thought I was dangerous. Hell, the bastard was probably right.

So why did his goddamn lies hurt so much?

Roughly, I pulled away, not caring who saw. "Don't make fun of me."

"Not my intention, I assure you." He didn't touch me, or try to quieten me down. Just looked at me, candid and raw. "Is that one word so hard to believe?"

"Do you think I'm stupid, is that it? Because I'm not a mega-mind weirdo like you? Screw you."

"Okay. I suppose you don't believe whatever the hell happened when I laid eyes on you at that press conference, either."

Air stole from my mouth, sucking me dry. *Oh, hell.* "Don't know what you mean," I said faintly.

189

"Don't you? I still can't quite breathe. Don't pretend you didn't feel it too."

"What are you…?" My voice cracked, and I struggled to tone it down, keep from making an even more abject idiot of myself in front of all these people than I already had. He was a professional liar. I'd fallen for it. More fool me. "You know what? Fuck it." And I whirled to walk away.

Now he did touch my arm, pulling me back around. I stumbled on my stupid heels, and had to grab his hand for balance. Shit.

His dark gaze stormed. "Wrong answer. I think we should continue this discussion somewhere more private."

"What for? I've got nothing to say to you, Caine. You win, okay? You can have your story in the *Chronicle*, telling everyone what a mighty peacemaker you are. I don't give a shit."

"I don't care about the *Chronicle*. This isn't about the campaign. It's about you, me, what we are underneath. I think you know that."

The irony choked me. I wanted to laugh. Grab him with an invisible fist of mindmuscle, shake him until his eyeballs rattled. *This is what I am underneath, you moron. Like it?*

I clenched my fists, shaking, barely holding it in. "You expect me to swallow that? Just how dumb do you th—ugh!"

He'd dragged me off my feet, along the mirrored wall and into a dim corridor shielded by a row of those massive orchids. Downlights gleamed onto the dark carpet, and a few doors led off discreetly, ladies' room, janitor's closet, whatever.

"Get your hands off me." I thrashed my arm until he let me go.

"Okay. Fine." His bronze hair shimmered faintly in the dim light, and I fancied it was his anger. Certainly it showed in his tight mouth, the force of his dark gaze on mine. "But please, just hear me out for a second. You don't like me, fine. That's your prerogative. But I won't have you thinking me dishonest."

"Look, I'm not—"

"You think I care about your scars? Of course I care! It's your scars that make you magnificent."

190

"Huh?" My brain was dazzled, slow to catch on.

"You fascinate me, I admit it." His presence burned me breathless, just like it did in the IRIN lobby, and I couldn't move or deny him. "I guess it's inappropriate, us meeting like this. But I'll take the risk. It's too important. I needed to see you again."

I gulped. Now he was getting intense… and my flesh still tingled in response. My pulse quickened, pleasurable yet dangerous.

Oh, yeah. That gazelle on the nature shows, drinking from the waterhole while the hungry jaguar stalks her from the long grass? That's me. "Listen," I said, trying to keep calm, "let's just walk away, okay? I don't want to cause some kind of scandal here."

"Ashton will buy us a few minutes. That's his job."

I stammered. "Heh. Right. Look, this was a mistake—"

He silenced me, a finger on my lips. "This isn't just about physical attraction, Verity. Believe me, I wouldn't be standing here if it was. But the moment you started asking me those questions? I knew you were special. I knew you understood me. And your scars only prove it. It wasn't an accident, was it? Someone tried their hardest to break you, but all they did was make you stronger."

I stuttered, terrified. Tears fizzled in my eyes. His simple words made no sense. They made the most perfect sense in the world.

"That's what I call magnificent, you stubborn, angry goddess." He leaned against the wall, close in the near-dark, and stroked one fingertip over my scarred cheekbone. "I did warn you. I see things others don't see. This face… it's ashes on the breeze. But strength lives in your soul."

My hands shook. God, I wanted to believe him. Wanted to press my cheek into his palm, let him touch me, pretend for just a moment that it was true, that the inside mattered more than the outside, and that if I showed him my inside he wouldn't turn from me in disgust. I wanted to rip myself open and tear my augment out. Get rid of all that rage and hatred. Banish the Seeker to hell where she belonged, and be just plain Verity forever…

I shook myself, incredulous. Jeez. I'm *such* a sucker. If he wanted to get laid, all he had to do was lock his goddamn office door this afternoon.

Deliberately, insolently, I angled my face away. "You're *so* full of shit."

He slipped his hand into his pocket, with a half-smile, as if he couldn't care. "Don't hide. I knew this was real the moment I saw you tonight. We're alike, you and I. You know what it's like to be... apart."

Apart. My heart shivered, warm. He spoke with such feeling about it, I almost wondered if he was trying to tell me something, that he wasn't just strange and clever and off-center, that he was augmented too.

But he couldn't be. I didn't sense anything. And there was no way an augment would fight for the persecution of his own kind. It was unthinkable. Besides, I'd seen him handle his Sentinel. He'd waved his hand right over the sensor and it hadn't gone *pop!*, and then it got one whiff of Patience Crook and all hell broke loose.

I laughed, bitter. He had it so wrong. "No, we're not alike, Caine. Believe me, we couldn't be more different."

"That's a lie."

I bristled, my cheeks warm. "Excuse me?"

"I said, you're lying." Harsh. Cold. "I warned you. I can tell."

He didn't touch me. Didn't fight. But somehow, I couldn't move away. Some weird magnetism between us dragged deep like a burning tide in my blood, and no matter how I struggled, it pulled me under. "That's not tr—"

"Then tell me you don't feel this." Suddenly he was close, too close, his body heat dangerous, the minty scent of his hair intoxicating. "Do you believe in fate, Verity? In accidents that change your life forever? I do. Tell me this isn't one of those moments. It's fucking crazy, I know it. But I can't look away. Tell me the bravest woman in the room will turn her face in fear." He caressed my wrist with a warm fingertip, searching for reaction.

I shivered, and yanked my hand away. "I'm not afraid."

192

"Lie," he murmured. "That's two."

My throat clogged with vile truth, and try as I might, I couldn't spit it out. Because I was, of course. Desperately. Madly, bone-numbingly terrified that he was right. That like my augment and his gift, this was fate.

Because it'd kill me.

I couldn't hide forever, not like this. Not the way he made me feel, real and strong and special. And when my façade failed, and he discovered my true identity, my life was over.

Shit. Guilt tore me raw. He thought we were alike, the poor filthy-rich ultra-clever weirdo that he was. He thought I knew what it was like to be smarter, stranger, more perceptive than everyone else, and he wanted me for it.

But I didn't know. My empathy was a lie. I just knew what it was like to be augmented. And the truth would disgust him.

And even if it didn't? It didn't matter. He had too much at stake. His warped compassion for the weird counted for nothing, not with City Hall up for grabs. He'd use me, like politicians the world over used everyone, a weapon against Equity. Expose me in public. Disillusion all those clueless voters who'd bought into her pretense, show her for the dangerous liar she was.

Flay my life away to win votes.

No escape from that. No ignoring it. No matter how badly he made me want to.

"Stop it, okay? Just stop it. What do you want from me?"

"I want you to be honest with me." Shadows sparkled darkly in his gaze. "No more lies. Be honest with *yourself*."

And there he goes.

Asking for the single goddamn thing I can never give him. Because I *am* dangerous. I *am* a threat. I'm the Seeker, and I could crush him right now like a bug if I felt like it.

I shove my thumbs beneath my mask. It's wet with my tears. My hands shake. I don't care. My heart bleeds raw, and I crush the leather in my fists and tear it off...

193

Scalding rage exploded in my blood, and I shoved him backwards with both hands, lest my power erupt and give me away. "I'll give you honesty. I have no fucking *idea* what you're talking about. Fate's bullshit. I don't feel anything."

"That's three." His dark minty scent caressed me, too sweetly. God, how had I ever thought him unattractive? He was mesmerizing, the angles of his cheekbones, his ink-black lashes, the way his hair glistened in the pale light.

But it meant nothing, this mindless attraction, except that I was weak. The Seeker was strong. Let her fight him off, him and his bizarre games. "You're right about one thing," I announced boldly, leaning close. "I *am* a stubborn goddess, by hell, and you have nothing I want, Vincent Caine. Not a damn thing."

"Four. I'm not giving up, Verity." He didn't retreat. He faced me, unafraid, kindling dark challenge deep in my heart.

Fuck! My fists clenched, painful. His know-it-all attitude cut deep into my composure and tore it apart, and all my bottled-up anger spilled out to poison me.

"Then you're a damn fool," I retorted, shaking. "You don't know me. You know *nothing* about me. And you can keep your fancy talk about gardens and tribes and protecting the weak, because..." My rage boiled over, and in a red-dimmed haze I grabbed him by the lapels, threw him against the wall and slammed my mouth over his.

...because right now, I don't give a damn about any of them.

My teeth banged his. Coppery blood stung, and it mortified me. What was I doing?

But my selfish rage overflowed, bubbling, hungry for this dark release, and it felt too damn good to stop. Was I using him? Honestly? I didn't give a damn about that, either.

"Fuck it," I said aloud, and kissed him again.

For the tiniest moment, he was shocked rigid... and then he was right there with me. Leading me on, cupping my head in his long fingers, his mouth alive, tasting, feeling, knowing...

Oh, hell. My desire ignited, mixing a heady cocktail with my rage. I pressed closer, demanding more. He tasted of mint and champagne, dizzying and dangerous. I didn't care. I kissed him harder, thirstier, his body on mine a hard-won triumph.

My thick-headed common-sense nerve screamed at me to stop. We were right outside the ladies' room. Anyone could see us. No-brainer that this was a bad idea. But the danger only made me hotter, the ache inside me darker and more painful, and I murmured in sweet confusion...

...a fist in my hair, tugging my head back, demanding my surrender. Sweet perfume dizzies me. My heart aches, lost. Stupid to imagine I could resist. My eyelids flutter, closing, and when he kisses me, the tears flow...

No. I gasped, shaking myself. Not now, for God's sake. No bad memories. Please, just this, him, here, now...

I felt Caine hesitate, withdraw, his touch gentling. "Verity...?"

"Shut up. Just kiss me." I barely recalled our argument, my rage, all the reasons this was a mistake. I just wanted to kiss him some more, taste him, live for a while in that magical world where none of the bullshit mattered and we were just him and me, Vincent and Verity, clean and fresh with no cryptic baggage to hold me back.

Another kiss, hotter than the last. He murmured in delight and pulled me in tighter, hands around my waist. I slid my arms around his neck, and when he spun us around to crush me against the wall, shy female muscles melted deep inside me and I was lost.

I wrapped one leg around him, desperate to get closer before this magical bubble broke. He gripped my bare thigh, lifting me. Fuck, I was wearing a dress. Probably making a mess on his clothes. He could touch my naked flesh, right here, right now, if I wanted.

And I did want. The thought of it scorched away my reason. I burned to take him right here. Push him down beneath me, get naked, let him see me as I really am...

He pulled back, breathing hard against my lips. "Verity... it doesn't have to be about this. Not if you don't want it to."

Fuck. If he was pretending, that was trying way too hard. I

didn't want him thinking. I wanted him lost, wild, out of control.

I pressed closer, showing him what I wanted, right there in his lap. "Do *you* want it to be about this?"

His eyes glittered, and he stole a rough, possessive kiss that thieved my breath. "I want it to be about everything."

"Then stop thinking so bloody much." I wrapped my thigh tighter, and dragged his glossy head down to me. This time, our kiss was slow, hot, delicious, drawing out every raw-slashed emotion I'd tried to hide. I wanted to strip naked, show him everything, pour out my soul. Or strip naked and have wild, biting, skin-clawing sex, so I wouldn't *have* to pour out my soul.

God, I was dizzy again. Kissing him made me exult and quiver at the same time. He teased clever fingertips up my thigh, and my head ached. I trembled against him, hot and exquisite like a fever. I wanted to fuck. I wanted to fight. Desire, rage, vengeance, the same sweet delirium. My limbs shook, and I felt my mindmuscle stir, stretch, awaken… "Mmm. Perhaps we should… oh, shit, that feels amazing… perhaps we should stop…"

A dark laugh that tingled deep into my flesh. "Is me taking you right here on the carpet a bad idea?"

"Fuck, no… umm, I mean, yeah, probably."

"Later, then," he whispered hotly, and took my mouth again, and I groaned and yearned against him, and holy fucking Jesus, what *was* that he was doing under my skirt? "Tonight, somewhere we can be alone. It's better that way. I want you to remember it."

I want you to remember…

Toxic white light seared my eyelids, and my mind shattered open.

The steel rooftop glitters under the moon. Wind nips at my cheeks, dragging my hair back. Stars glitter, reflecting the city's neon sprawl below… and a dark shape huddles in blood at my feet. Not moving, not breathing. Folds of wet black leather lift in the wind, revealing the crushed ruin of a handsome face, a bloodstained shock of faded hair…

It's my father. Blackstrike. Dead.

Tears sting my wind-burned eyes. My muscles ache. He's gone. Broken. Blood filling his blank blue stare. I can't ever bring him back.

But there's the weapon, shimmering bright, so close. It's what I came for. It's the only thing that can make this ugly business worth-while. My heart beats faster. I stretch out my hand...

Slam! My face hits the deck.

I struggle, but someone pins me down, knee between my thighs, weight on my torso, hand grabbing my neck and forcing my face down. "Let her go, you bitch. I know she's still alive. Don't you dare hurt her!"

I spit a laugh, and struggle. It's no use. He's too heavy, too strong. "It's over, you dumb fuck." It's my voice. It's not my voice. "Don't you see? She's gone!"

Again, the man I can't see bangs my face against the steel. Crunch! My lip splits. "Last chance," he forces through clamped teeth. "Don't hurt her. I'm warning you..."

Jesus in a hot plum pie. Sweat soaked my new black dress. I whimpered, but Vincent held me close. "Let it out, Verity," he whispered, a burning imperative on my ear. "Whatever it is, it's hurting you. Trust me. Let it out..."

"Don't hurt her. I'm warning you."

I flex my mindmuscle, ram my invisible fist upwards. He grunts with the impact, and I struggle and twist and force myself onto my back.

Handsome blue eyes drill into mine.

For an instant, my heart stops.

Because the guy holding me down is Adonis.

Adonis, who knees me in my guts, making me retch acid. My own brother who pins my wrists to the wind-chilled steel and listens to me shriek, while someone I can't see grabs my shoulders, jams something sharp and metallic onto my scalp and screws it tight...

"It's for your own good, Verity." Adonis stands, catches his breath, adjusts his ruby tie. There's blood on his swollen lip, and he licks it off. "Take her away."

I yell, froth splashing, and thrash my talent, but nothing happens. Just a horrible empty space. Terror claws my heart to ribbons, and I scream.

My own fucking brother.

And nothing's burning, I realize dimly as they drag me away, the hot metal helmet already singeing my hair. We're not under attack. No melted steel or sliced glass, no dripping molten rain. My father's body isn't scorched or charred.

A stinging needle pierces my arm, and drugged sleep claws from the black depths like a monster to claim me, leaving one last, fading, excruciating realization to torment me in my nightmares:

Razorfire isn't even here...

"Verity."

My name, that voice... Cool hands stroked my hair. I struggled, mindless. The hands persisted. "Verity, stay with me. Please."

Caine. Not a dream. I forced my aching eyes open. Downlights glared. He knelt on the floor, cradling me in his arms. "Hush. You fainted. It's okay."

I retched, wet. Probably stained his suit. He didn't seem to care. My body shook. I wanted to weep, scream, beat the horrid memories away.

A black blur materialized, and dragged Caine away from me. "Let her go!"

I tumbled to the carpet. Caine stepped back, hands raised in peace. "Excuse me, who are you?"

Glimmer ignored him, and knelt at my side, feeling my skull for bumps, peeling my eyelids back to check for concussion. He still wore his mask, his skunky hair crazy over his black-and-white penguin suit. "Jesus. What happened? Are you okay?"

The Dread Pirate Glimmer, I recalled hazily, and laughed. No, my friend. This girl is most definitely not okay.

"What did you do to her?" Glimmer rounded on Caine, fire in his eyes. "Can't you see she's ill? Did you call the paramedics? Christ, if you've hurt her I'll—"

"Nothing of the sort, I assure you," said Caine coolly. "The lady fainted."

"Yeah," Glimmer retorted, his angry haze blackening the air. "I saw. That's one hell of a campaign strategy you've got there."

"Adonis," I croaked, groggy. I didn't care what Glimmer saw. Didn't care that Caine and I had been kissing, touching each other, that I'd probably have fucked him and his election campaign both, right there on the carpet, if we hadn't been interrupted.

None of it mattered.

"It was Adonis, that night on the roof. He gave me to those... And Razorfire..." My throat seized. I couldn't talk anymore. Didn't want to say the words.

Fresh rage made me shiver like a fever, burning my confusion away. I'd thought I remembered fire that night, flame-whips, Razorfire's evil weapons. But it wasn't true. Wasn't real.

My fucking prick of a brother. He'd lied to me all this time. I'd drag him from his lofty perch next to our sister and thrash his handsome head into the glass until he told me what the fuck was going on.

Tears scorched puddles in my eyes. He'd betrayed me. The brother I thought loved me more than anything, who'd always been there for me, no matter what...

Caine touched my arm. I shook him off, woozy. Glimmer said something, probably *what the hell are you on about?* or *have you finally gone completely batshit?* I didn't hear. The screaming in my head drowned everything out, ripping at my senses until my head exploded in confusion.

Everything I'd believed. Everything I'd clung to, to keep me alive in that vile asylum while those bastards tortured me. Everything I'd carved in stone since, to give me purpose, keep me from diving into the howling void of *who the fuck cares.*

All lies.

Dad tried to help you, Adonis told me. *Razorfire killed him.*

Razorfire wasn't even *there.*

At least, not in the part I remembered now. But someone killed Dad. Someone planted that appalling weapon on the roof at FortuneCorp, the one I'd nearly died trying to recover.

And I'd beat the awful truth out of my scheming, lying, vile-hearted brother if I had to kill him doing it.

My nerves flamed bright with rage and vengeance, and I dragged myself to unsteady feet and strode out into the ballroom.

And the mighty glass ceiling imploded.

21

A massive pile of jagged glass fell, and shattered on the tiled floor with an ear-splitting crash.

I dived for cover, rolling under a table. Glassy shards rained, like stinging sand. All the ceiling lights had popped out, leaving only the tiny lights around the ballroom's fringe and a threatening forest of shadows.

I wrapped my head in my arms, and ducked up, risking a glance around through glassy raindust like snow. All hell had broken loose. People screamed, ran in all directions, and for a moment I couldn't see through the mess.

Then, I spotted her. Equity, her long silver gown splattered with blood, clambering over a pile of shattered furniture. And helping her, Adonis-the-asshole-bastard-traitor, glass shards in his hair, his nose bleeding.

Go ahead, help her, I wanted to scream, *you're both in this together!*

But Adonis was calm, composed as usual, already shielding his eyes from the deadly-sharp rain with his other hand to look up.

In search of the culprit.

Cursing my slowness, I looked up, too.

A fresh pile of glass rained down on me. I screamed, and instinctively flung out my talent. The glass crunched into my force field, and broke into a million tiny pieces. They showered, scattering on my barrier like I was inside a cocoon, and spilled to the floor.

I flung the glass away and dived back under the table. I lay there, panting, my heart pumping. That was close. But what the fuck was going on? A bomb? Did someone fire a gun?

I shivered, suddenly cold. My breath clouded white. I glanced again at that shattered glass, scattering into puddles of water...

Not just glass. Ice.

I'll be the one stabbing an ice pick through your face.

Glacial laughter crackled down, chilling my blood. "Hello, citizens," Iceclaw yelled, from some vantage point high above. "Thought I'd drop in. Any free drinks left?"

Frustration charred black holes into my heart. Damn it. Adonis would have to keep, or this maniac would kill us all.

"Iceclaw!" I screamed, my voice ragged, and primed my muscles to sprint out there and tear his greasy ass from the sky. "You fucked-up son of a bitch!"

A dark shape dived in beside me, and Glimmer rolled into me with a thump. He grabbed me, calmed me, fought for my hands when I tried to thrash him away. "Hey, take it easy," he said roughly. "You'll not beat him angry. Jesus, what happened to you?"

I sucked in chilled air, trying to stop lashing out at anything and everything I could see. But my mindmuscle spasmed, dangerous. The table above us skittered on its legs, and out there in the dark, Iceclaw cackled and froze more glass to smithereens.

"It doesn't matter," I said desperately. I wanted to get away from Glimmer. He was warm, safe. I didn't want warm and safe. Look where warm and safe had gotten me. "Just make sure those security clowns get Caine out of here, can you? This is our goddamn fight."

And I didn't want Caine to see me. Didn't want him to know I'd lied, that I'd used him to make myself feel better about being such a fuck-up.

That I was weak, afraid, potentially dangerous. Everything he'd said I was.

Glimmer's mouth tightened. "He'll be okay. They're watching him like hawks."

"They weren't doing a bang-up job five minutes ago! Please, just take care of it. Iceclaw's mine."

Glimmer smoothed my hair. "It's okay. I'm with you, you know that. See you at the other end. And Verity?"

"Yeah?"

"Take care," he said, and he was gone, an eye-boggling shimmer in his wake.

I sat up, rubbing my arms. Already, it was frigid in here, and snowflakes danced on chilly breeze. Iceclaw's talent, liquid nitrogen mixed with bad attitude. The Gallery's answer to global warming.

Great. Still, it could be worse. Could be Razorfire up there.

But I glanced at the clear blue ice creeping inexorably down the walls, and a finger of unease tickled my spine. Crystal Towers was a sixty-story building, held up by a network of steel girders.

At ultra-low temperatures, steel became treacherously brittle. That evil cracking sound I was hearing? Not good.

I crawled out. My stupid shoes had fallen off somewhere, and broken glass crunched on my toes, under my knees. Blood smeared. I didn't care. The pain felt good. It sharpened my nerves, focused my mind, stretched my senses to a razor-bright edge.

People still screamed, huddling under broken tables littered with glass. All those fine clothes were torn and bloody now. Some ran for the doors, but ice licked down the walls two inches thick, coating hinges, doorknobs, elevator buttons, everything in its path. The doors were frozen shut. No one could get out.

Some people weren't moving. A dozen or more, they just lay there in puddles of glass and blood.

I couldn't see Caine, or Glimmer. I looked down at my own dress. Blood, vomit and tears stained the front, and the neckline was torn. I didn't remember doing that.

Remember. Ha. That was a laugh.

Over on her table, surrounded by her security guards, Equity cursed like a sailor and shook off Adonis's placating hand. "Everyone keep calm," she called, lifting her hands like a preacher. "We have a Gallery situation here. Please, stay calm."

"I'm sorry, did someone say something?" From somewhere above, Iceclaw unleashed a fresh blast of icy rain at her, and she squealed and ducked, fury flashing in her eyes. Adonis sheltered her, holding her close as she crouched.

But she didn't unleash. Didn't burn the air with blinding light.

She couldn't, I realized with unhallowed glee. Couldn't melt Iceclaw's flesh with ultraviolet rays or scorch his retinas blind until he convulsed with agony and fell to his death. No more than Adonis could charm him into giving up, or coax him to jump with a wink and a lethal smile.

Too many people watching. Too many cameras could be rolling. If Equity showed herself as Nemesis, her campaign was screwed.

Right now, I couldn't give a fuck if they both died.

But I was still in shadow. No one could see me.

I fumbled in my clutch bag for my mask. My nails tore on the sharp sequins, but I dragged it out. Knotted it around my eyes, and tossed the bag onto the table.

I felt stronger already.

Pity I wasn't wearing my shiny new outfit. But no help for it. I'd just have to fight scruffy.

I stepped onto the tiles, and skidded on ice. Forty feet above me, Iceclaw swung like a big-ass monkey in the metal spider's web that once supported the ceiling. He wore the same dirty jeans, ragged mittens with no fingers, an old-fashioned leather aviation mask with round goggles to keep out the snow and glass. His long, greasy hair whipped in the breeze.

He saw me, and laughed, flipping me a cheeky wave. "Seeker. Fuck me, they let any old gutter trash into these charity gigs, don't they?"

Equity whirled, and shot me a glare, sharpened with menace. "Seeker," she hissed in turn. "You've got a nerve showing your face here."

I wanted to laugh. Let her wonder how I'd gotten an invitation. And she wouldn't say my name, I realized gleefully. She couldn't risk anyone knowing who I was.

Not even Iceclaw would say my name, even if he knew it. It was a superior villain thing. That information was his alone, to torture me with. He didn't want just anyone figuring it out. Where's the fun in that?

I vaulted onto a table, into a shaft of light. "What do you want, Iceclaw?"

I'd do him the same courtesy. Not that it'd do him any good in thirty seconds when I crushed him to pulp.

But a hundred people remained trapped in this ballroom, and if I'd forgotten that, their damn wailing would've reminded me. The glass ceiling was gone, mostly, but tons of sharp metal still hung up there. If I dragged the roof down, they'd all be crushed.

Fuck. Frustrated, I started calculating how far it was, the wind effect, how much energy I'd need to fling myself up there, hopefully without hurtling out into empty sky and falling to my death.

"I want you, and all your worm-grubbing friends, of course!" Iceclaw landed on an unbroken ledge near the roof's summit, and held on to the exposed metal brace above his head. Snow swirled around him, whipping up his hair. "Sorry, love. Boss's orders. Nothing personal... actually, fuck *that*. It is personal, ha ha! Wipe your scum from the face of the planet, Seeker. You and your whole muck-loving crew."

Yeah, that was himself talking, all right. "Wow," I yelled back, "having Razorfire's hand shoved that far up your butt must really hurt."

"This glass is a nice touch, eh? I like that. How many more of 'em d'you think I can crush before you catch me? Hell, maybe I'll just freeze the whole goddamn building down on their heads!

How'd ya like that?" Frost crackled on his laughter, and he lifted his face to the sky and *a-hooo!*ed like a hungry wolf, calling down the chill.

Hailstones pelted, clattering on the tiles. Freezing rain needled my skin. Wind howled, and tables skidded and tumbled. I braced myself, feet apart. Sheets of ice crystallized on the walls, crackling downwards like hungry glaciers, and steel girders began to creak under the stress.

I didn't stop to listen to any more.

I dragged in a fistful of power. The rubbery air *stretched*, the kinetic energy scorching my palm and melting the snow to raindrops. I dragged it tighter, a popping noise like over-stressed rope, and let fly.

It fired me into the air, a gigantic slingshot. I sailed towards the broken ceiling, wind buffeting me in all directions. The freezing air clawed my lungs bloody. Icy knives stabbed into my sinuses. I couldn't control it.

I hit the metal spider's web, grabbed for the metal spars, and missed.

I flailed, desperate. My palm slapped icy metal and stuck there like glue. Skin ripped. Chill stabbed up my arm, and I screamed. Wind flung my body outwards, tearing at my limbs, hungry to rip me off and fling me into oblivion.

But I held on.

I fought for my footing on the sharp metal web, and gripped on tight. My teeth chattered, and my face stung, bruised by hailstones and chilled raw. Shivering, I tore a fistful of neckline from my dress and used it to wrap my hand, but already frostbite blistered.

Ten feet away, his ass jammed into a fork in the web, Iceclaw laughed, swinging his legs. Inside his goggles, his hate-crazy eyes gleamed white. "Glad you could make it," he called. "Let's do this, Seeker. You and me. It's been far too long."

Fuck. I wasn't dressed for this. He'd freeze my half-naked ass in seconds. No time to lose.

"Give it up." The ultimatum felt dull and hollow in my mouth, like something I'd rote-learned but didn't really believe in anymore. "This is between you and me. No one else has to get hurt. Let's take it outside, like civilized people."

"Fuck civilization," he growled, spitting icy shards. "What's civilization ever done for us? They treat us like shit. Fuck 'em."

It's for your own good, Verity... The memory of my brother's treachery punched me in the guts, and my vision blurred. All my so-called heroic family had done for me was dump me in the shit.

I clutched the iron spar tighter, the wind flapping my hair, stinging my eyes, threatening to drag me away. "Us?" I yelled. "There is no us, you sick freak!"

But images swamped me, all the times I'd hidden or fled, concealed my power from morons who'd hurt me for it. Those assholes who kicked the crap out of me in that alley, ignorance, fear, the dumb stupid hatred of animals... and Caine, for God's sake, who wasn't ignorant or scared, who touched me and made me burn and actually fucking *understood* and still wanted to ping us with his rotten gadget and lock us away.

And still, in spite of all our sacrifices, the Gallery won.

They always won.

I shivered, and clung on tighter. Below, the frozen walls shuddered and cracked. Plaster exploded, forced from its fittings by the ice-swollen steel girders beneath. But how far down did the freezing go? Would the entire hotel collapse? How many people were inside? How many would be crushed?

But selfish rage thudded in my blood, obliterating everything but the sound of Iceclaw, laughing at me.

"You know you don't give a fuck about them," he sang. "And they sure don't give a fuck about you. So what's the problem? Lost your nerve? Aren't you up for it anymore?"

"Try me, asshole," I spat, that rage spilling hot. My greedy mindmuscle flexed in response, and I grabbed for him with invisible fists, but he was too fast. He leapt about like a circus dwarf on monkey bars, always a step ahead. I couldn't catch him, and snide remarks about knives and gunfights sniggered in the back of my mind.

Fuck. I sure could do with that pistol now.

"They stuck you in the nuthouse, that's what I heard. Carved your brain into popcorn chicken." Iceclaw leered at me, gleeful. "Can you still get it up, Seeker? Or are you frigid, is that it? Did they cut your ladyballs off? Because that'd be a real shame."

Red mist drowned me, and before I knew it I'd grabbed the iron bar above his head in a fit of rage. "Come over here and find out," I growled, and pulled.

The brittle metal creaked, and with a glacial crack, it broke.

A vast section of webbed roof came loose. It folded, an icy lattice twenty feet wide, dangling above nothing.

With me on it.

I hung on tight, my naked legs swinging. I couldn't feel my toes. Hell, I couldn't feel my tongue. Only my elbow, hooked around the steel, aflame with the effort of bearing my weight. And my head, the holy mother Mary of all headaches, screaming fit to split.

Below, people squealed and ran to and fro, enraged ants. Hail thundered, a deafening iron monster that wouldn't let up. I could barely hear some woman's voice, yelling at everyone to stay calm, don't panic, keep close to the walls, help is on the way. Equity? I couldn't tell amid the screams.

Iceclaw tumbled, a crazy-ass acrobat, and swung from the lattice's edge on one muscled arm. Fucker was strong. "Ooh, ooh!" He whooped, insane. "That's the spirit!"

He howled again, and more cold air swirled in. Tiny ice crystals pierced my eyeballs. The walls shuddered and cracked. More glass splintered and fell. "Come on, Seeker," he crooned. "You can end it all. Fuck 'em. Drop the damn ceiling and let's go out together. You and me. Blaze of glory, all that."

He thinks I won't do it.

The truth hit me, a hammer in the face. He thinks I won't

209

sacrifice innocent lives just to kill him.

I'm not a bad person. The words tumbled in my mind, stones in a barrel, coming around again, again, faster, louder. *I'm not a bad person. I'm not.*

My mindsense shuddered, hungry. Grimly, I held on, pain screaming in my elbow, but pale compared to the shrieking agony in my heart. Tears spilled and froze on my cheeks. *It's for your own good...* Adonis's fatal words echoed, endlessly mirrored, a dark tunnel into my soul. My own family had betrayed me. They were all in on it. I'd disarmed a lethal Gallery weapon—a weapon my own fucking sister stole for them—and all I got for my effort was a beating and nine months of torture.

My whole damn family had turned out to be Gallery stooges. That's what you got for keeping the moral high ground.

That, and Razorfire's mocking black laughter in my dreams.

Lust for vengeance clawed holes in my reason, and truth bled out, cold in the shine of the moon. What the hell did I care for those people down there? They hated me. They feared me. I'd devoted my life to helping them, and they wouldn't even meet my eye. They used me when it suited them, and then they spat on me and left me to rot...

No! a distant voice inside me screamed. *Don't let* him *have his way. Don't dive willingly into that abyss...*

Iceclaw sobbed like a girl, mocking me. "Boohoo. All those squashed dead people. Can't face it, can you? Can't look yourself in the eye and say 'good job, sister, they fucking well deserved it'."

"No!" The wind snatched my yell away. My mind splintered, spinning in all directions like ice crystals shattering on glass. *Glimmer's midnight-blue eyes, his warm hands on my face... my father's shadows, writhing out to choke me... kisses burn my throat, and I shiver and weep... a dark chuckle, a voice that strips my heart raw...*

Haven't you learned yet? You have no god...

"Go on, then," Iceclaw taunted. "Back to your sad little hero's world. I'll tear this goddamn building down. You're a weakling, Seeker. You're weak and we're strong and you ain't never gonna win!"

...you have no god but me.

"Just you fucking watch me!" I screamed, and tore the ceiling free.

22

With an almighty screech of twisting metal, the lattice cracked and fell.

I tumbled. My grip slipped. Hail and snow lashed my face. Broken steel slammed into my body as I fell, and frantically I lashed out with my power, grasping for something, anything to keep me alive.

My invisible fingers slammed into a broken window and held on. Glass sliced. I screamed, and the power flung me sideways, slamming me into the icy wall six feet from the ground.

But the lattice was too big. My power couldn't hold it. Glass fragments spun in the wind, and the whole thing smashed into the floor two feet away.

Crash! It bruised my ears, a tangle of steel and broken furniture. Screams echoed. And then silence throttled me.

Just the aimless clatter of hailstones, the wind's fading howl.

I slumped to the floor, wheezing.

People didn't scream any more. They moaned, and stumbled, disoriented. Already, Iceclaw's eerie storm was fading, weakening, drifting away. Ice melt dripped from the frigid walls.

Weary, I hauled myself to my feet. Broken glass cut my soles.

I wobbled, slipping in blood.

A lot of blood. It oozed from beneath the wreckage in puddles. I stared dully. Pale flesh glared at me from the mess. A staring eye, a face, a shock of red hair. A hand, slack and lifeless, wristwatch clotted crimson. Bodies. Lots of bodies.

I looked away, dumb… and my gaze snagged on a pile of shimmering silver cloth, stained with blood.

I ran, clambering wildly over twisted steel and bodies and roses of broken glass. My hands sliced bloody. I dragged away a twisted lump of steel. It snagged in her silly auburn-dyed hair. It wouldn't come free. I yanked, desperate, and her head fell to one side, revealing her face.

Equity's eyes stared, already fading to empty gray, her light forever darkened. Blood spilled from her mouth. Slowed to a trickle. Stopped.

Reflexively, my mouth opened to scream. But I didn't have the will.

I just knelt there on the rubble, staring. Scream, damn it. Cry. Puke. Do *something*.

Feel something.

But I just stumbled up, and climbed numbly back down to the floor.

I couldn't see Adonis, or Caine, or Glimmer. Didn't mean they weren't there, dead and bleeding under the rubble.

To my left, a heavy body heaved and groaned beneath a pile of broken metal bars. Long sandy hair crusted with blood-soaked snow, jean-clad legs bent at crazy angles. I weaved over to him, fatigue blurring my eyes. Iceclaw's goggles lay askew. One lens was pierced by a shard of steel, right through to his eyeball. Gross.

He grinned up at me, a gory mess of crushed bones and teeth. He tried to talk—to say *fuck you, Seeker* or *I knew you had it in you* or even *say a prayer for me, darlin', God knows no one else will*—but bright crimson blood frothed, and only a guttural choke came out.

I stared down at him, and finally, jagged guilt drove into my heart, ripping in opposite directions until I didn't know which way was up. *This is all your fault!* I wanted to scream. *You made me do this. You made me like you. It wasn't my choice. I'm not a bad person. I'm not!*

My legs trembled as I bent over. My cold-bitten fingers shook as I closed them around an ice-rimed iron spike.

He glared up at me, a cold curse, and a baleful gust blew my hair back. *I'll be the one stabbing an ice pick through your face...*

I gripped the sharp metal tightly, and stabbed the pointy end into his throat.

Putting him out of his misery.

Or me out of mine.

Blood gushed. He gurgled, heaved one final drowning breath, and died. The frosty wind faded, and I was alone.

I let the cold spike slip from my fingers. It clattered on the broken floor, lost.

Above, a helicopter's searchlight sliced in, banishing the darkness. It glared, hurting my eyes, but I didn't shield them. The chopper's blades thundered, *thwockthwockthwock!* in the night, an inexorable mechanical monster. Already, frantic fists hammered on the ballroom doors. Emergency services, police, paramedics. The ice was melting. Soon, they'd get in.

Maybe, I'd just stay here and let them find me.

I didn't pull my mask off. I just found an empty patch of ground, and let my lifeless legs buckle.

And then hands settled on my shoulders, pulling me back to the light.

I moaned, uncomprehending, the sweet scent of vanilla and spice forcing only slowly into my darkness. Glimmer, so gentle and warm, my God, he was so wonderfully warm, his strong arms around me, his rough silken hair on my face. He slipped his jacket around my shoulders, and his whispers calmed me without words, soothed my battered soul.

I shivered, my deep-iced core melting at last. It felt so good.

215

So forgiving. But my frostbitten limbs were unwilling to move me to safety, to let me be absolved. I didn't deserve his warmth. I didn't want it.

But I let him drag me to my feet and take me away.

#

Outside, the summer air burned my bitten skin. It hurt, like poison deep inside, where Iceclaw's vile chill had taken hold. I shivered and sweated on the back of Glimmer's bike, huddling in his jacket, my cheek pressed against his warm back. When we got home, he tried to carry me inside, but I muttered and fumbled and pushed him away, stumbling down the stairs and into his dim lair on my own.

He didn't speak. He just threw himself into his high-backed chair, unknotted his black bow tie, scrunched a fist in his glossy hair. Blood and dirt stained his white shirt, and his sweet bottom lip swelled, bruised.

For some reason, that hurt more than anything.

My heart stung. I wanted to wash him clean, let him pretend none of this had happened. He didn't deserve this. He didn't deserve me.

He glanced up, and I got my first real look since the ballroom at his face. Slick with sweat, pale skin stark against his dark-shadowed eyes. Like he'd suffered a shock, and come out the other side with nothing to say.

An evil ache rotted my skull like a corpse's, and my stomach salted sick. I didn't want his silence. I wanted him to shout, accuse, condemn me for the murdering maniac I was.

His jacket was warm, smooth, imbued with his goddamn vanilla scent, and I shrugged it off, furious. My dress was torn, and the air was cold. I grabbed the Seeker's shiny gunmetal coat from the sofa and yanked it on. It didn't make me feel safer.

I planted my butt on the desk and folded my arms. "Well, that could've gone better."

Glimmer shrugged sharply. "At least Iceclaw's dead, right?"

Bitter guilt stung my mouth like bile. "Glimmer—"

"Isn't that what you want me to say?" He skewered me with his dark-and-angry stare. "Job done? All's fair?"

"No! That isn't what I want." Now, at last, I was crying. Not because my sister was dead. Not because I'd killed all those people.

Because I'd disappointed my only friend, and it tore my heart to mincemeat.

Because deep inside, some wild, defiant part of me didn't give a damn about those people. And it fucking terrified me.

Glimmer just looked at me. Unblinking. Refusing to fill the silence. It dragged, excruciating, broken glass across my skin.

"Iceclaw was going to tear that whole building down." My voice grated, nails on steel. "Imagine the body count then. What was I supposed to do? Answer me that."

"That's not the point."

"Then what is?" I jumped up, shoved his chair backwards, lest I claw his damn eyes out. Jeez, I'd been up for thirty hours. We both had. My body shook with fatigue and all of tonight's ugly madness. I could barely keep my eyes open. I wasn't up for this. "It's always us who have to care about collateral damage. Iceclaw sure didn't give a damn. He put all those people at risk, not me. I just finished what he started and now the sick motherfucker is dead and he'll never hurt anyone again. What the hell else do you want from me?"

He rose and grabbed me, trapping my wrists between us. I fought. He didn't let go. "I want you to make your choice," he insisted. "Draw a line and pick a side and stay there. Is that so much to ask?"

"It's not that simple." I struggled, useless. He was too strong. My mindmuscle thrashed in fiery anger—how *dare* he force me—and I nearly let it strike out.

Nearly unleashed on him.

My stomach lurched, aghast, and I stopped fighting.

But his midnight-blue eyes drained of warmth. His lip quivered, and he released me, hands dropping to his sides. Like I'd sucked away his strength.

My eyes burned, blind. "Glimmer—"

"It is that simple, Verity." Soft, but chilled, like he'd put himself on ice. "I know which side I'm on. Best you decide, and fast, or I've got nothing more to say to you."

I felt like clawing my eyeballs until they bled. I'd wanted him to judge me, so I could scream and rant and unburden my sins onto him. Now I had what I wanted, and fuck me raw and bleeding if I wouldn't suffer that guilt for a hundred years unrelieved, if it meant I could take it back.

Rage, I could cope with. Disgust, sorrow. But his coldness was unbearable. I wanted passion. Hatred. Jealousy. Anything, except this emptiness. "Is that a fact?" I mocked. "And what the fuck were you doing, Glimmer, when Iceclaw attacked? Did he take you by surprise? Or were you too busy spying on me and Vincent Caine to notice a Gallery villain climbing on the roof?"

His eyes smoldered, a lick of flame. "You can talk. You were a mite preoccupied at the time."

"Oh, so now we get to the real issue. You're sore at me because you're jealous. I shoulda known."

"Don't be ridiculous. Were you even listening to what he said? The guy was screwing with your mind!"

"Yeah. And you're the fucking expert on that, aren't you?"

"Excuse me? Was that an accusation?"

"Damn right it was."

His jaw tightened dangerously. "I've never unleashed on you, and you know that. Not once. I thought you trusted me."

"Oh, right, sure." Now it was getting childish. I didn't care. I just wanted to pick a fight. "Don't come all self-righteous with me. You've done nothing but flirt your pretty-boy lashes at me since I got here. If that's not screwing with my mind, I don't know what is."

218

He folded his arms. Leaned closer. "Yeah? Well, maybe you just see what you want to see."

I laughed, cruel. "You have *got* to be kidding me."

A loud clatter of wind chimes strangled my voice.

My phone. Ringing. Inside my dented clutch bag.

I stalked over and grabbed it, answering without looking. "Who the fuck is this?"

"Verity? Are you okay?" Stress cut those ever-calm tones ragged.

Perfect timing. Just fucking perfect.

I pointed one finger at Glimmer, and speared him on a *don't-you-dare* glare. "Vincent. Hi. Umm... yeah, I'm fine. I, uh, got out before it started."

Jeez, did I hear relief, coloring that sigh? He actually sounded like he gave a shit. "It's carnage in there. Unbelievable. So many casualties, I just wanted to..."

"I'm fine. Really. Uh... thanks." I took a deep breath. "Listen, can I call you back? I'm kinda in the middle of something."

Crack! A massive weight thundered down above our heads, and the world shuddered.

The floor quaked. I stumbled, my bare feet stinging. Stuff fell from shelves. "What the hell?"

"What was that?" Caine's voice tightened.

"No idea." Another rumble. The concrete walls cracked, dust puffing from the gaps. "Earthquake? Hell of a time for the fault to slip."

Glimmer leapt for his screens, checking his surveillance. "Do you think we're that lucky...? Shit."

One by one, the screens flickered, and died.

Glimmer cursed, and flicked switches, but the power was gone. "Could use a hand here," he snapped. "That's no earthquake, Verity."

"But the power's cut—"

"Then why are the lights still on?"

Good point.

The phone line crackled against my ear. "Verity, listen," Caine insisted, "wherever you are, get out."

I braced myself against the table as another quake shook the basement. Books and cups slid sideways. The kitchen rattled. "We're under attack. I don't know… it's something strange…"

"Where are you?" The line was breaking up. I could barely hear him above the quake. "Verity, listen to me… can protect you… tell me where you are…"

"I…" Hot gritty air blasted me in the face. I coughed, and smelled gasoline, and the air exploded with the tart sweetness of *augment*.

Glimmer looked at me. I looked at him. And then, the lights blinked out, plunging us into dusty darkness.

The ceiling tore open, a gigantic shudder that knocked me on my ass, and the sky rained fire.

23

My chin hit the concrete floor. Blood splurted into my mouth. My breath knocked away. I struggled to inhale, and coughed on a lungful of dust.

Flames ribboned around me, orange and scarlet like a demon's eyes. Radiant heat scorched my face, singed my bare legs. Glimmer crawled up beside me, covered in dirt, blood seeping from cuts. "Okay? Nothing broken?"

No, I fucking well wasn't okay. But I shook my head, and coughed, spitting black goo. Glimmer's scalp was bleeding, I noticed. It dripped down his masked face and through his hair, painting his skunk stripe crimson. I was probably in better shape than he was.

Furniture lay broken, screens smashed and burning. I spied my phone, lying in the dust, and scrabbled for it. The plastic was hot in my hand. Dead, no reception bars. I stuffed it into my coat's buttoned pocket. Through the dancing shadows, I could see where the ceiling had ripped apart. The smoking black edges were sharp, sliced with precision that chilled my blood. The stink of gasoline licked my tongue—*no, not gas,* I realized dimly. Something richer and less volatile, hotter when it ignited.

No point lighting it if you can't watch it burn.

Flames swirled, and a dark figure dropped from the ceiling's gaping hole.

I scrabbled backwards like a crab, trembling. My bowels watered. God, I wanted to disappear, turn tail and flee, squeeze my eyes shut and pretend this wasn't happening.

He'd found us.

Damn lucky we weren't dead already. But then, he wouldn't just kill us, would he? Tormenting us was far too much fun.

Razorfire landed, and rose gracefully from his crouch into the flickering firelight. Tall, poised, catlike. Crimson silk flared around his legs, that high-collared coat he always wore. Flame danced in the palm of his left hand, crept whimsically up his wrist, that strange fiery trick of his that had wrought such destruction on so many. A shiny metal mask covered his face, hawk-like and rusty red like dried blood. But his piercing eyes shone through, scarlet like the devil himself.

My limbs shook. Knives and gunfights, I recalled dimly. But this psychopath had dodged bullets all his life. It was a point of pride.

Beneath him, you see, to be so easy to kill.

Glimmer was quicker than me. In a flash, he rolled and reached behind his back for his weapon.

But Razorfire just skewered him with that flaming stare. Glimmer yelped and dropped the pistol. It clattered to the floor, glowing red, and the metal parts started to melt. Glimmer shook his burned hand, locking his teeth on a shriek of agony. Lucky he hadn't scorched his palm through to the bone.

Razorfire stalked forward, and his tall shadow loomed monstrous on the broken wall. I trembled. Christ on a crispy cracker. We'd wanted our enemy to come to us. Now he had, and I wanted to leap up, fight, tear him to pieces.

But I couldn't move.

A smile curled his mouth, mild yet terrifying. "Hello, Seeker." Smooth voice, dark and rippling like hot honey. "Consider me

223

snared in your little trap. Well done. I confess, I got tired of waiting for you."

"Generous of you." My voice croaked in the smoke.

"Isn't it? That's the kind of guy I am." Razorfire glanced around the burning basement, and where his gaze lingered, flames licked eagerly, like they wanted to impress him. "Nice place," he remarked. "Very techno-grunge. And look, it's the striped puppy dog! Did he follow you home? Seriously, son, do something about that hair. You're making us all look like a bad circus act."

This wasn't how I'd imagined our meeting. I wanted to scream acid hatred at him, rip his face off with my teeth and spit the flesh away. Pin him to the floor, wrap my power around his throat and make him talk before he died, make him tell me what he'd offered Equity that made her turn her coat for the Gallery. How he'd brainwashed Adonis into locking me in that asylum, when I was the one Adonis loved most in the whole world.

How the death-loving bastard had managed to kill Blackstrike that night, when so far as I could tell, he wasn't even *there*.

I shuddered, cold despite the searing flames. Behind us, another screen exploded, hot glass showering. Sweat dripped down my face, stinging my bruised lips. Hell, I just hadn't remembered that part properly yet. Right?

But the answers scared me more than not knowing.

"Fuck you," I said. Best I could do at short notice.

Razorfire clicked his tongue, scolding. "And I thought we were old friends. Speaking of: how's your father?"

My heart squeezed, agonizing. Treacherous rage boiled again inside me. Fucking prick. I'd tear his skin off.

My vision blurred, and Glimmer's voice slipped into my head, strained tight but calm. *Don't, Verity. He'll burn us both. Find out what he wants.*

Screw that. In the dust beneath me, my fists tightened, and quietly I collected a handful of power, finger by finger…

Razorfire's eyes flared, hellish. He flung out his hand, and flame like red-hot wire lashed from his palm.

The table beside me sliced in half and exploded into a fireball, and his flame-razor hissed and crackled, snapping back on his command like a whip. "Belay that," he warned, "before I melt your eyeballs from your skull. You're far too easy to provoke. Always were."

My nerves hacked ragged. I forced my mindmuscle to relax, but only slightly. "And you always talked too much. I'm bored, asshole, so just roast us and get it over with."

A sweet dark chuckle. "You know that's not the way it works. I say when you die, Seeker. Not you, or your glimmery little pet."

"Yeah, yeah," I said carelessly, but my mind sprinted crazy circles. So what the hell did he want, then? "You know, there's something I've always wondered. What stupid bastard died and made you God?"

You have no god but me, my memory intoned inexorably, and I shuddered.

Razorfire's mouth curled, and the flames around us leaped higher, hotter. "God did," he said acidly. "When he put us above the rest and left them all to rot at our whim. God doesn't care, Seeker. God's dead. There's only me."

"You and your maniac ego, you mean."

"I prefer to think of it as class. Their maker despises them behind their backs. I just do it where they can see. I don't make false promises, Seeker. That's the difference between their god and me."

My face scorched, and I smelled burning hair. I had to shield my eyes from the flames. Behind him, in the kitchen, a slab of broken concrete shuddered and fell another foot or so, crushing the fridge and splitting the burning bench into pieces. I eyed the debris surreptitiously. Could I grab a piece in time, I wondered? Could I crush him with it before he burned us both to meat?

Glimmer touched my shoulder, a calm warning, and called out hoarsely. "What do you want?"

Razorfire regarded him, amused, like a parent with a precocious toddler. "It speaks. Fascinating. How's your pretty wife, son?"

Glimmer froze, rigid, and it occurred to me I'd never asked him exactly what Razorfire did to his wife to make him break his cover. The usual, just deliberate violence and threats? Or something more… personal?

Glimmer gritted his teeth hard. "Better off without me. Thanks for the lesson."

A slick, sadistic grin. "That is my pleasure! Seriously. Nothing like learning who your real friends are. But enough cozy chitchat, time's burning. A word with you, Seeker."

"I've got nothing to say to you." I edged my fingers loose, trying to relax. *Don't give yourself away this time. Feel for the power. Let it flow on the air, gently pull it tighter…*

Razorfire crouched, resting forearms on knees, his glossy red coat flowing in the dust. Fire played lovingly between his fingertips, and he teased it, coaxing it into fluid shapes. "Now, that's not true. I only wanted to say I thought you were marvelous tonight."

"You were there?" Dumb question, I realized. Of course he was there. As if he'd miss a chance to see carnage like that.

"Are you kidding? I experienced every heart-stopping moment." He panned with one hand, as if to visualize the scene, and orange flames trailed from his fingers, mesmerizing. "Such theatre! Glass everywhere, blood on the tiles, all that running and screaming. Two ancient and powerful adversaries, a battle of wits and a fight to the death. I assure you, your audience was entranced from the very first line."

I squeezed my eyes shut on images of death, pale faces under that mess of steel, the staring eyes, the blood, my sister's torn silver dress… Oh, Jesus. He'd seen me. Watched me crush all those people to death. Relished every scream.

Maybe he'd even sent Iceclaw there to provoke me. *Just wanted to say I'll be seeing you tonight,* Iceclaw had said on the phone. *You and your new friend.*

Wouldn't be the first time Razorfire had pitched one augmented against another for his own twisted amusement. Maybe the whole thing was part of his plan.

But plan for what?

I blinked, chasing the horrid images away. What's done is done. I couldn't take it back. Not now. Not ever.

Razorfire leaned closer, confidential, and that peculiar incendiary scent thickened. My pulse skittered. He was so close. I could see the tiny beads of sweat on his face, his neat fingernails, the curl of hair at the nape of his neck.

Pretty flames danced over his knuckles, and he watched them, entranced, turning his hands to the light. "Wanna know a secret?"

"No, actually. Any hope I can shut you up?"

"For a moment, when you hung there on that rooftop, I confess I lost faith in you, Seeker."

"So sad," I muttered between clenched teeth. A little more. Just one inch at a time…

He licked his lips. "I know! I really thought you'd shame us all with your weakness. I admit, it brought a tear to my eye. But you didn't let me down."

"I'm sorry, did you say something? I forgot to listen."

"You knew you could survive the fall, you knew he couldn't." His pirouetting flames hypnotized me, seductive. "That was all that mattered. A truly magnificent finale."

"It wasn't like that. It was an accident, you psychopath!" The lie fouled in my mouth, stinking of fear. I flexed my muscle. Behind him, the concrete shuddered and shifted another inch closer.

"No, Seeker. No. It was…" His breath caught, and his eyes flamed brighter, terrible desire that made me tremble. "Invigorating. Seriously. Let's get a room."

"You don't say that to me!" The denial burst from my lips, buoyed on a surging tide of guilt and bitter anger. His poisoned praise sickened me to my soul. And yet… "You don't talk to me, you sick fucking animal. I'm not like you. I'm nothing like you!"

He sighed, a tiny huff of exasperation, and straightened. "Must we go through this again? I'm getting tired of repeating myself. Tell her, will you, puppy dog?"

I'll buy you a few seconds, Glimmer murmured in my head. *Be careful.* He crawled to his feet, stepping into Razorfire's leaping shadow, and hurled a black shimmer of confusion.

It hit the wall of heat haze and sizzled away like water, and Razorfire eyed it, sardonic. But Glimmer just laughed, and threw another one. "Tell her what? That you're a sorry loser with no friends who gets off on tormenting people with party tricks?"

"Well, that wasn't precisely what I'd envisaged…"

I inched the ragged chunk of concrete closer, lifted it from where it lay. It hovered above head height. Dust and rubble rained. The roaring flames and crash of burning furniture obliterated the sound. At the very least, I could throw it at him, slow him up for a few seconds so we could get away. My fist clenched tight with the effort, and sticky sweat poured down inside my coat. Just a little further…

"But if you want to be like that?" Scarlet flame lashed from Razorfire's hand, spearing for Glimmer's face.

Glimmer was quick. He dived, and the flame coiled past him with an angry snap.

But Razorfire was quicker. He unleashed with a stinging wall of fire, and when Glimmer skidded backwards, Razorfire leapt like a crimson-clad spider and grabbed a smoking fistful of Glimmer's hair.

The flames licked his face, his shiny coat, his glossy mask. They didn't burn. He hurled Glimmer against the crumbling wall, and wrapped him in a glittering wreath of purple flame.

"Like my party tricks now?" Smoke hissed from Razorfire's teeth. "How about you tell her that if she moves that chunk of ceiling one more inch, I'll melt the skin from your face?"

Glimmer hissed, and squeezed his eyes shut against the heat, but he couldn't move or escape.

Radiant heat steamed the sweat from my face, and the convection updraft whipped my hair vertical. I screamed, frustration bubbling acid in my heart. "Leave him out of it. This is about us, right? So come get me."

Razorfire just grinned and, with a flick of his outstretched hand, let the flames lick closer to Glimmer. "He'll die slowly, Seeker. In exquisite agony. I've had quite a lot of practice, you see."

The concrete block shuddered in mid-air above our heads. My head ached, squeezed in a horrid vise of tension. My control was slipping. If I dropped the block now, it'd all be over. Razorfire would be crushed. But so would Glimmer. "I'll kill you, you crazy son of a bitch, I swear to God."

"Not before I peel your little pet down to the muscle." Razorfire stood fast, the hot breeze swirling his silken coat around his legs. "Come on, Seeker, admit it. Those jeweled apes in the ballroom meant nothing to you. That test was too easy. You ready to level up?"

Do it! the angry voice inside my head screamed. *Kill the bastard! You might never get this chance again. Think of all the lives you'll save. You killed dozens tonight at Crystal Towers. You're already going to hell. What's one more?*

"I'm not a patient maniac, Seeker." Razorfire's hot-sweet voice ran like evil treacle into my thoughts. "Don't waste my time with your platitudes. Choose."

Around us, walls crashed and burned. The place was filling up with smoke. Soon, the inferno would consume us all.

My overstretched mindmuscle shrieked in agony. Fatigue blurred my eyes. The concrete chunk began to shake, ready to fall. *It isn't your fault,* the seductive voice whispered. *You tried. You weren't strong enough. These things happen. It wasn't your choice. No one will blame you.*

I stared at Glimmer wreathed in deadly flame with sweat running in rivers down his face. He caught my eye, and incredibly, the corner of his mouth twitched, a shadow of that sweet crooked smile.

Draw a line. His angry words flushed back to me, a hot skip

229

in my pulse... or was it Glimmer, right now, whispering in my head? *Pick a side. Stay there.*

I wanted to. God, I wanted to so much, it tore me apart inside. But it was all for nothing if Glimmer died anyway, and Razorfire's lies were legendary.

"Promise me!" I yelled, my voice sucked away by the scorching wind. "Promise me you'll let him go!"

"I would. Truly. I actually think that well of you." A lilt of mocking surprise. "But what's my promise worth to you? No, Seeker, you'll just have to trust me."

He knows you won't do it, the voice cackled, mocking now. *He'd never die to prove a point. He knows you'll give in. Don't give the evil motherfucker the satisfaction. Crush his crazy carcass and be done with it. Why go along with his sick-ass plan?*

Because the evil motherfucker's right.

My heart quailed, and I knew any courage that vengeance-sharp voice gave me was false.

I couldn't do it.

Couldn't kill my only friend to save the world.

I'd let my father's murder go unavenged, let Razorfire go free to pursue his happy-sick plan for that Pyrotox. Let all those innocent people suffer, because I couldn't bear one more stain on my conscience. I was selfish, stupid, weak. A coward. Everything Razorfire despised me for.

Surely, I languished in hell.

I screamed, helpless, and with my last wavering ounce of strength, I hurled the concrete harmlessly against the flame-licked wall.

Crash! The floor shuddered. Jagged fragments tumbled to the ground, lost in dust and smoke, and along with them vanished my last hope of redemption.

Razorfire laughed, dark and delighted and damaged to the core, and deep in my soul, something good and gentle screamed and died.

"We're not finished, Seeker." His tone wasn't gloating or triumphant. More like... satisfied. "The lesson's not done. But there's hope for you. I know it. Be seeing you." And he whirled, and vanished into the smoke.

I howled, and tore after him, but the stinging smoke choked me backwards, and by the time I recovered, he was gone.

I cursed, rich and blistering. Without Razorfire's strange tricks molding them to his will, the flames reverted to nature, roaring hungrily up to the sky, and the spooky wall of fire surrounding Glimmer died.

He stumbled, coughing. His face was scorched, red like sunburn. His shirt had burned through in patches, smeared everywhere with charcoal. A gap had singed into his hair, making the dirty skunk stripe stick up even more.

And his mask was gone. Torn, or burned away, I couldn't tell. But for the first time, I saw his face.

Pale. Haunted. That was all. Not disfigured, not revealing any secrets. Just a young, weary face, darkened by sorrow and soot. He'd told me the truth.

I wanted to thrash my head against the wall, split the aching bones open and let my hideous power bleed out on the floor to die. But I didn't. I just staggered over to Glimmer, and dragged him to his feet. Razorfire was gone. We were still alive. But at what appalling cost?

He gazed up at me. His eyes were reddened from smoke and stinging heat. Around us, everything he'd built burned.

He didn't speak. Just gripped my hands tightly, and let his bruised forehead rest on mine.

I closed my scorched eyes. My burned face stung. He smelled of charcoal and sweat, of everything we'd lost, everything Razorfire had seared away.

I wanted to kiss him. Or slap his face. They seemed equally pointless. Equally false. He thought I was strong because I'd saved him. Thought I'd drawn a line, chosen a side.

All I'd done was fail. Him. Myself. Everyone. And all because I'd let this strange, precious, valiant boy touch my heart.

"Damn you," I whispered tiredly, and turned away.

24

On the surface, everything was burning. The warehouse was gone, jut a pile of blackened, twisted steel and razor-sliced concrete. Smoke and flames billowed four stories high. Sparks shot into the night like malignant fireworks. Broken steel cracked and groaned and, somewhere, glass exploded. The heat was intense. Already the fire had spread to the next building, and a fire crew in their black-and-yellow suits swarmed like bees around their engine, rolling out hoses.

Glimmer and I crawled away into the dust, and ran.

The dark streets loomed with hideous shadows. The rough ground grazed my bare feet. My lungs ached, and so did my head, and fatigue made my limbs shake. I'd torn off my mask and stuffed it inside my coat. Not a good time to be recognized. We were incognito, unremarkable, exposed in the worst way.

I collapsed against a bus stop, where the trolley cars rattled to and fro, and the neon lights of drugstores and pizza joints mingled, dazzling me. I fought to catch my breath. "I can't run any more. Please, just a moment."

"Not yet. Just a little further." And Glimmer supported me, held me by the shoulder, urged me on.

At last, we halted, in a dark and lonely grotto under a railway bridge, where long grass poked between the concrete slabs and a rushing drain gurgled and stank beneath a rusty grille. I sank gratefully to my butt on an upturned milk crate, the remnants of some absent hobo's home-sweet-home. A dead rat rotted by the long concrete wall, ants crawling on the carcass. Above our heads, a train rattled by.

Glimmer collapsed against the wall beside me, and for a few moments, we panted for breath.

I huddled in my silvery coat. I still wore only my stupid black cocktail dress beneath, and though my skin still stung like sunburn from our ordeal, the summer night's warmth had vanished, leaving an empty chill. Above, stars glared, cold and foreign.

"I'm sorry about your place," I said at last. God, what a futile little word. But I didn't know what else to say.

"Yeah," Glimmer replied softly. "Me too."

"Can you save anything? I mean..."

"Data? No. Well... maybe." He shrugged, exhausted, and didn't elaborate.

"Well, I guess we've gotta start somewhere." I emptied my coat pocket. One hand was all I needed. Just my mask, and the phone, with battery half full. "I got this. Whatta you got?"

He searched his pockets. "Phone. Keys. ATM card, account watched of course. And, uh... forty-two dollars and sixty-four cents."

"Dude, we are set." I sat in silence, fingering my phone. Caine's card was still tucked into the case, a sliver of white against the black. For a moment, I even considered it.

Yeah. Call him, Verity. And explain to him why a crazy archvillain chose your *house to burn down.*

Glimmer rolled his shoulders with a sigh. "Look, I'm wasted. Okay if we stay here a while?"

I nodded, numb. Where else did we have to go? And fatigue was dragging me under, a hungry sea monster, into the depths. I couldn't stay awake much longer, let alone run.

Glimmer settled himself on the ground a few feet from me, his back against the curved tunnel wall, and shivered, wrapping his arms tight. He didn't have his jacket on, just his scorched shirt. He'd given the jacket to me, and I'd thrown it aside as we quarreled.

I flushed. That all seemed so stupid now. I didn't even remember what we were arguing about, except that it involved me and Caine and a healthy dose of embarrassment.

Fuck me raw if I wouldn't welcome all that back and be happy as a pig in shit, if it meant things could be the way they were between Glimmer and me. So I'd dropped a ceiling on a few dozen people, and kissed Vincent Caine when I knew Glimmer didn't want me to. We could get past that.

It sure beat the hell out of him knowing I was selfish, a hypocrite and a failure, that I'd lost the courage of my convictions and he could never trust me again.

But we'd never be the way we were. I'd broken that. Me and that sly devil, Razorfire. Who could be out there right now, burning people to death because I hadn't killed him.

I couldn't look Glimmer in the eye. But I wanted to. I wanted to crumple to my knees, grab his gentle chin in my fingers, force him to stare into this scarred face of mine that wasn't half so ugly as the person inside. *Forgive me!* I wanted to implore. *Give me another chance. You're still alive. That has to count for something!*

But I knew it wasn't true.

"Well," Glimmer said after a moment. "Good night, Verity."

"Adonis did it." My voice shone dully, tarnished with my guilt. "I remembered. That's why I fainted. Adonis put me in the asylum. They're all in on it. Every stinking one of them."

A moment of silence, his face in shadow. "I'm sorry."

"Tomorrow, I'm going to ask him why." I said it before I realized I had a plan.

Confront Adonis, make him tell me what happened that night. He was there. He'd seen everything. And then I'd know, for good or ill, and Razorfire could never play his lying guess-me games with me again.

Glimmer's midnight eyes shone in the darkness, bluer than I'd ever seen them. Almost purple. Maybe it was just because his face was stained dark with dirt and blood. Maybe because he wasn't wearing his mask.

Maybe, I'd never really looked before.

"Okay," he said softly, "sounds like a plan." And he closed his eyes, hands loose in his lap.

I swallowed. My body begged me for sleep, but already that nightmare headache lurked behind my eyeballs, threatening to pounce. I cleared my throat. "Glimmer?"

A flutter of feathery lashes. "Yeah?"

My mouth swelled dry. "I can't... I don't want to dream. Not tonight. Can... can you...?"

He didn't say anything. Didn't ask me why. Just extended one hand to me, palm upwards.

He never did ask why, I realized, humbled. All this time. Not once.

Slowly, I crawled over to him, and laid my head on his shoulder. His skin was cold, but underneath, he was so warm. I curled in. He wrapped his arm around me, and for a sweet, elusive moment, his breath lingered in my hair. And then his fingers flickered before my eyes, and the world shimmered and warped, and I sank gratefully into silent darkness.

Seconds later—or was it hours?—Glimmer was shaking my shoulder. "Verity, wake up. You gotta see this."

#

"Huh? Whassup?" I swallowed, thick, and blinked crusty eyes. Sunlight glared, and traffic noise zoomed. Overhead, a train clattered on the bridge. I groaned, and rolled over to bury my face in my elbow.

Glimmer crouched beside me. He kept shaking me, wouldn't let me slip back into the void. "Wake up. Your brother's on TV."

"Uh." That got my attention. I sat up, shielding my eyes from the glare. Our hidey-hole under the bridge looked different in sunlight, no shadows or monsters, not desolate but just empty. Harmless. My muscles ached, but it was a good and distant ache. I'd slept deeply. No nightmares, at least not that I could remember. I rubbed my eyes. "What is it? Show me."

Glimmer leaned against the wall beside me, and we both held his phone and watched.

It was Adonis, all right, and I recognized the meeting room at FortuneCorp that we used for media announcements and Q&As. Apparently, he'd called a conference. Cameras flashed, and the ticker tape across the bottom of the screen read FAMILY OF TERROR VICTIM EQUITY FORTUNE DENOUNCES GALLERY VIOLENCE. On the podium behind the lectern, Adonis looked immaculate, as usual, perfect black suit and red tie... but his face was pale with shock, like he couldn't quite comprehend what had happened.

Behind him, I saw Uncle Mike in a sober suit, the edges of his silvery bracelets shining. And all three of our cousins. Pointy-faced Jeremiah, twitching and tugging at his hair like he always did when he was visible; Harriet, skinny and blond, whose laugh could curdle steel, a teenage version of Equity with her sullen pout and flashing eyes; and shifty-eyed Ebenezer, whose talent was to give people the creeps, limping and twisted in his black greatcoat, his mismatched face for once scrubbed clean.

Jeez, what the hell was he doing there? Uncle Mike didn't let Ebenezer out much. Accidents tended to happen when Eb was around.

"Last night's awful events at Crystal Towers are a tragedy, not only for Sapphire City and for the nation, but for each of us personally." Adonis's face was cold, closed, not giving anything away. "Forty-six families have lost their loved ones. We at Fortune Corporation offer our condolences, and share in your grief. You all know by now that my sister, Equity Fortune, lost her life in the attack. Her courage and dedication as one of this city's assistant district attorneys were second to none. Her influence in the boardroom at FortuneCorp was intelligent and forward-thinking. And she earned a lot of friends and admirers during her campaign to become the city's next mayor. But to me, she'll always be my big sister, gone too soon. I'll miss you, Equity. Rest in peace."

I stared, numb. I wanted to feel something. Equity was my sister, too. We'd grown up together, fought together, argued over company policy and picked fights at Thanksgiving like any other family.

But my sorrow and grief was poisoned with a swift arrow of rage. *She's not worthy to be your sister,* that voice in my head hissed. *She stole from Dad's company and put a lethal weapon in the hands of a villain. She got what she deserved.*

I dragged my attention back to the screen. "But Equity's death will not be meaningless," Adonis was saying. "None of those who lost their lives last night have died in vain. I've spent the early hours of this morning in conference with the city and the Department of Elections, and I'm both proud and humbled to announce that I've been given special dispensation to continue my sister's campaign, in her memory, and in memory of all those whose lives were treacherously snatched away at Crystal Towers. Ladies and gentlemen, I'm Adonis Fortune, and henceforth I'm running for mayor."

A shocked moment of silence, and then applause. More cameras flashed. I laughed, irony like ash in my mouth. "He's got to be kidding."

Glimmer shifted beside me, uncomfortable. "I dunno. He's got charm, you gotta give him that."

"Maybe, if you're a starry-eyed debutante," I grumbled. "Equity at least had gravitas, and a respectable career. Everyone knows Adonis is a snake-oil spin doctor who chases anything in a skirt. No one in their right mind would vote for him. Vincent Caine will kick his ass."

On the tiny screen, Adonis lifted a hand for silence. "But I am not my sister," he continued, "and I cannot in good faith continue with those elements of her platform that rest heavily on my conscience. I'm talking about Equity's policy of conciliation in crime. We all know the Gallery threat has intensified over the past months. After last night's tragedy, we can no longer pretend these people have anything but evil intentions. They wish nothing less than death, terror and the total dissolution of law and order in Sapphire City. I can tell you now, friends, I will not tolerate this. I will not let our city sink into an abyss of fear."

My spine tingled warning. My senses always told me when Adonis was up to something, or so I'd thought. But at this distance, I couldn't tell for sure. And I couldn't see the faces of the press corps. Couldn't see if Adonis was using his augment. "Damn it, where's he going with this?"

"Shh," said Glimmer absently. "Listen."

"Therefore, as the new chairman of Fortune Corporation, I'll be making some key changes. I'll personally be taking over as head of operations, and we'll be putting the full weight of our security resources to work, in concert with the Sapphire City PD and with the full cooperation of the DA's office, to make our streets safe for ordinary citizens. That offer's regardless of the outcome of Tuesday's election, friends, and you have my personal assurance, as well as the full agreement of FortuneCorp's board, that we will dedicate our full resources to getting these Gallery terrorists off the streets and into the county lock-up where they belong."

"Full agreement of the board, my ass," I grumbled. "They didn't bloody well ask me." FortuneCorp contracted out private security personnel by the thousand. To deploy them in concert with the PD, with full police powers and a mandate to scour the streets clean…

A privateer was just a pirate with a license, after all. It sounded all too much like a private army.

But would I have dissented? I wondered uneasily. After last night?

"But that's not all." Adonis's voice took on a strange, delighted tone. It gave me the heebies. "For too long, entities like FortuneCorp have operated in secrecy, our everyday operations hidden from the public eye by legal firewalls and commercial confidentiality. No longer, friends. If the people of Sapphire City are to invite us onto their streets, into their homes and businesses, give us the privilege and grave responsibility for their safety, I believe they deserve nothing less than one hundred percent transparency."

My mouth dropped open. "Oh, holy Jesus," I whispered, "he isn't…"

"If you honor me with your vote, I promise you complete and abject honesty. And to show you how deeply I believe in this promise, I'm prepared to act on it in advance." Adonis lifted his arms at his sides, to encompass Uncle Mike and our cousins, who stood behind him in a row like the usual suspects, a line-up of four of the most dangerous people on the planet. "And so, I give you Fortune Corporation," Adonis announced. "Michael, if you please."

My blood stung, somehow hot and cold at the same time. *Oh yes, he certainly is.*

Uncle Mike stepped forward, stretching out one hand, and a ball of blue static erupted in his palm.

Shocked gasps, murmuring. Someone screamed. Flashbulbs went crazy. Uncle Mike clapped his hands, and the crackling electricity vanished in a wisp of smoke.

"Illuminatus." Adonis's voice was flat, matter-of-fact.

Jeremiah inhaled, and vanished. "Phantasm," said Adonis.

Harriet giggled, and behind her, a glass wall shattered. "Melody."

Ebenezer grinned his slimy grin at a woman in the front row, and she dropped to the floor on her knees, shaking, her face drained of color. "Bloodshock."

Seductive light glittered from Adonis's fingertips, so subtle I'd have missed it if I didn't know what to look for. An augmented glow tainted his smile, and around the room, rapt silence fell. "I'm Adonis Fortune. I'm Narcissus. And this is my family."

241

"Jesus," I whispered. "He's unleashing on them. They'll lap up every word."

"I know that some of you are already turning from us in fear." Adonis was talking directly at the camera now, that practiced orator's cadence lifting his words. "So let me put your minds at rest. We are augmented, but we're not the Gallery. We'll fight to protect you with every last trick at our disposal, and we won't shrink from meeting those Gallery villains on their own despicable level. In fact, with your mandate on Tuesday, I intend to instigate a policy of engage-on-sight. We won't wait for the villains to attack innocent people again before we strike. We intend to take the fight to them."

"Vote for me at this election and we'll face a harrowing time, I won't deny that. It won't pass in peaceful safety, this dark night of Sapphire City's soul. And it won't be pretty. Blood will be shed before we're through. But when that glorious sunrise comes, I promise you, the Gallery will be banished forever."

Rabid horror gnawed at my bones. Fuck. Had this been his plan all along?

Events played in my mind, an awful silent movie jerking in fast-forward. He'd gotten sick of Dad's insistence on secrecy, so when Dad died, he'd taken his opportunity. Rid himself of me because he knew I'd never go along with it. Dad putting Equity in charge must have been a setback. But Adonis just bided his time, waited for Equity to become vulnerable. Perhaps he'd even unleashed on her, used his power to talk her into stealing Pyrotox for Razorfire. And Uncle Mike was obviously in on it. Look at him, standing up there like this wasn't everything Dad despised.

Create a threat, convince everyone the only possible response is war. Oldest trick in the warmonger's book.

And when I'd showed up again to throw a bomb in the works, Adonis had eliminated me a second time…

Razorfire wasn't even there… The words jabbed at my chest, a sharp accusing finger, and I couldn't speak.

Jesus. What if Adonis had murdered Dad, too?

I trembled. It was all just speculation. I had no evidence. The only way I'd know for sure was to confront him and demand the truth.

But I wanted to howl, climb through that tiny screen and scream at them all that they were being manipulated, that my handsome brother could make them believe anything with a flick of his fingers and a smile.

That Iceclaw and Weasel and Witch and the rest were just minnows in the shark pond. That Razorfire had dirtier, more destructive weapons at the ready, that he'd poison the city and burn it to a puff of ash, just to catch Adonis in a lie.

It wasn't just about death, no no, death was far too bland for the likes of us. We'd all die tortured, broken, corrupted, knowing we were headed for hell.

These poor, powerless, normal sods had no idea who they were dealing with.

But I couldn't do anything. Not abandoned and alone under this grotty bridge in the suburbs. I could only listen, aghast, as my brother undid everything it had taken my father thirty years to achieve.

But even as I shuddered, sick, part of me relished it.

Open battle. No rules. Just me and my enemies, to the death.

Adonis was coming to the end of his declaration of war. "Anyone who isn't with us is against us," he called. "To that end, I implore all the augments out there who don't wish to be hunted down as villains to come forward. You'll find us generous to those who prove themselves friends."

I snorted. "Yeah, right. Good luck with that."

"But this is no amnesty," Adonis warned. "We will not offer mercy to those who have shown by their actions that they are enemies of the people. You know I'm talking about the multiple murderer, Razorfire, and his allies. In particular, those responsible for last night's tragedy at Crystal Towers." On the screens behind him, images flashed up, masked faces in close-up. Razorfire. Iceclaw. Weasel. A bunch of others I only vaguely recognized.

And, of course, Glimmer and me.

"These villains are our targets. May their capture be swift, and justice be served." Adonis swept the watching crowd with his sparkling blue gaze. "In conclusion, friends, this day heralds a new era of hard-won peace and power to the people. In memory of my late father, Thomas Fortune, otherwise called Blackstrike, murdered by Razorfire and the Gallery. And my sister Equity, also called Nemesis, tragically killed at Crystal Towers. We are augmented. We are Fortune Corporation. And we are on your side."

Applause broke out, rapturous.

And if they'll believe that, they'll believe anything.

I switched the phone off, appalled, trying to beat down the treacherous, seductive fire in my blood, that passionate revenge-thirsty beast in my heart who screamed for war. "Jesus on a jumping bean. Did we just get conscripted into the global war on common sense?"

Glimmer chewed his lip. "Nice move," he commented. "Pulled the rug out from under your buddy Caine, that's for sure. A moment ago Caine was the take-no-prisoners, law-and-order candidate. Now he's the bleeding-heart civil rights advocate. Hell of a reinvention."

"Is that all you've got to say?" I wriggled to my feet. "Adonis just started a damn war. What do you think Razorfire's gonna do when he hears 'engage on sight'? Break out the popcorn and catch some cable re-runs?"

Glimmer shrugged. "Isn't that what we've been doing? Engaging on sight?"

"Well, yeah, but… fuck me raw, Glimmer, don't tell me you agree with this?"

For a second, his eyes darkled with indefinable desire. "No, I do not. But what choice do we have? You heard the man. We're public enemies. Any cop, or security guard, or citizen with a grudge and a shotgun will be coming after us. You planning to lie down and take that?"

My lip trembled. "Surely they won't believe him. Will they?"

"Hey, you tell me." Glimmer didn't mention that Adonis was right, that Crystal Towers was my fault. But his tact only maddened me. Then, his mouth twisted. "That glittery thing he does? Looked like world-class mindfuck to me. Apparently I'm the expert on screwing with people's minds."

My face heated at the reminder of those accusations I'd flung at him. I glared daggers. "Not funny."

"Wasn't meant to be."

"Fine. Fuck it." I dragged my hands through my scorched hair, and fresh determination soured cold in my heart. "You wanna know what we're gonna do? There's only one thing we *can* do."

"And what's that?"

25

"Kill my brother."

There. I said it.

But it didn't feel good. I couldn't just brush it off, like an unpleasant task that I knew had to be done. It made me want to scream, tear the ruined skin from my face. Howl to heaven that I'd do anything, I'd make up with Equity, toe the company line, take back every fight and disagreement and petty sibling squabble, if I could only put things back the way they were.

But I couldn't. Adonis had destroyed everything I'd ever been, everything I ever wanted to be, for his own selfish ambition. And if he got his way? The city would burn and we'd be left standing in the ruins.

This was the only way. I'd failed Razorfire's test with Glimmer. I wouldn't fail this one. And when I was finished, and my beautiful, beloved, treacherous brother had breathed his last?

I'd hunt Razorfire down, and kill him, too.

Glimmer stared at me, shadows flitting across his eyes. "You can't do that."

"Why the hell not?" I warmed to my subject. "He's destroyed everything my father worked his life away for, to get thirty seconds of glory on TV. He's betrayed me, my sister, my entire family. And now he wants to plunge the city into war. I'd say it's a fair trade, wouldn't you?"

"But..." For once, Glimmer was lost for words. "Your own brother..."

"Didn't stop him when he fed me to the murder machine, did it?" My anger flared, hot and prickly, and my mindmuscle coiled tight. "Didn't stop him brainwashing my sister and handing her to Razorfire on toast."

"You can't be sure that's what happened."

"What other explanation is there? Why else would he get rid of me like that, if it wasn't to cover his tracks?"

"I don't know," said Glimmer fiercely. "But that doesn't prove he's a traitor. It doesn't mean he deserves to die. It only proves what we've known all along, Verity, which is that you don't have a fucking clue what happened."

"I know enough." I rounded on him, air stretching with an invisible groan at my fingertips.

"Do you?" His midnight gaze snapped onto mine, and wouldn't let go. "Why do you really want to kill him, Verity? Is it because you want justice? Revenge? Or is it because you're afraid to find out what really happened that night?"

"What the fuck is that supposed to mean?"

"Think about it!" he snapped. "If Adonis wanted you out of the way so badly, why didn't he just kill you?"

"Wh...?" I swallowed, confused.

"Blackstrike was already dead, right? Adonis could do whatever he liked. If he's the monster you say he is, why bother with all that nonsense at the asylum? What's one more corpse?"

"But..." I stared, cold. He had a point. "Then what?"

"I have no idea." Glimmer's gaze was steadfast. "I just know there's more to this than meets the eye."

"Okay, fine," I snapped. "But that doesn't change the fact that Adonis is hijacking FortuneCorp and starting a war."

"Oh, right, I forgot," said Glimmer sarcastically. "FortuneCorp versus the Gallery, heavyweight championship of the world. Party time for villains everywhere. And your solution is to kill the only person who's got a chance in hell of winning?"

I stared, aghast. "I don't believe this. You're taking his side!"

"I am *not* taking his side." Glimmer yanked his skunk stripe, frustrated. "I'm just saying you can only fight one enemy at a time. You've gotta choose your battles."

"That is such a load of crap. My battle got chosen for me. Adonis chose it, the night he bolted augmentium to my head."

"Look. I'm sorry for what happened to you, so help me I am, and if Adonis did it, then you deserve your reckoning. But right now I'd rate Razorfire and a truckload of Pyrotox as a bigger threat!"

He made sense. I knew he did. But insane cackling voices in my head drowned out my reason. *Hot soulful kisses, tearful sighs, musky feminine perfume drifting from my hair… My father's voice, cold and rippled with shadows: Get your hands off that, you're not fit to touch it… Don't hurt her, I'm warning you… You have no god but me…*

I gritted my teeth, fighting off a burning headache, but the pain crushed my vision to splinters. I reeled, my stomach bubbling with bile and bad memories I didn't understand. "I can't live like this," I gasped. "I have to know. I have to make him tell me!"

Glimmer held me, forced me upright, his silken hair rough on my face. "Verity," he said urgently, "listen to me. You can't go to him. He has your entire family on his side. You can't win. They'll kill you!"

"What do you care?" The words burst out, stained with bile and sorrow. I wanted to swallow them, but it was too late, and my cheeks fired like fever.

His face drained white. "That is one hell of a thing for you to say to me."

"Don't pretend you give a damn," I said spitefully. "Aren't you the white knight of Sapphire City? Fighting for justice? Willing to die for your stupid cause?"

"Yes," he retorted. "I'd die for my 'stupid cause', if I thought my death would mean something. But this is just a waste. It achieves nothing."

"It'll fucking well make me feel better!" I turned away, grinding my scarred cheek against the wall. I wanted it to hurt. But the gritty pain only made me feel worse.

"Oh, right. So you'll just give up, is that it?" Glimmer wouldn't let me hide. He strode around in front of me and wrenched my chin up, forcing me to look into his eyes. "I thought you had more courage."

I laughed, sick. "Don't you *dare* accuse me. You're not so gallant as all that." And I grabbed his scarred wrist and forced it to the light.

He tore it away, but not before I saw the burning shame in his eyes. "Yeah," he said, softly, as rough with rage and sorrow as I'd ever heard him. "Yeah, I walked that road once. I couldn't see a light in the darkness. But you know what changed my mind?"

I shook my head in disgust. I was ashamed that I'd punched so low. But I was too enraged and upset to care.

But he wouldn't let me avoid his eyes. "I realized what happens if I die."

"What?" I asked grudgingly. "A mess on the carpet? No more cheesy puffs?"

"Nothing," he said steadily. "Not a goddamn thing. Except Razorfire wins. Think about that." And he released me, and turned away.

"But…" I stumbled after him, grabbed him, forced him back around. "But he's already won! Can't you see that? He's already proved how weak and corruptible I am. I had the chance to kill him and I couldn't go through with it."

"Because you decided life meant more than victory. Doesn't sound like a defeat to me."

I laughed, crazy rainbows flashing before my eyes. "But that's how he does it, don't you see? That's how he wins. He makes us think we're heroes. We think we're taking this admirable moral high ground, when all we're really doing is losing, Glimmer. Over and over again, we lose."

His night-blue eyes crackled black, and a silver shimmer wrapped his clenching fists. "So you should've killed me," he said flatly. "Is that it? You should've killed me to get to him."

"Damn right, I should have." Fuck, I was crying now, acid tears that carved hot trenches in my face. Fiercely, I scraped them away. They kept coming. "I should've burned us both, if that's what it took. At least I would have taken that sick psycho motherfucker with me."

"Then why didn't you?" His words speared me like arrows, relentless, unstoppable. "Huh? Tell me that. If you're so sure that death is the solution, why the hell didn't you kill us both?"

"Because I'm weak." My stomach cramped, poisoned, and I fell to my knees, gripping my aching head in my hands, to stop it splitting in half and spilling my selfishness out where everyone could see. "Okay? I'm weak and pathetic and afraid, and Razorfire's strong, and that's why we'll never win!"

Glimmer was on his knees, too, holding me. "That's what he wants you to think. It's just a filthy game he plays with your mind."

"No!" I screamed the word, and my voice broke. I scrabbled to my feet, unsteady. "No, I won't back down this time. I'll go to Adonis, find out the truth. And if it's like I think…"

"Okay." Glimmer was still on his knees in the dirt. His hands clenched in his lap, and muscles bunched in his arms, twitched in his thighs, like he was ready to explode. "Say it all works out like you say. Say you somehow get in there, past Illuminatus and Phantasm and all the rest of them, without getting yourself killed. Say you confront Adonis, and he says, 'yeah, you got me! I stuck you in that asylum. Hell, I killed Blackstrike, too, and brainwashed Equity into giving Pyrotox to Razorfire. I even got her killed on purpose so I can be mayor.'" Shadows flitted over Glimmer's face, coiling in his hair. "What then? Can you really kill your own

251

brother, just to prove Razorfire wrong? What'll it achieve? The war will still go on. Do you care so much about revenge that it's worth your soul?"

Yes! I tried to scream, but hot stickiness blocked my throat.

Glimmer snaked to his feet, and stalked up to me. So close I could taste the sweet vanilla-spice scent of him, under sweat and dirt and charcoal-smeared pain. He leaned over me, his lips in my hair, like he didn't want anyone to hear whatever terrible secret he told me. "I like you, Verity." His whisper tingled the skin below my ear. "I care what happens to you. Believe me, that doesn't happen every day."

My nerves grated across a sharp edge. "Listen, you don't have to—"

"Shh." He stopped my lips with a warm finger, and he tasted of fire and blood. "Just listen. I have this little problem with promises, you see, and I promised you I'd do anything I could to help. It's too late for me to back out. I will follow you into the fire, if that's what you want. So I'm going to ask you a question. And please, answer me honestly if you can."

I held my breath, my thoughts muddling like watercolors in the rain. Jeez, was he going to ask if I'd do the same for him? I already had, damn him. I'd already followed him to hell, down in that inferno of a basement, the moment I couldn't hurl that concrete and let him burn…

"Why do you care so much what Razorfire thinks of you?"

All the air sucked from my lungs.

I gulped like a beached fish, and reeled away.

Red hot knives stabbed my skull. I squeezed my eyes shut, tore at my temples with shaking fingers, but it didn't help. It didn't make the awful truth any easier to bear.

I'd failed, sure, as a hero. I'd killed Iceclaw when I should have handed him over to the police. I'd crushed those people at Crystal Towers when I should have let the villain go rather than waste so many lives. And I'd let Razorfire escape so I could ease my conscience, when the right thing to do was kill him and wear the pain.

Yeah, I'd failed as a crime-fighting hero. Dad would be disgusted with me, and the thought of his disappointment jabbed poisoned thorns deep into my heart.

But it hurt worse that my archenemy didn't think me a worthy adversary. That after all I'd endured, I was still just easy game.

That I'd thrown everything I had at Razorfire, and he'd just *laughed* at me.

And as for Glimmer...

My skin crawled, mortified, like hungry worms festered under there, ready to burst out and consume my living flesh. Glimmer saw through me like glass. He knew I was selfish, proud, too scared to suffer for my convictions. He knew that if I went to find Adonis, I'd back down from the hard decisions and get myself killed.

And still he'd come with me anyway. For the sake of a stupid promise I barely remembered him making, this brave and talented boy would give his life.

Glimmer had a moral core of steel and the courage to match. Me? All I had was my stupid pride.

Shame poured like molten metal over my soul, and set it on fire.

"I thought you were my friend," I spat. "Just stay the hell away from me." And I turned, my face aflame with tears, and ran.

#

Half an hour later, I stumbled off the trolley car downtown, with golden late afternoon sun hammering my aching skull. Workers poured from office buildings, time to go home, and the trolley car lurched away with a fresh load. Traffic inched by, taillights flashing red, on, off, on, off. A skinny guy in a suit hung out his window, staring at me.

I hunched in my sweaty coat and walked on.

Glimmer hadn't followed me. He hadn't called my name. He

just stood and watched me go.

I slouched in an office doorway, catching my breath, wiping the sticky remnants of tears from my face. Would I ever see Glimmer again? I didn't know. But I had the feeling that this was one insult he wouldn't accept in silence. I'd gone way too far this time. He'd never forgive me.

I'd hopped the train a few blocks from the bridge. I didn't have money for a ticket, so I had to steal, grabbing a handful of change from a street performer's guitar case as he played "Stairway to Heaven" on the station steps. He cursed at me, shaking his dreadlocked head like it happened all the time. I didn't turn back, though rote-learned guilt stung my tongue bitter. *I need the money more than you do, you damn welfare cheat. Play some Kings of Leon and shut the fuck up.*

Now, I pushed myself upright, straightened my clothes. I still wore my cocktail dress, torn and smeared with dirt, and the Seeker's shiny gunmetal-gray coat. Dirty scabs crusted my bare feet, and my once-elaborate hairdo was disintegrating. I looked like I'd dressed from some warped charity store and then rolled in the dirt for a few hours. I didn't care. In a few minutes it probably wouldn't matter anyway.

Across the street, the FortuneCorp tower glittered in the falling sun. Workers exited through the lobby, suits and briefcases and weary eyes. Above them, those sheer glass walls flashed, flawless, stretching endlessly to the sky.

Casually, I surveyed the lobby, checking exits, lights, manpower. Increased security, four men on the desk when before there were two, only normals but armed and alert for trouble. CCTV would be on and recording. Panic screens ready to slam down, alarms waiting to shriek my doom. I didn't see Uncle Mike, or the rest of my family. Maybe they were waiting for me inside.

Inside my coat pocket, I wrapped my mask tightly around my clenched fist. It didn't give me comfort, like it used to. It just made me feel like a fraud. The smell of scorched leather only made me remember Razorfire, and I let go.

I darted across the street, dipping between traffic. Masking up was useless anyway. My disguise had already been peeled away, by Glimmer's misguided tact and Caine's creepy sympathy and Razorfire's fucked-up mind tricks. I was well and truly in the clear, in all my tarnished, ugly nakedness.

Verity Fortune, once known as the Seeker. Coward, liar, slayer of innocents.

The shimmering glass lobby doors slid open for me. I strode in, walking briskly but not running, and headed straight for the granite-topped security desk, where the black-suited guards did their unobtrusive business. I wanted them all to see exactly who I was when they tried to kill me.

Not that I was planning to give them the chance.

I flung my fist out in front of me, ripped the desk from its foundations and slammed it into the wall.

Glass shattered and tinkled. Tiles exploded. Trashing this place was becoming a habit. I broke into a sprint. The desk bounced and smashed on the floor, its granite façade snapping like plastic. Two security guards crumpled, groaning, bones broken.

The third guy had dodged the flying desk by a few inches, and he staggered to his feet, his brain taking a few precious seconds to assimilate what was going on. I sprinted for him and crash-tackled him to the floor. Big guy, muscled hard, and he fell hard too. The back of his crew-cut head cracked into the tiles, and he grunted, his mouth wobbling slack.

I jumped to my feet, standing over him. Groggily, he reached for his gun, but I swept it from his hand with a flex of mindmuscle, and the butt slapped into my palm.

I caught hold two-handed, and leveled it swiftly at his face. "Hit that alarm and I put a bullet in his throat," I snapped, and behind me, the fourth guy halted with his beefy hand an inch from the button.

Black satisfaction roiled through me like a storm. Ah, yes, I knew the secret now, and it was so easy I laughed, strange and beautiful.

Normal people? They don't want to die. And they don't want their friends to die. To win, you only need to be willing to jump into the void.

Or be so desperate to escape the void that you'll do anything.

The alarm dude, a big bald African-American guy, looked at me like I'd sprouted a second head, and his expression only made me laugh harder.

But he had the presence of mind to move while he thought I was distracted. His hand edged towards that alarm button, and I flicked the pistol's safety off with my thumb.

"Nuh-uh. Back it away," I warned, still chuckling. "You guys don't get paid enough to be heroes. All I want is to see Adonis. You can make that happen, and go home safe and happy tonight. Or, you can fight me, and there'll be blood on the floor to clean up and a pretty wife and kids crying on the news. Your choice."

He made the right one, of course, and in a minute or two, I rode the elevator up to the fifty-sixth floor alone. The semi-weightless lurch as I ascended, combined with the familiar pine scent of air freshener, made me dizzy. I gripped my gun tighter, warding off the flashbacks. Last time I'd made this journey, I'd done it with Adonis at my side and thirst for justice in my heart.

Was that what I wanted this time? I wondered, as the figures on the floor display flickered, 35, 36, 37... Justice? Did I want my brother to pay for what he'd done? Or did I just want to hurt him? To watch him suffer as I'd suffered, to force an explanation from his bleeding mouth before I shoved this pistol barrel in it and blew his lying head off?

My skin tingled, warm. The floor number reached 56, and stopped, and the weightless world hissed to a halt beneath my feet, returning me to gravity and sunlight and other unpleasantly real things.

Guess I'd find out soon enough.

The elevator door whispered open, and I gripped my pistol firmly in my sweaty hands, and strode out.

26

The receptionist's desk was unattended, and the glass security door stood ajar.

Light spilled in, stained blood-red by the sunset. Shadows lurched, grotesque, the plant's misshapen leaves, the sofa a hulking beast preparing to spring.

Beside Dad's brown leather chair, a single circle of light sprang from a metal lamp onto the glass table. And on the table sat a yellow plastic crate.

My blood clotted cold. My vision shimmered, pain and disbelief. But I didn't need to read the writing to know what it said:

BIOHAZARD
KEEP REFRIGERATED
INFECTIOUS WASTE – DO NOT OPEN

I stumbled forward, blind, my thoughts a whirlpool of gritty black poison I couldn't penetrate. There must be some explanation. Some other reason for that foul crate crouching in my brother's office. Some saving grace that didn't mean I'd been lied to like a child from the very beginning, that Adonis never loved me, that everything I'd ever believed was ashes on the wind.

"Hello, Vee," said Adonis. "I've been expecting you."

In Dad's chair. Immaculate suit, red tie, his blond hair unruffled.

My heart pounded. I tried to talk, but my throat seized dry. My mindmuscle froze, impotent at the sight of him. All I could do was extend my shaking hands, aim the pistol at him.

But I didn't even do that.

I couldn't.

My nerves shredded, hacked to bits by my own weakness. I wanted to howl. My knees shook. Sweat seeped from my hair, trickling down my burned face. Fresh agony drove spikes down through my skull into my spinal cord. *Don't hurt her, I'm warning you… It's for your own good, Verity… You have no god but me…*

I made some strangled sound, like a drowning person struggling to the surface, and choked out the only word I could manage. "Why?"

A sky-blue stare, unreadable. "Give me the pistol."

I scrabbled to hold the gun, my sweaty palms slipping. "Tell me why! I'll shoot you, I swear to God."

But golden come-hither glittered in his gaze, and numbly I let my fingers relax, let him reach out and steal my little metal friend from my unresisting hands.

So easily, he'd unleashed on me. So coldly. Like we'd never trusted each other at all.

Adonis set the pistol neatly beside the crate. My sweat dripped from the grip onto the polished glass. "I told you I had something to show you. Do you want to see it, or do you just want to accuse me?"

"Why did you do it?" My voice tore itself free, and cracked like crystal in a vise. "You had me tortured. You lied to Equity so she'd do your dirty work. Christ, Ad, did you kill Dad? Is that what happened?" I collapsed onto the sofa, hugging my arms to my chest and rocking there. Back, forth, like clockwork, but it didn't soothe the chaos in my soul. On the table, the yellow crate sneered at me, sniggering with snide cratey laughter, and I shuffled away from it, lest it bite. "And what's *that* doing here? Did Razorfire give it to you? Are you going to…?"

"That's, like, eighty-five questions. Which answer do you want first?"

"Don't be so goddamn reasonable. Just tell me the fucking truth!"

"All right. You want the truth? Yes, I sent you to the asylum. Did it ever occur to you to ask why?"

"Every damn day." My stomach boiled, salty soup. Finally, I had the truth from his mouth, and it didn't make me feel vindicated or satisfied. It just made me want to throw up.

"I mean, really ask," he insisted, harsh. "You're my sister and I love you. Do you think I'd make that decision lightly? Don't you think I'd rather do almost anything than put you through that pain?"

"I didn't—"

"No, you didn't. Can you really face the truth about what happened, Vee?"

"Enough with the platitudes, okay? I don't believe them anymore. Just tell me why."

Adonis laughed, sharp with bitterness that shocked me cold. It wasn't like him. "Do you even care? Or did you just want to blow my head off to make yourself feel better? Seems that's your style lately."

My head throbbed, and behind me something smashed. My stomach heaved. I fisted my blurring eyes, fighting off the sickening pain. My mindsense teetered out of control, and desperately I held on. "Don't provoke me, Ad," I forced through teeth set on edge. "It's not a good time."

He stared at me, eyes narrowing. "Jesus, you really don't remember. You haven't figured it out. Those doctors really did the job on you, didn't they?"

Sinister laughter echoed in my soul. I huddled, shaking, bathed in sweat. "Please. I can't take this! Just tell me what the fuck's going on."

"One question first," he said coolly. "You answer, I'll tell you what I know. But you might not like it."

Numbly, I nodded. I'd lost my family, my livelihood, my only friend. I had nothing left to lose.

"When you dropped that ceiling at Crystal Towers, how did you feel?"

The memories burst in, black and stinking, as if some dam had broken and all the poisons lurking in the mud flowed out to swamp me. *Vincent Caine, kissing me, the seductive flavor of mint and danger. I murmur, pressing closer, and slip into desire's sweet darkness... Iceclaw, laughing, swinging from the roof to taunt me, you're a weakling, Seeker, he says, you're weak and we're strong and you're never gonna win, and I scream, just you fucking watch me... and then Equity's silver dress in a pile of twisted iron and glass, torn and soaked in blood...*

"Sick," I whispered. "Guilty. Out of control."

Kind of like I felt right now.

Adonis's deep blue gaze stripped my soul bare, and I shuddered in horror I didn't understand. What did he see, when he stared at me like that? His sister, gone rogue? A villain, an enemy to be hunted? Something once valued, now broken, fit only to be discarded?

At last, he nodded. "Fair enough. I promised you answers." He pointed at the laughing yellow crate. "Where did *that* come from? Someone express-couriered it to me this morning after my press conference. No return address. But I can guess. Do you know what's in it?"

I nodded, numb. "It's Pyro—"

"Pyrotox," he finished for me, cold. "Do you know who invented it?"

"We did."

"Very good. I learned that this morning, after I had the contents

261

analyzed. And now it's in Gallery hands. An unfortunate accident, wouldn't you say?"

"That's what I was trying to tell you." I hugged my elbows tighter, shivering. Did I really believe he knew nothing about it? "Equity stole it."

"Did she?" Adonis's gaze sharpened like ice. So different from my Glimmer's gentle midnight blue. "Are you sure?"

I swallowed, uncomprehending. "I saw her. We hacked the security footage in the lab."

"Ah, yes. Security cameras. Come, take a look." Adonis walked to his desk. I followed, and stood there, rubbing my goose-pimpled arms.

He woke up his display, and the screen sprang to life, muted colors hovering a few feet above the desktop. He flicked through a few files until he found the one he wanted. "After what you said last night at the party, I had my suspicions. So I went hunting, and this afternoon, the lab rats found this."

I already knew what I'd see. The science lab, 6:45 a.m. Desks and consoles, everything blurred out by the camera so no one could poach any secrets...

I gasped, ice shimmering through my veins.

This footage wasn't blurred.

Adonis had the original recording, direct from the camera, before the digital smearing was applied to safeguard the company's secrets. You could see everything, in perfect, full-color high definition.

My heart quailed. I didn't want to watch. But I had to know.

Adonis swiped through the film with one finger, speeding along until Equity's slim figure appeared. There she was, walking in from the bottom of the frame. Dark suit, pony-tail, bracelets gleaming. She sat at the computer console, pulled out her mobile device, plugged it in.

I pointed. "There she is. She did it. Right on camera."

But Adonis just smiled, ghostly. "Look again." With two sliding fingers, he zoomed the image in.

Not on Equity.

On the glass partition in front of her.

Where a reflection of her face shone back at her. Obscured in the blurred footage I'd seen at Glimmer's. In this one, it shone pristine like a mirror.

My eyeballs swelled, aflame. Something in my head stretched like creaking rubber, a squirt of desperate agony, and *snapped*.

The thief wasn't Equity.

She was me.

27

I stumbled backwards, falling over the desk. My heart burst in two, and my blood coursed cold. My hands flew up to cover my face, and I gasped for air, but it wouldn't come, only hot black emptiness, flooding in to smother me...

A chart slices my finger, stinging. A paper cut. I suck it, the blood a coppery spritz in my mouth, and keep flicking through, weapon schematics and diagrams and patent applications and... Hmm, what's this? A chemical formula. Diagrams of a molecule, like a spiky spider with carbons and hydrogens, aluminums and a single, sinister sulfur... I read the specifications, and my pulse quickens. Looks interesting. Might be of use. It's stamped PROJECT DISCONTINUED, with a date last year and my father's scribbled initials. Curiouser and curiouser. Maybe there's more on the computer. I note the file number and the date, and keep flicking... A shuffling noise pricks my ears, and I glance over my shoulder. Someone's coming. Best not be seen. Better get out of here...

My vision blurred black. Adonis steadied me, kept me from falling. He didn't accuse, or judge. He just held me, and let me fight my way back from the edge of the abyss.

At last, I wheezed in a breath, my eyes bulging. "That's me," I gasped. "It's me. I did it. But… I'm wearing her clothes. Her haircut. Her damn bracelets, for fuck's sake. Why would I…? Oh, Jesus."

I collapsed on my butt on the desk's edge, panting, my body aching and screaming and avoiding the truth with any noise it could make.

I'd framed her.

I'd stolen the Pyrotox formula, and made it look like Equity was to blame.

Adonis let me go, stepped back. His face was cold, an impenetrable mask. "You don't remember."

I shuddered, the horrid images gnawing at my soul. "No! I mean, not until now. But didn't you already know? Isn't that why you…?"

"I had no idea," he interrupted. "I told you. I only found this today. I'd never even heard of Pyrotox until this morning, let alone the fact that we invented the rotten stuff."

Icy dread spiked my spine. If this wasn't the reason he'd imprisoned me, then… "There's more, isn't there? Tell me!"

Adonis didn't answer. He just dragged two hands through the hair on the nape of his neck, scrunching it tight, a startling reminder of Glimmer that I really didn't need. "You're honestly telling me you have no idea why you stole those files?"

"No." But the word made no sound. Horror had already sucked my voice away.

Because it was pretty damn obvious what had happened to those chemical schematics. Razorfire had sent Adonis the finished, improved, more deadly product this morning. Just to gloat. Which meant…

Adonis stared at me, despairing, and the bleeding blackness in his gaze made me want to scream and hide. "I didn't want to show you this. But I can see there's no choice. I'm sorry, Vee."

Then don't! I wanted to scream. *I don't want to know. Please.*

But he'd already flicked through the files on his screen, and popped up another video recording. A broad expanse of steel, gleaming beneath scudding storm clouds. Security spotlights shone over an access door, a steel-railed stairwell, the square tops of air-conditioning ducts. In the display's corner, a date-time counter showed 00:47.

FortuneCorp's roof, forty-seven minutes past midnight.

The missing security footage from the night Dad died.

My pulse scrambled, a frightened animal trying to escape. "But this file was gone," I argued. Like denying it could make the awful thing go away. "We checked the code. It was like someone deleted it—"

"I deleted it," Adonis said gently. "I didn't want anyone to know."

My eyes squeezed shut, so tightly my head wanted to explode from the pressure. I didn't want to see.

But I forced my lids open, and though my eyes burned like I'd hacked at them with acid-dipped sandpaper, I made myself look.

For once, my helplessness made me strong. I'd already lost everything. I'd come too far to shrink away now.

Let me see, for good or ill. Let me gaze upon my soul.

The footage began to play, and as the lightning crackled and thundered over FortuneCorp's roof, it stabbed deep into my mind and ripped it open. I gasped, agony crushing my skull until my vision flashed purple and white like crazy stars....and in a splash of raw, blood-soaked certainty, I *remembered*.

#

I climb, six stories over smooth glass walls, the glittering city lurching a dizzy distance below. Clouds scud overhead. The storm is on its way, and the air smells of ozone, sharp and fresh. Its power energizes me. My feet scrabble for the cracks, and my sweaty hands slip, but I carry on, muscles aching. The pack strapped to my back is mercilessly heavy, weighing me down like death. Lightning crashes, deafening. The glass wall flashes its reflection, stained like fire in the reddish moon. I hold on, the world shaking.

My limbs shudder with fatigue. My head aches like poison, my thoughts stretched to ripping point in too many different directions, and somewhere inside me, a lost, distant voice I barely recognize screams raggedly at me to stop this madness.

But I clamp my will down tight, and the voice strangles to silence.

I have to reach the top. The building is full of enemies, and even if it isn't, it's too dangerous. I got as far as I could on the inside, but I can't risk Adonis finding me, cornering me, trying to talk me out of this.

It's too late for talking.

For weeks, I've seen them all watching me, suspicion and fear creeping cold in their eyes. Uncle Mike keeps asking me how I am, like something's wrong with me that only he can see. I shrug and tell him I'm fine, but I know he doesn't believe me. Cousin Jem and that sly freak Ebenezer drop by my office far too often, slinking about in the corridor to keep tabs on what I'm doing. Even skinny Harriet tried to make friends with me, and I coldly told her to go elsewhere.

They don't need to know where I've been spending my nights.

My body tingles warm in memory, of dark and dominant caresses, tears, breathless ecstasy I'd never imagined. But not just passion, though there's that in plenty between us. Admiration. Understanding. Secrets, hot and painful on my breath in the dead of night, ideas and sins and desires so dark and terrible I never dared whisper them to anyone, not even my brother. And always, stark, raw and bleeding between us: the truth and nothing but the truth.

I'm giddy, excited like a girl. I'm horrified. I'm terrified. My heart sings and screams at the same time.

I'm utterly, fatally besotted with this man. I don't need my so-called family any more. I have Him.

But Adonis… Adonis is the worst. I never could lie to my brother properly, not since I cried in his arms the night Mom died and he kissed me and promised he'd always take care of me, never leave me, always be there for me no matter what. And the pain and questions and bleak despair in his gaze are more than I can bear. He doesn't know—he can't know for sure, or he'd already have handed me over to Dad—but he suspects.

He suspects. And my brother's disappointment is harder than anything. Especially now that He won't return my calls...

I grit my teeth on treacherous tears, and keep climbing. This is no time for weakness. It isn't all for nothing. It can't be. Only He understands. Only He knows. Too long, I've pretended this away, kept my real self hidden inside, fought our petty battles and lost, over and over again while the real evil just laughs at us.

Fear. That's the real evil. Hiding, skulking in the darkness, wearing a mask so no one has to face what you are and accept that you're more and brighter and better than they.

Self-denial. Living in terror. Slavery, when in truth, we're the masters.

That's true evil.

But no longer. Not tonight. He'll see, and He'll come for me, and at last everything will be as it should be. Like it was before I lost my nerve and broke His beautiful, brittle heart.

At last, I reach the top. I haul myself over. Lactic acid screams ragged in my limbs, but I make it. For a few seconds I lie there, panting. Lightning splits the sky, and I bathe in it. Exult in it, the smell of rain and ozone, the sharp taste of power on the air. My hair springs alive, crackling with charge. Raindrops sting my face. It invigorates me, lends me energy.

Almost there. Just another few yards.

I scramble to my feet. Below me, the city sprawls, glittering and oblivious, the bridge's neon arc shining through the mist. From the broad expanse of roof, spires knife the sky, aerials, microwave dishes, satellite receivers. Spotlights gleam over a stairwell leading down to the roof access door in a little alcove. Big cubic aircon ducts poke up in orderly rows from the corrugated iron surface.

The roof is deserted.

Only seconds, now.

I unclip my backpack. My shaking fingers fumble as I open the zipper and take out my salvation.

It's so beautiful. So lethal. A perfect sphere, glass and silvery metal, bolted to a little steel frame and a cell phone timer. Inside, the transparent gel sparkles, catching the stormy light and scattering it like jewels. I glide my fingertips across the glassy curve. It feels cold, calm, focused.

It's an aerosol weapon, ionized particles for maximum adhesion. The building is fifty-six stories high. From this altitude, the poison will spread rapidly, blanketing the city center within minutes. Maximum loss of life. And then, the rain will wash the poison away. The storm is my ally. It's not a persistent chemical, and it's a big ocean.

For a second, my resolve wears thin. Surely, it won't come to that. He won't let it come to that...

My fists clench around the steel. Not a moment to lose.

Swiftly, I chain the frame to the aircon duct, snapping the padlock tight. Not much, but for a few seconds it'll slow anyone who tries to thwart me...

"Stop."

The command cuts effortlessly across the sharp wind. I whirl, and my guts shrivel hot, like I'm a little girl again, punished for some naughty game.

It's Dad, standing at the top of the stairwell, his long black coat whipping in the wind. His faded blond hair sweeps back, splashed with eerie sunset bloodstains in the stormy light. His handsome face is cold, and shadows flicker and threaten at his feet. "Get your hands off that. You're not fit to touch it."

Beside him, Adonis stares at me, power glittering golden in his empty blue eyes.

My heart jumps into my throat, and inside me, that little voice erupts again, kicking and banging her fists against the wall I've built to keep her trapped. Adonis! *she screams.* Help me! Don't let her do this...

But she's weak, that trapped girl. I'm strong.

There's no helping her.

I crush the cell door tighter in my mind, cutting off her screams.

I yank my phone from my bag, and brandish it so Dad can see. "Don't you come near me!"

"You have to stop this." Dad walks slowly closer. His voice is calm, measured. Talking me down from the edge. "Think, Verity. You don't want to do this. Give me the weapon."

"I said, don't come any closer!" My yell slices the rising wind. "It's too late. I'm done."

More lighting strikes, closer now, eerily illuminating Dad's face and painting his shadows like inky wreaths around him. "Verity, please..."

"Don't call me that! I'm not your daughter, Fortune. Not any more." It sounds alien, strange in my ears. But it's true. I'll never be Verity Fortune again. She's wasting away in that cold cell, screaming into silence until she dies.

I'm something new and special. Better.

Dad's shadows writhe and gibber, living things, and he clenches his fists, holding them back. "You're not making sense! He's messing with your head, can't you see that? Whatever he told you..."

"No." I struggle against the vicious ache behind my eyeballs. My mind is tearing in two, the edges raw and ragged, and I don't know how to keep it together. "No! You're the one messing with my head. You and your false promises. You've lied to me all my life!"

"It's too late, Dad." Adonis's voice is flat, empty of emotion. "She's gone. Let's end this, once and for all."

"No!" Dad shakes him off, his face cold with pain. Shadows thicken at his feet. "There's still time to make this right, Verity. Come inside. Come back to us." For the first and only time, Dad's voice cracks. "Please."

I laugh. Crazy, unholy laughter, bursting my lungs and cramping my guts until tears spill onto my face and whip away in the wind.

I drag in a fistful of power, and flash it out to ride the lightning.

Shadows throttle me. Suddenly, it's black as death. I gasp for breath. Dad's little shadow-creatures crawl over me, hungry, gnawing, into my ears, up my nose, down my throat, searching for food...

271

I strike out blindly. Something crashes, steel bending. More lightning erupts. Footsteps thump over the steel, and Adonis screams. "Verity, for God's sake, you'll kill us all..."

I fall in the dark, my head cracking against the aircon duct. Wind lashes my face. Raindrops sting. I scrabble for the weapon, lest it smash, but I can't find it. Panic crunches cruel claws into my heart. I've lost the weapon. I've lost my phone. I can't see anything but stars. I can't breathe. And Dad and Adonis are going to kill me...

Blindly, before I can rein it in, my cornered mindmuscle lashes out like a wild thing.

Metal ruptures, a shrill screech that rips my ears raw, and impact shakes the roof like thunder.

I suck in a breath, burning for air. The obstruction in my lungs dissolves like fog on a mirror, and suddenly, I can see.

I struggle upright. The roof's torn like paper, a massive section curled up and broken. A severed aircon housing bounces away, caught by the wind. Adonis crawls to his feet, his face drained pale, no color except the dark blue whirlpools of his eyes. Lightning flashes, and illuminates a dark shape huddled on the steel.

My heart stops.

Black leather flaps in the wind, shining wet, and uncovers Dad's broken face. He's not moving. Just lying there, in a spreading pool of blood. Blood fills his eyes. His mouth. Everywhere, blood.

I scuttle backwards on my hands, a frightened animal. I didn't mean it. I couldn't see. I didn't know where he was.

But I can't get away from this thing I've done, and I thrash my legs in impotent defiance and scream bitter rage to the uncaring sky.

Adonis yells, and unleashes on me, his talent poisoned, perverted by raw grief and denial. Golden-black glitter ignites at his fingertips, and he hurls his hatred at me in a stinging black cloud.

Crippling loathing sinks into my flesh, and my muscles seize. I can't move. Can't flex. Can't do anything but wait for death, and in an agony of tearing mindflesh, the last tiny shred of Verity Fortune withers and dies.

I cackle and spit laughter. It hurts. But it feels good to hurt. Razorfire taught me that, and I fell to my knees in his dim scarlet-lit chamber and begged him for more. "What you gonna do, Ad? Kill your own sister? You haven't got it in you!"

He dives for me—so graceful, my brother, when he moves like that—and together we roll, fight, claw for each other's eyes. But he's too strong, too good at dodging my power. We played too many fights as kids for him not to know my moves. At last, he grabs my hair, wrenches it tight around his fist, snaps his glitter-poisoned teeth an inch from my ear. "You are not my sister!"

And slam! My face hits the deck…

28

I reeled, and crashed into Adonis's desk. Paper and a tablet computer tumbled onto the floor. I stumbled, my vision in pieces, a vile poisoned axe splitting my head apart. Before me, the security video rolled on, but I didn't need to see. I knew what happened next.

"It was for your own good, Vee." Adonis gripped my shoulders, forced me to look at him. "You weren't yourself! Razorfire brainwashed you. I knew you were seeing him. I tried to warn you, but you wouldn't stay away. Those doctors were supposed to fix you. They were meant to undo all the damage Razorfire did, make you hate him again like you always had, until he..."

He didn't say it. But I knew. I'd known all along. I just couldn't admit it.

Couldn't cope with the raw and bleeding truth.

Adonis hadn't done it because he hated me. He'd done it because he loved me, and I'd betrayed him. Killed our father. Collaborated with our archenemy, at the very least. But what else?

Adonis's cheeks flamed, and for a moment, his gaze slipped. "I couldn't... I didn't tell anyone. No one else knew, I'd kept them all out of it. I had the weapon destroyed, I erased the footage and told everyone Razorfire killed Dad. I didn't know what else to do! And then you came back and I thought you were fixed, I really did. You didn't remember anything, and you were so…" He swallowed, his eyes sparkling. "I missed you. I really wanted to believe you were cured. But you wouldn't listen to me, and you got so angry at Equity, and then you unleashed on her. Your own sister, Vee. Just because she wouldn't give you what you wanted right away. My Verity would never do that."

"But… I wanted to kill him, Ad." My mind galloped, stumbled, fell by the side of the road and picked itself up with skinned palms. "I came out of that asylum with one thing on my mind. Surely that means I've changed! I can do this. I know I can."

But he just sniffed, and released me to walk over by the sunset-streaked window. "Sure. The doctors did that much. But the rage is still there, isn't it? You crushed those people at Crystal Towers because Iceclaw challenged your courage—"

"I didn't mean it. I lost control. It was an accident." But I knew it wasn't, and deep inside, I laughed bitterly at myself for trying to muster a defense.

"No it wasn't, Vee!" He rounded on me, his eyes ashimmer with azure tears. "I saw you up there. You didn't give a damn about anyone but yourself."

"You say that like it's such a goddamn crime." My body shook. My aching head was ready to explode. I didn't care. The words just tumbled out, stained with rage and agony and the hurtful black shadow of all those years I'd locked my heart away. "You know what? You're right. I didn't care about those people. I'm just sick of losing, Ad. I'm sick of backing down from fights to save a bunch of stupid frightened pricks who hate me. I'm proud of my augment. I don't want to hide it any more."

But I remembered Blackstrike, limp and bleeding on that wet steel roof, and such vile black loathing for my talent smothered me that, for a moment, I couldn't breathe. I'd killed my own father. Slaughtered all those people at Crystal Towers. All because I had this evil power in my head that wanted to be free.

What the hell gave me the right to be proud of that?

My vision doubled, the halves pulling asunder, like some ugly creature inside me yearned to break out…

"Then join me," Adonis begged. "Come back to FortuneCorp. We can win this war. I know we can."

"With what?" I laughed at him. It was shrill and strange. Not my laughter. Like I was someone else, not Verity Fortune. "Self-sacrifice? You gonna keep the moral high ground? Save the people? Protect the city, when Razorfire doesn't give a monkey's bleeding balls about either of them? Good luck with that. He'll wipe the goddamn floor with you."

"So I've changed Dad's policy. Doesn't mean I've lost my honor." Calm, cold. Golden glitter wrapped around his fingers. He'd tamed his temper.

Which was more than you could say for me. "Honor's no fucking good when you're dead."

Adonis's jaw dropped. "Are you listening to yourself? There's no such thing as a selfish hero!"

"I'm no hero, Ad. I've learned that lesson, okay?" My mouth tasted odd, bitter. I swallowed. My skin itched, like it wasn't mine. Like some twisted, grinning doppelganger had snatched my body and sucked me out, dumped me in the gutter and made my skin her very own. I rubbed my arms, the hair standing up. "I… I met someone, while I was gone over the past few weeks. He's just a kid. No one you know. But Razorfire attacked us, he threatened to kill Gl… to murder my friend. I had the chance to kill the city's sickest psycho, and *I was too fucking scared to move*. What the hell kind of hero does that make me?"

"The best kind! Are you seriously standing there trying to tell me that *not* sacrificing your friend for victory means you failed? Can't you see how royally *fucked up* that is?"

My mouth fell slack, and I stared, shuddering.

Draw a line. Glimmer's advice clanged deep in my skull like helldrums, beating me inexorably to my execution. *Pick a side.*

And I'd so very nearly picked the wrong one.

Why do you care so much what Razorfire thinks of you?

My throat convulsed, and I retched and choked sour bile onto the carpet.

Adonis laughed, dazed. "He's still in your head, isn't he? You're still listening to Razorfire's god-complex bullshit. The doctors didn't cure you, Vee. They can't. No one can."

"No!" I screamed, squeezing my temples together with both hands. My eyes streamed. My skin squirmed. I wanted to slice it open and drag this parasitic monster out. But it wasn't that simple.

Not when the monster was me.

"What other explanation is there?" My brother's yell tore my nerves ragged. He was sweating, his perfect hair in a mess. He'd tugged his tie askew. His handsome face had twisted into something I almost didn't recognize.

I'd done this to him. I thought I couldn't bear his coldness. But his disintegration was worse.

"I don't know!" I ground my teeth so hard, my ears popped in protest. My mouth was bleeding. It tasted foreign, strange. Like it wasn't my blood. "Fuck, I don't know anything anymore."

Adonis was shaking, and visibly he controlled himself, fingers clenching. "Vee..."

"Just let me try," I begged. *Love me,* I wanted to implore. *Just love me again. That's all I want.* "Please, Ad, let me try. I just need time."

Adonis's lovely blue eyes streamed tears. "We don't have time," he replied stiffly. "I'm sorry, Verity. Truly, I am. But I can't let you screw up again."

And he aimed my pistol at me, sideways and one-handed like a gangster, and fired.

29

The bullet slammed into my chest.

I staggered back. It didn't hurt. Only a sharp hot-and-cold sensation, fire and ice, spearing me like a blade. Blood blossomed on my nice new coat. Glimmer would kill me. I put my right hand down to catch myself, and it buckled beneath me, numb.

Adonis fired again. Missed. The window behind me smashed, the second time in two weeks I'd made that happen.

He wasn't letting up. Already, distant voices raised in alarm, yelling and hubbub that meant they were coming. My family, I realized distantly. All those others who thought like Adonis thought. The way out would be blocked. Nowhere to go.

Once they arrived, I wasn't getting out of here alive.

I rolled, blood spilling on the carpet, and dived for the shattered window.

Broken glass grazed my cheek. Adonis yelled. My heart sprinted in terrified protest at the idiot who was hurling it to its death, but I couldn't stop. The ground lurched, sickeningly far below. And then the wind caught me, and my guts dropped out, and I fell.

I cartwheeled in mid-air, crazy, out of control. My coat dragged back. My hair slapped my face. Wind buffeted my body as I tumbled, faster, faster, flashing glass windows and steel pylons and spinning city lights rushing by. Fifty-six floors, I realized dimly. That's two hundred meters, give or take. I had five seconds before I hit the ground.

And I'd already wasted four of them.

Blindly, I flung out a fist of power.

My invisible fingers grasped upwards, hooked over a balcony railing. Stuck fast. The elastic force grabbed me, and bounced like a bungee. My bones rattled, and I hurtled skywards, a living cork popping from a bottle. I fell, and bounced again, more gently this time, and after a few more boings, my body banged and bobbed against the glass wall, ten feet from the ground.

I dropped. *Crunch!* My legs jarred. I rolled into the alleyway, bruising my hip on the gutter, and lay there, bleeding and panting and wondering why the hell I was still alive.

I pushed myself into a sitting position. I ached all over, and now I was out of danger for a few seconds, the damn bullet started to hurt, didn't it, a hot dagger stabbing through my upper chest on the right-hand side. I pressed the wound gingerly and had to suck back a shriek. I'd wear the bleeding, thanks. My coat was already soaked and clotting. I didn't want to even think about peering over my shoulder for an exit wound. I'd just have to hope the fucking thing was still in there, lodged in a rib or something.

Because I didn't have time to waste. Already, Adonis had raised the alarm. I could see through the glass wall of the lobby, where security staff ran to and fro, answering phones and calling on their radios. Soon, Uncle Mike and the rest of them would be down here, looking for my body, dead or alive. In my current state, I didn't like my chances of winning a fight.

I had to get out of here.

I dragged myself up, tucked my coat tighter over the bloodstain, locked my arms across my chest and my hands under my armpits, and hobbled out into the square as fast as I could.

The street was crowded, office workers and early bar-goers

rubbing shoulders with musicians and hobos. The smell of melting cheese and tomato drifted from a café, chairs scraping and glasses clinking. A saxophone wailed, some soulful jazz tune. Traffic growled by. No one really looked at me. So far, so good.

But what now? My family were my enemies. Glimmer... well, Glimmer was gone, and I'd only myself to blame for that. I had no money. No home. Nowhere to go.

I hugged myself tighter, and hard corners jabbed me in the ribs. My phone.

I dug it from my pocket, my heart racing. That stupid pocket that buttoned. Only reason it hadn't fallen out.

The screen shone up at me, reflecting the lights overhead as I hobbled along. I switched it on. Not broken. A tiny corner of white card poked out of the case...

Sweating, I ignored it and called Glimmer.

No answer. Straight to voicemail. I sighed. "Hey. It's me. Umm... you were right, okay? Adonis told me everything, and... well, you were right. I, uh, just wanted you to know." Tears stung my eyes, and swiftly I swiped my thumb and ended the call, before I could say something stupid like *I'm sorry.*

Sorry. What a useless, pathetic little word.

Caine's card winked at me again, beckoning.

I squirmed. I wanted to see him. Hell, I needed his help now the whole of FortuneCorp was after me, as well as Razorfire and the Gallery. But something dark and hollow and hungry inside made me shrink away...

Fuck it. So what if he finds out I'm augmented? Like I've got other options.

I pulled out the card. *Vincent Caine*, it said, *Iridium Industries.* An email address. A cell number. I tapped the screen for the keypad, and started to type...

I frowned, my skin wriggling. The digits seemed familiar. Like I'd seen this number before.

Well, of course, dumb-ass. Caine called you once already,

remember? Right before Razorfire showed up and burned the place down…

Crunch! I bumped into someone, reeling. I held out my hand in apology, and staggered on, not paying attention.

He'd called me already.

But I'd never given him my number.

I'd never given anyone this number. Glimmer said it was secure, untraceable, and I believed him. But Iceclaw had it. And so did Caine.

Whatever. The guy's good with gadgets. And there's definitely an aura of *stalker* about him. I typed in the next few digits, and true to form, the number popped up as a Recent Call.

Twice.

Once in the incoming. And once in the outgoing.

My throat tightened. It didn't make sense. I'd barely used this phone. I checked the date on the outgoing call. I hadn't called anyone the day before yesterday, except Glimmer. Had I?

My mind jerked backwards, mental whiplash, a movie flashing by in reverse… Glimmer, sitting at his console, digging up information about the night Dad died. *Did I call anyone?* I'd asked, and he'd told me about my three calls, all to the same cell, the one whose number didn't seem to exist.

And then I'd called it, and got the invalid number message.

This was that number.

I stared, and slowly but inexorably, like rusty mechanical puzzle pieces, the truth ground into place.

The night I killed Dad, I'd called Vincent Caine. Three times. And he'd refused to talk to me…

My blood boiled, burning yet freezing, just like the bullet, draining me dry.

Oh, shit.

The last piece of the puzzle scraped into its hole.

And I cancelled the call with shaking fingers, and ran.

30

By the time I got to IRIN, distant thunder rolled, and purple storm clouds bruised the sunset sky. I screeched to a halt by the big white gate of the compound. Violet shadows crept, heralding the coming storm.

I jumped out of my stolen car—the world was already chasing me, right? What's one more crime?—and ran for the gate. Wind played in my hair, and sharp ozone stung my tongue. My skin tingled, warm and alive, a seductive promise of power. It felt beautiful, evil, delicious. I wanted to exult, laugh, stretch my arms to the crackling electric sky and howl.

The security guard at the gate came out of her booth. "Excuse me, ma'am, I'll need to see your identification—"

I hit her with an invisible fist, and she slammed back against the gatehouse, unconscious. I didn't have time to talk to her. Besides, identification was useless. I didn't know who the fuck I was anymore.

I leapt the gate on an elastic snap of power, and landed on the other side. My body jarred, and I took the impact on bent knees. Pain stabbed my torn chest, and I sucked in breaths as gently as I could, but my lungs still speared hot and swollen, my ribs moving stiffly at best. Getting shot really sucked.

I staggered to my feet, my headache still spinning. The vast lawn was dark, dappled by solar spotlights, deserted. At the top of the rise, the broad white buildings shimmered, eerily backlit against the purple sky. A golf cart was parked beside the gate, and I jumped in and twisted the key, sending it skidding down the slippery black road.

The lobby lay quiet, the lights dim, TV screens showing silent pictures. On the white sofas, a few young guys played video games, shooting each other with huge guns in ruined post-apocalyptic streets. Always, when the apocalypse comes, we reach first for weapons. It's war technology that survives while the pleasant stuff rusts to dust. When you're faced with that proverbial thirty seconds before the sky falls, you don't dash back into your burning house for the microwave oven and a coffee plunger.

You grab your guns, and run.

I wondered if it'd be like that when he finally got his way and set the world on fire. Guns and bullets, lasers sweeping the broken streets, gritty smoke and roaring flames. The bitter-rich glory of war. Or would it be civilized, the defeated lined up in orderly rows, a silent, rationalized, inevitable surrender?

No one stopped me. No one even looked at me. The elevator seemed to take forever to climb the four floors, tiny lights blinking like mischievous fairy eyes. I shivered, and rubbed my arms, willing the wriggling under my skin to go away. Were they my hands? My arms? Or was my skin just a body snatcher's suit, worn like a cheap disguise by someone cleverer, more determined, more sinister by far than I?

The door hissed open. I didn't need Ashton's swipe card. Like I was expected, that *he* knew I was coming.

And of course, he did. He knew me better than I knew myself.

His office lay in darkness, only the pale lamp over his Perspex desk piercing the night. On the desk sat a shiny metal-and-glass globe filled with ruby-red gel. It glittered inside, catching the light like jewels. The floor-to-ceiling windows lay open all around the perimeter, and storm-heavy air poured in, expectant, smothering yet alive.

He stood a few feet from the edge, his back to me, hands clasped behind him, gazing out at the thundery sky. Dark suit, neat bronze hair. Nothing frightening or exotic. Just a man.

Conflicting emotions roiled inside me like fighting serpents. My heart clogged my throat, and my stomach quavered with sickness. My skin crawled. I could unleash right now, grab a handful of ozone-rich air and hurl him out the window. Four floors was pretty far. It might be enough.

But my muscles shook, inside and out, and my clenched fist trembled and fell limp.

Beneath him, to be so easy to kill.

The floor seemed to roll beneath my feet, dragging me inexorably onwards.

I halted beside him. The stormy breeze stung my mouth, ripe with his elusive scent of mint. Mint's what you use to mask the smell of gasoline, I realized, dim memories of crime-scene cleanup glimmering in the distant recesses of my mind.

Mint. All that stuff about fate and accidents. That damn phone number. He'd hidden in plain sight, and like a weak, stupid little girl, I'd seen what I wanted to see.

On the horizon, lightning forked, and the flash lit his face in silhouette. His height intimidated me—he'd always been taller than me, I realized dimly. The fact that I hadn't noticed was just another slice of misdirection, another way he messed with my mind.

He didn't speak. Didn't look at me. Just let me struggle against the silence, until I couldn't fight any more.

"All that stuff about gardens and tribes," I burst out. "It was all bullshit. You didn't mean any of it. Why do you even want to be mayor? You hate them. All of them."

"This is my world." He spoke softly, calmly, and I was mesmerized by the dark timbre of his voice, the way his lips moved in the warm twilight. "I do as I please. Besides—" The ghost of a laugh. "It's amusing, don't you think?"

"I killed my father." My bones shook, rattling inside me until I trembled. Tears bruised my cheeks. "But you knew that, didn't you? I did it to impress you."

Quiet, tense and volatile. At last, he turned his head, and his deep gray eyes sparkled with sunlit flame. "Verity," he said, and such wonderful warmth flowed in his honey-hot voice that I quivered and melted inside, "just the taste of you on the air impresses me."

And in the space of a single breath, I fell into the fire and was lost.

His hands dragged my hair back. His lips, so fiery and intense, a kiss filled with rage and thirst and broken memories that cut like glass. I gasped, his rich dark flavor only making me thirstier. His body heat, enveloping me like an inferno, his strength an immovable force I couldn't escape. I didn't want to escape. I held on, drowning, burning, overcome with sensation and danger and the bittersweet glory of being alive.

I didn't know what I'd thought would happen when I came here. But not this. Never this.

I trembled, dazed in his embrace. He was so beautiful. How could I ever have forgotten this? This was love, obsession, fascination, a raging torrent of emotion and need that I couldn't control. My body ached to be filled, needed, possessed. I couldn't breathe. I didn't need to breathe. All I needed was this, him, now and forever.

I pulled back, gasping for air, his taste sweet and terrifying in my mouth. "You left me alone. You wouldn't take my calls. I had to do something. Why did you make me do it?"

He gripped my hands, held them tight, pulled me tighter against him like he didn't want to let me go. I fought, but he wouldn't relent. "*Make* you? It was magnificent! I knew you'd come through for me, but you exceeded even my expectations…"

He captured my mouth again, and again I couldn't resist. I inhaled him, thirsty, and it made my senses drunk. Lightning exploded overhead, and the thunder's power resonated in my chest. "But you let them take me away," I sobbed, overcome. "You let them torture me. How could you?"

"Because I knew you could take it!" His eyes flamed hotter, and he caressed my hair, his fingers trailing fire that made me shudder for more. "Once I figured you weren't dead, it was only a matter of time. And you did it. You survived. And look at you now, my precious beauty." He stroked my scar, a single fiery fingertip along my cheekbone, and it tingled all the way down inside me. "Even more stunning than before."

I wept, undone. He kissed my tears to tiny flames. "I thought about you, firebird," he murmured, easing his hands beneath my bloodstained coat to caress me. My bruises ached and swelled for his touch, a pleasurable kind of pain. "I imagined you chained up in that place, at the mercy of those fools. They dared to lay hands on you. It made me so hot." His grip jerked tight on my ribs, hurting me as he crushed me against him. "This is how you've gotten to me. You make me lose control. You have no *idea* how much I wanted to scorch them all to ash."

"But you didn't." Exquisite agony, sweet razors slicing my heart. "You left me."

"I respect you too much! I could never love a woman who needed rescuing. I hope you know that."

"Of course," I murmured, breathless with tension and emotion and the fucked-up craziness of it all. He made no sense. He made all the sense in the world... but deep inside me, in a tiny iron cell packed with stifling darkness, the starved, bleeding shadow of a girl I used to know thrashed and wailed and clawed her eyeballs raw. *Listen to yourself, you crazy motherfucker. You're insane!*

I ignored her. I wanted this feeling too much. This powerful heat, this passion for life I'd never known anywhere else. "They made me hate you. I was so confused. I wanted to..."

"I know. I saw it in your eyes in that basement. You were so strong, fighting so hard. I wanted to take you right there." He caught my bottom lip with his teeth, possessive. "And now you've come back to me. There's so much we'll do together, Verity. A whole world that belongs to us."

You sick bastard, get your hands offa me!

I murmured, pressing closer. God, he felt so good. So real. "But... didn't you hear... Adonis has unmasked... the whole of FortuneCorp are onto us."

He laughed, dark and gentle. "Let me worry about that, firebird. In fact—" He swept me into his arms and laid me down beneath him, inches from the floor's edge. Thunder burst overhead, ozone-fresh. All the hair on my body sprang alive. He tilted my chin up with his mouth, tasting my throat, my collarbone. I shivered, delirious. God, my nipples were hard. "Perhaps that'll be my gift to you," he whispered. "Get this party started. Which do you want to kill first?"

"Huh?" Lightning flashed, blinding me momentarily. More thunder. He was already easing my coat off my shoulders, nuzzling my torn dress aside, tasting my blood as it seeped from my aching wound. I gasped, shuddering with need. I longed to be naked, feel his body on mine, inhale his precious scent, push him inside me and soak him up, let him take me, brand himself on my body and my heart until I never forgot where I belonged again...

My head fell back, dazed with desire and heady memory. But tingling discomfort crept into my bones, and my headache returned with a sharp and jagged vengeance. Something was wrong...

"Your brother or your uncle." My nipple burned in his mouth, so hard it ached as he suckled me. His body felt so powerful on mine, demanding, unrelenting in his passion. "They both deserve to die. They tried to break you. Make you weak like they are. They had their chance to win my respect and they wasted it. So I'll crush them..." He bit me, and the sting felt so good I moaned. "And I'll relish every. Excruciating. Second of it." He punctuated his words with his teeth, harsh and delicious. "Which?"

Adonis, I wanted to murmur. *He wanted to tame me, chain me up like a dancing bear. Let Adonis die first. Now strip me bare and fuck me, before I explode.*

But deep in my heart, that slave-girl Verity yelled and kicked the walls, and my mind thrashed, confused. Surely, my master was right. Adonis had betrayed me. He didn't love me. How could he love me, when he wanted me to be weak? Only my master understood me. Only he loved me, always and forever to the death.

He wants to kill your family, slave-girl Verity howled. *He'd let you murder hundreds of people to impress him. He'd rather see you die than save you pain. This is not love! No!*

I blinked, dizzy. "But... umm... do we have to?"

He froze, his lips suddenly cold on my belly. "Come again?"

Just two words, dark and dangerous. But my every nerve jumped alive in warning, my heart aching that I'd said the wrong thing, disappointed him again. He'd punish me, and I'd welcome it. I *deserved* to be punished...

My memories shuddered and broke, flowing. Adonis, weeping, his bright blue eyes shimmering with remorse. *He's still in your head, isn't he? The doctors can't cure you. No one can.*

Can't you understand how royally fucked up this is?

I squeezed my eyes shut against it, but it kept coming. My brother, leveling a gun at me for the first time in my life. *I'm sorry, Verity, I truly am. I can't let you screw up again.*

My father's body, limp and bleeding on the roof, Adonis's sparkling black rage erupting around me like a swarm of wasps. *You are not my sister...*

You are not *my sister!*

An axe of agony came whistling down on my head, and my crystal-sharp world shattered.

Blackness throttled me. I struggled for air, fought to crawl away, get him off me, break free of the darkness. My blood throbbed afire, and everything that was so horribly wrong with this situation slapped me in the face like a thunderclap.

Look at me, I'd screamed at him long ago. Torn my mask off and bared my true face, streaming with tears, burning with raw longing for absolution I couldn't find in conscience or common decency. *For God's sake, look at what you've made me...*

I wasn't Adonis's sister. I wasn't Verity Fortune. Razorfire had made me into someone else. Someone aloof, angry, self-obsessed, the one who wore perfume I didn't recognize and dropped ceilings on innocent people and sacrificed her friends for the sake of petty victory.

Someone who could actually feel affection and desire for *him*.

"Oh my God." My voice drained, barely a whisper. I scrambled up, and stumbled backwards. "You evil son of a bitch. Get away from me."

He coiled to his feet. His coppery hair was tangled out of place. Messed up by my hands. That bruise on his lip made by my mouth. "Verity..."

"Shut up." I backed away, inch by inch, my legs weak. Slave-girl Verity was right. But I'd locked her away, the only person with any hope of saving me. "Don't say another word. I'm not listening."

"We've been through this. You're mine. You belong to me. That's the way it is."

"That is *not* the way it is! I'm not a bad person. I'm not!" I tore at my hair, the precious words I'd clung to for all those months of torture still scarred into the depths of my brain.

But it wasn't me who'd put them there.

The doctors had tried to help me. Tried to cure me. And they'd failed.

He caught my hand, caressed my fingers, pressed my palm to his cheek. "Think, Verity. They've confused you again. You're not yourself. You just have to remember..."

"I don't want to remember." I pulled away from him, shame and sorrow and disgust mixing an acid cocktail in my heart. Lightning tore the sky, dazzling me, and it didn't feel good anymore. It just hurt my eyes, power I was never meant to harness. The memory of his touch, his kiss, his lips on mine made my flesh creep. God, I wanted to be sick.

He clenched his fists, quenching angry flames. "Don't deny me. It never works."

"You brainwashed me!" My voice quaked. "You fucked with my head. I'm not like you. I'll never be like you!"

"That's not funny." Fire curled around his fingertips, a subtle threat. "Don't make me show you how I love you, Verity. It always ends in begging and tears. I thought we were past that."

"You don't love me, you sick fuck." Sour bile stained my mouth, blessedly rinsing out the flavor of mint. "You don't know what love is."

His fiery eyes drained to black. "Don't say that." His whisper cracked, empty. "Please. Tell me you don't mean it. Tell me they haven't *spoiled* you!"

He sounded so desperate. So sincere.

I laughed, it was so fucking insane. But fear tingled in my belly, so recently aflush with passion. Getting away might not be easy if he lost his temper. "This is crazy. Okay? *You're* crazy. I'm leaving."

"No, you're not." Soft, deadly.

"Yes, I damn well am." I whirled and strode for the elevator.

In a fire-sparkled flash, he landed in front of me and grabbed my arm. Flame kindled in his eyes, and a warm flush of memory shivered along my skin. "Did you just challenge me?" he whispered, running his thumb over my wrist. "We can play, if you like. You know I always win."

At that forceful caress, longing caught fire in my blood, aching, desperate, screaming in denial... I shuddered, disgusted, and shook him off. "Don't touch me—ugh!"

Slam! My chest hit the Perspex desk under the spotlight, and my brain rattled. Blood smeared from my wounds, sticky copper on my lips. That evil glass globe leered at me, inches from my face, that ruby-red death glittering like a devil's spell.

He forced my hands behind my back. I kicked, but he dodged me easily. I pummeled him with invisible fists, but he wore it, holding me against the desk's edge with his thigh, and dragged me around to face him, his expression set tight. I struggled, but his grip was steely, hot, immovable.

I spat at him, enraged. "Get your filthy fingers off me. What you gonna do, rape me? Good luck with that."

He grabbed my hair, forcing me to stare into his flaming eyes. "Quiet, firebird," he said calmly. "This isn't your fault. They've brainwashed you. You're not yourself." He reached behind me, and metal clicked, a tight band crushing my wrists.

Of course he'd have handcuffs. Every self-respecting lunatic has handcuffs. I struggled, but something yanked my wrists tight.

He'd cuffed me to the table.

For a hyper-intelligent evil criminal mastermind? Fucking stupid mistake.

"Oh, I'm myself, all right," I hissed. "This is me, telling you to go fuck yourself." And I scrunched my mindmuscle in a tight ball, and unleashed into his face.

And… nothing happened.

I tried again, frantic. Nothing. Just an empty space.

"Augmentium," he confirmed calmly. "It's a new alloy. Stronger, lighter, more effective. IRIN's latest innovation. I knew you'd be impressed."

My bones clattered cold, and for a moment I couldn't breathe.

Augmentium. Just like that god-awful helmet at Mengele's hospital. I was helpless.

He searched me swiftly, digging into my pocket for my phone. He tossed it a few feet away, out of my reach. It burst into flame. Plastic hissed and dripped, a puff of brown-smelling smoke. "I've been patient with them, Verity, and they spat it back in my face. I won't let them come between us again."

I struggled, wild. "Let me go, you fucking lunatic."

But he just planted a hot kiss on my forehead and stroked my hair back, making soothing noises. He picked up that glittering ruby globe, and rolled the cool glass along my cheekbone, a sinister caress. "You stay here, firebird." His burning gaze shone, beautiful,

294

besotted, utterly unhinged. "I won't be long. I'll finish what you started, and everything will be like it was before. You'll see."

He backed away, pressing his hand over his heart, a promise or a threat. And then he whirled and walked out, humming, tossing the glittering sphere from hand to flame-wrapped hand.

31

Fuck.

I struggled, useless, that vile metal cutting into my wrists. He'd cuffed me tight, and the desk's edge was sharp against the small of my back. I couldn't feel what he'd fixed me to. Some handle or something. Whatever it was, it wouldn't come free.

I strained my head around, trying to look over my shoulder. A neat pile of stuff on the desk, pens and a remote control and other things I couldn't see. Maybe something I could use to free myself. I twisted with all my might, but I couldn't reach, not even with my feet.

I tried to pull the desk over, tip the stuff onto the floor. It was heavy, or bolted down. It wouldn't budge. I strained harder, leg muscles screaming. Blood gushed afresh from my bullet wound. I yelled. Something fragile popped in my ankle, a sharp spike of pain, and I relapsed, defeated, aching all over.

Without my power, once again I was useless. Trapped.

The irony didn't escape me.

Fuck fuck fuck.

I locked back a scream of frustration. My blood boiled, an urgent fire I couldn't quench. I knew where he was going. What he was doing. And it soaked my guts with bitter terror.

Finish what you started.

What I'd started, that stormy night on the roof of FortuneCorp.

In my mind, I saw that evil weapon, gleaming in my fingers as I bolted it to the aircon duct. Smooth glass, gel sparkling like pristine ice inside. So pretty. So lethal.

And now he had a better one. A sicker, more lethal one. He'd go to FortuneCorp, just as I had. He'd kill Adonis and Uncle Mike and my cousins and anyone else who'd ever tried to help me, tried to set me back on the road to humanity. Kill this war with shock and awe before it was even born, make certain he and his Gallery were the only ones left alive to win. And he'd asphyxiate half the city doing it.

All because the crazy-ass bastard thought he loved me.

Goddamn it.

I wanted to cry. Scream, beat my head against the Perspex until it bled. *Why does this have to be my fault?* my bruised heart wailed. *Why did he have to pick me?*

But as I shuddered and struggled and banged my mindmuscle uselessly against that immovable augmentium wall, my soul ripped ragged with shame.

I knew why.

He hadn't picked me. I'd invited him in. I'd questioned, grieved, raged against my conscience, that core of humanity that means we'll never be as ruthless or dangerous or deadly as the villains are.

I'd questioned what it meant to be a hero. But it was more than that. I'd hated it. Turned my back on it. Let my grief and anger get the better of me, torn out my own soul and spat on it. And Razorfire was there, waiting.

My vision blurred like rainbows, flashback unrolling with a shiny tinfoil crackle. *I'm on my knees in charcoal dust, the ruined apartment block smoking around me. The roof's gone, sliced away by his evil talent. Bodies, contorted and burned. Ashes, charred bricks, the sharp-cut edges of metal girders ripped bare. And in my arms, the lifeless corpse of a child.*

Her pale hair is smeared in dirt and blood. A hostage. I'd tried to save her, tried to untie her little hands, while across the street, my enemy scorched the earth. He'd offered me the hero's choice: the fight or the girl. And I couldn't let her sit there, screaming, while the flames licked at her feet.

Now everyone was dead.

And there's Razorfire, striding satisfied atop the only wall left standing. His crimson coat swirling in hot breeze, flames caressing his ankles as he surveys his masterpiece.

I scramble up, grief and rage lighting molten acid in my blood, and drag in a handful of power, ready to explode.

But my enemy just grimaces, shaking his head. "Such a mess. Seeker, I'm disappointed in you. All you had to do was let her die..."

And I'd listened. Oh, at the time I'd cursed at him, unleashed, hurled chunks of brick and steel. But his words had planted a slick poisoned seed deep in my heart, and in the dark of the morning I lay awake, chilled, staring into the black depths of the void and wondering what it might be like down there...

And now it had come to this...

Midnight on the bridge, neon blinding me in tears. Chill winter fog coils cruel shackles around my limbs. I grip the upright girders, the metal cuts my palms until they sting like poison and drip crimson, but I don't care. What's more blood? More pain? It won't bring back the ones I've failed. Won't repair all the damage I've done.

My muscles twist and shudder, tension too long unrelieved. I'm messed up inside like a frustrated lover, afire with impotent rage. Longing for release, oblivion, an end to it all. My eyes burn, and I scream wordless agony to the uncaring night.

It doesn't echo. No birds flutter away in shock. There's no evidence I'm here, that I make a difference. That the world would care if I ceased to exist.

The sound just vanishes into the dark.

And in the raw space of a breath, he's next to me, sleek and dangerous in crimson silk and lies. So close I can feel his unnatural warmth, radiating from his body like sweet fever.

I jerk in fright. Stumble back, scramble for my fragile, reckless talent.

But he just smiles, slight, calm. Moonlight gloats over his rust-red mask, the sharp edges spiking glittery light. "Peace, Seeker. It's a beautiful night."

I've never seen his smile. Not this one, untainted by triumph or deceit. I'm repelled, but I'm fascinated, too.

Carefully, I relax, my pulse alive. "What do you want?"

He laughs, not sadistic but warm and intimate, wrapping me like black velvet. Another first. "That's a strange question."

I feel like crying. I wipe my nose, defiant, but my lips tremble. "I'm tired, okay? I'm not in the mood for your games."

"Very well. The truth, then. If you can handle it." A warm glance, dark and rich like a storm. "I've always admired you, Seeker. No"—he lifts two fingers, expecting a protest—"it's true. You kill and bleed and suffer for them, yet your heart lies empty. You fight to exhaustion rather than surrender, yet the air shimmers with your rage. It's beautiful, Seeker. You've already given me so much! And now here you stand. Alone. Weeping. Screaming into the dark. Tell me: what do you think I want?"

I shrug, careless, but swift pain slices into my heart. Of all the people to see me like this...

He touches my arm. Just a brief brush of fingers, a flicker of rosy flame. But my spine rivets rigid, a hot nail gun of shock, and I can't help but glance up at my enemy.

And now I can't look away. His storm-dark eyes ignite, fiery compulsion I can't escape. He leans closer, his strange warmth enveloping me, my first breath of that piquant scent of mint and fire, and whispers, "I want your soul..."

I thrashed against the Perspex table, madly rattling my cuffs until my wrists bled. Fuck. I knew it was useless, but my nerves fluttered like a trapped bird, compelled to escape. Lightning split the sky, deafening. The wind whipped my hair, stinging my eyes, the taste of raindrops and ozone and wild insanity, and I screamed, my skin ripping apart.

"Verity, stop it." Calm voice, dark. Hands on my face. Blindly, I kicked, wailed, snapped my teeth for flesh. I'd not let him touch me again. Not let him poison me. I'm not a bad person...

"Verity. It's me. Calm down." Light flickered, a flash of silver blinding me. I gasped, the precious scent of vanilla and spice.

I forced my eyes open, willed the light to fade, struggled to hear over my thundering heartbeat. My tongue was clogged with cotton, I couldn't talk. "Ughmph—"

"Shh." Glimmer cupped my face in his hands. He still wore black and white, his shirt bloody and torn, revealing the bruised muscle of his chest. His hair was wet, that skunk stripe plastered down over one eye. "It's okay. I've got you."

Relief shuddered my weak limbs. I sucked in stormy air. The taste of thunder reminded me forcibly of *him*, his mouth, the pulse in my throat thudding against his lips... "Glimmer," I gasped. "Jesus Christ. How did you...?"

Swiftly, he examined my cuffs, hunted for something to break them, his midnight blue gaze darting over the desk. "I got your voicemail. Figured you'd come here." He rummaged through the stuff next to the display, and his gaze flicked up briefly. "Guess that didn't work out so well."

Heat squirmed under my skin. *You were right*, I'd said to him. *About everything*. "Caine," I forced out, "he's..." My throat swelled hot and tight. I couldn't speak.

But the tears spilling molten down my face told Glimmer all he needed to know. His face blanked, just for a second, shock and disbelief. "Shit," he said softly. "Well, that explains a few things."

"He's got Pyrotox," I added incoherently, facts and memories mixing to ignite, feeding the heat on my fevered brain. "Adonis shot me. He's going there... I mean, Razorfire's... it's just like the night Dad died." The memory smashed like a train wreck into my face, and I sobbed afresh, trying to swallow my tears but choking on them instead. "I killed him. Adonis showed me the video. I killed him because we're... Razorfire and me, we're... fuck, how can you even look at me?"

Glimmer swallowed, his throat bobbing. His eyes shimmered wet.

My heart ripped raw, stinging like I'd stuffed it with salt. Surely, he'd leave me. He'd never forgive me. How could he forgive me? He'd given me everything, bared his valiant heart to a stranger and I'd savaged it with lies.

The fact that I didn't know was no excuse. He'd every right to spit on me, grind my face into the glass, walk out on me without looking back.

But he just blinked. Sprung his skunky hair. And kept hunting through the stuff.

I trembled, my courage lost. "Won't you even say anything?"

"What do you want me to say? That it's okay?" He swept the pile aside, casting about for something else. His eyes lit, and he grabbed the framed gadget from the wall and smashed it on the desk's corner. The plastic frame splintered, and he ripped off a long shard and shoved it into the lock on my handcuffs. The action pressed him tightly against my shoulder, his hair prickling my face, his breath an acid accusation on my neck. "It isn't okay, Verity. It's not okay at all."

"Then what are you still doing here?"

"Everyone can be saved." The shard slipped, slicing into my arm, and he swore and tried again. At last the ratchet popped, and one cuff cracked open. He dragged the chain through the space—I'd been cuffed to a metal bracket on the desk that looked strangely built for the purpose, and Jesus, *he'd* probably locked me up here before—and I tugged myself free and stood, wincing at my torn ankle and rubbing my remaining metal-belted wrist.

Glimmer tossed the plastic spike onto the table, and flexed his cut palm, grimacing. He didn't look up.

"Even me?" My voice sounded small and feeble.

At last, Glimmer looked at me, and the sharp shine in his gaze wasn't hatred or scorn or even sorrow… well, maybe a little. But mostly, I saw resolve, the dark hungry glitter of scores unsettled. "Even you."

"What about *him*, then?" I didn't dare say his name aloud, lest I howl or vomit or otherwise embarrass myself. "Does that apply to him, too?"

A crooked Glimmer smile, rich with vengeance. "They say God can forgive anyone."

God's dead, Razorfire had said. *God doesn't care. There's only me…* "Yeah, well. Ain't no one gonna save him from me when I get my hands on him." I picked up the spike and levered my remaining cuff open. The augmentium had cut bloody welts, and they stung like a bastard. I flexed my wrists. Ouch. Still, it took my mind off the bullet wound.

I tossed the cuff away, gratitude mixing sweetly with hot mortification in my blood. If Glimmer hadn't turned up, I'd have been stuck there until *he* returned…

I could never love a woman who needs rescuing. He'd said it with such passion.

Well, good. Fuck off, then.

I took a steadying breath. "Glimmer?"

"Yeah?"

"Thanks. I, uh… needed a hand."

His mouth twitched, that cute crooked smile. But he didn't say anything. Didn't embarrass me. He just scratched at his burned hair, making it stick up. "Plan?"

Blessed warmth eased the tension inside me. Good, honest warmth, untainted by evil. Damn, it felt good to have Glimmer back.

I coughed, suddenly conscious of my ripped dress, the blood, the fact that I smelled of passion and probably had marks on my lips and my neck and God knows where else…

"FortuneCorp," I said. "The roof. That's where he'll be. He likes the symmetry. And I, uh, told him Adonis shot me. He wasn't happy about that."

A quirk of dark brow. "Ain't love a bitch?"

My stomach watered sick. Too early to be making jokes about *that*. "You wouldn't believe the shit he said to me, Glimmer. The guy is batshit crazy. It was horrible." Horrible, too, that his twisted words of love had shocked me breathless, melted my insides to a puddle of desire, made me shiver warm and willing under his kiss...

Glimmer winced, bashful. "Sorry. I guess that wasn't so funny."

"It's okay," I said steadily. I didn't know how to deal either. At least he was making the effort.

"Right. The roof, Pyrotox, don't let him kill everyone. Doesn't seem like rocket surgery. You ready?"

"Yeah. Bring it on." A thought struck me. "Wait. What day is it?"

A blank look. "It's Monday night. Nearly Tuesday morning, in fact."

"So tomorrow's election day, right?"

"So?"

"So we're gonna make sure the bastard doesn't get away with this." My mind raced downhill, skidding ahead. "A camera. We need vision. There must be something in this shiny geek den we can use."

Glimmer skunked his hair again. "I saw a game console in the lobby, with webcam?"

"That'll do." Already I strode for the elevator, my thoughts careering in circles, a recursive loop with no exit but death. My actions felt strange, foreign, like someone else's blood in my veins... yet so familiar. Truth skewed ugly, a glaring mirror image of my past.

Maximum loss of life. Not a moment to lose.

Only this time, I really was saving the world.

Glimmer skipped to catch me. "Do I have to guess?"

I grinned at him as the elevator door slid shut. My first real smile since everything fell apart. It hurt my face, and made my guts ache with fatigue. But it felt good, too. "You're the mind reader," I teased. "You figure it out."

32

The storm cracked and boiled overhead, illuminating the glass skyscrapers with hellish flashes of doom. The overcast sky scudded, reddish, bruised like a broken heart. Hot wind lashed, dust and grit flying. Rain refused stubbornly to burst, and thunder boomed and threatened, ozone stringing the air tight.

Beside me, Glimmer peered up at the FortuneCorp building across the street, its spire stark against the bleeding sky. He had the webcam, on a digital headset he'd taken from IRIN, and clipped it over my ear, making sure it wouldn't fall off. "So how are we getting in there, again?"

I wiped trickling sweat from my temples. My pierced shoulder still ached, but now it stung, too, salt and dirt, that peculiar fevered brand of itch that means infection. My bare feet scuffed on the side-walk, leaving a reddish smear. Lightning exploded again, lighting the lobby in garish sunflash. Security en masse, dudes in suits everywhere. Like a fucking fortress. Not to mention Adonis and Uncle Mike and the rest of them, on watch for us, ready for war.

My pulse tightened, thudding in sympathy with the tension on the air. I didn't doubt for a moment that *he* was already in there. "Same way I got in last time."

Glimmer frowned. "And that would be?"

"We'll have to climb."

"Excuse me?"

"We'll never get there by elevator. We break in through the parking lot. The fire stairs go all the way up to fifty-six, but the roof exit will be watched. You have to ditch the stairs at fifty and climb."

"You want me to run up fifty flights of stairs with security guards shooting at me, and then climb a vertical glass wall."

"Uh-huh."

"Five hundred feet above the ground. In forty-knot winds, with lightning all over the place."

"Sure. What are you, a weakling?"

"You're insane, you know that?"

"Dude, compared to what I've seen and heard tonight, this is positively reasonable."

He rubbed sweaty palms together, shaking his velvety head in disbelief. "You're the boss. You know he'll be expecting us, right?"

I nodded. It was exactly how I'd done it last time. It was what he'd want. I knew that, and yet somehow... I also knew it was the only thing to do.

What the hell was that? I wondered uneasily. Respect for my enemy? A nod to old times? Some part of me that still cared what the sick motherfucker thought of me?

Or just the only way I'd ever get on that roof without Adonis blowing my goddamn head off?

Stay frosty, soldier.

Glimmer looked at me, and shrugged. "Okay. Let's do it."

And I punched his shoulder for luck, and we did it.

#

I heaved myself over the sharp glass edge and onto the roof.

The wind snatched my breath, a horrible vacuum sucking at

my lungs. I choked, bleeding, my shoulder on fire. Above, the sky threatened bloodshed. The shadow of the aircon housing smothered me, but at least it meant I was out of sight.

Lightning sheeted, God's wrath come alive. A bloody hand slapped onto the edge, and Glimmer reefed himself up beside me.

Fatigue screamed a tantrum in my muscles. I was so bone tired. I just wanted to sleep forever. For a few seconds, we lay there, dying, the wheeze of our tortured breathing beaten into silence by thunder.

And then we dragged ourselves to hands and knees. Nowhere else to go but onwards.

"Camera?" I panted.

Glimmer adjusted my headset. "Yep. Not that we'll get much audio in this damn wind. What am I recording, exactly?"

"Everything." I crept to my feet, silent as I could be on an iron roof with bleeding bare feet. My coat whipped around my legs in the gale. I wore no mask. I'd offered mine to Glimmer, and he'd waved it away.

Ready or not, we were in the clear.

My heart thumping, I crept to the edge of the aircon housing and peeked.

Déjà-vu. The rippled steel rooftop, broad and flat. Flashing lightning, spotlights shedding white pools on the stairwell.

And Adonis.

Steadfast and strong, like always. His blue eyes dazzled, electric, his hair swept back and his neat suit tugged into disarray by the storm.

But this time, it wasn't me he faced, with that shining glitterball of death in my hand.

Razorfire, calm and quiet, his coppery hair gilded by the lightning. He and Adonis were neck-deep in convo, shouting at each other from twenty feet apart, their voices lost to me in the howling wind. Razorfire had done the same as I had, of course, chained the weapon to the aircon housing so it couldn't be removed.

Halfway between him and my brother, the poisoned globe glittered, hungry ruby-red.

The inevitability pounded my guts like a sucker punch. Never say he doesn't appreciate irony.

But something was wrong. Something was different. My mind stumbled, reeling, playing spot-the-difference with knives in the dark... and blindly it hit something, and drew blood.

Razorfire wasn't masked.

I could see his sharp features, those stirring gray eyes, the arrogant facets of his cheekbones. And he wasn't wearing the crimson silk that struck terror into all but the craziest, most lovesick hearts. Still dressed in the same suit, in fact, probably still with my blood on his shirt. Mass murder in menswear.

The bastard was in the clear.

At my side, Glimmer hissed between his teeth. "What the hell is he doing?"

"I don't know!" My mind boggled cold, and I remembered that strange chill in my guts after his press conference, when I'd realized I'd played into his hands without even knowing I'd made a mistake. Was there some part of his plan I didn't understand, hadn't anticipated?

Well, of course there was.

He wasn't Sapphire City's archvillain for nothing.

Lightning struck almost directly overhead, and my teeth rattled. My shadow leapt, suddenly huge, spilling like a monster onto the roof at Adonis's feet.

I cursed, and jumped back into shelter. But too late.

Adonis's head snapped around, burning blue eyes locking onto me. Razorfire did the same, a stormy thunderbolt that rooted me to the spot.

Glimmer's hand clenched tight on mine. My guts hollowed, sick. We were made.

33

Razorfire—no, Vincent, his name was Vincent, and no matter what I thought of myself now, he'd carved himself into my heart so deeply I'd never be rid of the scars—Vincent ran straight at me.

Just a couple of steps. Enough so I could hear him. And he flung out his arm towards Adonis.

I cringed, ready for a hail of flame.

But he didn't unleash.

He just pointed, accusing. And called out to me, his voice stretching like a rubber sheet on the wind's cruel surface. "Nerve gas!" he yelled. "If it's released it'll kill everything in a six block radius. It's on an automatic timer, only a minute left. I can try to disarm it. But you have to evacuate the area!"

Reality blurred. My head ached with fatigue and confusion. Like the asylum all over again, truth melding with lies like molten plastic, colors swirling until I couldn't tell one from the other... "What?"

Wind whipped his hair. "It's nerve gas. He's insane. Get everyone out!"

"What the fuck—?"

Clunk! The penny dropped, and so did my guts.

But too late. Adonis had already crash-tackled him.

The two men skittled to the rooftop, rolling towards the edge. Adonis fought grimly, and let rip with a fistful of black-glitter hatred, a cloud like gnats that nipped at Vincent's face.

But still, the sly bastard didn't unleash. He just fought, grim, clawing for Adonis's eyeballs and wrestling ever closer to the roof's edge. And on the weapon's digital timer—nice big bright figures, of course, so everyone could see—the seconds counted down, 58, 57, 56…

He knew.

Inside my head, a seething little voice screeched my idiocy, and beside me, Glimmer banged his head back against the aircon duct in pure frustration. "Fucking *wise*-ass," he growled.

To think I'd imagined I could outsmart *him*.

Of course he knew. That I was recording this—what there was of it, while lightning ripped the reception apart, shredding the audio and breaking up the picture and conveniently concealing anything that wasn't quite right—and streaming it live to an internet server so the city could see.

He knew me too well. He knew everyone was watching. And he'd stage-managed it perfectly.

I didn't even need to look up at the FortuneCorp surveillance camera, the one that had so effectively proved my guilt over Dad's murder. Because I knew it would be smashed, missing, deactivated, whatever. There'd be nothing to show that Razorfire was the one who'd planted the weapon.

Our word against his. The promise of a family of reviled augments and weaponeers, versus Vincent Caine, philanthropist and creative genius, the city's latest darling.

Knives and gunfights, I thought dimly, and laughed. I'd brought a fucking toothpick to this one.

Adonis grabbed Vincent's collar and slammed his head into the rooftop, power sparkling from his fingers. And Vincent just let him. I'd seen him burn condominiums to the ground for lesser insults.

313

Glimmer grabbed my arm. "That timer can't be real!" he yelled. "He'd never kill himself."

Only one thing an archvillain won't do to win.

But could I trust that? After he'd so ruthlessly manipulated me? *What's my promise worth to you, Seeker?* He mocked me from my memory, and it stung like salt in my bloody wounds. *You'll just have to trust me.*

I stared at Glimmer, for one helpless, bewildered second. And then we turned as one and sprinted for the weapon.

Malicious wind tried to fling me off my feet. I staggered, my coat flapping wildly. My hair blinded me. I dragged it back, and kept running, slamming into the side of the aircon duct and holding on. The evil ruby globe glittered, flashed magical by lightning. Clipped to it, the tiny duplex transmitter from a cell phone, and a little silvery button that looked suspiciously like a high-frequency sound emitter.

A detonator, in fact.

Ultra-pitched sound wouldn't explode, of course, not like a regular detonator. But it did shatter glass.

And that was enough for a weaponized incendiary like Pyrotox. That bad boy ignited on contact with air. If the glass broke, we'd all die in choking agony.

The crimson figures on the timer flicked over, sinister and inexorable. 38, 37, 36...

Glimmer poked at it, squinting to see in the volatile light. A warning spark flashed, and he jerked his hand back, swearing. "I can't!" he yelled. "It's too small, I can't see. The fucking thing's triple-wired, I need my gear. If I smash the oscillator, it'll just go off. We'll have to..."

A hoarse yell whipped my head around.

Adonis clung crablike in the gale to the roof's edge. I couldn't see Vincent. My heart jumped into my throat like a hot frog... but then hands gripped the edge, fingers and then palms, slick with blood. Dragging himself back to the top.

I ran over, weaving in the buffeting wind. Thunder shook the building. I tripped, and skidded on stumbling feet for the edge.

Adonis clawed for Vincent's eyes. His face was twisted with loathing, his blue eyes afire with a lifetime of pent-up rage. "I'll fucking drop you, you son of a bitch. I've wanted to do this for years."

The timer flashed, taunting me. 27, 26, 25... And still, Vincent didn't unleash. He tried to climb up, his fingers scrabbling wet on the metal rooftop, and latched onto Adonis's arm with a grip like steel. He didn't speak.

He didn't need to. Everyone watching on my camera already knew what to think.

Vincent Caine, genius gadget-maker. He was the only one who could defuse that weapon. If Adonis dropped him, we were all dead.

Lightning burst over me, prickling my skin with static. All over my body, hair sprang tight. Female muscles tightened in my belly, and power kindled, seductive. I exulted, lifting my face to the light.

Razorfire had ruined my life. Adonis had tried to kill me. All I had to do was shove Adonis over the edge, and they'd both die. I'd be free of them at last.

Free of everything.

Everyone who knew my terrible secret would be dead. No one would ever know who I'd nearly become.

Hunger for vengeance dizzied me, along with a fresh thirst for justice that I thought I'd lost forever. Glimmer must be rubbing off on me. Razorfire was a criminal psychopath. He didn't deserve to live. Imagine the lives his murder would save. Even if I had to kill innocent civilians to do it, I'd be doing the city a favor.

Of course, I'd die too. The storm might dissipate the evil chemical, blow it away, spread it too thin to do more than a few city blocks of damage, but I'd still get a lethal lungful.

Did I care? I was a villain, a bad person, the lover of a murdering maniac. Maybe I didn't deserve to live, either.

In the corner of my eye, figures counted down. 20, 19, 18...

Below, Vincent gazed up at me, grabbing on tight to Adonis's arm like a slick hungry leech, and for an instant, his eyes flashed with triumphant flame. It could have been the lightning. No one watching would even know.

But I knew.

And I knew that the man who'd poisoned my willing heart to love him—more than honor, more than conscience, more than the primordial drive for life itself—had seen through me, one last time.

The one thing a villain won't do to win... is die.

My mind struggled, bursting with confusion and shattered memory and unknowable desires, and with one final defiant thrash, it flashed clear as daylight with newborn resolve.

Maybe I didn't deserve to live. But it was just like Glimmer had told me. *I realized what happened if I died,* he'd said. *Nothing. Not a goddamn thing.*

If I gave up now, I'd never atone for my sins. Never be able to make up for all the bad things I'd done.

There's one thing a hero won't do to win, too. And that's surrender to the darkness.

I'd sacrificed victory to keep the moral high ground. I'd saved my friend's life rather than win at all costs. And now, I'd keep those innocent people alive, even if it meant saving my most dangerous enemy and alienating my best-loved brother forever.

Even if it meant I'd never be free.

If that makes me weak, then fuck 'em all, and sign me up.

I grabbed Adonis's arm, trying to pull him away. "Ad, for God's sake, let him up. He can disarm it—"

Adonis elbowed me in the guts. Hard.

I retched and staggered, spitting bile. Vincent struggled to hold on. Time was slipping away. I had no choice. I braced my feet wide, stung my mindmuscle with all the nervous energy the lightning could lend me, and *flexed.*

An invisible fist ripped the air apart. Thunder poured in, boiling over me like a tide. The empty air sucked Adonis backwards, dragging him like a rag doll to thump onto his back on the rooftop. And Vincent came with him, tumbling head first over heels to land gasping at the foot of the aircon shaft.

Glimmer pounced on Adonis, but my brother wasn't moving all that well. He just groaned, blood dripping from a wound on his forehead.

I whirled to face my enemy. Behind him, the counter ticked down. 11, 10, 9…

He scrambled gracefully to his feet. For one magical moment, our gazes locked, and under his commanding gray gaze, my heart did a shivery somersault. He wasn't stupid. He'd thought of everything, always did. What if he'd somehow made himself immune to Pyrotox? I'd gambled. Played his game. Had I lost everything? Would he kill us all, just to make his point?

7, 6…

And he spun on the spot and grabbed the weapon.

4, 3, 2…

I slumped, and closed my eyes. I didn't see what he did. I didn't need to. By the time I looked up again, the thing was in two pieces in his hands, and the timer flashed twin zeroes like Christmas lights.

I knew my love, see. And I knew he didn't want to die. He'd do whatever it took to save himself.

Even if it meant saving us all.

The wind blew my hair wild, stinging my skin fresh and electric. I lifted my face to the storming sky in exultation, and with a wild crash of thunder that throbbed like victory in my blood, the rain fell.

34

By the time the storm passed, the whole of Sapphire City had seen our little home movie.

Early morning sun bathed the wet concrete in Union Square. The rain had washed everything clean, and the blue sky shone fresh and untainted. Glimmer and I sat on the steps, nursing our wounds. I'd slipped my coat off—shiny gunmetal was kinda conspicuous at the moment—and the wooden planks felt rough under my thighs. I'd wrapped up some newspaper and pressed it over my bleeding chest. My dress was torn and bloodstained, but no one really noticed that. It was election day, or it would be, when the polls opened in an hour, and they were all too busy watching the fun on TV. Like us.

Glimmer slouched next to me, in a T-shirt that said I HEART SAPPHIRE CITY. We'd stolen it for him so he didn't have to wear the torn and bloody half of a tuxedo. We'd stolen a phone, too—what did the stupid woman expect, if she left it on the Starbucks counter while she sweetened her coffee?—and together, we huddled over the little screen and watched Razorfire take our city by storm without firing a shot.

Just a few minutes of shaky, broken footage from a thunder-soaked rooftop, and a press conference.

It was the steps of Sapphire City PD headquarters, a shiny metal building with dark glass windows. As usual, he stood with no lectern, no notes or prepared statements. Cameras flashed at him, sparkling in his eyes, a pale imitation of the lightning we'd soaked in. I watched him, admiration and loathing cooking a salty stew in my belly. He was slick in front of the camera, my love, smooth and dauntless, unflappable.

"No," he said in response to some question, "it was just an accident, I'm afraid. A late-night meeting in the city. I alerted security, but..." He spread his long hands. "I got there first. These things happen."

"A meeting with whom?" the journalist asked.

A slight smile, charming. "I'm entitled to a personal life. And before you go starting rumors, Caroline, I'm quite single. For the moment."

"Asshole," I grumbled, but I couldn't help wondering if he meant me.

"Who took the video, Mr. Caine? And why aren't they in police custody?"

"They called themselves Glimmer and the Seeker. Perhaps Mr. Fortune can shed light on that. As for police custody..." A flicker of perfect regret. "That isn't my job. I trust our police to do *their* jobs with the same level of skill and attention they've always displayed. No doubt those two pseudo-villains will soon be apprehended."

"Can you explain how you disarmed the weapon?"

"Easily. I'm an engineer."

"But neutralizing a bomb is an intricate job, Mr. Caine. A job for specialists. Or were you just lucky?"

"Luck didn't come into it. The device used an IRIN cell phone for a timer. I invented it. It wasn't difficult to dismantle."

"You just happen to come across a bomb made with one of your cell phones? Isn't that something of a coincidence, Mr. Caine?"

"Not really, Ms. Mason. What model's your cell?"

Laughter. I rolled my eyes. She deserved that.

"Frankly," he continued with a smile, "it makes me shudder that violent people use my technology for violent ends. But when I'm selling to ninety percent of the market I'm bound to net a few crazies. It isn't the weapon that kills, Rachel. It's the person who wields it."

Heh. That one made me laugh. *Guns don't kill people...*

"Are you aware that the substance in the bomb was made right here in Sapphire City, by Fortune Corporation?"

An elegantly raised eyebrow. "That's a shame. I've always had the deepest respect for Fortune Corporation's ethical weapons charter. If they've opted for profit over principles, then I condemn that unequivocally. As should any decent citizen."

On the steps, I snorted. "A shame. That's funny..."

"Shh," said Glimmer, still watching.

"Did Mr. Fortune say anything to you?" a reporter asked.

"I believe you all heard what he said on the rooftop, as well as afterwards," Vincent answered. "It's all on the police record."

"And what's your response to his accusations? He claims you tricked him, that you're some kind of criminal supervillain who instigated the whole affair?"

Vincent laughed, easy. "Mr. Fortune is augmented, Simon. He'd know more about criminal supervillains than I would."

"He even said that you were Razorfire," the kid persisted. "The Gallery mastermind. What do you say to that?"

An amused twist of his brow. "If I were, I'd hardly be standing here giving a press conference, would I? I believe I've made my position on that topic clear. Our city has the right to be freely informed about this menace. I can only say it's providential that Mr. Fortune has exposed his villainy so soon after what seemed such a frank and open disclosure of his own and his family's augments. Which, I have to admit, I was on the brink of congratulating him for."

"Are you aware that since being taken into custody, Mr. Fortune has been subjected to testing with your Sentinel device?"

I leaned forward, my pulse tight. "Yes. Ask the question. Come on, ask him."

"No, I wasn't," said Vincent. "I hope the test was voluntary."

"Are you aware that the test showed what your device called high-level mental-energy augmentation? Potentially very dangerous?"

"It doesn't surprise me. He struck me as a dangerous man."

"Would you agree to submit to testing, Mr. Caine?"

"Yes!" I pumped my fist. He'd avoided the issue the day Witch was arrested. Hadn't touched the sensor. But this time... "That's the way. Let's see him get out of this one."

His gaze stormed, that dangerous darkness that made me shiver. "I don't see why that should be necessary."

"Mr. Fortune has requested that you submit."

"With all due respect, Mr. Fortune is in custody pending charges—"

"But wouldn't it clear you of suspicion?"

"Suspicion of what, Ms. Mason? I answered the police chief's questions. I don't believe I've anything to prove."

"Except your innocence," said Ms. Mason sweetly.

"I'm sorry, since when did proving innocence become a legal requirement?" More cameras flashed, lighting his eyes.

But I thought I saw a hint of flame, and my heart squeezed tight. "He's feeling threatened. Jesus, he could burn the whole stinking lot of them if they don't shut up."

"But isn't that what your Sentinel is designed to do?" Mason pressed. "Prove our innocence? Or are you rejecting your own policy because you don't think it should apply to you?"

He stared, silent.

My throat tightened. "Fuck. They've got him. He's gotta walk away."

"Very well." His voice sliced smoothly through the hubbub. "Since you insist, I see no reason for delay. Bring out the Sentinel."

I gasped, and so did the entire press corps. A uniformed officer jumped to, and soon he hustled back out with a humming blue

Sentinel in his thick hands.

"Is it in working order?" Vincent asked softly.

The police officer cleared his throat. "It's the same one as tested Mr. Fortune, sir. Full contact sensors. You just have to touch it—"

"Fine," Vincent snapped, and thrust his palm on the sensor. I plugged my ears against the screams.

Nothing happened. It just sat there, blue, winking at him.

He took his hand away. Planted it there again. Same result. "Satisfied?" he asked coolly. "We can do more tests, if you like. Calibrate it however you want. Frankly, I've got better things to do. More questions?"

Beside me, Glimmer grimaced. "Seen enough?"

"Well, bugger me," I breathed. Reluctant admiration coursed through my veins. I didn't know how he'd done it, but he had. Some piece of code, a genetic indicator, a biochemical blocker... "Wait a second. Wind that back."

Glimmer skipped the video back a few seconds. Once again, Vincent stuck his left palm on the Sentinel's sensor... in a tiny glint of sunlight.

His wristwatch, silvery in the sun. Always, he wore that watch. Only it wasn't silver, was it?

IRIN's latest innovation. Stronger, lighter. Effective enough to mask even Razorfire's lurid augment, for a few seconds. But a few seconds was all he needed.

I swore. "He's wearing augmentium. He's had that damn thing on the whole time."

No wonder I hadn't smelled the power on him, like I did on Iceclaw and Weasel and every other augmented Gallery nutbag. He'd crippled himself, just to keep up the charade in public.

Glimmer laughed, humorless. "You've gotta admit, that's ballsy."

"I guess so," I admitted grudgingly. "Shoulda known he'd never let his own device incriminate him."

"Well, he's sure as hell incriminated us."

"Yeah." I mustered a grin. "Fine. If we're the city's new villains, time we started acting like it." I grabbed Glimmer's arm. "Come on. We've got work to do."

35

I sprang from shimmery vanilla-scented shadow into full view, and blew the cell door off its hinges with an invisible fist of power.

The solid iron door flew into the cell and crashed against the opposite wall. "Fire in the hole," I said calmly, and strode in, my newly cleaned coat-tails flaring around my legs.

In the corridor, police officers shouted and flailed, but Glimmer threw out his hand and silenced them with a rippling wave of sleep. They slumped, unconscious, before they'd even drawn their guns.

"Time's wasting," Glimmer snapped, watching the corridor with his pistol cocked. "Say what you've gotta."

From the cell's bench, Adonis gazed up at me in silence. His handsome lip was cut, his blue eyes dark with bruises. Not all of them had been there when he was arrested. His wrists were locked together in front of him. Augmentium cuffs, silvery and innocuous. I shuddered. I'd seen those before.

"Well, aren't you a pretty picture?" Like I could talk, I realized. They'd done worse to me when I was locked away. But at least I wore my mask again. Now, no one could see my shame.

Except me.

"Fuck off," Adonis said stonily. "I don't talk to villains."

"Then shut up and listen," I ordered. "I don't have much time. Not sure if you get the six o'clock news in here, but tonight Sapphire City's already toasting Vincent Caine as the new mayor. This morning's little stunt has placed FortuneCorp firmly on everyone's shit list. I don't know where Uncle Mike and the others are hiding, but you can bet it's nowhere within shouting distance of a CCTV camera, which cancels out pretty much everywhere but the forest and the sewers, and I'm thinking Jem and Eb aren't too flash at woodcraft. Oh, and I almost forgot: there's a pair of clowns called Glimmer and the Seeker—this is Glimmer, by the way—who are the new public enemies number one and two."

Adonis shrugged coldly, but I saw a flicker of his old handsome smile. "Congratulations. Not a lot I can do about it in here."

"My point exactly." I folded my arms. "Razorfire's the goddamn mayor, Ad. FortuneCorp's in pieces. Crime's happening. Do you want to fester in here until he decides to play with his food some more? Or do you want in?"

I offered him my hand. Take it or leave it, brother.

Adonis stared at me, hard. I stared back.

He grabbed my hand with both of his. I pulled him up, his cuffs clinking, and for a second, he yanked me close. "We're not done," he whispered. "If you think this means I trust you, you're even crazier than I thought."

I swallowed, hot. I wanted him back. Wanted us to be like we were before. I didn't like that icy glint in his eyes.

But he'd shot me. I'd let him down. We both had something to prove to each other. And I needed all the help I could get.

"Fine," I said shortly. "Whatever you say."

Glimmer unlocked Adonis's cuffs, and we stole three handguns from sleeping cops and fled into the night.

CPSIA information can be obtained
at www.ICGtesting.com
Printed in the USA
LVOW03s2156310317
529236LV00002B/6/P